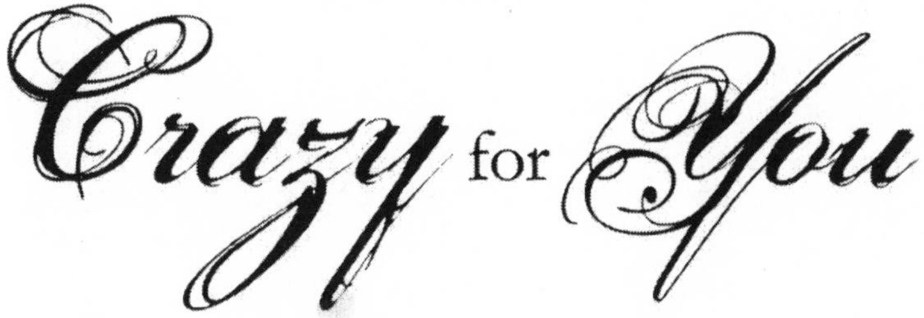

A MEPHISTO COVENANT BOOK

STEPHANIE FEAGAN

Pink Publishing, LLC

ISBN:
eBook: 978-1-940431-07-9
Print: 978-1-940431-05-5

FIC027240FICTION / Romance / New Adult
Key words: paranormal romance, New Adult romance, alpha male, sexy romance, Mephisto series, fantasy romance, dark angel romance books

Please Note
This is a work of fiction. Names, characters, places, and incidents either are the product of the author's imagination or are used fictitiously, and any resemblance to actual persons, living or dead, business establishments, events or locales is entirely coincidental.

Cover Photograph © Selina Kolokytha
Cover Design and Interior format by The Killion Group
http://thekilliongroupinc.com

DEDICATION

For Michael – They're all for you.

ACKNOWLEDGEMENTS:

Many thanks once again to Kristen Droesch for stellar editing. Thanks to Selina Kolokytha for her beautiful photograph, and thanks to Kim Killion for transforming it into such a lovely cover. Thanks to Jennifer Jakes for interiors. My heartfelt gratitude to all the Facebook Peeps who are so lovely and supportive. To readers, bloggers, and fellow bibliophiles, thank you for sharing your passion for storytelling!

LEXICON

~~ Who's Who and What's What in the World of the Mephisto ~~

Aurora – First child of Adam and Eve, born before the fall of mankind, who was lost from Eden and began a line of descendants born without Original Sin who came to be known as Anabo.

Mephistopheles – The dark angel of death who ferries souls bound for Hell. He is Lucifer's second in command, and has many thousands of minions to aid him in his work.

Elektra – An Anabo Mephistopheles fell in love with over a thousand years ago. She bore him seven sons, in secret, without God or Lucifer's knowledge. Before her eldest was compelled to jump to his death and be resurrected to immortality, he murdered Elektra to release her spirit and alert God and Lucifer to the existence of his younger brothers, to save them from his fate of losing all light in his soul. The remaining brothers were blessed by God at death, ensuring they retained the light of Elektra when they came back as immortals.

Mephisto – Six immortal brothers, sons of the dark angel, Mephistopheles, and the Anabo, Elektra. Their sole purpose is to capture those who've pledged their souls to their oldest brother, Eryx, and imprison them in Hell on Earth. By virtue of the blood of Mephistopheles, they are bound for Hell when the world ends, or when Eryx is finally defeated, unless they fulfill the Mephisto Covenant.

Anabo – Pronounced *uh-nah-bo*. A human born without Original Sin. Extremely rare. An Anabo may be recruited to be a Lumina, or she can become Mephisto via a change in

DNA when she's kissed by a Mephisto. If she's immortal, the change to Mephisto is permanent. If she's not immortal, she can ask Lucifer to be returned to how she was before the kiss. If an Anabo wishes to become like other humans, she can request to lose Anabo and Lucifer will make it happen.

Eryx – Eldest brother of the Mephisto, oldest son of Mephistopheles, Eryx lost all light in his soul when he became immortal. An anomaly, his soul belonging to neither God nor Lucifer, to fill the hopelessness within, he wants to take the reins of Hell from Lucifer and thereby control all of mankind and eradicate free will, dooming all humans who are not Anabo to Hell.

Lucifer – Ruler of Hell, the down to God's up, dark to the light, he is mankind's conscience, the reason for free will. Mankind is fallen and have the choice to rise above it, or not.

Lumina – Exceptional humans with extraordinary light in their souls, recruited by the Mephisto to become immortal and live and work with them on Mephisto Mountain. A recruit dies and is resurrected by God to be a living angel. Luminas may marry other Luminas, but are discouraged from interacting with humans.

Purgatory – A spirit meant for Heaven, but unable to ascend because of their anger at God, usually because of something occurring just before or during death. They are sent to work for the Mephisto to learn humility, acceptance and forgiveness from the Luminas.

Hell on Earth – A labyrinth of caverns deep within the Earth, carved out by Lucifer to imprison those who pledge their souls to Eryx.

Lost soul – One who pledges his or her soul to Eryx. Upon death, their soul is absorbed by Eryx, making him stronger. When he believes he is strong enough, he will declare war on Lucifer and attempt to take over Hell. The Mephisto and Luminas know the lost souls by the shadow across their eyes. If captured, they die in Hell on Earth, their spirit unable to escape and add to Eryx's strength.

Skia – In Greek, *skia* means shade, or shadow. Skia agree to become immortal followers of Eryx, and hand their soul to him upon resurrection. They are drones, incapable of free will, enslaved to Eryx's commands. The Skia are Eryx's recruiters, and search constantly for humans who are vulnerable, who are likely to pledge their soul. The shadow across Skia eyes are much darker than the lost souls because their spirits already belong to Eryx. Unlike the lost souls who die when they're sent to Hell on Earth, the Skia are immortal, and live in eternal misery and horror if they're captured. They have strength equal to the Mephisto and are specifically chosen by Eryx for their exceptional intelligence, which makes them cunning and more difficult to capture.

The Mephisto Covenant – God's promise to the Mephisto of redemption and a chance of Heaven if they win the love of a woman and selflessly love her in return. They are limited to extremely rare Anabo females because all other human girls are afraid of them.

Kyanos – A small island in the North Atlantic, surrounded by a mist created by Mephistopheles over a thousand years ago to hide Elektra and his sons from God and Lucifer. When the youngest Mephisto became immortal, they left Kyanos, but still return for councils, or for punishment.

Council – A meeting of the Mephisto on Kyanos, a trial of sorts to determine guilt and punishment of a Mephisto who's broken a hard rule. Punishment is usually a period of solitary time on Kyanos, which is primitive and cold.

Mephisto Mark – An internal mark made by a Mephisto to an Anabo during sex, allowing the Mephisto to mentally search for and find her, as they do with each other. If the Anabo is immortal, the mark is permanent. If she's still human, it is not and can be replaced by another mark, or erased entirely by Lucifer.

Scent – A particular scent attached to an Anabo, Lucifer's way of indicating which Mephisto she is meant for. If an Anabo is found and any of the brothers could go for her, it would be a free-for-all, a fight to the death – and they can't die. To keep order, Lucifer attaches a scent to an Anabo, and the Mephisto who don't catch it are instinctively not attracted to her.

Mephisto Mountain – Several thousand acres of land high in the southern Colorado Rockies above Telluride, populated by Lumina cottages, the Mephisto mansion, and outbuildings. The boundary is circled by the Kyanos mists, making everything Mephisto on the mountain invisible to humans and inaccessible to anyone but the Mephisto, Anabo, and Luminas.

"I am part of the part that once was everything,
Part of the darkness which gave birth to light..."
Mephistopheles, from Goethe's *Faust*

CHAPTER 1

~~ EURI ~~

I was expecting a delivery, a new laptop, a gift to Miles for his twentieth birthday, but the knock at the door on Friday afternoon was not a courier. Instead, my mother stood in the hallway outside of Miles's flat, a tiny fourth floor walkup in the dodgy end of Brixton in southwest London. She was out of breath and her eyes had that wild, manic look to them. I decided she must be skipping her meds. Again.

"Hello, Mum." I waved her inside. We didn't go through the motions of a maternal embrace, or a typical greeting between a mother and daughter who haven't seen one another in over a year. What was the point, after all? She was as apathetic about me as I was about her. I did wonder what she was up to, however. My mother never did anything without a specific reason, usually of benefit to herself. "What brings you to London? Have you been to visit Dad?" It was a loaded question, considering she spent most of her time with her lover in France.

"He won't see me. The man is impossible, always buried in those damned dusty books. He should have married a book."

I agreed. He'd have been happier married to a book. Or a wounded rhinoceros. Or shards of glass. My mother, for all her colorful life and lavish shows of affection, was at heart a spoiled child, prone to mean tricks and endless pouts and tantrums. My father was a serious man, steady and stalwart, a scholar of Greek tragedies, which is how I came to be named Euripides, and my twin sister named Sophocles. Mother allowed it because she wasn't overjoyed at the prospect of motherhood. In short, she didn't want children. So of course she had twins.

"Mum, why are you here?"

Her beautiful face lit up with a wide, happy smile. "Darling! I've come to take you on holiday. Sophie is waiting in the car. We will all go to Ink Lake and catch up. Miss Mildred is lending her cottage for the weekend. Do pack a bag, there's a good girl. We've only a few hours of daylight left."

Holiday? Sophie in the car? I was terrified already.

"Euri, I hear voices. Have you fixed the telly after all?" Miles walked out of the bedroom and saw my mum, his grey eyes widening in surprise. "Lady Longbourne, how extraordinary to see you here."

Mum didn't speak to him, but gave him a quelling look. "Euri, I haven't the smallest notion why ever you want to live with him. You are an aristocrat, daughter of an earl, from one of the oldest families in England. You might have your pick of any young man, even a royal, yet here you are in a hovel with the chauffer's son."

"He is my best friend and has always been. I'm only here for the summer, until the start of fall session at Cambridge. And I resent your misguided pride, Mum. You are the daughter of a pig farmer." I knew better than to provoke her, but the wounded look on Miles's face had to be assuaged.

"Who became one of the richest men in the UK. I doubt Harold's son will make much of himself, as my father did."

"Lady Longbourne," Miles said, coming to stand beside me, "I'm immune to your insults, but as it upsets Euri, I'll have to ask you to stop. Or leave."

"I intend to leave as soon as my daughter has packed a bag for our holiday."

"What holiday?" he asked, looking at me.

"Mum wants to take Sophie and me to Ink Lake."

Miles frowned. "Countess, did you get permission to take Lady Sophie from her home?"

Bless Miles for asking the logical questions. I was too

blindsided to think straight.

Mum shrugged. "She is my child. I don't need permission."

Gathering myself back to sane rationality, I said, "She's in need of constant care, and you and I are not competent to do that. Did you bring her medicines and her supplies? She wears a diaper, and must only eat certain foods because of her digestion issues. Mum, please, I will go with you and we'll return Sophie to Hertfordshire, then you and I will go to Ink Lake." It was a lie. As soon as we had Sophie settled back into her room at Hawthorn House, I would call Miles to come for me and tell my mother to go back to France. Then I'd call Dad and let him know. He needed to remind the assistants at Hawthorn House of my mother's mental instability. Maybe he should hire security to ensure Mum couldn't spirit Sophie away whenever she chose.

Mum argued with me. Of course. "We are perfectly able to take care of her. It's only that you don't wish to, which is cruel of you because she is, after all, your sister. I insist we go together to the lake."

"I will go, but without Sophie."

I could see the wheels turning in her head, the plots and plans only a loose cannon like my mother could make. She was up to something and my blood ran cold. This would not end well.

"Very well, we will take her home. Now do go and get your things. I will wait in the hall." Her sudden acquiescence unnerved me. She gave Miles a look much like she'd give something stuck to the sole of her Jimmy Choos.

He nodded. "It was no pleasure seeing you, Lady Longbourne. I hope it will be a very long time before I'm forced to see you again."

"Humph!" She turned and walked out, slamming the door behind her.

"I'm sorry," he said immediately.

"Don't apologize. She deserves your scorn."

"I wasn't apologizing. I am offering sympathy that your mother is completely selfish, narcissistic, and mean. I can't fathom how a woman like that could have a daughter like you."

He followed me into the bedroom and sat on the bed

while I packed a few things for appearances sake, because I intended to be back in the flat by later tonight.

I was shaky and scared, and before I could stop myself, I went into a dream. I was in the back seat of a car, staring at the window, watching cars go past, seeing a guy on a bicycle, hearing kids shouting. I was uncomfortable and so tired. I wanted to be home, watching Denny's Neighborhood on television. I wanted my soft bear, the one Euri gave me last Christmas. I wanted to never see Mum again. I knew why she came for me. She would finish what she'd started when I was little. I lived in this body because of her. I was a burden, but I was alive, a soul, one who could still love, and I did love my sister and my dad, more than they would ever know.

"Euri, stop it. You've got to stay in the here and now, do you understand?" Miles shook me, hard.

My head wobbled and I blinked, refocusing on the room, on the clothes I'd laid out to fold into my bag. "She's afraid. I have to get her back home. As soon as I leave, call my dad and tell him what's happened. Maybe he can meet us there. Can you beg off working at the restaurant tonight and come for me?"

He hugged me and held my head against his shoulder. "I will call your dad, and of course I'll come for you."

"Since I'm making you lose money, I'll help with the rent."

He chuckled against my hair. "This month, I may let you."

Ten minutes later, Mum and I clattered down five flights of stairs and out to the curb where she had parked the car, a vanilla rental of some kind. A nondescript sedan. I thought it odd. My mother was all about showing off, and why wasn't she in her own car, the one she kept at the car park at the airport?

I tossed my bag in the boot, on top of my sister's wheelchair, then got in the back seat with Sophie. I took her hand and she flopped her head toward me, drooling a bit on my sleeve, looking at me with a smile of happiness in her eyes. "Hello, Sophie, love." I kissed her cheek and she made a guttural grunting sound that meant she was glad. I had seen her just this Wednesday when I went for my weekly visit, but this was different. Unusual. She knew Mum was up to something, and she was afraid. I leaned close to her ear and whispered, "I won't let her hurt you. I'm here for you. Don't be scared."

Mum had taken off almost as soon as I closed the door, and was on her cell while she drove, speaking in French. She was angry. I gathered from her conversation that Stefan, her lover, had broken off with her.

As soon as she ended the call, she started to cry and said with heavy bitterness, "Everything is wrong, and it's your fault."

I sighed and made no response. This would get so bad, and there was nothing I could do about it. I had to stay for Sophie, had to make sure she got back home safe and well.

"My father has cut me off, and because I no longer have money, Stefan has tossed me aside. Your father is divorcing me because he's found a fresh young thing who he's certain will give him his blasted heir. I've lost everything." She looked at me in the rearview mirror. "Except my children. No one can take my babies away from me, no matter what lies you've told. My father loved me until you came along, lying and turning him against me."

I didn't point out the ridiculous contradictions in her passionate speech. I didn't respond at all. She wouldn't hear me anyway.

She drove north, out of the city toward Hertfordshire. We would be at Hawthorn House within the hour. I tried not to let Sophie see my fear, but as much as I was able to know what she experienced in times of high emotion, she knew what was within me.

A tear rolled down her soft cheek. I wiped it away and kissed her and pulled her into my arms.

We were passing through a tiny village and Mum had to slow the car. She scowled into the rearview mirror, watching me hold Sophie. I did it all the time, but she didn't know it. As far as I knew, she hadn't seen Sophie in at least five years. "You always blamed me, but I am *not* responsible for what happened to Sophie. You weren't there. No one was there but her and me."

I didn't argue. I'd come to believe that Mum had long ago convinced herself that Sophie really had fallen and hit her head. She would never own up to what actually happened. How could she? If she drowned her own child, what kind of monster must she be?

Riding in the back seat of that sedan with my mentally, physically challenged twin, the memory came to me as it always did, in startling, horrifying clarity. Sophie finding the Indian headdress in the attic of the London house. Sophie putting it on, taking off all her clothes, decorating her naked body with 'war paint' which was Mum's lipstick. Sophie running through the roomful of London society ladies during the luncheon Mum was hosting, whooping and hollering as if she were an Indian. I tried to stop her, told her Mum would be furious. But Sophie was always one for a lark, and the Sioux war bonnet with all its feathers, a gift to our great grandfather in a previous century, was entirely too tempting to her joyful six year old heart. Maybe if she hadn't been naked, Mum would not have been quite so angry.

As it was, she marched Sophie upstairs, sacked Nanny Green, and hauled Sophie to the bathroom where she ran a bath and made her get in and scrubbed until my sister's skin was raw. She shouted at her and Sophie only laughed. Mum was in a rage, and that's when she held my twin beneath the water until she stopped breathing.

I had returned to the attic, was nosing through old trunks, pulling out hats and gloves and opera glasses. I looked through the glasses and went into one of my dreams. It was me beneath the water, me thrashing and trying to save myself, me that my mother was determined to kill. I was still dreaming, couldn't see where I was going, but I managed to get down the attic stairs, and down to the ground floor of the house, screaming for Jenson, the old man who'd been the butler at the London Longbourne house since forever. He went with me upstairs where my mother was running in circles in her bedroom, hysterically screaming her grief and horror, wailing, "My baby! Oh, God, my baby! She hit her head! She fell and hit her head!"

Jenson was able to resuscitate Sophie. She lived, but she was forever altered. Her body grew as mine did, but housed a child-woman with limited motor skills and an inability to speak.

No one believed me. They all passed it off as the hysteria of a twin whose sister had been compromised. But I knew the truth. And later, I knew when Sophie was being mistreated at the sanatorium in Yorkshire, the first place my father took her. She was examined and a doctor verified that her injuries were due to abuse. Dad took her to another place, where she was also hurt. I was nine by then. I rang up my grandfather, Mum's dad, and told him he should make sure Sophie was safe. He bought Hawthorn House, hired the very best nurses and assistants and household help and that was where Sophie had been the past nine years. Safe and comfortable, away from our mother who never visited. She was taken in her wheelchair for walks in the lovely park surrounding the old house. Sophie loved it there and I went to visit and spend the night once every week, usually on Wednesday. I was friendly with all the staff, because I wanted to know them, and I wanted them to know I was on top of things. If anyone had any ideas about mistreating my sister, they'd have to answer to me.

My mother continued to rant and rave and go on about what a horrible person I was to tell tales and lie about what happened. "You're the reason my own papa has cut me off. How will I live? I have nothing and no one, all because of *you*."

She'd turned off of the thruway onto a narrow wooded unpaved road. "Where are you going? This isn't the way to Hawthorn House." I sat up, extremely concerned. "Mum, I'm sorry about all of it. Don't fret, all right? I will take care of you. I have money from Grandfather, from the trust he gave me. I have money from my concerts. I will share all of it with you, and when I'm twenty-one and the trust goes away and I get all the money, you can have it. You can live just as you always have. Now please, can we turn round and go back to the thruway? Sophie needs to get home."

"It won't be the same, don't you see? I can't live off of you. It must be mine. I must be the daughter he loves, and so long as you are here, a reminder to him of my failings, he will not love me. He is cruel to me. How can you know what that's like? Your own father hating you! Your father adores you, so you *don't know*."

I knew what it was to have a soulless mother who tried

to murder my twin. She had become more worked up and angry, and nothing I said could bring her back to earth. If she stopped, even for a moment, I planned to open the door and get out and take Sophie with me. If I had to carry her back to the thruway, I would.

I never got the chance.

Mum continued her tirade, louder and louder, more and more angry. She sped faster and faster, low hanging branches beating against the car, making a terrible racket. We bounced and jolted when she hit ruts and dips in the road. I held Sophie, her mouth open in a silent scream while tears cascaded down her cheeks.

And then, suddenly, we broke free of the trees and seconds later, the car was airborne. We landed with a sharp jolt in water, which instantly began to fill the car. We were sinking into a lake.

So this was her goal all along. She would drown the both of us, and then her papa would love her again. I saw her struggling with the door, trying to get it open, but all my effort was for Sophie. It was amazing how quickly the car flooded. I had cracked my window, which contributed to the swiftness of flooding, and because of that, because the pressure was quickly equalizing, I was able to break it by kicking with the heel of my boot. I turned for Sophie, but she looked at me in the green gloom and shook her head, her blond hair swaying in the water. She pushed me away and moved her eyes toward the front seat, to my mother, who was desperately trying to open her door.

My sister wanted me to choose our mother over her. The look in her eyes broke me. Changed me. Altered my soul. She wanted me to save the woman who'd stolen her life in a fit of pique, because she'd been embarrassed. Sophie was meant to be a happy soul, a light in the world, someone who would have made a difference. Instead, she lived in a diaper and drooled because of our mother's total disregard for anyone beyond herself.

It wasn't a choice. Not really.

I grabbed Sophie and pulled her with me out the window. I left my mother to drown.

In the end, it didn't matter. By the time I broke the surface, my sister was dead.

She was eighteen years old. She was the other half of me, and she was gone, and I didn't know how I'd go on without her.

The water dragged me down, back into its murky depths, but I wouldn't let go of my twin. I clutched her to me and knew I would die, too, and we would be together in Heaven, whole and healthy and sisters for all time.

But it wasn't meant to be. Strong hands grasped my arms and pulled me up, forcing me to let go of Sophie. As I rose higher, her beloved face disappeared into the deep shadows and I knew what it was to be alone. Completely, utterly alone. The hands dragged me through the water, up and out and onto the bank, lying me down in soft summer grass. I blinked up at a man with dark hair and a handsome face and a solemn look in his black eyes.

"Euri," he whispered, "it's not your time. Not yet."

He knew my name. And I realized that I knew him, just as all of humanity knows him.

Ironically, incredibly, inconceivably, my savior was Death.

CHAPTER 2

WE ARE ANONYMOUS.
WE ARE LEGION.
WE DO NOT FORGIVE.
WE DO NOT FORGET.
EXPECT US.

One Year Later

~~ EURI ~~

"Are you sure about this, Miles? I'm a pianist, not a hacker."

"You're a hacker. Wasn't it you who broke into records at Cambridge to find out your scores?"

"That's not hacking."

"I am certain the chaps at Cambridge would disagree."

"They never knew. That's why I'm not a hacker."

"Semantics, Euri. And are you forgetting the time you hacked into the Milford Retreat website and coded it so that all the text was in pirate English?"

"It was just a lark. I hate that place. They make empty promises and charge an enormous fortune for what amounts to a week of swim lessons. And their telly advertisements are bugger annoying."

Miles laughed, shaking his head as he refocused on his laptop screen. "You're a hacker, love, and after tonight, you will be quite official, a member of Anonymous, inducted and initiated by this op."

"Do you suppose Anonymous ops really do any good?"

He sobered and looked at me, sitting just next to him on

his old sofa, my own laptop on my thighs. "They bring international attention to something somebody wants to hide. Kovalev went too far when he shut down the Internet in Azbekastan. He already closed the borders, and hijacked the airwaves. There's no TV but his propaganda. No radio except what he provides. From a group of Anonymous who escaped, we know his regime has begun ethnic cleansing, killing anyone who wasn't born in Azbekastan, anyone who isn't Russian Orthodox. He's burned entire villages to the ground and his loyal guards and army have tortured and raped and stolen. After tonight, everyone in the world will know what's going on. People will see tweets and Facebook posts and Instagram photos from people in Azbekastan. And there won't be a bloody thing Kovalev can do about it." He refocused on his screen. "The Azbekastan government's homepage will redirect to the U.N. homepage, which will have OCCUPY AZBEKASTAN across it in flashing red letters."

"Shouldn't we be doing this under shadow IP addresses?"

"You and I are doing nothing illegal. All we're doing is visiting the Azbekastan government's website. We'll just be doing it with hundreds of thousands of others, all at exactly the same time, which will crash the page long enough for someone to code it to redirect to the U.N. website."

"Who will do that?"

He glanced at me. "No one knows. That's why it's called Anonymous."

"Yes, but you know it's going to happen. How?"

"From IRC, but there were also posts about it on 4chan. If you'd ever get off the music boards, you'd have seen it as well."

"I'm not so enamored of 4chan as you are, Miles. It's like walking into a room of twelve-year-old boys. They post photos of naked girls and lewd disgusting stories that could never be true, and I swear I can hear them giggling."

"Sometimes they're funny. Sometimes, in all the ridiculous, there are insights so brilliant, they take my breath away."

"I visit the music boards because I enjoy talking to people about what they like and listen to, how they discover new bands and music. I've become friends with a guy named 4Jane, who I'm pretty sure is John Jamison, the lead guitarist for Arcadia. Someday I'm going to see them live."

"You'll have to go to America. They don't tour outside the U.S."

"I know." I stared at the blinking cursor on my screen, just behind the link pasted into my address bar. My finger hovered over the mouse, ready to click at 11:11. "Miles, I had a call from Stu today."

I felt him stiffen and wasn't surprised. I'd known this wouldn't be easy. Swallowing, I went all in. "He offered to sponsor me for a three month tour that will include select cities in Europe, and the last month in the United States."

He didn't look at me. "Did you say yes?"

"Not yet."

His grey eyes met mine and I could see how sad I had made him. "But you will."

How could I explain it to him? He knew I wasn't always in my head, knew I had been connected to my sister in some strange way that allowed me to know what she knew at certain times. I told him it stopped after Sophie's death, which wasn't exactly a lie. I no longer channeled my sister.

What I couldn't tell Miles was that I still went into my waking dreams, except now I knew what a stranger knew. A guy named Z. And what he knew was so messed up, I had begun to wonder if he was merely a figment of my imagination. I wondered if I'd stepped off the edge and fallen into madness. I wouldn't know, of course. Madness is the best of all liars and charlatans, insidiously making insanity appear normal.

But what if Z was real? He lived in the United States. Colorado. He was a huge fan of Arcadia. If I was there, I could go see Arcadia and maybe, just maybe, Z would be there and I could meet him. I could find out if he was real. I would know why he was in my head.

I couldn't say any of this to Miles. It sounded ridiculous. Crazy. But I had to know, and so I jumped at the chance to do a concert tour that would take me to the United States.

"When will you leave?"

"In two weeks. I'll be back in London twice before the end of the tour, so it's not like I'll be gone the whole three months without seeing you."

He was very quiet, and I hated it so much that I hurt him. He'd always been sensitive and easily wounded. I was typically non-confrontational and laid back, so it wasn't in me to be hypercritical or judgmental. I had always believed that's why he and I were so close. We fit. We complemented one another. But he never failed to take it hard when I left for tours, and now was no different.

I didn't try to cajole or talk him back to happy. He needed to let it be for a while. He would deal with it in his own way.

A few minutes later, when the alarm went off on his computer, we both clicked on the link to the Azbekastan homepage and received error messages. The page was not available. We waited five minutes and tried again and just as Miles had said, we were redirected to the U.N. homepage, and OCCUPY AZBEKASTAN flashed in red across the screen. We checked Twitter and Facebook and tumblr and already there was an explosion of images and retweets and shares of horrific photographs and desperate stories of misery and suffering.

"It will be a short window of time that the Internet is open within the country. I'm sure they have people working right now to shut it down. They'll have to bypass what Anonymous did which will take a bit, but they'll get it, and the country will go dark again."

Looking at the photos, I broke out in a sweat and my stomach churned. "Why, Miles? Is he just pure evil?"

He sighed and closed his laptop and drained his beer before he said, "Kovalev believes this is what needs to happen for his country to be whole and healthy again. He's convinced himself that those who are not native Azbekastan and Russian Orthodox must be taken out of the picture. Once every man, woman, and child in his country is homogenous, he believes all the problems will be solved. There will be no homelessness or hunger or unemployment or economic crisis. He's wrong, of course, but you asked if he is evil and my answer is no, his intentions are not evil. His actions are, but he sincerely believes he's in the right."

On Instagram, I saw a photo of Kovalev, wearing a mink Cossack hat, his arm around a brunette with enormous breasts. "He's a megalomaniac, an arrogant fascist dictator.

The people are starving, but he's no doubt fabulously wealthy with homes all over the world and yachts and women and every luxury known to man."

Miles nodded. "He feels he's worth it because he's the answer to the people's troubles. He's empowered by divine right. He says God talks to him."

I continued clicking through the photos, until I came to one of children lined up before a firing squad. I began to cry. "I wish God really would talk to him and tell him to stop." I swallowed. "I hate him. I hate anybody who's so determined to make everyone else bend to their will, they'll do anything to win."

He reached over, closed my laptop, took it from me to set aside, then drew me into his arms. "Because of your mum. I know."

I cried for a while and he murmured kind things and when I was spent, he led me to bed and made love to me. It was comforting and familiar, just as it had been since the first time, when I was seventeen. He was shy, sweet, tentative. He kissed me softly, came into me gently, and it was over in a matter of moments. I wondered sometimes what it would be like if he lasted longer, or was a little less shy. He was always almost apologetic, despite how many times I told him I wanted him as much as he wanted me. But Miles was what I needed. He posed no threat to my peace of mind.

After we brushed our teeth and he'd checked the lock and switched off the lights, we slid back into bed and he was asleep almost instantly. He'd been jazzed up by the Anonymous op, then sex. He was all done with the day.

Lying awake, I stared at the shadows on the ceiling and felt myself slipping into a dream. I didn't try to hold it back, but before it consumed me, I got up and went into the front room and sat at the upright piano Dad had sent for me last summer, after Sophie died. I played and dreamed and lived in Z's world for the next several hours. The screams in his head were muffled, almost muted by the music, and I wondered, not for the first time, if he was soothed at all, if the screams were less in his head when I played. I was within his mind for these stretches of time. Was he ever in mine?

~~ Zee ~~

LadyAnon wasn't on the music boards tonight. I was killing time until the takedown we had planned for later, and decided to pop onto 4chan and see what was up. Once I realized she wasn't there, I went to all my usual pages, and saw the latest Anonymous op. I saw all the photographs. Azbekastan was crashing into full-scale genocide. The atrocities were epic. I wondered again if Eryx was involved. There were certain elements to the crisis in Azbekastan that bore our oldest brother's signature. He'd tried before to take control of a country, but it backfired because we were on top of it and wiped out his carefully placed Skia before they could convince the populace to give their souls to him.

I would have to go there and see if the Mephisto needed to get involved, or if Kovalev was acting on his own. He might be like the maniac currently in charge of North Korea, who was so egregiously arrogant, he wasn't susceptible to Eryx. He believed he had everything he needed, his authoritarian control absolute and his chokehold on his people complete. What could Eryx promise him that he didn't already have? Kovalev might be the same. I'd have to wait and see.

I glanced at my cell phone. Still over an hour before we'd leave for Panama, where we'd be taking out an odd pocket of lost souls, a group who'd travelled there to start a colony, a cult of Eryx's followers. It had surprised me when I'd found them. Eryx typically advised his followers not to congregate, not to call attention to themselves, but these people had run ads in papers, offering a solution to worry and stress and problems. They'd found the answer and others could join if they wanted.

I had gone there and found forty-two lost souls and the Skia who'd suckered all of them. He'd been immortal a very short time, and I wondered why Eryx would make such a lame guy one of his minions. Skia were typically extremely intelligent and capable. That's why Eryx chose them. They had an innate ability to charm people. Their sole purpose was to convince people to hand their soul over to Eryx.

The Skia who led the group of lost souls in Panama was

dumber than a box of rocks.

Tonight's takedown would be a piece of cake.

I was slightly dizzy. Aware that the latest incarnation of my insanity was about to take hold, I laid back on my bed and stared up at the ceiling. Just as it had before, the screaming in my head dialed down several notches and I heard a piano. Soft and beautiful. I floated on it for a while, allowing my imagination to run loose, until Jax came across the intercom. "Covey up at the M. We leave in ten."

I sat up and wished the music wouldn't stop. When I popped downstairs to the great hall to stand in our circle around the onyx M inlaid in the marble floor, the music was still there. I wondered where it came from. The pieces were difficult, beautiful melodies from symphonies I'd not attempted to play in at least two hundred years. It was strange that I'd hear them now. If music was to be my madness, why not something I was currently obsessed with?

Not that I'd quibble. It was a gift from the ether, from the maze that was my mind, and it was infinitely better than the endless screams.

Phoenix looked at me quizzically. "What's so funny?"

"Nothing's funny."

"Then why are you smiling?"

"Maybe I'm happy."

Key stood next to me. He frowned. "You're never happy."

"Untrue." I glanced toward Sasha before I said to Key, "I'm generally happy having sex."

"Well you're not having sex now, so what's up?"

"Back off. Can't a guy smile if he wants?"

Jax slid an arm around Sasha. "Phoenix will find you, okay?"

She pulled a face. "Maybe this time I'll go to the right place."

"Maybe," Jax said, pressing a kiss to her forehead. "Or maybe you'll land in some other P location, like Peru, or Perth, Australia."

"Panama is in Central America," she said with a nod. "I looked it up and saw pictures and imagined what it would be like. I will land in Panama."

I made no comment, still bemused by the music, but I

doubted she could do it.

Jax began the count and the seven of us disappeared from Colorado. We materialized on a side street in a small village sixty kilometers from the outskirts of Panama City and, as expected, Sasha wasn't there.

Phoenix drew a hard breath and let it out noisily. "Jax, I'm already tired. You mentally search for your Anabo. Where is she?"

Jax stared up at the sky for a few beats before he said, "Pittsburgh."

We all laughed, then waited while Phoenix left to find Sasha. Ty looked down the street at a stray dog and Key said, "Don't even think about it. This takedown is going to take some time, and we can't spare you."

Ty shot him a resentful expression. "Is it okay if I *look* at him?"

"Fuck off."

Denys stepped between them, grinning as usual. "Children, children! Let's all play nice, yeah? I for one want to get this done and over. I've got a date."

"You don't have a date," Jax said. "You're hoping to get laid. That's not a date."

Denys shrugged. "It's a date. I just don't know who it's with." He grinned again. "Some pretty lady is going to get real lucky."

I rolled my eyes.

Key said to me, "It's your turn to stay at the gates."

"Yeah, okay."

Phoenix appeared, holding Sasha's hand. She took one look at Jax and said angrily, "Dammit to hell, why do I suck at this so much? I'm not stupid. I can read a map. I'm always so certain I know where to go. How could I end up in freaking *Pittsburgh?*"

I admired Jax for not laughing, because it was damned funny, but clearly Sasha didn't think so. She was seriously bothered by her inability to transport to the correct location. But she had other talents we had put to good use, and that's what Jax told her. "We've all got some flaw to us, Sasha. Don't be so hard on yourself."

"It's embarrassing. I've been Mephisto for over two months, gone on countless takedowns. I should have this by now. And I know you're all laughing at me." She looked around at each of us, no doubt searching for a stifled grin. We all stared back with complete sobriety, as solemn as Jax.

Key said in his usual leader alpha dog way, "We have to get moving. The group's dinner hour is almost over."

Jax always commanded takedowns, and he stepped forward. "Ty and Denys take the south side of the building and Key and I will take the north. Zee, check the lodging cabins for any outliers. Phoenix and Sasha, bring the first round of doppelgangers." He looked around at each of us before he began a count and on three, we transported to a clearing in the jungle, where the lost souls had built a compound.

While the others threw a freeze across the dining hall, I popped to the men's lodge and checked inside. Nothing but neatly made bunks. Likewise, the women's lodge was empty. I popped to the dining hall, grabbed the arms of a young woman and a middle-aged man and transported to the gates of Hell on Earth. After dropping the lost souls to the sand, I lifted my arms to the sky and began the chant that would open the gates. Before I was done, Key, Jax, Ty, and Denys all appeared with two lost souls each.

As the ground shifted and swirled and began sucking them into the vortex that would lead to a pit deep within the earth, Key said gloomily, "We can't find the Skia. The son of a bitch must have skipped out."

No way. The guy was way too stupid to give us the slip. He was hiding somewhere on that compound. I lowered my arms. "Do you want me to find him?"

Key jerked a nod before he looked at our tallest brother. "Ty, take over for him."

I left the Arabian Desert and returned to the oppressive hot humidity of the Panamanian jungle. Wandering the periphery of the compound, I allowed my mind free rein, waiting for the ever-present screams to separate, for the voices to distinguish one from another so that I heard female, male and child. Tonight, however, it was different. The screams remained coalesced and muffled and it was the music that became distinct and crisp, as if there was a piano right behind me. It was a Brahms piece, one of my favorites. I kept walking, focusing on the Skia. All my senses sharpened immeasurably, including the one I'd had the misfortune to be born with. I knew what the Skia looked like. I'd been here before for reconnaissance. I was always reconnaissance. Because of my sixth sense.

Walking around the clearing in the jungle, I sweated profusely and barely noticed, my mind running in hyper mode. When I passed the back of the dining hall, the music reached a crescendo, the screams escalated, and the hair at the nape of my neck prickled.

I popped inside, into a supply room, and there he was, crouched behind a stack of crates. This one was younger than most. Probably in his mid-twenties. Too bad he'd fucked himself over by believing Eryx. Now he'd spend eternity in Hell on Earth, a fate worse than death. He'd wish to God he could die, but unlike the lost souls who'd die as soon as they landed, he wouldn't. Ever. He'd pray for Lucifer to take him to Hell, a paradise compared to Hell on Earth.

Fuck, why did they do it? Why did this guy do it? What was so necessary to him that it was worth his soul?

I felt no pity. I never did. He had a choice and he made the wrong one. All the lost souls and all the Skia were less than zero to me. I'd give anything for a chance of Heaven. Because I knew what this schmuck did not – there is life after death, even for immortals, and spending it in Hell would be eternal misery. I was doomed to it, but this wanker had a chance and he threw it away for some bullshit lie my brother fed to him.

He began to cry and beg for his life. I didn't speak or respond. When I reached for him, he stabbed me, but his knife skills were abysmal. Had Eryx taught him nothing? Despite his inhuman strength, I easily captured him and moments later, we were at the gates of Hell on Earth. I tossed him to the sand and Ty began the chant.

Key appeared with the last of the lost souls and looked at the Skia, his mouth curving into a pleased smile. "I don't know how you do it, but thanks."

"Welcome." I popped away, to the basement storage room at the Mephisto mansion where we kept doppelgangers provided by our father. I gathered up a couple and transported them to Panama. Jax was busy setting the dining hall up for a fire caused by a gas explosion while Sasha and my other brothers and I continued ferrying the doppelgangers, placing some at the long tables, some close to the doors, as if they'd tried to escape.

When we were done, we congregated at the edge of the clearing and watched while Jax fixed the propane tank, then popped to us in the nanosecond before it exploded, sending fiery propane into the air, onto the thatched roof of the wooden building that was the dining hall. We watched it burn, waited until we were sure there would be no question why all the people inside were dead, then went back to Colorado.

Another takedown done. Sometimes I wished I could enjoy a sense of accomplishment, but I'd long ago lost that feeling, I guess because I knew there would be a bajillion more takedowns in the years ahead. We had another one scheduled for two nights from now, some people in a small village in Italy. They were scattered, so it would be more complicated, and the reasons for their fake deaths would have to be different. But that wasn't my concern. After I reconnoitered and had the deets, I handed them off to Phoenix, who made all the plans and ordered doppelgangers from M.

Until the Italy takedown, I intended to do as little as possible. Well, as soon as I had sex. So, sex, then music, maybe some movies, and some long surfing of the Internet. I'd do all of it with the screamers in my head, but maybe, if I was very lucky, I'd also do it with the piano. It still played, and I realized it made me feel less anxious, less afraid of what might pop into my head, some random bit of conversation or thoughts from strangers. My mind was like a beacon, signaling an outlet for human travails. Why couldn't I hear happy, nice things? It was always so damned depressing. And the screams. I'd decided centuries ago that the screams were all of mankind, reflecting the terror every human held in their heart, delivered to my mind on a different plane of existence. Nobody else heard it. Only me. And it never, ever stopped. So long as there were people, there would be these screams of fear. Every human was terrified of life, of inevitable pain, and ultimately, what lay beyond death. Because nobody knew. It was a big question mark.

I knew. And wished I didn't. I'd have given anything to be just a regular guy.

Since I was nowhere close to normal, even for a son of Hell, I'd at least pretend. I'd do normal guy things, like finding a hot girl to hook up with.

In the great hall, Denys said, "I'm going to Max's in Vegas. Who's with me?"

I liked Max's. There were always beautiful girls, the bar stocked decent whiskey, and the music didn't suck. "I'm filthy and hungry. As soon as I eat and shower, I'm in."

Ty nodded. "Me, too."

Key shook his head. "I've got a lot to do. Not tonight."

We didn't bother waiting on an answer from Phoenix. He never went out, never looked at girls. He'd buried himself for over a century, penance for the death of Jane, because it was his fault she died. He'd abandoned her and Eryx murdered her. So Phoenix stayed home while we went out.

Jax and Sasha walked toward the dining room. Of course Jax wasn't going. He had Sasha. I felt a familiar pang of envy, but not because I wanted Sasha. She was my sister now and I would always think of her that way. My envy was for what I didn't have, what I would never have. Each of my brothers would eventually find an Anabo. We had a promise from God that it would happen. Granted, no one thought it'd take a thousand years, and patience was not a Mephisto strong suit, but we would live until mankind no longer existed, many more thousands of years, so eventually, we would each find a girl who could stick around long enough to fall in love. Except me. I had no hope because I was batshit crazy. My brothers would have someone to share their life with. I would always and forever be alone.

Except for those few moments when I was having sex. I could pretend. It was pathetic and lame, but it was what kept me going.

"Meet back here in thirty minutes," Denys said.

We agreed, and after I grabbed a couple of sandwiches and a glass of milk from the dining room table, I popped upstairs. I inhaled the sandwiches and stripped out of my clothes. Ordinarily, I'd switch on some music, as loud as possible, but tonight, incredibly, I had a piano playing in my head. While I brushed my teeth, I looked in the mirror and debated shaving. I decided not to and went to the shower.

I was soaping up, running lather up and down my chest, down to my semi hard cock, around my balls, when the music faltered and I heard a girl say, "Oh, *my*."

I leaned against the tile wall of the glass shower and looked all around the bathroom. No one was there. The voice had been inside my head. *Fuck.* I slid down the slick tiles into a squat and slumped over, feeling lost and despondent. How could this be happening to me? *Why?* Who hated me *this much?* God, or Lucifer?

My madness had gone to a whole new level. I'd spent over a thousand years with the screams, with the woman in the ocean who called out to me, with the sixth sense that struck even when I didn't want it. I had all my crazy nailed down. Even the sleepwalking, the nightmares, and the monochrome world. Today had been a good day. Everything was in color. I might wake tomorrow and the whole world would be purple, or red, or shades of gray.

Yes, I was mad as a hatter. But the crazy I knew was familiar. No surprises. Just day after day, year after year, century after century of the same psychosis.

Now I had a British chick in my head, one who played the piano more beautifully than anyone I had ever known and who knew every move I made, and would evidently be judgmental. What would she say when I took a girl to bed, a girl I already knew I'd forget by tomorrow, and whose memory of me I'd erase as soon as I left her? Because no woman would think that was a cool thing to do. Not even an imaginary one in my own mind. Was I going to have to give up my one small consolation in this fucking nightmare that was my endless life?

The piano music became louder, more dramatic, sexier. And I heard her humming. Then she whispered, "If you are real, I will find you. Until then, I'll leave you to your own thoughts. And sex with strangers."

"Who are you?"

Shit. I really had gone walkabout. Now I was talking *out loud* to the voice in my head.

"I'm who you play for," she whispered, and then the music stopped.

CHAPTER 3

~~ EURI ~~

Almost two months into my European tour, I sat on a bed in a hotel room in Moscow with my cell to my ear and listened in silent shock and dismay to my best friend, the sweet, gentle soul I'd loved all of my life, rant and rave about organized religion, the oppression of the British government, and the injustice of the aristocracy.

"Your family is a shining example of what's wrong with everything," he said, only one decibel shy of shouting. "Why the *fuck* should anyone call you *Lady* Euri? Because you were born to a man whose ancestors raped this country for God and king? They got the spoils of war, the land of honest Englishmen, and have passed it down over the centuries so that someone like you will be called *Lady*."

"What's happened, Miles? Stop shouting and tell me what's going on."

He was silent for so long, I looked to see if the call had been dropped, but he was still on the line. At long last, he said in a monotone, "I've done something. I can never change it."

"What have you done?" No response. "Miles, *please*, what have you done?"

"There's another board now. It's not like 4chan."

I fell back on the bed and stared up at the plaster rosettes around an old light fixture that looked like something from a hundred years ago. Probably, it was. My heart hurt. Miles was all I had. If he left me, and it seemed pretty evident that this was to be a send-off of the worst kind, I would have no one. I didn't count Dad. I loved him;

he loved me. But we weren't close. Miles was everything to me, especially since I'd lost Sophie. I'd always thought I was everything to him. We were there for each other, always. But that was apparently no longer true.

I sternly told myself not to cry. I was certain it would make him angrier. I swallowed. "What is this other board?"

"Six-six-X."

"That's it?"

"That's it. I found it through a note on 4chan, and it changed my life. Literally and completely changed my life."

I didn't tell him that if this was the result of his change, it sucked hard. He seemed inordinately pleased with himself and evidently didn't realize he was acting like a monumental prick.

I got up and went to my laptop and typed in 66X. A page came up that was similar to the 4chan home page, with a greeting and a list of all the available boards. There were a gazillion forums on 4chan, ranging from music to movies to gaming to anime to politics to NSFW porn pics.

On 66X, there were three: Religion, New Life, and Covet.

I clicked on Religion and scanned the posts about varying religions and why they were wrong. All wrong. Lots of comments about God and how he'd failed the world and there had to be a new world order and on and on. I clicked on New Life and scanned the comments there about a new way of living, an oath, a promise, and a guy who went by Anon66X, who was the be all, end all. The naysayers were trolled and threatened. I clicked on Covet and all the messages there were about what the posters wanted that would make their life complete. For some, it was material things, like a new car or house. Some wanted to be more attractive, or thin, or have big muscles. And some wanted someone to love them. Someone to be with them.

Besides the infinitely smaller number of boards, there was another huge difference between 66X and 4chan. The posters on 4chan were commonly juvenile and frequently irreverent, but there was almost always a sense of camaraderie, even from the trolls. A lot of the 4chan posters thought of trolling as a sport. But the people on 66X were not funny or teasing or trolling. These people were angry and desperate and hateful. Every post I read made me want to bathe, to wash away the filth and the rage and hate. Who *were* these people? And how could Miles be so enamored of them?

Just like at 4chan, most everyone posted as Anonymous, except Anon66X, who'd evidently started this forum. I wondered what kind of psychopath he must be, and what did he do to make people change completely? Because Miles was nothing like he was even two days ago, when I'd talked to him while I was in St. Petersburg.

"Well?" he asked. "I know you're on the boards. I can hear you clicking."

"I don't understand, Miles. What did you do that you can never change?"

He sighed heavily. "I am a convert. Anon66X is more than you could ever imagine. He's a mystic being, not human, something from a long time past, a prophet who says he will lead the world back to how it was supposed to be in the beginning."

Miles was talking like a nutter, like one of those demented fellows who stood on street corners and shouted that the world must repent or burn in Hell. "A convert. What does that mean? Has he started a new religion?"

"He's led a life entirely devoid of God or Lucifer, of Heaven or Hell."

I didn't think that was possible, but didn't say so. It was sure to set him off again. "I see. So you've joined his movement, is that what you mean?"

"More than that, Euri. I pledged him my soul. And I know you'll think it's not possible, not real, but trust me, it is. I belong to him now, and when I die, I won't go to Heaven or Hell. I'll just . . . stop existing. My death will give him more strength, more power. He's been doing this for centuries. He's trying to be stronger than Lucifer, to take Hell away from him. He wants to abolish free will. He wants everyone to belong to him and be at his mercy."

"It's a lie, Miles. He's a maniac, like Kovalev. He's trying to con people. Has he asked for money?"

"No, Euri. I wish you were right, but you're not. My soul is lost to any purpose but his. I'm subbed onto a private board and we've been learning all about what is expected of us. I've learned I have to be careful who I talk to, who I associate with, and always be on the lookout for his brothers. Their sole purpose is to capture and kill people like me. To keep their brother from becoming more powerful through the acquisition of a soul, they lock us away so our spirits can't escape when we die. This is what I have to look forward to, Euri. This is what I signed up for. And nothing I do can change it."

My mind was rushing back in time, to the night I stayed up almost until dawn, playing the piano, living in Z's head. Since then, I'd tried to stay away as much as possible because it frightened me and made me doubt my sanity. And if he turned out to be real, I didn't want to know what was in his mind. I didn't want to be with him when he had sex with strangers, or when he carried those people to the desert and sent them into the ground. It was freakish. And so I had done my best to put Panama out of my mind, but now it all came screaming back to me. Z had called them lost souls. He'd attributed their loss to his brother, a guy named Eryx.

Z *must* be real. And his brother had lied to Miles so he would hand him his soul.

I sat back down on the bed. "Why would you do this, Miles? *Why?*"

He began to cry, deep, racking sobs. "For you," he said in a harsh whisper.

Tears instantly popped into my eyes. "What do you mean?"

"I wanted to be a guy who isn't just the chauffer's son, somebody really worthy of you. He promised . . . he said I would become what I needed to be."

Lies. Isn't that what Z had said about the guy he captured in that storage room? *Too bad he'd fucked himself over by believing Eryx. What was so necessary to him that it was worth his soul?*

"I've loved you since I was old enough to talk. How could you ever imagine that you're not enough?"

"Why did you leave, Euri? If you just hadn't left London. I thought you'd give up the tours after Sophie was gone. I thought you'd stay here with me, and marry me. But you left, and I realized nothing I ever do or have will be good enough for you."

I was crying in earnest now, my heart breaking. "Miles, I've *never* cared about money or things. You know that. It's always been you and Sophie and the music. Everything else can sod off. I just don't understand how you could think you needed to be anything but what you are. You're my love, my . . . everything."

He didn't speak for a while, crying too hard. Finally, he said in a hoarse voice, "You need strength, Euri. You're strong, but sometimes, you're not. Sometimes, you're . . . you need someone who can take care of you. Because you're off, my darling. Do you know?"

"Yes," I whispered, "I know."

"And so I thought I could be that for you, and believed him when he said I would become stronger, smarter, and more capable. You've never seen me as I am, Euri. You never see anyone as they really are, except your mother. You always knew just who she was and what she was about, but everyone else, it's as though you see them through a glass, a magical portal that grants them qualities that don't exist. I wanted to be who you thought I was, and now, I'm nothing. I'm less than nothing. So I'm saying goodbye. For what it's worth, I did love you. I did this for you. I am sorry. *So* . . . sorry."

"Miles, I'll come home first thing tomor—" I stopped talking. He'd ended the call. I called him back and he didn't answer. I texted and he didn't reply. I emailed. I called again. Over and over. He never answered.

~~ ZEE ~~

There were no screams. For the first time in my entire life, I didn't hear anyone screaming. I didn't hear music. I heard nothing but that British voice, the one I'd first heard in the shower over two months ago. I'd wondered if I'd ever hear her again, if my mind might bring her back, and here she was, but she wasn't speaking to me. I stopped walking and abandoned my reconnaissance of a Skia in Montreal. Leaning against a building, I shoved my hands into my coat pockets and listened. This couldn't be in my head. I wasn't imagining this conversation, or her thoughts. Wherever she was, this was happening in real time, and like a radio, my head was collecting the signal.

I was so completely blown away by this, so determined to hear the entire conversation without interruption, I knew I had to leave and go somewhere that my brothers would not be tempted to follow. Somewhere they hated. If I stayed in Montreal much longer, one of them, probably Denys, was bound to show up to see what I was doing. To ask me to go somewhere for a drink or a burger or to pick up girls.

I didn't want any of that. I wanted to hear what this girl was saying.

I transported to Kyanos, the tiny island in the north Atlantic where I was born, where I'd first heard the lady in the ocean. All my brothers except Key hated Kyanos. It was where we grew up, but it was where our mother was murdered by Eryx, where he'd become the monster he was. We'd finished growing up, the younger ones, on Kyanos, and as soon as Denys was eighteen, as soon as he became immortal, we left and went to Greece. Key still liked to go to Kyanos, but the rest of us didn't.

Perched on the edge of the cliffs in moonlight, I watched the rolling surf as it crashed against the rocks below and listened to her. Yuri. A strange name for a British girl. Every Yuri I'd ever known of was a Russian guy.

Yuri. Who was she and why could I hear her? How had she heard me? I was bemused. Enchanted. Absolutely breathless with wonder.

Nothing like this had ever happened to me. Without the screams, I could hear the ocean clearly and it was beautiful. I sat there and inhaled the clean, pungent, salty air and smiled like a fool. Her voice was melodic, cultured and beautiful. I closed my eyes and could see what she saw. A hotel room, an old one with faded antiques and cloudy windows.

I heard the sorrow and desperation in her voice while she talked to Miles, who must be her boyfriend. He was very dear to her and she was devastated by his news. I didn't feel sympathy for her. Miles was a loser she was well rid of. She just didn't know it yet.

When he wouldn't answer her calls or emails or texts, she said a prayer. "God, please bring Miles back. Forgive him and take him back." She began to mutter, walking around the room, stopping to look through the windows at the city below. I recognized it as Moscow.

She texted again, then called, then sent another email. She did this over and over and when she still had no reply, she said almost in a shout, “Bloody, sodding, evil bastard!”

I knew she wasn’t cursing Miles. She cursed Eryx.

When she sat at her laptop to send yet another email, I paid particular attention. Her name, I realized, was not Yuri, but Euri. She addressed it to Miles Gordon. I knew he was in London, a chauffer’s son. I knew she was Lady Euri, so she was the daughter of an aristocrat. I would go to London and figure out where Miles lived. We’d have to take him out, of course. He couldn’t be allowed to live and sucker in more people, or die and increase Eryx’s strength.

I wondered how long she would be sad. She’d said she’d been in love with him since she was a child. I guess it might be hard to get over losing someone like that. But not when he’d chosen to throw it all away. I just couldn’t feel any sympathy for her. She really was well rid of him, and us taking him out would cut the tie that much quicker. She’d think he died. She could move on.

She left the laptop and went to the bathroom. I stayed with her, which was extremely weird and I felt like a perv, but I didn’t want to break the connection. I was obsessed. Then she went to wash her hands and looked at herself in the mirror and I nearly fell off the cliff, I was so startled.

She looked exactly like Jane. Not similar. Exactly. It was as if Jane was in the mirror.

I saw her through her eyes, not mine, so it was impossible to see if she had the light of Anabo around her. But her resemblance to Jane was freakish. I was shaky, sitting there on the edge of the cliffs. My memory tugged at me, wanting to go back, to relive those few months that Jane was a part of my life. But I resisted. It was too depressing and what was the point? She was dead and it was as much my fault as my brother’s.

Euri was so like Jane, I had to know if she’d been born Anabo. I wished I knew where she was so I could go there now. But Moscow was a very big place, and finding her would be like the proverbial needle in a haystack.

I’d wait. I’d go to Miles’s funeral, and then I’d know.

~~ EURI ~~

Three days later, I was still calling and texting Miles. He still never answered.

I was in Prague for the last European appearance, set to go to London the next day for a short holiday before I left for the U.S. I was so anxious to go home, to see Miles and try to fix this. I had already made plans. We would visit the bishop, a friend of my father's, and ask him what was to be done. Maybe we needed an exorcist. Or a blessing from the archbishop. Whatever we needed to do, we would do it. I would get Miles back.

While I was dressing for the performance, my cell rang with Miles's number. I answered quickly, but it turned out to be his dad.

"I've some terrible, distressing news," Harold said. "Miles is . . . he's . . . Lady Euri, he's gone from us."

I was instantly reeling, dizzy and lightheaded. I dropped to the floor, to my knees. "He's dead?"

"Aye, that's the truth of it. An overdose, the doctors say." He sniffed. "I thought you'd want to know. I'm here at his flat, getting his suit to carry to . . . for the . . ." He stopped talking.

I couldn't speak beyond saying, "I'll be there."

I poured my soul into that night's performance. My sponsor, Stu, and his wife, Zoe, told me it was the best of my career. I wanted to care, but I didn't. I just wanted to go home, to the little walkup in Brixton, to Miles's sweet face and gentle arms and the safety and comfort of his affection.

That night, I drank all the little bottles in the mini bar and got totally pissed, all by myself. I went out on my balcony and sang the aria from *Rigoletto,* because that was Miles's favorite. Then I threw up for hours and was wretchedly hung over the next morning.

At Gatwick, Harold was waiting for me, wearing his chauffer cap and suit. He'd brought the Bentley, he said for old times' sake. We didn't hug or anything like that. He was far too proper for such displays. But as he opened the door for me, he said quietly, "I am glad he had your friendship, Lady Euri. It was the very best part of his life. He loved you so."

I looked up to meet his eyes, the same grey as Miles's, and saw tears. I didn't say anything. I didn't trust myself not to throw myself at him and sob all over his nice wool suit coat. I nodded and got in the car, he closed the door, went round to the driver's side, and we were off to the London house, to my father.

The funeral was two days later, and lightly attended, mostly people who knew Miles from his work at the restaurant and some school chums and all of the staff from Longbourne, my family's estate in Yorkshire, and the staff at the London house. There were a few of Harold's family members there, and the woman who owned the bakery we went to every Saturday. Miles would have loved that she came.

At the back of the group of mourners at the graveside, standing beneath umbrellas because of the heavy fog and mist, I saw a very tall guy with very short dark hair, a tattoo of a question mark on his neck, and a large diamond stud in one ear. He was dressed in a dark suit with a white dress shirt and a somber gray tie, in keeping with the occasion, and despite the gloomy day, he wore a pair of Wayfarers. From behind the dark lenses, I knew he stared at me. And I knew who he was. This was my daydream. This was Z.

Before I could wonder why he was here, *how* he was here, they were lowering Miles into the cold ground. I watched and remembered all of my life with him, all the happy times and sad times and defining moments, turning points in our relationship. The first time he kissed me, when I was twelve and he was fourteen. We were in the stables at Longbourne. The night he drove all the way to Edinburgh to get me after I'd gone off with a school friend who turned out to be a wanker who tried to make me do something I'd no intention of doing. I ran away and hid in a church and that's where Miles found me. The summer we spent in France at my aunt's small villa, running through the vineyards, driving down to the coast, taking cooking lessons. And the first time he made love to me, in my own room at Longbourne, just before I went back to school for my final year before university. It had been my idea. So many of my schoolmates had done it, and I wanted to know what it was all about, and so I seduced Miles. When it was over, we laughed, because it was such a peculiar thing to do.

He was gone, and I couldn't wrap my head around it, couldn't fathom that I would never see him again. I remembered every word of our last conversation, and knew why he'd taken an overdose. He'd rather be dead than to live with what he'd done.

And because of Z, who I now knew was definitely not a figment of my imagination, I didn't doubt the reality of it. When I turned to look at him again, I was disappointed. He was gone.

Then he startled me by appearing right next to me. No one else noticed. I leaned close and whispered, "You're Z."

He was staring down at me from behind the shades and he slowly nodded. "You have a scent," he said in a low murmur, sounding vaguely surprised.

"It's Prada."

"It's the ocean."

"No, it's Prada Iris."

"Come with me."

"Where?"

"Anywhere that's not here."

"I want to stay here and bury Miles."

He moved closer and inhaled deeply. "He sold out. He doesn't deserve your grief."

"He's getting it anyway." I swiped at my tears. "Go away."

"As you wish." Without another word, he disappeared.

I caught the scent of hot cross buns and wondered why? We were in a graveyard, several kilometers from anywhere that might serve food.

Returning my focus to the grave, I listened to the reverend finish his blessing, waging a silent battle within myself. Z was so tall, and big. He was more than handsome. He was irresistibly masculine and powerful. He was not gentle and he was not kind or compassionate. He was nothing like Miles. But I couldn't be indifferent to him. I wanted him, and not entirely in a sexual way. I felt a curious need for him, which defied all logic and decency. I was standing at the grave of my best friend and lover; the one person besides Sophie who'd ever really loved me. He'd sacrificed himself for me, or so he said, and yet here I was pining after someone I'd literally just met.

Except it didn't feel as though we had only just met. I'd traveled about with him in his head for months, and while I'd tried to avoid him after Panama, I wasn't entirely successful. I knew many things about Z that I didn't know about people I'd known my entire life. The ability to see into a person's thoughts was intimacy that flipped between wonder and shock. He was a very large, very virile male, an otherworldly bloke who had the ability to transport himself across the globe in a matter of moments, who took down those who turned their backs on God and pledged their souls to his oldest brother. But he was also a musician of rare ability, and when I wasn't trying to avoid his thoughts as he went about his duties to humanity, I listened to him play. And was captivated.

I would find Z later, while I was in the United States, and I'd find out why, of all the people on the planet, he was the one I dreamed of. For now, for Miles, I intended to let everyone at 66X know what happened to him. Maybe if they knew before they pledged, they'd have second thoughts. Maybe they would leave the boards and forget Eryx and his lies.

I had to try. After all, what did I have to lose? Hadn't Death told me I had a specific purpose? I couldn't die because I had a responsibility to humanity, something I was born to do. I'd thought he meant the piano. I'd begun playing at six, just after my mother tried to kill Sophie, and my teachers declared me a prodigy. I didn't know about that. I just knew it was my solace, my escape, and I could dream to my heart's content when I played, and no one knew, no one scolded me for woolgathering.

But maybe I was wrong. Maybe this is what Death had meant when he pulled me from the lake. It was my responsibility to tell people that Anon66X was a liar and a con artist, and no matter what they wanted, he wouldn't give it to them. It was a one-way contract. He got their soul and they got nothing except screwed.

After the funeral, my father and I hosted a reception for

the mourners, and as soon as the last one had gone, I went upstairs and hurriedly packed for the U.S. tour. When I was done, I settled on my bed and opened my laptop to begin my campaign to stymie and thwart the force of evil who'd stolen Miles's life and destroyed his spirit. I wasn't afraid. I was resolute.

~~ ZEE ~~

For the first time in my long life, I had no idea what to do. I'd essentially been on my own all these years, because there was no one who could help, no one who would have the smallest inkling of understanding. When I had a dilemma, it was generally something to do with reconnaissance and takedowns. I took those problems to Key, or Phoenix. Anything personal, I handled myself, on my own.

I remembered that Lucifer visited me once, just after I became immortal and we were still living on Kyanos. He appeared while I stood on the cliffs and listened to the woman in the ocean.

"You hear her, don't you?" he'd asked.

I was fucking freezing because he was Lucifer. He was death, absolute and forever. I nodded.

"Do you know who she is?"

I looked at him, but never got an impression of his face. "She's balance. She's hope."

His voice was dark and low, just as it had been when I died, when all was darkness, before I was resurrected. "She's you."

She was stability. The solid side of me, because I wasn't nonfunctioning. I was able to go about and live my life and I only occasionally checked out. The woman in the ocean talked to me, soothed me. She was me, only kinder and gentler. I'd wished more than once that she was a real woman, that she would appear one day on the rocky beach of Kyanos and stay with me and scare away the yawning loneliness that was my reality.

But, of course, that wouldn't happen. She wasn't really a woman. She was me. And I was mentally unbalanced. "It's difficult to be me," I'd said to Lucifer.

"I'll see what I can do."

That had been over a thousand years ago and I was more batshit now than I'd been then. Evidently, Lucifer couldn't do much.

I walked around London, because she was here, and because I had a love of London. We all did. I stopped into a pub and had a beer and a slice of steak and kidney pie. I debated what to do.

My instinct, of course, was to pop over to the Longbourne house in Mayfair, to her bedroom, and tell her she was supposed to be with me, and there was no point in dancing around it. I'd tell her Key's rule that newcomers to Mephisto Mountain could bring no worldly possessions. Then I'd take her hand and take her home with me and kiss her all the rest of the day and into tomorrow, when I'd take her clothes off and make love to her forever.

I supposed she'd not like that.

She was an independent soul. She'd had to be, it seemed. I'd found out about her sister, and her mother. She'd spent a lot of her growing up years on the road, playing the piano across Europe. She had few friends. Her father was distant and proper. Miles really had been her everything.

She would have to forget him and move on.

The screamers got cranked up about then, as if to remind me I was the worst kind of fool. I threw back the last of my beer, paid my ticket, and left. Wandering around Piccadilly, I reminded myself why I could not have her. I was a horror movie in real life, an unpredictable mix of violence, rage, and sexual proclivities. Every day was an adventure. I never knew who I'd be when I awoke.

How could I take her with me? How could I subject her to that?

I couldn't. Ever.

Walking toward Hyde Park, I shook it off. Because I had to. If I didn't, I'd be suicidal. I needed to focus on my family, on my brothers, who I loved. I'd continue looking for mindless, meaningless hook-ups with blue-eyed blondes so I could feel happiness for tiny moments in time.

Back in Colorado, I took off my suit and dressed in leathers and went out looking for lost souls. I found a few in Cologne, staggering drunk, looking for a psychic they hoped would help them get their souls back. They saw me, and despite being shit-housed, they knew who I was. They turned and ran.

I didn't chase.

Tonight, I decided I didn't care.

Instead, I went in a bar where a band was playing bad covers of seventies pop songs. It was painful. I had a whiskey and waited. It took less than ten minutes. She was tall, with long blond hair and pretty eyes. Maybe blue, but it was too dark to tell. It didn't much matter. She looked at me and I looked at her and decided she was the one. I'd take her home and fuck her. I didn't doubt she'd go with me. My brothers hadn't ever figured out why girls would go anywhere and do anything with any of us, but I knew. I'd known since the very beginning, when we left Kyanos and went to live in Greece and discovered girls, and realized there was something infinitely more enjoyable to be done with a dick than what we'd done with ours since puberty.

Because we were sons of Hell, humans were hardwired to be afraid of us. We were temptation. We were humanity's siren song of very bad things. To be with us exponentially increased the probability of giving in to dark desires, so they were afraid, and while we were charming and handsome and strong and masculine and all those things most women liked, we scared the bejesus out of them, which added an irresistible element of danger.

My brothers spent a lot of time wooing girls to convince them to sleep with them. I didn't bother beyond being courteous – I wasn't an animal, after all – because I knew they would go with me. They always went with me. I suppose if I went to a church to find a lady, I'd strike out, but I couldn't go inside a church without catching fire and dying an agonizing death, which would pretty much put the kibosh on getting laid anyway, so it wasn't an issue. I went to high-dollar restaurants and cafes, or dark, extremely loud concert venues, where the liquor was plentiful and the music screamed like a lover, making men hot and women wet. Everybody was looking to hook up. I knew because I knew what went on in their heads. I could feel their thoughts, knew what they wanted.

Her name was Leona. Or maybe it was Laura. She asked

me to take her home.

I was on my way out of the place, ecstatic to escape the German version of Captain and Tennille's 'Love Will Keep Us Together,' a suckass song in any language, and had just slipped my fingers around Linda's arm when I heard Euri say, *"Bollocks."*

I slowed and Lorna shot me a quizzical look. I apologized and mentally thought of my cell phone number. Seconds later, it rang. "I've got to take this," I told Liesel. Moving toward the door, I ducked into the foyer and answered. "This is terribly inconvenient."

"Do not take her home. She's a nice girl."

"Spoiler alert: Nice girls like sex as much as not nice girls."

"She wants more than a shag. She wants somebody to love her. What will you do? You can't even remember her name. Leave. Now."

I did. I walked right out of there and off down the street. "You're not my fucking mother. Get out of my head."

"I'd love to, but you keep intruding. I can't play the piano but what you're there. In case you don't know, I play the piano for money. I can't stop."

I kept walking. "You couldn't stop even if it wasn't for money."

"You think you know me?"

"As well as you know me."

She was quiet for a moment. "How did you find me?"

"I knew you'd be at Miles's funeral."

"How did you know he died?"

"You were distressed and hyperemotional. That's when your thoughts pay a visit. I can close my eyes and see what you see."

"Did you have anything to do with his death?"

"No."

"Liar."

"I'm a son of Hell. It comes naturally."

She began to cry. "He was so sweet, so gentle and kind. He deserved a chance."

I stopped on the steps of a place I'd wished I could go inside since it was built in the 1300s. "Can you see where I am?"

In a moment, she said, "You're at a church."

"The Cologne Cathedral in Germany. I've wanted to go inside for over seven centuries, but I can't because I'll burn to death. I can't walk on holy ground. Miles could. He had the very best chance, and what did he do with it? He threw it away for a lie. He wanted you, Euri. He wanted to be strong and successful and everything he could never be and still be sweet and gentle and kind. The fool couldn't see that even if Eryx had given him what he promised, he'd have lost you in the end. You loved all the things in him that would have disappeared. He had his chance, and he fucking blew it. Be sad for his death as if he committed suicide, but not because he was sent to Hell on Earth. He knew the risk when he turned his back on God and all of humanity, but he took it because he wanted you."

"He sacrificed—"

"*Bullshit.* There was no fucking *sacrifice.* Don't make him into a martyr."

"You're angry because you have no chance. Is that it? Is that why you have no compassion for the lost souls?"

"Damn straight."

"What about people who are susceptible to your brother's lies? Do you feel bad for them? They're down on their luck, or abused, or hungry. Maybe they think he can give them what they need to survive."

"They should reach out to other human beings and ask for help and give help when they're able. They have options. They see Eryx as a get-it-quick solution, an answer to their problem without any hard work or real effort. All they have to do is tell God to fuck off and agree to pledge their soul to a tyrannical liar with mommy issues."

"*What?* Did you say *mommy* issues?"

"He murdered our mother. Did I fail to think about that? I'm a little unclear about how often you've been in my mind, so it's impossible to know what you know."

"After Panama, I tried very hard to avoid your thoughts, especially when you go on takedowns. It's a special kind of horrible, isn't it?"

"It's worse in person."

"But in all the times I've been with you in spirit, I've never known Eryx killed his mother."

"*My* mother. He lost the right to call her his mother. He killed *my* mother."

"She must have been an extraordinary woman, giving birth to seven sons, raising them alone on a remote island."

"Not entirely alone. Our father was there some of the time. He made things not so difficult for her. He loved her, in his way."

"The dark angel of death in love with a human. And his eldest son murdered her. You've a very dysfunctional family, haven't you?"

"Doesn't everyone?"

"Indeed. And it appears you and I are destined to have our own cocked up relationship. I'm occasionally successful at blocking your thoughts, but just now, when I sat down to play, I couldn't keep you out."

I'd caught her scent. Chances were excellent that she'd caught mine. Whether I wanted it or not, we'd bonded during those few moments at Miles's funeral. "Seeing each other in person reinforced whatever it is that connects us. I suspect that from now on, the mind games will only get more intense."

"It's no bother, actually. I rather like you, Zee, despite what you do for a living."

I smiled. "I like you, too, Euri, despite knowing we will never be together in real time."

"Why?"

"Because I . . . it just wouldn't work."

"Is it because *you* have mommy issues, since Eryx killed your mother?"

"I assure you, my issues are unrelated to my mother. Have you noticed there is always a cacophony of screamers in my head?"

"I've noticed. You also hear strange snippets of conversations, and sometimes you have violent thoughts, and sexual thoughts, and once, you spent half a day wondering what might have happened if Mozart had become a Lumina and lived with the Mephisto."

"You have to admit to curiosity. If he knew he would live forever, would he have written more music? What would he have thought about the Beatles? Led Zeppelin? Beyoncé?"

She laughed, as I'd hoped she would, but then she grew

quiet and asked soberly, "Why would Eryx kill his own mother?"

"If I tell you, will it upset you?"

"I don't think so. Why do you ask?"

"I know what happened with your mother."

"I didn't save her, but that's not the same as murdering her."

I had a feeling there was an enormous lot more to the story, but what was the point dredging it all up now? Best to move on and put it behind her. "Eryx turned eighteen, which is when all of us were hardwired to die so we could come back as immortals. No one knew about us. Not God and not Lucifer. Eryx knew when he died that he'd come back with no light in his soul. To make God aware of our existence, to keep the rest of us from the same fate, he murdered our mother. Then he jumped, and came back just as he'd known he would, with what amounts to no soul at all. He's not evil for evil's sake. He's evil because he is incapable of anything else."

"Why does he want to sack Lucifer and take over his job?"

"Why does Kovalev want to kill off half of his country's population? Why has he closed the borders and shut down the Internet? How can he in all good conscience live a life of luxury while his people are starving? He wants to feel important. He wants everyone to see him as a brilliant illustrious hero of mankind, a guy who really has it all figured out. He is incapable of seeing the truth. Eryx lost sight of the truth a thousand years ago, the night he jumped to his death. He can't be anything but what he is, and he hates it. He will do anything to be something he can never be and he knows it, which enrages him. He has no hope. And a man can't survive without hope. I think he'd off himself, except he would simply cease to exist. At least we have Hell, which won't be a picnic, but it beats not existing."

"Do you have hope?"

I took a seat on the cathedral steps and stared down at the space between my boots. "If I didn't, I'd walk into this beautiful church and die and go to Hell and call it done."

"What do you hope for, Zee?"

"You."

She didn't say anything for a very long time, but I knew she was still there. Finally, she said, "I don't know why it's me."

"Because you're meant for me. You're Anabo, born without Original Sin, something rare and wonderful. Of all the females on the planet, you are the only one who isn't afraid of me, who might stay with me for the rest of time. You're all I hope for."

"What do I have that you want?"

"You can love me."

"I don't even know you."

"Don't you, Euri? You've been poking about in my mind for months now."

"I've seen you in person only just today, for a total of three minutes. Love generally happens in real life. And besides all that, why would I love the guy who murdered my best friend?"

"I didn't murder him."

"He's dead, isn't he? Don't the people you send into the ground die? The body they buried today wasn't really Miles."

"It's my job. It's been like this since Eryx jumped and came back, and that was over a thousand years ago. I'm not going to apologize for it. It makes no difference anyway. I'm not fit for you, or anyone."

"Evidently, I'm unfit as well. He gave his soul to your brother because I was so intrigued by you, I accepted a tour that would bring me to the United States, on the very slim chance that I might find you and know why, of the billions of people on Earth, my dreams are of you. He was genuine, and gave me the greatest gift of love and affection. I thanked him by ditching him because of a voice in my head."

Overwhelmed by an unfamiliar emotion, I sucked in a deep breath. "No worries, Euripides. I will leave you to your life."

"So that's it then?"

"That's it. Now I'm going back to find Loretta."

"Her name is Lissa."

"Yeah, Lissa. Will you not play the piano for a while?

Give me at least the illusion of privacy."

"I'm going to bed as soon as I'm finished online."

"Goodnight, Euri. And goodbye."

"Goodnight, Zee. And you know as well as I do that this isn't going to be the end. We haven't even gotten started."

"It can never happen."

"We'll see. For now, I hope Lissa has gone off with some nice German chap who will love her and give her lots of babies and a charming cottage with geraniums."

"She'll be waiting for me."

"Then I hope you can't get it up."

"You can be very harsh."

She ended the call and I sat there on the steps and stared at my phone and then I laughed. I really did. And I went home. I was sure not to be up for shagging anyone, especially a *nice* girl like Leslie.

"*Lissa!*"

I looked up at the ceiling of my room and said out loud, "Go to bed."

She was dogged in her determination, I had to give her that. Night after night, for hours on end, I saw her post as LadyAnon at 66X, always with absolute conviction. She was trolled, insulted, and threatened, but she never backed down. I wanted to admire her, but I didn't. She was wasting her time, her heart, her life, engaged in a battle she would forever lose. Eryx didn't care what she said, and the people she tried so desperately to reach, to save from themselves, were already gone. Once a human even thought about the idea of selling out, they were as good as gone. It might take them a few weeks or months to finally take the leap, but if they were at all interested to begin with, they were already lost. Every soul who posted at 66X would eventually belong to Eryx.

I posted as 4Jane and tried to talk her into laying off, but she told me to mind my own business. So I left her alone.

Except when I was asleep. After seeing her in the real world and catching her scent, my dreams of her became more graphic, more vivid, more frightening. It was a mystery to me why I was violent toward her. If I believed in romantic love, I would be madly in love with her. I wanted her with a bone-deep need. Of all the people in the world, she'd be the last one I'd hurt. I'd cut off my hand before I touched a hair on her head. So why did I have such horrific dreams about her? I had always had them. Since I became immortal, I dreamed of a girl who looked just like Euri. I always killed her. Or tried to. I wasn't angry, or upset. I was determined.

It might have been my subconscious desire to kill her so I could bring her back as immortal, so she'd have to stay with me, but typically in my dream, she was already immortal. I took her down, then sobbed my regret after she left me all alone.

It was just another mutation of my insanity, something I had to live with. The reason I could never be with her in reality. Who would want to be with a guy who harmed them every night, even if it was only in his sleep?

So I stayed away from her thoughts as much as I could, ignored her when she talked to me. Pretended I didn't hear. She knew, and she'd sometimes laugh at me for the pretense; other times, it made her cry.

I spent time on the Internet gathering IP addresses from 66X, coding them before I placed them in an Excel spreadsheet. Once a week, I sorted the data based on several criteria, and deleted those who had pledged as soon as we'd taken them down. Kyros was happy about staying on top of the 66X boards. I was happy to have something to do that intersected with Euri's life, even something as lame as seeing her posts on the forums.

She was crazy, like me. Maybe not as severe, but she was scarily close to madness. She was even less a candidate for me than Jane had been. Sweet, reserved, ladylike Jane, who was not a whit mad. Totally sane. Being with me would have been her own Hell on Earth. I wished I'd handled it differently, because in the end, she died and it was as much my fault as Phoenix's. He never knew she was meant to be mine. None of my brothers did. If I'd owned up to it and been honest with them, maybe Jane could have found happiness with one of them. Maybe she'd still be alive.

I wouldn't let the same thing happen to Euri. I would stay away from her. I would never tell my brothers about her. She would move on with her life, meet somebody and marry him and have babies and die, like everybody else on Earth.

And I'd go on with my crazy. Alone. I was always pretty much alone. It's what it meant to be me. So I'd carry on as I had for the past thousand years, and for this brief interlude, which might be her entire life, but only an intermezzo in eternity, I'd have her in my head. Then she'd be gone and I'd be left with the screamers and a voice in the ocean. It's how it had to be. I knew this.

That was my intention.

But, as they say, the road to Hell is paved with good intentions.

CHAPTER 4

~~ EURI ~~

I left the tour before it was done, burned a bridge with Stu and didn't care. I skipped out on the performance with the New York Symphony and went instead down to Hell's Kitchen to a club called Blackbriar because Arcadia was playing. I stood in the middle of all those screaming fans and, during a break, one of the roadies invited me backstage. I met John Jamison, a tall, lean bloke with a dark beard and warm brown eyes. He reminded me a bit of Miles and I immediately liked him.

"Will you play keyboard on a couple of songs?" he asked.

"I'd be delighted."

It was magical and I loved it so much. During the encore, the drummer winked at me, the bass player gave me a thumbs up, and John Jamison grinned at me. When it was over, as we left the stage, John said, "How much would it cost me for you to stay with us?"

I named a figure and he laughed. "Seriously? That's all?"

"I have enough," I said. "It'd be really excellent to travel with Arcadia."

And so I joined a rock band. I never went back to my hotel. One of the roadies went to collect my things and deliver a note to Stu. "I can bring you to court over this," he said when he called.

"There are only three more concerts on the tour, Stu. I'm sorry, but I can't do this anymore. Keep all the money if you want. Just let me go. Let me be."

"Losing Miles is catching up with you. I was afraid of something like this."

It wasn't just Miles. I was slipping further and further into my psychosis. I was now as much in Z's mind as I was in my own. I spent hours every day in a vague fog, which I know made me appear quite mad, but I became less able to stop, to remain focused. I needed to be with people who didn't expect anything from me but music. It was all I had, all I could offer. When I played, no one knew I was living another life. My only other option was to go home, to Longbourne, and live as a recluse, away from people. No doubt I was doomed to that, but not yet.

Stu said he'd talk to Dad and assure him I was fine. We ended our call and I knew I'd never hear from him again. My career as a concert pianist was over.

I had another call later that same night, in the wee hours, waking me from deep sleep. I answered and Z said, "I heard you play with Arcadia. It was fucking genius. You're a genius."

"No, only lucky. Some people are born smart, some beautiful, and some with a talent for music. Whatever I am, it's luck."

"Call it what you want, that was incredible. Did John ask you to join the band?"

"He did, and I said yes and dropped my remaining piano concerts. I'm going to tour with Arcadia. Will you be a groupie and come to our concerts and try to sneak backstage so you can see me?"

I felt his presence in the dark, heard his movements from the corner of the tiny hotel room. I ended the call and whispered, "Or you could go all out stalker and just appear in my bedroom."

He stayed where he was, and I heard him inhale deeply before he said, "I came to say good luck on the road, and to give you a warning. You're very innocent, Euri. Or naïve. Everyone is both good and bad, but you can't see past the good in anyone, and I worry that you'll be hurt by someone you wrongly trust because you can never believe anyone is capable of cruelty."

I sat up in the narrow bed and turned on the lamp. He was dressed all in leather, including his coat, an ankle-length duster. I was struck once again by his size. He was enormous, especially in the cramped hotel room that was perhaps smaller than a utility cupboard. "You could sit down, if you like."

"I would like it very much, but no, thank you. I can't stay. I came in person so you'd understand the gravity of your situation."

I didn't see anything particularly grave about my circumstances, but he seemed quite sincere and concerned, so I said, "You're very kind to worry, Z. I will be vigilant, I promise, and at the first sign of a problem, I will take steps to ensure I am safe."

He came a bit closer. "What steps?"

"I will contact the coppers."

"That's not always your best bet. Police frequently ignore crimes against women."

"I could ask John's help. He seems a gentlemanly sort who wouldn't allow anyone to take advantage."

"He may be held up elsewhere."

I finally gave him what it was he came for. "I will call you, Z."

He nodded his satisfaction. "Good." He glanced at my practice keyboard, still in its case, taking up a large portion of the miniscule room. "Try the bridge in A during rehearsals and see how it plays."

"In 'Franklyn Lies'?"

"No, in the oil of Olay song."

I laughed. "It's 'Spoil and Obey'."

His black eyes fairly glittered and his smile was definitely wicked, even predatory. I didn't mention to him that my greatest danger going forward was this crazy-making attraction I had for him. A son of Hell. I'd take my clothes off and climb all over him until lunchtime tomorrow if he'd let me.

He was still giving me that wolfish smile. "You do realize that's a song about sexual bondage, right?"

"I'm aware. I am optimistic, Z, not naïve. Don't worry about me." When he was standing next to the bed, I bent my neck and gazed up the height of him, at his handsome face. "Kiss me."

He bent toward me and my breath hitched, my stomach fluttered, and my sex came to attention. Just before his lips touched mine, he moved to the right and kissed my cheek.

His warm, soft lips on my skin was as erotic as anything I'd ever experienced. He traveled south and nuzzled my throat, his big hands holding my head, his duster swinging to either side of me, encasing me in his scent. Hot cross buns. And men's cologne. And a musky smell that was his essence, what made him male.

When he pulled back and unbent, I was breathing harder, and so terribly needy. "Why will you not kiss me on the mouth?"

"Because it will turn you to Mephisto, and that can never happen. My apologies, Euripides. I shouldn't have come. Shouldn't make this more intolerable. Try to stay out of my head. Move on and find a new love to replace Miles, a solid guy who won't sell out."

"I don't want that. I want you."

"No, you don't." He smiled crookedly. "You want romance. Go and find it, just be careful. Especially with the roadie named Rulon. He's a misogynistic piece of shit who gets his jollies fucking drunk girls. Promise me you'll stay away from him."

"I promise. What about Joe?"

"He's cool." He lifted a brow. "You like Joe, do you?"

"This is secret Z code, fishing to see if I might have sexual thoughts about Joe?"

"Well? Do you?"

I did not, but said, "I fail to see why it matters."

I noticed his hands clenched and he shoved them into his coat pockets. "You're right. It doesn't."

He disappeared and I blinked at the space where he'd been. Why hadn't he said goodbye or goodnight? How very peculiar he was.

Moments later, I received a text from him: DON'T FORGET – TRY THE BRIDGE IN A.

I texted back that I wouldn't forget. Then I smiled, turned out the light, and went back to sleep.

Nomadic in an old charter autobus, Arcadia went all over the United States over the next several months and I went with them. We stayed in cut-rate motels, and I lived out of a suitcase while traveling with a band of geeks from MIT who still acted stupid about female genitalia. It was like taking a road trip with 4chan. I endured pussy jokes and silly grins and red faces and awkward, poorly hidden boners for the sake of the music. I was doing what I'd always wanted to do. I'd never pursued anything like it because I knew Miles would never get over me being away for so long.

He was gone now, and Sophie, and my Cambridge education. I figured it would still be there when I went back, if I had the mind to do it. I feared I would not, that I'd be lost to reality long before I could return to university.

I just didn't care. I played music, saw America, fielded concerned calls from Dad, continued to post at 66X, and grew ever more entwined with Z. He tried not to. At least once a week, he tried to block me from his thoughts, but after a day or so, he'd give up. He invaded my thoughts, sometimes during awkward moments, like when I was in the shower. He'd chuckle in his deep, low voice and say, "Turnabout is fair play."

My mind began inviting him in more frequently, even when I wasn't playing piano, and I slowly lost the ability to stop it. I concentrated as diligently as possible and, after much practice, became quite adept at carrying on conversations with people in real life at the same time I heard conversations between Z and someone else from a thousand kilometers away. Sometimes, when it was impossible to focus, I pled a migraine and the band left me alone. If we were on the bus, I'd cover my eyes and allow his conscience to override mine.

Traveling across the United States, I saw amazing things, landmarks and cities and spectacular scenery. Behind my eyes, within my head, I saw things I could never unsee, like the sweaty, desperate faces of the lost souls as they were sent below the ground. Like the cries of sorrow from those left behind, who were hoodwinked into believing their loved one had died, who they thought they'd see again someday in Heaven. I saw victims of the lost souls and Skia who weren't found by the Mephisto before they could commit atrocities. There was a dark side to humanity I'd never known before. It was frightening and sad and eternally horrifying. I grew to understand Z and knew why he had no pity. What I saw through his eyes was enough to turn the kindliest angel of God into a jaded cynic.

I thought a lot about Miles during those months on the road. I swung widely between terrible grief and bitter anger. I missed his sweet, melodic voice, his kindness. I missed knowing he was there, in London, and would be there when I went home. But he wasn't there because he'd sold his soul. I realized why Z said it wasn't a sacrifice. Every human is responsible for their own spirituality, and Miles had lost his center, not because of what he perceived as my abandonment of him, but his own lack of self-worth. Still, he'd been a lovely man, and I loved him without prejudice.

He'd said that I never saw anyone as they really were, and maybe he was right. I did tend to focus on positive characteristics and ignore the rest.

With one exception.

I knew all of Z, the bad with the good.

He was at times funny, frequently sad, and always fighting our connection. And yet, I know he searched for excuses to see me, to pop into my physical life for brief interludes that usually left me frustrated and lonelier than before.

He told me one night, "There will come a day when I regret seeing you, listening to you, wanting you. I should go home and never talk to you again. It's like chasing a drunk buzz, wanting it to last but knowing how much it will hurt in the morning."

"Being with you is like the edge of an orgasm, when you're oh, so close, and given only one more moment, you'll fall right off into bliss."

We were lying on my bed in a motel in Kansas City, staring up at the bumpy ceiling. He had come to bring me some sheet music he'd written, because I begged him for it. He said he would do this one thing, and then he wasn't coming back.

I didn't believe him, but I went along to allow him the illusion.

"I like your analogy better," he said to the ceiling, "but the aftermath of an orgasm is contentment. It's almost as wonderful as the climax. A hangover is not a happy time."

"And you believe when you're not with me, when this is over, you'll feel rotten like a hangover?"

He sighed and rolled to his side and propped his head in his hand to look down at me. "It'll be infinitely worse than a hangover. Besides, my hangovers don't last all that long. Immortality means we don't suffer illness like mortal people do."

"Why does it have to be over?"

"Because I'm not right for you. I have . . . issues."

"I know, Z. I'm getting to know you very well. So much, in fact, I know exactly why you believe you're bad for me, but I'm not afraid of you. I will never be afraid of you."

"You should be."

"Then if you won't be my love, at least be my friend. Of all the people in all the world, you're the only one who gets me." I laughed. "I can't believe I just said that. But it's true. If other people knew what goes on in my head, they'd have me sent away. They'd never believe it's all you. My daydreams are simply what runs through your mind, what you see and hear, and nothing in your life would be believed by ordinary folk. You know, I've done a bit of study on psychosis, and a doctor would certainly label me psychotic, delusional and hallucinatory. It would be assumed that none of this is real, just like they were so sure that what I knew of Sophie wasn't real. But I knew I wasn't imagining it."

"What you call your daydreams are not something ordinary people can understand. It's abnormal. Extraordinary. And not crazy. But just like me, you sometimes have other things going on in your head that follow no logic. And that's what makes you insane." He sat up and looked toward the telly, tuned to an old episode of *Friends*. "Last week, when you were in Denver, what happened?"

Bloody hell. I'd thought he wasn't aware. It came and went and I heard nothing from him, didn't feel him in my thoughts, and so I was certain it had passed and he was unaware. I was wrong.

I turned to my other side, facing away from him. "Please, let's not talk about it. It's not an ordinary thing, you see. It's only happened a handful of times and it distresses me terribly to think about it."

Suddenly, he was behind me, gathering me close to him, blanketing me in warmth and affection. "Next time, I'll come to be with you."

"Maybe there won't be a next time."

"It's your madness, Euri. How you were made. There will always be another time. I've been insane for a thousand years and every episode I have, I wish with all my heart and soul that it will be the last, but it never is. Crazy doesn't heal itself. There's no logic to it, no way to predict it, anticipate or prepare for it. The best you can do is accept it."

"If anyone knew . . . if John or anybody in the band were to know, they'd call my father and he'd be on the first plane to America. He'd take me back to England and lock me up."

His arms tightened and he breathed into my hair. "For now, while you're traveling with Arcadia, I'll be your friend. I'll know and I'll be with you. Don't fret."

I'd said I didn't want to talk about it, but now I was curious. "How much did you see?"

"All of it. I wanted to pop in and maybe make it stop, but sometimes interrupting is worse than letting it run its course."

"Did you see—"

"I saw everything. I saw you press your whole body against the mirror and stay like that for almost two hours, but I also saw what was happening in your mind. It's all right, you know. It doesn't change who you are."

I began to cry, because it all felt so hopeless. "But it does," I whispered. "Every time it happens, it takes away a little bit more of my soul."

"Hey, what's this?" He tugged until I rolled to my back and he looked down at me from his beautiful black eyes. "You're the eternal optimist who can put a happy spin on anything. You live for silver linings. And it's not as though your episode was a terrible thing. Not like mine. You saw your twin, someone you loved, someone you miss. It wasn't real, but you were so happy to be with her."

I swallowed and swiped the tears from my cheeks. "Yes, I'm so happy, so anxious to make her whole again, I give her a piece of me. I know that someday, she'll have all of me. I will cease to exist. It's not as though she takes it, Z. I give it freely."

"It's just your mind's way of dealing with survivor guilt. She was handicapped and you weren't. She died and you didn't. You fall into these episodes as a way for your mind to deal with the grief and guilt."

"I loved her so. You have no idea." Crying hard now, I clung to him and hated myself for this weakness, for what I was powerless to combat. "She was so bright and beautiful and such a force of nature. I was the quiet one and she was always laughing, always the instigator, the smart one. She was the leader and I was happy to follow. If I can share myself with her, if I could make her into what she was meant to be, I'd go to any lengths, even giving her pieces of me."

"You're not giving her any of you except love and adoration. This is not real. You know that, Euri. When you have an episode, when you believe you walk through the mirror and are with her, it's not really happening. That's the horror of psychosis, that what seems so solid and real is nothing but a glitch in your brain."

I wanted to believe him. But I didn't. Just as ordinary people would never believe I could read the thoughts and see the actions of a bloke from many kilometers away, Z didn't believe I sometimes saw my sister's spirit in the mirror, that I crossed into another realm to see her, touch her, share my life with her. She walked and talked and laughed and when I left her, I always felt smaller, as if the world had narrowed. I was less able to talk to people. My soul shrunk. It was real. I knew this. I supposed Z would believe me when I ceased to exist.

He was staring down at me with a look of concern. "Okay, let's go on the premise that it's real. Why would God let something like this happen to you? Why would he allow you to gift the soul he gave you to your sister? And why does she need it? She has her own soul, her unique spirit."

It did seem out of synch with what I believed about God.

"Why would you be intended for me if you're going to disappear? Because that's so fucked up, I can't even get my head around it."

"Maybe because you don't want me, God allows me to

give myself to my sister." It sounded ridiculous when I said it aloud like that. And completely discounted all he hoped for. "Sorry. So sorry. That was a singularly cruel and stupid thing to say."

His lips curved into a soft smile and his eyes were warm and affectionate. "It's all going to be okay, Euri. Do you believe me?"

I nodded because I did believe him. Somehow, it would be okay in the end. He would make it so.

"Come here." He slid his arms around me and pulled me close and my head rested in the warm nook between his shoulder and his neck. Our legs entwined and he held me like that for the longest time. I heard the laughter of *Friends* from the telly, and I whispered, "I'm so very happy and glad that you're my friend, Z."

He answered by moving his head to kiss my cheek, then resettled and we stayed like that until I drifted off to sleep.

When I awoke, my cell was ringing, sun shone through the break in the curtains, and Z was gone.

"Did you write this?" John continued riffing Z's music on his guitar while the others sat with idle instruments and bemused smiles on their faces. We were in the practice studio of a newish club in Manhattan, Kansas, home of the Kansas State Wildcats.

"It came to me in a dream," I said, not wanting to lie, but not able to tell the truth. I had added lyrics, some of my meandering thoughts after I lost Sophie, after I lost Miles, and after one of my mirror episodes. I'd titled it, indulgently, 'All Of Me.' I'd emailed it to Z, and he said, "This is fucking genius. If Jamison doesn't like it, you have to bail from Arcadia and go on your own."

John appeared to like it very much, which meant I could continue on with the band.

Two weeks later, we were back in New York for a break and while we were there, we cut a new record. The first single release was 'All of Me' but the song fans liked best turned out to be 'Send Me Down', which was all Z's. He'd handed me music and lyrics, and John was blown away. I felt guilty taking credit for it, but Z assured me he was over the moon to have his music heard by people outside of Mephisto Mountain.

On the road after the time we'd spent in New York, I grew restless, and every late night visit from Z became a hardship because he always left. I begged him to stay a little longer, but he was resolute. And constantly berating himself for coming to see me at all.

In Virginia Beach, at a Best Western that was a cut above our usual dated, shabby inns, I decided to have it out with him and issued an ultimatum. “I want to be with you, Z. I want to know you, but you only allow me these tiny little visits and bugger if you don't spend half the time complaining that you shouldn't be here. Either come to see me and make it count, or don't come at all.”

He was just done with a takedown and so was dressed in his leathers and long duster. It swirled around his boots as he paced the length of my room and mumbled curses and debated what to do. Although he appeared absolutely certain he should leave and never come back, he tortured himself because he couldn't make himself do it.

I had ordered a pizza, and when the phone rang from the front desk to tell me it had arrived, I turned toward the door. “Either be here when I get back, ready to eat pizza and talk about anything other than your blasted guilt, or go home.”

He made it to the door before me. “I'll get your fucking pizza. Just sit down.”

And so he stayed and we ate pizza and talked about what England was like in previous centuries. His favorite place they had ever lived was Yorkshire, only a few kilometers from Longbourne. The symmetry of that appealed to me.

He stayed later than he usually did, until I was in bed, and sat beside me and petted my hair until I began to drift off, and then he disappeared.

This became who we were. He came to me every third or fourth night. We'd have something to eat, we'd talk, and he'd stay until I went to sleep. He held me, touched me, kissed my cheeks and my neck and my arms, but never my mouth. We became friends.

But I wanted so much more.

~~ ZEE ~~

During those weeks after Euri joined Arcadia, I couldn't stop myself from going to see her, couldn't save myself from inevitable pain. My obsession brought to mind the frog analogy. If a frog is placed in a pan of room temperature water, he's happy. He sits in his water and thinks about lady frogs, or flies. The heat is increased by small increments, and the water slowly becomes hotter and hotter, but the frog remains, still thinking about his lady, or those flies. Or, hell, maybe he doesn't think at all. He has a tiny little frog brain. Until a certain point, he is perfectly able to hop out of the pan and gain his freedom – his life. But he doesn't. The silly fucking frog stays until he's a boiled frog.

I was no smarter than that idiotic tiny-brained frog. I knew I should hop out of the pan. Self-preservation demanded it.

But I couldn't stop seeing her. Every time I went, I'd think, this is the last time. I'd make it two days, maybe three, and then I was compelled to go back. I loved touching her. The instant we came into contact, the screaming in my head stopped. Completely. I could hear her breaths, her heartbeat, the whir of the inevitable ice machine at the end of the motel hallway. I knew what it might be like to be normal.

She was so beautiful, tall and blond, with soft skin and that lilting, cultured British accent. She smiled a lot, always more happy than not. Just sitting in the same room with her felt good. Felt right.

Then I'd go home, go to bed, and dream of her. And I always killed her. The means varied. One night I might strangle her, the next might involve a knife, and every so often, I'd smother her with my hands. The location never varied. I took her into a church, laid her on the altar and while my body burned and my own life slipped away, I killed her. My Anabo.

I knew I should tell her about the dreams, explain why I could never be with her. I might kill her in my sleep. If she were immortal, as she was in the dreams, I couldn't kill her, but who'd want to be with someone who hurt them night after night? I had no idea what I was capable of. Many years ago, when we still lived in Yorkshire, I'd woken up in the barn, standing over a newborn calf. I was covered in blood and the calf was dead. Had I gone there in my sleep to help the cow deliver, and the calf was already dead? Or had she given birth to a healthy calf and I killed it?

I didn't know. My horror was enormous. And shame. I couldn't tell Ty I'd been there, that I knew the calf was dead. He thought more of his animals than he did of people. If he thought for even a moment that I'd killed the little calf, he'd never forgive me. I'd never forgive myself.

I futilely railed against the insanity, more so now than I had in centuries. Because now it kept me from Euri and I wanted her so badly, it became a pain in my chest. I knew I should stay away from her. Going to see her, even for an hour or two twice or three times a week, was cruel to her and the worst kind of self-flagellation. I was all kinds of a masochist.

But every few days, I'd be right back at her door, wherever she was, asking to come in and be with her and bask in her perfect light for a few hours.

It wasn't just the pleasure of her company I craved, or even the blessed silence she could bring. I became obsessed with thoughts of sex with her. My imagination made love to her again and again. I dreamed of making love to her. Then I'd kill her. I wished I'd wake up after the sex dream and never again have the horrible nightmare of killing what I wanted above anything. But I never did. I'd gather her up from where we'd just sent each other to the moon and back, and a church door would appear, open, and I'd carry her the length of the aisle to the altar and she would die by my hand.

Jesus Christ, I was so fucked up.

But, then, so was she. Not in the horrifying way of my mind, but she was equally batshit.

She had another mirror episode while she was in Deadwood, South Dakota. This time, she wasn't in her hotel room, but the lobby of the hotel. She caught something in a large mirror behind a potted palm and went for it. She pressed her entire body to the glass.

I was just home from a particularly difficult takedown in Tokyo, where a couple of Skia had escaped and I'd spent five hours searching for them. My brain hurt. I was exhausted. I came home, stripped, and sat at my piano, thinking to soothe myself a bit before I showered.

As usual, I slipped into her mind, but instead of hearing her soft voice and gentle thoughts, I was with her as she stepped through the mirror and walked toward Sophie, who stood beneath a broad elm, wearing a wide straw hat and a sunny yellow dress. She opened her arms and Euri hugged her.

I saw all of this while I scrambled to get into a pair of jeans and a T-shirt. I slipped into some flip-flops and popped myself to Deadwood. I knew that lobby. It was an old Victorian hotel, renovated for modern times but kept to look like an old west saloon with red flocked wallpaper, velvet settees, and Tiffany lamps.

People were staring at her. Of course. Who wouldn't stare at a young woman plastered to a mirror? As always, as soon as I was close to her, I was no longer in her mind, couldn't see what she saw. But I didn't need to see to know she was deep in her delusion.

I walked up behind her and said with a laugh, "Sugar, I've told you, nobody can see your moustache, so stop looking at it. Let's get out of here and grab some lunch, yeah?" I pulled her away from the mirror, immediately put my arms around her to shield her from the stares, and walked her out the back door, into a small garden area. As soon as we made it to the alleyway, I popped her to the hall upstairs and walked until my mind told me to stop. Room 211. I popped inside and laid her on the bed. She was still with Sophie, her eyes glazed over and her mouth moving as though she were talking, but no noise came out.

I decided maybe it would be best to wake her up, to bring her out of her trance.

"Euri, come back. Come and be with me, Euri. Tell Sophie goodbye now."

She couldn't hear me. She was smiling. I leaned over her, was mere inches from her face when she reached up and held my head and whispered, "I love you."

I went very still and knew within a nanosecond she wasn't talking to me. But it was maybe the best nanosecond I'd ever had. How much would it blow me away if she looked at me and said she loved me? I wished it could be so. I was envious of a dead handicapped girl because Euri went to see her and told her she loved her and she wasn't even real.

Still close, I said again, "Euri, say goodbye to Sophie and come with me."

Her mouth continued to move without sound and her smile softened.

Ten more minutes into it, she showed no sign of returning to reality and I was all out of patience. I debated leaving, just going home and letting her come out of it on her own, but some devil inside wouldn't let me do that. I was compelled to wake her up, to connect with her.

I kicked off the flip flops and lay down next to her, gathered her close and sang to her. I have no idea why. It just came out and before I knew it, I'd sung all of the Beatles 'Golden Slumbers' and my favorite rendition of the national anthem of France.

She was still smiling, still mouthing words, still a zillion miles away.

I moved her slightly and kissed her cheek. Good Lord it was soft. Her scent was crazy strong, almost as if I stood at the cliffs of Kyanos above the crashing waves. I had one arm curled around her, holding her close. I smoothed her hair away from her face with my free hand, then I stroked the soft skin of her throat, and skimmed down, across her breasts to her belly, to her hip. I ran my hand around to her backside, soft and round and perfect inside a pair of jeans. I kissed her forehead, her cheek, her nose, and the corner of her lips. God, I wanted to kiss her full on the mouth. What would she taste like?

Just like always when I was this close to her, I acquired a desperately deprived boner. My sex life had withered to nothing since I'd found Euri. It was fucking impossible to fuck a girl while Euri was watching. And since I couldn't have sex with Euri, that pretty much made me the most frustrated son of a bitch alive. I was dating my hand. And I hated it.

The temptation to kiss her, to bring her back to me and then make love to her all the rest of the day was enormous. I made up all kinds of justifications for it. She wanted me, wanted to be with me. I knew this. We'd be happy together. Batshit, but happy.

Until I woke her up in the middle of the night with my hands around her throat.

I sighed and pulled her closer.

And waited.

Finally, she moved with conscious purpose and, without saying a word, slid her arms around me, rolled me to my back and lay on top of me. Her cheek was against my chest and she lifted her arms and ran her fingers through my hair. "Thank you for being here."

"Welcome. Maybe in future you should avoid mirrors in public places."

"Capital notion."

"What do you talk about during your visits with Sophie?"

"What might have been. It's different, you see, because she can talk, and walk. We're always in a park with lovely trees and we sit on a bench and she tells me all the things she'd do if she had the chance."

"Like what?"

"Simple things, like swimming, or horseback riding, or knitting. She says she would volunteer at a school for disabled people because she knows what that means."

"She doesn't want to have what you have? No desire to be musical, or a writer or something creative?"

"She was always pragmatic. Much more grounded than me."

"But she could see into your thoughts, couldn't she?"

"Yes, but she didn't like to, and had the ability to stop it from happening. I remember after the first time Miles and I had sex, she was angry with me."

"Did she not like Miles?"

"She loved Miles. Before she became disabled, they were inseparable. They'd go off from the house at Longbourne and pretend to be Power Rangers."

"And what did you do?"

"I listened to music and read books. I was always content just to be in my room at Longbourne."

"Until Sophie was disabled?"

"That's when I began playing my own music. Miles was with me a lot, and we became close as the years passed, solace to each other, I suppose."

"And Sophie?"

"She always loved him, and it hurt her that he and I became lovers. That was the only time she seemed resentful of her circumstances. She wouldn't let me visit for over a month afterward."

"Did she know because she could read your thoughts?"

"She knew because she was with me when it happened. In my head, I mean."

"That had to be rough. If she was in love with him."

"I was naïve enough not to realize she loved him like that. It wasn't possible for her to . . . she couldn't . . . I assumed her feelings for him were childlike and affectionate. She eventually forgave me, but it was never quite the same after that. I grew up and she didn't. She couldn't."

"Was she angry at your mother?"

"Strangely no, but she didn't like it when Mum visited, which was rare, thank God. She was afraid of her, and who could blame her? It irritated Mum, who insisted until the day she died that Sophie fell and hit her head. I don't think about it, Zee. I can't change what happened, and living in anger and resentment doesn't have an effect on anything except to make me unhappy. I know these mirror episodes are strange, but I can't not go to her when I see her."

"I understand." Oddly, despite the insanity of it, I really did understand.

We were quiet for a while and I was hyperaware of her supple body lying atop mine.

She lifted her head and looked at me in all seriousness. "You have an enormous hard-on."

"Your fair charms overwhelm me, Lady Euri."

"I want it inside of me."

Fucking killed me, but I said, "No."

"Kiss me."

It took a moment for me to say, "No."

She moved further up my body until her face was just above mine. She kissed my cheeks, as I usually kissed hers, and trailed her lips along my jaw to my throat, then around to my ear, and finally, the corner of my mouth. And all the while, she moved her hips, rubbing her center against me, making my dick throb with need and my heartbeat increase to inhuman speed. "I'd wager you taste divine," she murmured. "I want to kiss you, Zee. Please stop trying to save me. Put us both out of misery and accept me. Take me home with you and make love to me and never let me go."

I closed my eyes and turned my face away from her. "I can't, Euri. I just . . . can't."

She rolled away from me and sat up on the side of the bed, her back to me. "Then you'll have to go away. If you won't make love to me, won't make this what it's supposed to be, I don't want to see you any more. I can't endure this never ending push-pull with you, these tiny unfulfilling tastes of you when all I can expect at the end is being alone."

I moved to sit beside her and took her hand in mine. "Do you mean this? Or are you deliberately trying to be cruel so I'll cave?"

She looked up at me with resolution in her lovely eyes. "I mean it."

"We decided we'd be friends. You need a friend like me, Euri. What would be happening right now if I hadn't been here to rescue you? They'd be hauling you off to a hospital. At a minimum, John would be questioning whether you should stay in the band. He'd be calling your father for sure."

Her resolute look became a little less convinced.

I took heart. "Don't kick me out of your life, Euri. You're the only friend I've ever had. And I know that's as pathetic as it sounds, but swear to God it's true. The past few months since I've known you have been the best of my whole life, and my life's been a fucking long time, so that's saying a lot." I was begging and couldn't stop. The idea that I'd never see her again made my whole body hurt.

She breathed a heavy sigh and looked down at our entangled hands. "Sometimes, Xenos, you make me very tired. This isn't me. I don't want difficult, don't want painful. I know you and I together wouldn't always be easy street, but I'm absolutely sure we'd be wonderful for each other."

Feeling her capitulation, I pressed my advantage. "Then let's continue as we have, and I'll work on overcoming my concerns." Total bullshit, because what were the odds I'd stop the nightmares now, when I'd been having them for a thousand years? But I was desperate enough to lie to her, and I did it well, I suppose, because she rewarded me with a big smile.

"So what you're saying is that you just need more time."

I nodded. "Right."

And a lobotomy.

CHAPTER 5

~~ EURI ~~

There was a darkness to Z that was as disturbing as it was intriguing. He was a paradox, a gentle soul in the body of a warrior with the temperament of insanity – always a mystery who he might be when he awoke each morning. I'd come to know Z without the curtain of societal rules or the caution we all employ to keep others from knowing our real thoughts and opinions. I grew to know him as well as I knew myself. All of him, even what he tried so desperately to hide from his brothers. I learned him in increments, a bit of thought here, a visceral emotional reaction there. In spite of who and what he was, I liked him. And I wanted him on a deep, primitive level I'd not known existed. It was more than sexual need, even more than emotional. There was an invisible tie between us that felt so secure and certain, I sometimes lost sight of where I ended and he began.

As much as I couldn't stay out of his head, I knew he was frequently in mine.

In the beginning, it was awkward, but I became accustomed to his presence, always at the edge of my mind. And I became more settled into his routines, into what he thought about. I wondered if all guys were as preoccupied with sex? Because Z thought about it quite often.

Although, to be fair, I also thought about sex quite a lot, and it was always with Z. Not that I didn't have ample opportunity for sex with other blokes. I was hit on by every single band member, which I did not take as any glowing compliment to my sexiness, but that I had all the lady parts necessary for real, live, human contact sex.

Z turned out to be spot-on in his assessment of Rulon. Except Rulon didn't bother getting me drunk first. After repeated come-ons, which I refused or ignored, he became more aggressive, more insistent. He seemed to believe I was not a human being, but a vagina he deserved to deposit some semen into because, I don't know, he had a penis? He was male? I avoided him as much as possible, but that only served to make him more demanding. He was clever, somehow managing always to do his worst when no one was looking. The guys in the band and the other roadies were oblivious. I considered talking to John about it, and had decided I would have to, that it would be Rulon, or me. I couldn't take it anymore.

The last time I turned Rulon down, I told him I planned to tell John about his behavior, and as most guys like Rulon do, he went over the line between extremely scary and actually violent.

I was in my room at the Kirkwood Inn in Bozeman, Montana one night when Rulon knocked on the door. I knew exactly what he intended, but I asked what he wanted at the same time I texted Z that I needed some help. By the time Rulon had kicked my door to break the security chain and grabbed me and thrown me on the bed, Z was there and Rulon was almost instantly unconscious, laid out on the floor, bleeding. Z looked like controlled rage, his mouth set in a grim line, his eyes hard chips of onyx, and his hands clenched in fists. He didn't say anything before he picked up my phone from where I'd dropped it, and sent a text. When he looked at me, his face softened. "Are you okay?"

"Just a little rattled. Thank you."

"I texted John, so he'll be here in a few moments. He'll fire this fuckwad." He glanced at Rulon. "I've wanted to do that for a while now." He cocked his head. "I hear John running." Then he looked at me again and disappeared.

When John came in, he took one look at Rulon and said, "Holy balls, Euri, did you do that to him?"

I realized half of Rulon's face was concave. Z had broken his jaw. I couldn't come up with an explanation of how I could possibly break a man's jaw, so I resorted to crying hysterically, which gave me more time.

After the ambulance came and took Rulon away, John said, just as Z had predicted, "I'm firing that asshole from the tour. He's been a problem since the get-go."

After he asked me one more time how Rulon was knocked out, and I cried some more to avoid answering, he left my room and I sat at the end of the bed and looked at the bloodstain on the carpet.

I heard Z's piano in my head and he said in a low voice, "If he asks again, tell him you hit him with a baseball bat."

"I don't have a baseball bat."

The music stopped, and there was Z, holding a bat. He handed it to me, winked, and disappeared again.

And so it went. Outside of his infrequent visits, he'd come to me at the oddest times for varying reasons. Then he'd pop out without a goodbye, as if he'd never even been there.

Despite our agreement to just be friends, as time passed I grew more and more dissatisfied and told him he needed to stop this ridiculous and completely ineffectual avoidance and just come and take me home with him to Mephisto Mountain and make love to me already.

He wouldn't respond when I said things like that. Instead, he'd go out hunting for girls. I was terrified that he'd take one home and go through with it.

I called him one night while he was at Max's in Vegas, eyeing a tall blonde. He answered with a curt, "Are you in trouble?"

"No, but I might be."

"What does that mean?"

"If you take her home, if I'm in your mind while you're shagging her, I will never forgive you."

He sighed. "Euri, we've got to live our own lives."

"Someday the two of us *will* land on a set of sheets, naked, and I do not want another girl in my head. I don't want the memory of your hands on her. Your attention on her."

"Jesus, are you fucking with me? You're *jealous?*"

"It's way beyond jealousy, Z." Most girls worry about what their guy is doing when they're not around. I worried what Z would do when I *was* around. "I wonder sometimes, while I ride the bus and watch fields and forests and mountains and coastlines pass by the window, when you will realize you're fighting a losing battle. We're so intimately connected, I can't see how or when it might end. I don't understand why you torment yourself this way."

"Because of what I am, Euri. I have dreams. You don't know about my dreams. I want you more than you can possibly know, but it's just never going to happen. You'd be so miserable, and that would be the greatest sin against God and all mankind, making a beautiful, happy girl like you utterly miserable."

"We are meant to be together."

"Lots of things are meant to be that never happen. Leave me be. Let me live my life."

"You mean, let you fuck that blonde. I'm not stopping you, but I will be right there in bed with you, so remember that when you're giving her what I want, what you give freely to someone who will never want it as much as I do."

He ended the call and then he left Max's and went home and jacked off, mumbling curses at me the whole time. "Is this what you fucking *want?*" he whispered angrily.

"Please, Z, just come for me and end this. *Please.*"

"I'll come for you. *This* is for you." He came on his hand, then rolled over and tucked his pillow around his head.

"Stop acting like a wanker and just take me home with you."

He sounded close to tears. "If you have any feelings for me at all, if you believe you're my friend, you'll do all you can to get out of my head. Christ, Euri, I can't take this anymore."

I had begun to cry, because he was so desperately unhappy and I was certain he would be far less wretched if he'd only let me in, let me be with him. "I will try," I said, "but I can't promise. There's some greater power keeping us connected, and I'm not arrogant enough to believe I can override that."

I stopped playing my practice keyboard and put it away in its case and went to bed, where my imagination ran away with the mental image of his hand around his hard, straining cock.

Turning over, I forced my thoughts to music, to a tune that had been nagging at me, and finally, ultimately frustrated, I went to sleep. And had the most amazing sex dream in the history of all sex dreams.

The following week, I did try to stay out of his thoughts, out of his life, but I had little success. The best I could do was not engage. I didn't talk to him, or call him, or try to interact in any way. I simply observed.

And when I knew he was in my mind, I made no effort to communicate, but hoped he'd see what it meant to be content, happy, at peace.

Z didn't understand joy, had no idea what it meant to be happy. I know he saw the world differently when he was in my head, but he couldn't see that he was just as capable of contentment. He was lost in a wretched labyrinth of gloom and desperation, unaware of how he might make it less painful and horrifying. He didn't see that I was a gift for him, as he was a gift for me.

He was, truly, quite insane. Not in the way of modern thought, but a deeper, darker kind of madness, shared only by those born with the sight, an indefinable ability to see and hear what exists on another plane of reality. Modern definitions of insanity include syndromes and conditions like schizophrenia and bipolar disorder. Z was none of those things.

He had a gift. He just didn't know it. He thought he was bad, dark and evil, and he never believed it more than when he awoke to a color day.

When he was especially despondent, he saw the entire world in shades of purple. He moved slowly, avoided any interactions, couldn't eat. At times, his sixth sense was overactive and on those days, he saw everything in black and white. His emotions shut down and he moved as a robot, methodical and certain as he crossed the globe in search of Skia and lost souls.

Then there were the red days.

We were playing a venue in Atlanta when I first experienced one of Z's red days. While I ran through a keyboard bridge, my mind was over a thousand kilometers away in Colorado. He saw everything in red. There were no screamers. Only a horrible silence filled with his terrifying thoughts. He felt the madness as it rolled over him and, before it blocked out all of his conscious thought, he transported himself to the seashore, to the cliffs above the ocean where he went when he wanted to avoid his brothers.

I wanted to stop playing, to run away and do whatever was necessary to keep his insanity out of my mind, but there was nowhere to run, no way to keep his thoughts away. I was as powerless to stop his invasion as he appeared to be helpless against the madness.

In his head, he hunted along a dark, littered alleyway, searching for refugees. Behind a pile of rubbish, he found three children with great dark eyes and thin, hungry bodies. Their mother lay dead at their feet. Z lifted his weapon and shot them, each with a clean shot to the head. The children stood there passively, as if they knew they couldn't escape. Hopeless.

I played on, wondering how he could imagine anything this gruesome and horrifying. I heard his soul cry out in anguish and realized these were not *his* thoughts. Just as he channeled the screams of humanity's fear, his mind invited the conscience of a stranger, a man who hunted and murdered the hopeless. But Z was unaware. He believed his own imagination conjured his murderous rampages and fueled his hate-filled motivations. He despised himself for what he thought lay in his subconscious.

The realization of how tortured he was made me cry. I spent the last thirty minutes of the concert with tears rolling unchecked down my cheeks, unable to stop. I shifted on my bench so the audience couldn't see all of my face.

When we finished the concert, John, looking very concerned, asked, "Where do you go when you play?"

"Somewhere far away." Somewhere he couldn't imagine, would never believe.

He took my hand and we left the stage after a second encore. "Let's get some rest, yeah?" He was elated over Arcadia's growing popularity. He wanted nothing to stand in the way of our success. Any mental issues I had, which I'm certain became more evident every day, he passed off as exhaustion and stress. I didn't mind. Maybe because what was crazy for me was agony for Z.

When we were in our rooms at a small motel in the dodgy end of Atlanta, I sat on the rock hard bed and called Z. He didn't answer. Either he was too far into his madness, or there was no cell service close enough to his island. I didn't leave a message. I lay back on the bed and cried for him.

~~ ZEE ~~

She had called me and I hated to admit how bummed I was that she didn't leave a message. I knew why she called. She'd been with me during a red day. I wondered if she'd wanted to tell me how appalled she was that any human being could be this fucked up.

I was massively depressed. Which meant I wanted and needed sex with a twisted kind of desperation.

I told Denys and Ty and Key that I planned some reconnaissance in Moscow, so no, I didn't want to go to The Lotus in Miami to find girls.

Instead, I went to Jackson's in New York. I saw the girl I wanted within one minute of arriving. She was, as usual, tall and blonde. Whatever subtle finesse I'd managed to master over the centuries went right out the window when I approached her. I stared at her while we ran through the usual meet and greet and, despite the look of a cornered animal in her big, blue eyes, she took my hand and followed me out of the club. "Where do you live?"

"Brooklyn."

Fuck, that was a long-ass cab ride away. I almost told her to forget it, but she smelled like that perfume Euri wore. I was hard and so damned needy.

The voices in my head went to a fever pitch, even my own soul was screaming at me, but I ignored all of it and took the girl, who had a K name, like Kenzie or Kayla or something like that, all the way home to her walkup in Brooklyn, where she had a cat and a crocheted throw on the sofa, probably given to her by some old lady who told her not to sleep with strangers. Karen should have listened.

I kissed her. I wanted her. I had her clothes off and was jerking my shirt over my head when I heard Euri playing her practice keyboard. She did it on purpose, because it was easier to get into my head when she was playing. Arcadia was off tonight, on the road and staying in Jacksonville, Florida. She pulled out her keyboard and played and spoke aloud to me in that soft British voice I'd grown so accustomed to. "Don't do this, Zee. She's not for you. None of them are for you."

I couldn't respond, of course. Kelly would freak out.

And I couldn't take her down, couldn't bury myself in her soft, inviting body and lose myself for a few stolen moments of fake sanity. Euri was with me as much as if she were standing in Karla's little bedroom, watching us.

My cock lost it and, even if I'd been willing to fuck this girl despite Euri's intrusion, I couldn't.

My anger was epic. Stepping back, I cleared my throat. "I have to go."

"Why? Have I done something?" Tears welled in her eyes, and I felt like an ass. I *was* an ass. Why couldn't Euri see it? She saw everything else about me. How could she miss that I was a total ass?

I didn't answer Kathy. I walked out into her hallway, erased her memory of me, and popped myself back to my room at the Mephisto house.

I was still holding my shirt in my hand. Throwing it to the floor, I went to my piano and played something I'd written a century ago, a particularly forlorn bit of music that was as dark as it was loud. Euri was still with me. I cursed her.

"You don't mean that," she whispered.

"You don't understand what it's like, how lonely I am. It's just for a little while, and I need it. Why can't you go away? Why are you here?"

"Because I can't help it."

"You could help it. You pulled that fucking keyboard out just so you could climb into my head and screw everything up." I played with manic anger, pounding the keys.

"My keyboard isn't some enchanted pathway to your thoughts, Zee. I am with you as much when I'm not playing as when I am."

I stopped abusing my piano and slumped across the keys, resting my head on my arms. "Please, *please* find a way to leave me be, Euri."

"Maybe it's time for you to come for me."

"It will never be time. Don't you understand? I *can't* be with you. I can't be with anyone."

"Says who?"

"Says me."

"Come and get me. I'm at the Jacksonville Inn. We'll have a cup of tea like ordinary people and we'll talk."

"No."

"I'll be waiting."

I ignored her, put my shirt back on and popped down to Miami, to The Lotus. My brothers were already gone, already lucky. They'd each found a willing girl to go home with. Just like at Jackson's, I found a girl within ten minutes of arriving. I took her back to her apartment and this time, I got both of us naked before I realized I was all kinds of an idiot. I never even got hard.

Once again, I walked out, erased her memory and went home.

The strains of a tune I'd never heard were in my head. "I'm in room five. I'm waiting."

I Googled the Jacksonville Inn, placed it in my head, and popped there. It was an old, shabby motel, the kind where travelers park in front of their room. I walked to room 5 and knocked.

The music stopped, she opened the door, and I was immediately enveloped in her scent, that rich, invigorating fragrance of the sea. And Prada.

I could never, even if I spent a billion years trying, explain how desperately I wanted to pick her right up off of her feet, carry her to that bed I could see behind her, and hold her as close as possible, skin to skin, me buried deep within her sweet, beautiful body.

"Hello," I said unimaginatively.

She stepped outside, closed the door behind her, and reached for my hand. The instant she touched me, the screaming in my head stopped. We stood there and looked into each other's eyes and I let out a relieved breath. She smiled at me. "Better?"

"Yes. It would be even better if we went in there and you let me make love to you until next week."

She turned and was sliding the key into the lock when I tugged her back toward me. "It can't be, Euri. Why won't you accept that we will never be together?"

"We're together now."

Hypnotized and spellbound, I couldn't look away from her. Her blond hair was long, with a slight curl at the ends, gently teasing her breasts, braless beneath a thin, pale pink T-shirt. Her jeans rode low, exposing a stretch of smooth fair skin below the shirt. She wore sandals and her toenails were painted blue. My gaze drifted to her soft hand, enfolded in mine. "I only came here to make you understand. You've got to try harder to stay out of my head."

"Impossible. Maybe if I stopped playing it'd be less intense, but making music is as much a part of me and as essential to my existence as my heartbeat and breath." She began to walk and tugged me to follow.

I should have left.

I didn't.

I followed her to the street and walked with her toward an IHOP, making note of each step, every breath, every blink of her beautiful cornflower blue eyes. I looked at her more than I watched the sidewalk. I wanted to remember every minute.

When we reached the IHOP, it was half past two in the morning and we were surrounded by drunks hoping to sober up on coffee and pancakes before they went home. We sat at a booth and she ordered tea, then tossed aside the standard black tea served at most American restaurants and pulled two of her own tea bags from her pocket. They were wrapped in silk and she concentrated as she dunked them into the hot water. "You always seem to enjoy tea," she said in her soft, pretty voice.

"We lived so long in England, we grew to love most everything British, especially tea. Hans, the cook, tries to prepare dishes like blood pudding or steak and kidney pie, but he generally misses it. He's more attuned to German food and breads and pastries."

"Well, he *is* German."

"Mathilda, the housekeeper, is English and she occasionally cooks for us. Then we get things like bubble and squeak and meat pies."

She passed my cup after she'd poured and added two packets of sugar. Because she knew how I took my tea. Was there anything about me she didn't know? I supposed not, just as there wasn't much about her that I didn't know.

The tea was delicious. "Just like in England. That's nice, Euri."

She smiled and we sat there and gazed at one another and drank tea like we were normal people. I liked the feeling. I loved the quiet, without the usual screamers. I didn't even mind that I could hear every conversation in the restaurant, including the guy in the corner who was berating his girl.

I focused on Euri. "I like the new songs Arcadia is playing. I heard one on the radio a couple of days ago. Phoenix builds bikes, and he always has a radio on while he works. I was out in his shop asking him about a takedown plan when I heard it."

"How lovely that you did. I'm happy you like it."

"Did you write it?"

She nodded and took another sip of her tea. I watched her mouth, and hell if I didn't feel my jeans get a little tighter in the zipper area. I looked away and made myself not think about kissing her or touching her, or seeing her tall, slender body without anything covering it up. Not that her shirt was much of a cover. Wearing no bra, she was one step from naked. I could see her nipples, which meant others could as well. I didn't fail to notice a guy checking her out, until he met my gaze, then his slid back to stirring his coffee.

Incredibly, the guy in the corner became a bigger asshole, and I watched his girl get up and walk out, leaving him looking stunned. Son of a bitch deserved to be left.

"Don't," she whispered.

"Don't what?"

"Focus on the ugly." She nodded her head to the right. "Look over there."

I turned my head and saw a guy feeding pancakes to a girl with a broken arm. They sat within a group of others, but it was as though they were all alone, smiling at each other, casting longing looks at one another.

I drank more tea.

"Take me with you."

"No."

"I want you to explain why. I deserve an honest answer."

"You're never with me when I'm asleep, are you?"

She shook her head.

"I have dreams, almost all of them about you, and I always hurt you. I have something inside of me that I don't understand and can't control. I can't be with you because I know I will hurt you. It would never be intentional, but that makes no difference."

"It makes all the difference."

"The point is, you'd be just as hurt, or dead, whether I meant to do it, or not. There's a reason people don't keep wild animals as pets. They're entirely too unpredictable. I have no clue what I might do to you if you were with me all the time."

She looked as if she wanted to say something, but either couldn't find the words, or was debating the wisdom of saying it. In the end, she had a look of frustration, so I was well aware that what she said wasn't what she really wanted to say. "We're supposed to be together, Zee. Do you know?"

I drained the tea and she pulled my cup toward her to fill it again. "I know. I get that, but we have free will, just like everyone else, and I'm never going to take you. I won't subject you to the life you'd have with me. *Especially* you, Euri. You see all the world as if evil doesn't exist."

She frowned. "You say that as though it's a character flaw, a personality disorder."

"You can't face reality, so you retreat into a dream world that doesn't exist except in your own mind."

"If you care to engage in a war of words over which of us is most unbalanced, you should rethink the idea. It's utterly pointless because I will immediately concede. You, sir, are far more batshit than I." She lifted her cup in a mock toast. "You don't really believe in happiness, or love. You've decided they don't exist."

"In my world, they don't."

She looked sad and I wished we could go back to the pretense of normality.

"Jax and Sasha love each other. Some of the Luminas are married and they love each other. You love your brothers, and the Purgatories. You love your father, despite who he is."

"All true, but it's just like you to myopically see what you want to see and ignore the rest. Are you not going to mention the lost souls and the Skia? My brother, Eryx? Maniacs like Kovalev? Your mother? Hell, even Miles lost it and went dark."

"It's there, but does it have to mean everything?"

"There can't be the world you see without the one I see."

"I see your world, Zee. I saw it before I knew you. My mother tried to murder my sister and I was there, as if it were happening to me. Nurses and aides harmed Sophie and I was there, felt her pain, saw their evil enjoyment of her hurt. I've traveled all over the world to play piano and met thousands of people, some good, some bad. A man in Seoul tried to break my fingers because I played better than his daughter. Another one in Belfast tried to kill me because my father is a member of Parliament and an aristocrat. He locked me inside the practice room and caught it on fire. I get it, Zee. There is evil in the world. I simply will not allow it to control my every thought and action. I choose to focus on the good, on things that make us happy."

How wonderful to have that ability. How marvelous that God saw fit to give her a happy insanity. How infuriating of her to criticize me, as if what I had in my head was my own doing. I nearly choked on it, but managed to say, "You've been very fortunate."

"You are also fortunate."

I almost spit out the tea. "Are you fucking *kidding* me?"

"There are amazing things in your life, but you never see them. You've spent your entire existence wrapped up in misery and anger over who and what you are."

I drank the tea and tried to talk myself down, but all the tea in the world couldn't drown my rage. "You think it's easy to be me? How would you like it if this shit were in your head every goddamn day for a *thousand years?* Go do that, Euri, then come and tell me how *fortunate* you feel."

I expected her to tell me off. To get up and leave. To throw her tea in my face.

Hell, maybe I *wanted* her to do any of those things. I was scared shitless and in way over my head.

Of course she didn't get mad. She gave me a beatific

smile. Her glow was astonishing. And her eyes. I swear they became bluer. "Get mad all you want. Curse me, call me a fool, ignore me." She leaned in and dropped her voice. "I'm never giving up on you, Xenos. Ever. Unless God or Lucifer make me stop, I won't stay out of your head. I will be with you in spirit if you won't allow it physically. I will stay with you and you'll see the world as I see it. If you insist on unhappiness in your own life, you'll at least be happy vicariously, through me."

This was my cue. My exit strategy. I had to leave now or I would never. I would take her home with me and keep her and turn her happiness into misery.

I felt tears form in my eyes. I stared at her and swallowed and somehow managed to whisper, "I won't be with you, Euri. I'll do everything in my power to shut you out. Do you understand what I'm saying to you?"

"All you're doing is delaying the inevitable, and making both of us suffer."

I refused to argue any longer. I disappeared.

~~ EURI ~~

The wanker in the corner took Z's seat, looking dazed. "Did that guy just disappear out of here?"

"Don't be ridiculous. You're drunk. He left through the front door." I nodded toward the window. "There he goes, in that blue car."

He rubbed his forehead. "Man, this night."

"You can't talk to girls like that and expect them to stick around."

He peered at me, dropped his gaze to my breasts, then looked again at my face.

Before he could speak, I said, "Don't go there. I'm aware I have breasts. You're aware I have breasts. We're both aware this shirt is see-through. Pointing it out is crass and offensive. Look when I'm not noticing. Tell me I look very pretty. Ask me about my life, what I like, what I dream about. If you tell me I'm uptight and a snarky bitch and a tease and . . . let's see, what else did you call her? Oh, right, a whore who'd do the whole football team, but not you. Now imagine you're a girl. Is this going to make you say, oh, lovely, take me, I'm yours?"

He cocked a crooked smile. "I guess not."

"She's at the back of this restaurant, crying. Go out there and be a gentleman and apologize. Then take her home and go see her tomorrow and take her for ice cream. Getting a girl drunk doesn't equal hot sex. It amounts to rape. You're a handsome bloke, probably a good student and an athlete."

He nodded.

"You can get sex anytime you like, but not the way you're going about it."

"Who are you?"

"My name is Euri. I play keyboard for Arcadia."

His eyes widened. "For real? Man, I love Arcadia. John Jamison is like a god." He glanced at the window. "Who was that giant guy you were with?"

I smiled as I scooted toward the edge of the booth. "The love of my life."

"Do you sleep with him?"

I looked at the kid. "Not your business, is it? See, that's the other magical thing about sex. It's something to be shared between you and her and no one else. You can tell all your randy friends it's none of their business if you're shagging that pretty girl or not."

"You're English, aren't you?"

"I am. In fact, I'm an aristocrat and I sometimes have tea at Buckingham Palace."

"With the queen?"

"Right." I stood and looked down at him. "We're playing tomorrow night at the Crow's Nest. You're underage, but they'll let you in if you tell the bouncer I invited you. The password is Sophie. Bring your girl tomorrow night and we'll go backstage to meet the band and she'll think you're very cool. For now, go back there and apologize."

He got to his feet. "Why are you being so nice to me? I saw the look your boyfriend gave me."

I touched his arm. "I'm nice to everyone. It's not so hard, really. Just let it go. You've got nothing to prove to anyone but yourself. I'll see you tomorrow night."

He followed me outside. "Can I give you a ride? Where are you staying?"

"Thank you, but no. And you should let that girl drive. I

believe the coppers here in America will toss you in jail for motoring whilst pissed."

"I guess pissed means drunk in England."

"Right-o."

"Thanks, Euri. You're all right."

"I'll see you tomorrow night."

He turned and walked toward the side of the building, weaving only slightly. "Goodnight!" he called as he made the corner.

I made my way back to the motel, still preoccupied by Z's hasty exit. I'd seen his eyes well with tears. He hadn't wanted to go. He hadn't wanted to leave me.

It would take an enormous effort on my part, but I would convince him eventually that fighting this was a losing proposition. God, or Lucifer, or maybe his father wanted us together, and it would be extremely difficult to alter the plans of powers infinitely greater than us.

I sincerely believed this.

I was also very certain that I was deeply in love with him.

Nevertheless, over the following weeks, I grew weary of the fight, of his attempts to block me, his ignoring me, his absolute determination to win the war. He simply didn't see that winning the war was a loss for both of us.

I cried a lot as we made our way across the south. In New Orleans, I went to a psychic who sat at a card table in a corner of Jackson Square. She told me I was destined to die young. I told her she was a charlatan, then I went to Café du Monde and ate my weight in beignets.

Hoping to see into his head, I played constantly, but he'd managed to block me. All I ever got were vague emotions and quick glimpses of his life. He suffered several more red days, and I was there for all of them. Difficult to keep his mind on lockdown when it had been hijacked by insanity. But I was locked out more often than not, and I continued to grieve the loss. I constantly plotted and schemed, trying to come up with a way to get to him, but nothing ever quite worked out.

I prayed a lot, but began to wonder if God wasn't listening. I felt as far away from my spirituality as I ever had. Even after Sophie died, I hadn't been this despondent.

She was my other half, my heart, but Z had become the other half of my soul. I was lost without him.

I called him lots of times, but he wouldn't answer my calls. I tried faking him out by calling from different numbers, like John's phone and a hotel phone, but he never answered. He knew it was me the way he knew so many things. He would know if I was in real trouble and then he would answer. My need for him was becoming dire, not just sexually, but emotionally. I felt untethered and alone. Afraid. I left messages, begging him to let me in.

Nothing.

I talked out loud to him, and I knew he heard me, but he never responded.

I had another mirror episode in Dallas, and he came to be with me, but as soon as I came back through the mirror and woke out of my trance, he pulled away from holding me on the bed and disappeared. He never said a word. I spent the whole rest of the night alternately crying and drinking a bottle of cognac some music rep had given me. It made me drunk, then sick, and I knew misery on the cold tiles of the bathroom floor.

Christmas came and I was alone. The band had flown out to their hometowns to be with family. My father was in England, too far away to travel for only a few days, and I strangely didn't want to see him. Maybe I was afraid he would try to make me stay. Perhaps I worried he'd have me locked up. It's a strange thing to be crazy and know it. Some who are afflicted with madness are blissfully unaware.

I spent so much time wandering in the fog that surrounded Z's mind, I missed much of what was happening around me. While the band was gone, I stayed in a posh hotel in Houston and read and watched movies on the telly and wrote music and dreamed about Z.

On Christmas day, I ventured out to attend the church that was just down the street from my hotel. It had been a while, and I loved being there, but I couldn't focus on the message. I checked out and when I regained awareness, the church was empty and a caretaker was shaking my arm, asking if I felt all right.

Embarrassed, I left quickly. On my way back to the

hotel, my father called.

We'd barely finished the usual greetings and chit-chat when he said, "I think it's time for you to return to Cambridge. The longer you put this off, the less likely you are to follow through. We've never had anyone uneducated in our family and I do not intend to start now. I expect you to finish."

"The tour is done in just over a month. I'll come home after that and decide my next steps." I didn't tell him I planned to take up residence with a band of brothers from Hell. He already thought I was dotty. No sense throwing petrol on that fire, was there? "I hope you've had a grand Christmas, Papa. Please give my best to Mrs. Carlisle."

"Yes, I will. Happy Christmas to you, Euripides."

I rang off and went back to my hotel room, ordered room service and gave the waiter an outrageous tip, apologizing that he had to work on Christmas.

A week later, I was happy to see all the guys when they came back to the tour. We played New Year's Eve in Houston, then traveled south, through the Texas valley, and played at a little beach club on Padre Island. During rehearsal, I was afforded a longer look into Z's life, I suppose because he was more emotional than usual. They'd found another Anabo, a girl named Jordan. She was the daughter of the president of the United States. Meant for Kyros. Z liked her and was ever hopeful she would stay with them.

Then, a short time later, Key brought home an Anabo for Phoenix, the martyr Mephisto who never went after girls. Mariah was a sad case, an orphan who lived in poverty with a horrific history of abuse. She'd been separated from Jordan, who was her sister, when they were quite young. Jordan was adopted by a man who became the president. Mariah remained in Romania with an abusive relative. Z was terribly sad about Mariah, which is why I was able to see into his life. He couldn't block me during times of extreme emotion. He was oddly ambivalent about Mariah, as if he resented that Phoenix had another chance. He worried that Phoenix was too hard and too selfish to be what Mariah needed.

And yet, Phoenix was trying. He was giving it all he had

to make it right for Mariah. Why couldn't Z do the same for me? I felt as if I were drowning, frequently short of breath, the whole world muffled and gloomy.

For weeks I had agonized over Z, longed for a return to how it was before, grieved the loss of him in my life. And while my music went to a level I'd never dreamed possible, it was hollow and meaningless to me. A part of me rebelled at this incessant need I had for him. I was independent, smart, able to look after myself and my own. But my mental stability had become intrinsically tied to him, whether I wanted it or not, and the longer I lived without him, the more miserable I became.

I lost my way, but never let it show, never cried in front of any of the blokes in the band. I played and sang and smiled and talked and carried on as if all was well and perfectly normal.

Until Austin.

Everything got dodgy in Austin.

~~ ZEE ~~

I remember reading an article by Russell Brand, just after Phillip Seymour Hoffman overdosed on heroin. Brand talked about the mind of an addict, that in recovery, it all really boils down to one thing – just don't pick it up. Every day, there's that one thing to do – just don't pick it up. Everything else was only support for the To-Do List of One Thing.

I thought a lot about Brand's essay after I left Euri in that IHOP. There were no words to describe the draw she had for me. I wanted her. I needed her. I was mad with grief that I couldn't have her. Every day, I would say to myself, just for today, I won't go. And the next day I would think the same. I understood the desperation of an addict. I'd seen a million of them over the centuries. But none had ever been as desperate as I was.

I really have no idea how or why I stayed so strong. I began to despise waking up, weird for me because I generally couldn't wait to wake up. It was escape from nightmares. Now, I dreaded sunrise because it meant another fucking day alone, without her.

I went along like that for a long time. I vigilantly kept her out of my head and tried so hard to stay out of hers, but sometimes it was unavoidable. Sometimes, especially when she played, I could see through her eyes, and as much as I knew it was wrong, as confident as I was that this could only make me more miserable later on, those moments were sublime. I caught the tiniest notion of what it might feel like to be at peace and it was impossible to resist. She looked out at the world through those beautiful, tranquil blue eyes and saw beauty and kindness and loveliness. Her world was a marvelous place to live. I knew it wasn't real. Her idyllic universe was as much a construct of her demented mind as my horrors were of mine.

Maybe the two of us together would balance the other. Maybe two crazies could form a sane union. Wouldn't that be something?

I began to imagine what it would be like if she were here with me, lying next to me all night. Would I stop dreaming? I convinced myself she'd be enthusiastic about hunting the lost souls. She knew what was at stake, knew who Eryx was, understood what he could mean to humanity if we didn't keep a tight leash on him. I imagined her training, learning to use a blade, holding my hand when we went on takedowns. She'd go with me for reconnaissance missions.

Over and over I had these thoughts, even while I knew it would never happen. I didn't feel sorry for myself. This went far deeper than self-pity. I went to Kyanos and shouted at the woman in the ocean. She laughed at me. I wrote pages and pages in my notebooks, then locked them up in a chest in the attic.

Then, mysteriously, unimaginably, after months of living with her on some other plane of reality, she was gone. For two days I heard nothing – no music, no whispers from her in the dark, nothing at all. I began to worry that she had died. I decided I would go to the next Arcadia concert and see if she was there. If so, it must mean that our bond and mental connection was gone. And if she wasn't there, I'd find out from John Jamison what had happened to her.

I got choked up just imagining that she was dead.

After the second day of her absence from my mind, I was in bed, wishing I could be glad she was gone, because after all, that's what I'd wanted all along, but failing miserably because no matter how demented I was or how badly I might hurt her, the idea of her no longer on Earth brought enormous pain. I grew short of breath. I was bereft.

I'd just decided to get dressed and go searching for her when my cell rang. I knew it was her. Alarmed and relieved at the same time, I answered, "Where are you?"

Her voice was low and raspy, like she'd been awake for way too long, or smoked a pack of Camels. "I . . . don't know. I woke up here and I don't know where I am. I was hoping you could, um, maybe come here, and just . . . be with me, Zee. I . . . need to be in Austin, but there's a mountain here and I don't remember there being a mountain in Austin. Uh, maybe? I'm not sure. I had to find the baby. Did you hear it?"

I had gotten out of bed while she talked, and already had my jeans on. I stepped into my boots. "No, I didn't hear a baby. Can you look at something specific?"

I closed my eyes and concentrated very hard. She was looking at a garbage can. "Are you in an alley?"

"I think so."

"Focus on the garbage can. Is there a city name on it?"

"It looks to be . . . the rubbish bin . . . Telluride. This is not Texas. Not Austin. Where is the baby?"

She came for me. I ignored her and she came to Telluride to find me. And a baby, apparently. "Stay right where you are."

"I can't find the baby, Zee. I think we have to find it."

"We will, but I need to find you, first."

I kept her on the phone while I pulled on a T-shirt and my trench coat. Seconds later, I was on the main street of Telluride. "What do you see behind the trash can? Is it a wall, a yard, a house?"

"It looks like a flat, and I hear water running in a brook."

I transported to a possible location and came up empty.

"I smell pizza."

The Blue Moose. It stayed open late during ski season. I popped behind the restaurant and there she was, sitting on the ground, her back against the wall. She wore old Chucks without socks, a ragged pair of gray sweat pants, and a faded T-shirt from MIT. Her blond hair hung over her shoulder in a long messy braid. She was very pale, with dark circles under her eyes and she held a cigarette between her shaking fingers. "You look rough, Euri."

"I am so scared." She swallowed and held out a pack of Marlboros to me.

I squatted down next to her and took the cigarettes, slid one out of the pack and willed it to light. Even through the acrid scent of the smoke, I caught the fresh clean smell of the ocean.

"Hot cross buns," she whispered. "Not pizza."

"It's still pizza. I'm the one who smells like hot cross buns."

"I know." She took my hand and lifted it to her nose. The instant she touched me, the screaming in my head stopped. She had a faraway, dreamy look on her face. "It's always so marvelous, and peculiar. Why do you smell like this, Zee?"

"I'm Mephisto. You're Anabo. We're destined for each other, so we each have a unique scent that only the two of us can smell. It's how we're made, so my brothers and I don't get in fights over Anabo girls. There are hardly any Anabo ever, so when we find one, it's kind of a big deal."

"What do I smell like to you?"

"The ocean."

"How lovely," she whispered, her cheek against my hand.

"Yes," I replied. "The loveliest scent on earth."

"Hot cross buns," she repeated after she let go of my hand. "Nanny Green made them for Sophie and me when I was wee. Mum sacked her, but a week later, Dad reemployed her. She stayed with me until I went away to school when I was eight. She made hot cross buns at Easter, and took me to see Sophie and we had a bitty rabbit that Nanny Green smuggled into the sanatorium. That was before Hawthorn House. That was . . . I'm so very tired, Zee. I have never been so happy to see anyone in my life as I am to see you."

"It's all going to be okay. Do you believe me?"

She nodded and I thought she was foolish to be so trusting. I had no idea how everything could be okay. They were just words. Maybe a wish.

We smoked for a while in silence, staring at each other, and then she said, "I was sitting on a sofa in the lobby of an old hotel in Austin, so I could use their Wi-Fi, when I heard a baby crying. I asked the desk man and he said he didn't hear a baby. I asked John and the others and they also couldn't hear it. I walked out into the car park, looking everywhere, going past each room, hoping to hear it closer, but never did. The baby was forlorn, you know? Sad and helpless. I called you to help me look. I was sure you could find it. But you didn't answer. I don't remember anything after wandering around the car park. Until now, until I was here, smoking a cigarette and calling you. I have nothing with me but my phone and a credit card."

"And this pack of cigarettes."

She peered at it, lying in my outstretched palm. "I only ever smoke when I'm drinking and then they're always someone else's. I don't know where these cigarettes came from."

"Are you hurt?"

Shaking her head, blue eyes wide, she said, "I feel like I'm hung over, and my belly hurts because I'm starving, but I don't think anyone hurt me. And I'm freezing." She looked up at the starry sky above us. "What day is it?"

I told her and she whispered, "I've been gone for two days, Zee. Where have I been? How did I get here?"

"You must have flown. Let's check your credit card charges and find out." I took her smoke and dropped it next to mine and ground them out with my heel. Then I reached for her, gathered her up in my arms, and took her home with me.

As soon as we arrived, I set her down and stepped back. She was a tall girl, probably as tall as Sasha, but she looked small and vulnerable, standing there in ratty clothes in my huge room with its lofty ceiling and massive furniture. Her Anabo aura was strong and bright and as essential to my continued existence as the oxygen I needed to sustain my blood.

I would *not* succumb. I couldn't. She was as insane as I, maybe even more so. The two of us would never work. Ever. *Ever*. I'd do what needed to be done for her, then I'd take her back to Austin, or wherever Arcadia was now playing, and then I'd take myself out of the equation. I couldn't live like this. I couldn't want her *this* much and survive. I would welcome death. And Hell. Even Lucifer. I'd work for him all the rest of eternity and it would be horrible, but no way it could be as bad as this. Tears gathered in my eyes at the hopelessness of it all. "You're not well, Euri."

She blinked at me. "I'm sorry. You've tried so very hard to avoid me, and now here I am, where you never wanted me to be. Thank you for coming to get me. I need to use the loo, and I'm so bloody thirsty." She swallowed again. "And hungry. Would you mind if I stay long enough to have a bite to eat? Just a biscuit or two, and maybe some tea?"

I turned and walked toward my bathroom, stopped and waved her inside. "Go in there and take a hot shower. It'll warm you up and make you feel better. I'll find you some clean clothes and get you something to eat."

Before she could say anything else, I popped downstairs to the laundry, a large bright room close to the kitchens with several washers and driers and ironing boards and shirt presses. Our housekeeper, Mathilda, wasn't there, for which I was grateful. There would be too many questions and not enough answers.

I found some clean jeans that I was sure belonged to Sasha. Jordan wasn't living here yet, and Mariah only owned one pair of jeans, which she wore every day, and they had holes, so I knew these newish ones must be Sasha's. She was about the same size and height as Euri. These would do until she went back to Arcadia. I took them, and a soft blue sweater, and popped back to my room. Euri's clothes were in a small pile next to the bathroom door, which was open, so I could see her inside my glass shower. I watched her for a while before I asked, "Do you like sandwiches?"

"I like anything except mushy peas."

"What's wrong with mushy peas?"

"They're mushy." Rinsing her hair, she moved closer to the glass. Sweet Christ, even with dark circles under her eyes and the pallor of her skin, she was more beautiful than any other girl in the world, built perfectly, with just-the-right-size breasts, a curvy waist, slender hips and long, long, beautiful legs. I wished I didn't have a hard-on, but it was inevitable. In that moment, it was a toss-up whether my need for her was more mental or physical. I had an overwhelming desire to break the fucking glass and go in after her. I'd take her with my clothes still on. I drew in a ragged breath and cursed my body for betraying me, for wanting what it could not have.

Fuck. I was in pain. What did she say? Something about bread? *Shit, I don't know.* I decided she could eat whatever I brought, then I'd get her out of here as soon as possible. I turned away and adjusted my very hard dick inside of my jeans. In my hurry to find her, I'd gone commando, and the zipper was killing me.

"Don't go to a lot of trouble, Zee. I'll just have a bit of tea and a biscuit and be on my way."

I mumbled something I hoped was polite, then went through the bathroom and into my closet, where I stripped off the jeans. I pulled on some sweats, blew off shoes, and popped down to the kitchen.

Hans saw me and smiled. "I had a feeling you'd be down tonight."

"Why?"

"We had halibut for dinner. Of all your brothers, you can never eat enough fish, so you're always hungry late, so I always expect you on fish nights." He went to one of the three refrigerators in the huge kitchen and withdrew a platter, which he set in front of me. "Choose your meats and I will make you a sandwich."

He was dead right. I was starving. "Pastrami, salami, some of that ham, and this pepperoni. Use whatever cheese you think will complement the meat. Lots of tomatoes, and some lettuce, and hot mustard. And pickles. Also, make a second sandwich with a little bit of that turkey you always save for Denys, don't lie and say you don't, and some thinly sliced tomatoes and butter lettuce. Make that one on Mathilda's French bread and use the aioli mayonnaise. Make mine . . . I mean the big one, on one of your hoagie rolls."

He lifted one brow, but asked no questions.

When he was done, he placed the sandwiches on two plates, added chips and fruit, then poured a huge glass of milk. He set all of it on a tray, then added a smaller glass of milk. And some of Mathilda's chocolate chip cookies.

"Thanks, Hans," I said as I picked up the tray.

He mumbled something about secrets, but I ignored him and popped back upstairs with the tray.

Euri sat on one of the chairs in front of the fireplace, dressed in my Kings of Leon T-shirt, combing out her long hair. She nodded toward the clothes I'd laid at the end of the bed. "Do those belong to Sasha?"

"Yes." I set the tray down on the little table between the chairs. "I couldn't decide about swiping underwear."

"Good call. Girls will borrow anything, but never knickers. Perhaps before I dress, you could pop over to a shop for a pair?"

"Yes, Euri, I will steal knickers for you." I'd go to Victoria's Secret, one that was closed, and swipe a pair of black lace ones. So what I'd never see her wear them? I had my imagination, after all.

I sat down, anticipating food, but before I could reach for the first half of my sandwich, she picked it up and took a bite that was amazingly dainty and huge at the same time. I'm fairly certain she scarfed down the whole half without taking a breath. Then she went for the other half. And the chips.

So I ate the little ladylike sandwich and tried to hurry so I could have some of the fruit before she wiped that out, too. She chugged the ginormous glass of milk – of course – and if I hadn't snagged it, she'd have gone for the small one as well. I let her have all the cookies.

I couldn't help imagining how much she might eat if she became Mephisto. Like my brothers and me, Sasha and Jordan could put away the groceries, but Euri could totally give them a run for the money, even without being Mephisto.

When she was done, she sat back in the chair and stared at me. "Will you kiss me?"

"You don't waste any time, do you?"

"My curiosity is killing me."

"I see. So I'm a *curiosity* to you. Everything about you is all I want and need. I'm seriously contemplating offing myself because this is so fucking miserable, but to you, I'm just something intriguing, an oddity, a random guy whose mind you've been playing around in for almost two years, whose body you know as well as your own because you're with me all the goddamn time now. But you're merely *curious*." I admit, I got a little worked up, but not because I was angry. I think my feelings were hurt. But I'm a manly kinda guy. Acting angry is always preferable to crying. "No, Euri. The answer is no, I won't kiss you. Not tonight. Not ever. We're going to figure out where you've been for the past two days, and depending on the answer, take steps to ensure you don't go missing again in the future, then I'm taking you wherever you ask me to take you and that will be an end to it."

She tucked her long legs beneath her and smiled at me. "You're quite horrible at being mad."

"I assume you mean angry mad, not insane mad."

She nodded. "You're the very best at insanity." Then she leaned her head back and closed her eyes. "You're not really cross with me, are you?"

I collapsed against the back of my chair and stared glumly at the fire. "No."

"But you're still not going to kiss me, are you?"

"No."

"You wouldn't kill yourself. I know you wouldn't. You might consider it because you're looking for any way to escape the pain, but you wouldn't ever actually go through with it."

Yet more glum, I muttered, "I guess probably not. My brothers would be sad. For all that I'm batshit, they do love me. And they need me."

"Of course they do. And you're completely wrong."

"About what?"

"About me thinking you're only a curiosity. I'm mad about you, Zee. Don't you know that by now?"

"Well stop it. We can't be together. It's just never going to work. You should be afraid for your life, but instead, you sit there and ask me to kiss you like I'm not capable of murdering you."

"You wouldn't murder me. You will eventually love me and I'll love you, and when that happens, I'm going to ask God to make us not crazy. You'll see."

"Why don't you ask him now? Why wait until we're in love? It'll be a long wait. I don't believe in romantic love. It's lust wrapped up in a pretty package so people won't feel guilty about doing it."

"You have just teased karma, so you're going to fall hard." She grinned at me. *Grinned.* "You're doomed to be crazy in love with me, but I'll be nice and not say I told you so."

"If I say I love you, don't believe it. I'm only trying to get you out of your clothes."

She sat up and in one smooth movement, slipped the T-shirt over her head and threw it at me. "You don't have to lie. Here I am, naked as you like. Now will you kiss me?"

I tossed the shirt back at her and didn't look past her knees. "Put the shirt back on. I won't kiss you because you'll start turning to Mephisto, which is a bad, bad thing. And I'm done with this conversation." I went to the desk and got my laptop, then settled back on my chair, gratified that she was once again dressed. Sort of. I couldn't forget she wasn't wearing anything at all beneath that T-shirt. I focused on the laptop. "Give me your credit card."

She did and I pulled up her account. "Password?"

I typed it as she told it to me, then scanned the recent charges.

"I can do that, you know."

"I'm aware. You could hack into the database and scan every cardholder's charges. But you're exhausted. Just relax and let me see . . . you bought something at the Gas 'n' Go in Odessa, Texas two days ago. Then you bought something at the Wag-A-Bag in Amarillo, then at Clines Corners, New Mexico. I've been there. It's a huge travel stop on I40, where you get off the Interstate to drive north to Santa Fe. Today, you spent over four hundred bucks at Mama's Tattoos in Montrose, which is north of Telluride." I looked over at her. "Did you get a new tat?"

With her eyes still closed, she held up her arm and showed me the question mark on the underside of her forearm. It was just like the one on my neck. "You didn't get that today. You've had it since I've known you."

"I got it from a bloke in Brighton when I was sixteen. On a dare, actually. Miles said I was a timid rabbit and would never do anything so anti-aristocratic."

"Why did you choose a question mark?"

"Why did you?"

"Because my existence is questionable."

"There you go. I've wondered at times if any of this is really happening. Am I in a room somewhere in the sedate countryside of Sussex, in a house with others like me, weaving a fantastical life that exists only in my head? Maybe I was never real, but merely a segment of Sophie's existence, the part of her unencumbered by physical limitations. Her mind on holiday, you might say." She opened her eyes and looked at me with a serious expression. "You see, I've been dotty since I can remember. I asked for a question mark. He showed me a pretty, cursive sort, and one with a smiley face on the dot. I told him he was all wrong and drew him a picture of what I wanted." She held up her arm and looked at the tat. "Interesting that it's identical to yours, don't you think?"

"Coincidence. That's all it is."

She settled back and closed her eyes again. "If you say so."

"I wonder why you paid over four hundred dollars to Mama's Tats if you didn't get one?"

"I assume I was with someone who did get one."

"Do you remember anything at all?"

"No. It's as if I've been in a coma for two days."

"Has this ever happened to you before?"

"Not like this, but I do spend a lot of time lost in a fog because my mind wanders and I dream."

"Of me."

"Not *of* you. I *am* you. I can't really see what's around me when it happens, and yet, I'm aware. I know when someone talks to me, or sits beside me on the bench. I can talk to them, but it's all instinctive. I'm not really there."

"Do you still hear the baby?"

"No. It stopped crying the minute you appeared in that alley." She sighed. "I wonder why I was smoking? It's really a terrible thing. I used your toothbrush. I didn't think you'd mind."

"It has my spit. It could be enough to make you start turning to Mephisto."

Apparently unconcerned, she yawned.

I continued scanning her charges, going further back in time since the last one was the tat shop. She'd charged some meals and hotel rooms and lots of gasoline, I assumed for the bus. She was paying some of Arcadia's expenses and I wondered why? John and the band's manager should be covering all costs, and if the concerts weren't bringing in enough revenue, they should stop touring. I said as much to Euri, but she didn't answer. She was fast asleep.

I set aside my laptop and carried her to my bed, settled her against my pillow and watched her snuggle in when I pulled up the covers and tucked them around her.

I leaned down to stroke her silky hair and rest my nose against her cheek and kiss her chin. I wanted to climb in with her and hold her next to me all night long.

Only one thing kept me from doing it. She murmured my name. She dreamed of me even when she was asleep. Were her sleep dreams like her waking dreams? Did she see me as some heroic savior? A romantic leading man? Were her dreams as rosy as mine were horrific?

While I stayed close to her and inhaled the scent of the ocean and shampoo, I remembered the worst of my dreams, the one where I stabbed her, and she looked up at me and asked, *"Why?"*

Quickly straightening, I turned away and went to my desk and wrote a note telling her not to leave my room under any circumstances, to call me when she woke up. Then I left to do some reconnaissance. I had to know where she'd been, and with whom.

My first stop was the Gas 'n' Go in Odessa, closed because it was three in the morning in Texas. I found the office and woke up the computer to scan previous security surveillance, moving back to the date she'd used her card in the store. At nine in the morning, after the night she'd left Austin, there was Euri, handing her card to the attendant. There was no one with her, but that didn't mean anything. They were most likely outside, getting gas.

She walked out and the attendant went back to stocking cigarettes behind the counter.

I left and went to the Wag-A-Bag in Amarillo and found essentially the same scene. Euri handed over her card, signed a receipt, then walked out.

The travel stop at Clines Corners is open twenty-four hours, so I had to be a little trickier to get to their surveillance recordings. They also have more than one checkout counter, so I had several different video segments to watch.

When I finally found her, she stood at the counter, waiting for the attendant to ring her up, and a man in a dark suit walked up to her and smiled. She smiled back. He slid his arm around her shoulders and pulled her next to him in a friendly hug. A moment of affection.

He was older than her.

Infinity older.

He was my father.

CHAPTER 6

Once again, I went to Kyanos to avoid my brothers. I called M from the parking lot at Clines Corners and asked him to meet me there. I arrived before he did and took a seat at the old table in the great room of the stone house where I grew up, made from a hickory tree that was struck by lightning the night Eryx died. We held councils at this table. The table in the war room of the Mephisto mansion was made from the same tree.

It was early morning in the north Atlantic, the sun just rising, turning the snowy island to gold. I stared out the window and heard the woman in the ocean calling to me. Still angry at her for laughing at me, I ignored her.

M appeared and took the chair at the end of the table, where he'd sat all the years of my youth when he came for a visit. I could almost see Mana bringing him a platter filled with all the delicacies she'd spent three days preparing for him. To his credit, he was always appreciative. He would smile and laugh and tease her and pull her onto his lap and kiss her right in front of all of us. He really had loved her. Just not enough to fess up to Lucifer and save her and all of his sons.

"Is this a stroll down memory lane, Xenos," he said impatiently, "or is there a specific reason for this meeting?"

"What happened to Euri?"

"When?"

"The past two days. I know she traveled from Austin to Telluride, and I know you were with her in New Mexico. I need to know why."

He avoided my eyes, always a clue that he wasn't happy about the conversation. "She went walkabout. Right off the rails."

"How do you know? Do you keep tabs on the Anabo?"

"Your mother does. She knew Euri slipped off the edge in Austin, so she stayed with her, and when Euri walked all the way from her hotel to Bee Cave Road and hitched a ride on a tanker truck, she became alarmed. I can move about in the world with face and form, but she's limited to an angelic ghost, and no one can see or hear her unless they're unconscious. Or dead. So she asked for intervention and I'm who showed up to make sure nothing happened to Euri while she made her way to you." He leaned back, crossed one leg over the other and stared at me. "She heard a baby. She needed you to help her."

"There was no baby. She heard it in her head. It might have been a baby a thousand miles away. It might have been a phantom baby. She's completely wack."

"Maybe there is a baby. Maybe it's her version of sixth sense."

"If there's a baby, why did it stop crying as soon as I showed up?"

"Maybe the baby is her. It's crying for love and affection and attention." He scratched his eyebrow with his pinkie. "Maybe the baby is you."

I was growing very frustrated. I hated when he did this. "Stop talking in circles and just level with me. How did she get from Austin to Telluride? Why did she spend four hundred bucks at a tat shop in Montrose?"

He sighed and looked around the room. "We had some happy times here, didn't we? Do you ever think about that? What it was like?"

Okay, so we were going to learn by metaphor. I squelched the urge to shout at him. He was my father, after all. "Yeah, Pops, I remember."

"You were always fey, even as a boy. You'd know I was coming for a visit before anyone else knew, including your mother. And you knew when I would leave. It made you mad at me, and you'd run away across the island and hide in the caves until I came looking for you." His smile was wry. "I never failed to come and find you to say goodbye. Did I?"

I shook my head. "No."

"Do you think I would lie to you now? Would I do anything that might make your life worse than it is?"

"No."

"Well, then, I will say what I have to say, and no more. I've interfered way too much already, and it's bound to be noticed. All of you have to do this on your own. You have to find your own way. Do you understand what I'm saying to you?"

"No."

He uncrossed his legs and stood, then walked to the painting above the fireplace. It was a primitive oil Sasha had done of the six of us. And Ty's favorite dog, a mastiff named Gretchen. He'd had at least thirty Gretchens over the years.

M cleared his throat. "Twenty-five years ago, there was a takedown in Russia, a group of men who were all Skia. They had a plan to take over the government, to recruit as many as possible to follow Eryx, then to sow the seeds of discord all across the country. Phoenix planned well, and Jax did his best to lead you all through the takedown. It was complicated. Difficult."

"Stop beating around the bush. They kicked our ass."

"Yes, but you'd been beaten before. Rare, but it did happen a few other times. The difference was that this time, when all of you went home with your tails between your legs, you stayed like that. Do you remember?"

"I remember. Key drank vodka nonstop and lay on top of his greenhouse and shouted at God. Denys disappeared for days at a time, no doubt fucking every girl who'd let him. Phoenix built more bikes. Jax stayed in the gym shooting endless baskets. Ty went to auctions and bought more horses, which made Key mad, so they got in fights and I had to break them up, but then everyone jumped in and it always became a free-for-all." I nodded. "Good times."

He was still staring up at Sasha's painting. "That went on for almost two years, and that's when Eryx caught up to you. He had converts all over the world, in places you would never find them. He got a jump on us, and we've yet to recover. You and your brothers eventually rallied and got back to work, but your hope for the future had dwindled to nothing. I saw this and went to Lucifer and asked him to ask God for more Anabo."

I waited for him to finish, to tell me Lucifer told him no, then gave him a lecture about interfering in the world. Lucifer was all about never interfering. People did what they did and lived their lives and at the end, either they made a difference in the world, or they didn't. Either they went to Heaven, or my father or one of his thousands of minions took them to Hell. How a man lived his life was entirely up to him. It's what free will was all about. And free will was what my brother wanted to end. He wanted all humanity in Hell, where he could control them. Lucifer was determined not to let that happen, but he would be a hypocrite if he meddled in the humanity of the world. He would never allow interference that would bring more Anabo.

But that's not what M said.

"He agreed. He gave me permission to contact your mother."

I sat up straighter, all ears, fascinated. The worst part of my father's punishment for consorting with an Anabo and giving her seven sons was that, after she died, he could never see her or talk to her. She was gone from him forever. My brothers and I had talked about it, a long, long time ago. We felt bad for him, but also recognized that he'd brought it on himself. If he'd confessed before Eryx jumped, we were certain Lucifer would not have been so angry.

But that was all in the past. I was astounded to know that Lucifer had agreed to let my father ask for more Anabo. I'd think M was lying if I didn't know for sure he was telling the truth. My freakish intuition wasn't always a burden. "So you asked Mana to ask God for more Anabo?"

"I did. And she did, and he agreed. And so there were eight Anabo girls born within a couple of years of one another. We didn't know until they were born where they would be, or who they'd be. Your mother visits them in their sleep and tries to help them through growing up. They've each had their own kind of trials."

Eight? We'd found four. That meant there were four more out there.

"I know what you're thinking, but don't, Xenos. The stipulation from Lucifer was that I would not interfere, that if you and your brothers were meant to find them, you would. He only agreed because there were exactly five Anabo left on Earth, and three of them were men. The other two were nuns."

That made me smile. "I'd take a nun. What's the big deal?"

"They were in their sixties twenty-five years ago. One of them has since passed on, and the other has one foot on a banana peel." He walked around the room and stopped at the window to look out at the sea. "There are only three of the eight girls that haven't been discovered. The fourth was Euri's sister, Sophie."

I slumped back in my chair and felt a great sadness. I wondered whom she might have been intended for?

M turned and looked at me. "I think God had a plan when he made Anabo of sisters. There's Jordan and Mariah, and Euri and Sophie. It made finding them more of a certainty."

"I suppose Lucifer can't complain about interference when it's a matter of biology."

"Right. I also think God intended to make it less difficult for them. It's hard to leave their world and agree to be in yours for the rest of time."

"I'm aware."

He took a seat again and smoothed his red silk tie as he sat back and looked at me. "I've told you all of this, in direct opposition to Lucifer, because you're the one who needs to know, and the only one who won't ever tell anyone."

"I'm not complaining, but curious – why do I need to know?"

"Because you're the only one who might actually not take a mate."

"And if I understand what was done to provide this mate, I'll feel guilty enough to overlook all the reasons I should never take her?"

"Something like that. Why do you fight it, son?"

"I will murder her. I'm sure of it. Is that what you and Mana want for her?"

"You won't murder her. You couldn't. She's ill and needs someone to take care of her. She needs *you*, Zee. If she goes back to England, her father will put her in a hospital, or a home of some kind. Her only chance of any kind of normalcy is you."

"That's really sad for her, but no way she'll be happier living eternity with me than she'd be in a safe environment in England. She'd have her piano."

"She'll have no love, and I'm something of an expert on what the lack of love does to a person. I meet thousands of people every week who lost their way because no one ever loved them."

"God loves them."

"But they have to take that on faith, and when you're sad and alone and hurt, you want someone to touch, someone to be there. It's part of the human condition, a need that's as important as food and shelter. If she's not with you, she's with no one."

I thought back over the past month. I'd managed to block her from my mind most of the time, but no matter how hard I tried, I couldn't stay out of hers. She'd cried a lot. She'd prayed a lot, too. She'd been so sad and lonely and I'd felt like all kinds of a douchebag, but kept telling myself she'd get over it, that this was what was best for her. For the first time, I began to wonder if I was wrong. Maybe she was crazy for a reason. Maybe God made her this way because it gave her the ability to be with me in all my madness. I'd have to think more about this. Later, when I wasn't getting the eye from my father.

"Knowing what you do about her, can you imagine her without someone to love? She'll be more miserable than you, and I didn't think that was possible."

"This is pathetic. So we'll still be miserably mad, but at least we will do it together. At least we'll have a friend in misery. Do you hear yourself? Do you have any idea how ludicrous you are?"

"I have to try, Zee. I know you should do this. I'm your father. I care a great deal about you, and I want what's best for you. Accept Euri. Don't take her back to the real world. Keep her safe and make her Mephisto. Look after her all the rest of time."

I changed the subject. "Tell me about the tat."

He never blinked. Always was quick on his feet. "There was no tat. They charged her four hundred dollars for that pack of cigarettes. She had been going on no sleep and no food for almost two days and she was clearly not all there, so they took advantage of her. She went in the shop to ask for directions, because she knew she was close to Telluride, but wasn't sure where to go to hitch a ride, and they saw her coming. A guy offered to take her to Telluride if she'd buy him a pack of smokes, and she agreed. He intended to drive her south of town and make her get out of the car, but I convinced him it'd be in his best interests to take her all the way to Telluride. So he did, and when he let her out in front of the Blue Moose, he tossed the cigarettes to her."

"So she hitched rides all the way from Texas?"

He nodded. "She couldn't have flown without her passport, but I'm not so sure that choice ever occurred to her. She wandered around the parking lot at an old motel in Austin, looking for the baby, then she struck out for Bee Cave Road. No money, no luggage. Just that credit card and her cell phone."

"So you kept an eye on her all along the way. Why did you appear to her in New Mexico?"

"Because she was with a guy who intended to do something violent."

That made me flinch.

"I appeared in the back seat and told him to pull over at the first stop, which turned out to be Clines Corners. I knew she wouldn't remember me because she'd gone off in her head to a place none of us will ever know, and so I approached her and warned her about bad people, and suggested she ask a certain rancher for a ride to Montrose. He was an older guy who was hauling horses. He lost his daughter not long ago, so I knew he'd pull out his paternal instincts and give her a ride."

This was, without a doubt, the most extraordinary conversation I'd ever had. Not only was he admitting he'd interfered with human life, and Anabo were humans with all incumbent humanity unless we convinced them to become immortal and stay with us, this was also one of only a handful of times I could remember having a serious one-on-one talk with M. He just wasn't that kind of father. "Wonder what made her go off like that?"

"No telling. I think the salient point here is that she

came looking for you. What will happen when she's in a home somewhere in England? When she goes walkabout again, she'll try to swim the Atlantic."

The idea was so preposterous, I realized he was being funny. My father, the dark angel of death, was making a joke.

Maybe if this wasn't all so fucking horrible, I'd have found it amusing.

I left him and popped back to Colorado, to my room. Euri was still asleep. Smiling. Mostly uncovered, and the Kings of Leon were riding high, exposing the whole bottom half of her. Lady parts and all.

Shit.

I changed back into my sweats, sat at my piano and played and wished I knew what she dreamed. I only halfway wished she'd slide back beneath the covers. I expected her to wake up, but she just kept sleeping. I began nodding off, missing notes, playing garbage.

It would make sense to go up to the third floor to sleep. There were twenty bedrooms up there, all fully furnished. Mariah was in one of them, and another was technically Jordan's, even though she wasn't living with us yet. That left eighteen beds I could sleep on. The problem was, I'd have to explain to someone why I wasn't in my bed. Other than our own suites, which were sacrosanct, anywhere else in the house could never be private. There was always someone who would know, either one of my brothers, or Sasha, or one of the Purgatories. Especially Mathilda. She had eyes in the back of her head.

But I was exhausted, mentally and physically. I didn't know if I could stay awake until Euri woke up. Besides, it wasn't as though I could go to sleep as soon as she awoke. We'd have to talk about the future (as in, there wasn't one for us) and then I'd have to make a plan to get her back to Arcadia, who were playing tonight in Las Vegas. We'd have to come up with a logical explanation for her disappearance. I'd checked police records in Austin, and John had filed a missing person report on her. He was a stand-up guy, and I knew he was crazy in love with Euri. He had to be freaking out and scared, but he had a schedule to keep, money to make, managers to keep happy, so he had to continue the tour.

I had no concept of a story we could invent to explain her disappearance. My head hurt just thinking about it.

I'd also have to pop to a Victoria's Secret and swipe a pair of panties for her.

Thinking about all there was to do when she woke up made me more tired.

I finally said fuck it and crawled into bed on the opposite side, far away from her. I slipped into sleep easily, surrounded by the scent of the ocean.

~~ EURI ~~

As I awoke, two things came to me, simultaneously: Z was crying, and he was strangling me, his big hands around my throat, choking me so that I saw stars. I couldn't draw breath. I flailed my arms, slapped his head, and bucked my entire body, trying to get him off of me.

Nothing worked. I lost consciousness.

When I came to, he was holding me like a child, cradled in his arms, rocking me back and forth in the center of the bed, sobbing. "Euri, *Euri*, I'm so . . . aw, *God*, what have I . . . I want . . . don't be dead. *Wake up*. Don't be gone. I can't bear it. I can't do this without you. I don't know why . . . *what's wrong with me?*"

I spoke in a whisper, because my throat was bruised. "I'm not dead."

He held me closer, so tight, he nearly crushed me.

I let him hold me and croon to me and cry because he was a monster. I stroked his hair and kissed his neck and assured him I was going to be all right. "You're just confused in your dream," I said. "Don't feel so wretched about this."

He continued to rock me and cry.

In a little while, after the storm in his soul had passed, he would lay back down, and when he woke up, he would think he'd only dreamed all of this. He wouldn't know it really happened.

He never did.

But he surprised me tonight. Perhaps because we were in his room, where he would finish the night in sleep without dreams, he laid me down, then stretched out beside me and gathered me close and whispered into my hair, "I'm going to fix this. I want us to be together and I'll do whatever it takes to make sure you're safe." His arms tightened. "I don't know why this happens. I don't understand what's inside me that would hurt you."

Was he awake? I didn't think so, because he wouldn't hold me like this if he were awake. He was all about distancing himself from me, certain he would hurt me if he were too close.

He had no knowledge that he had come to me at least ten times over the past few weeks, since the night he left me in Jacksonville, and been extremely violent. I would tell him, I decided. He wanted me, wanted this, wanted to not be so alone.

And I wanted the same thing. Because this was what Death meant when he pulled me out of that lake. My purpose was to be here, with Z, and help in the fight against Eryx. This is what I was born to do, and no matter how difficult it would be to find a way around Z's violent madness, I owed it to myself, to him, to all of humanity and to God to keep trying.

He would hurt me, I had no doubt. Nothing about this would be easy.

But my life hadn't been easy since I was six and my mother tried to murder Sophie. I always had the feeling I was running from something, and now I knew I was running *toward* this strange, otherworldly guy who could crush me with his bare hands, who loved music as I did, who had a tender soul, dying to break free of his insanity.

I was suddenly overcome. With tears in my eyes, I whispered, "Don't fret, Z. We'll figure it out. Get some sleep and everything will look better in the morning."

I drifted off, and when I next awoke, I was spooned into him and he had one arm around me, holding me close to his body, while the other hand stroked my hair. He had a stiffy, and it pressed against my bum, but I made no move to do anything about it. I knew he was awake, and if he realized I was awake, he'd spring from the bed and move away from me. I wanted to enjoy this as long as I could.

A sliver of light peeked between the draperies and I

heard the deep bongs of a grandfather clock from far away. Downstairs on the ground floor, I assumed. I knew the brothers' bedrooms were all on the first floor, except in America it was the second floor. *One, two, three* . . . it ended at twelve. Then a solemn male voice said, with just a hint of an accent, "Lunch is served. Allah is good."

I'd heard it before, when I was within Z's mind. This was Deacon, the butler, who announced every meal over the mansion's intercom.

I was hungry, and wished I could dress in Sasha's jeans and go downstairs with Z and have lunch and meet everyone.

I also wished I could turn in his arms and he would kiss me. I wished he'd slide his muscled body on top of mine, make himself a part of me.

But wishes are worth exactly what you pay for them.

He whispered, "Are you awake?"

"No."

He began moving away and I turned quickly and wrapped my arms around his middle. "Don't go."

For a few brief moments, he held me, and I knew it killed him to let me go and roll away. The wall candles lit themselves as he sat up and got off the bed and went toward the bathroom. I watched, enjoying the play of muscles across his bare back and the definition of his very tight bum beneath his blue gym pants. He closed the door, and I slipped from the bed and stretched. I'd never slept so well, even considering that he'd tried to murder me in his sleep.

Just another crazy day for me and Z. I wondered how long he'd let me stay, and what would happen after he took me back? I was feeling slightly off, as if the world was a bit cockeyed.

I sat at his piano and saw a note he must have left for me last night. I wondered where he'd gone? He'd signed it, *Zee*. I'd thought of him as Z for so long, it was odd to see his name spelled that way.

I began to play, instantly in love with his piano. I'd wanted to do this so many times, and now here I was, coaxing amazing music from this magnificent instrument. It was an original Steinway, old and mellow and glorious.

Perfectly tuned. My heart soared, my spirit was overjoyed, my body tingled.

"You're not in my head," he said from behind me. "You're playing, but you're not in me."

"Would you let me in if I tried?"

"Yes."

I smiled at that. "I'm in your life. I don't need to be in your head."

"But you're playing. You said you can't help it when you're playing."

"I can't. But I'm with you now, so there's no need. It's the same reason the screams stop when we're together. There's something in each of us that complements the other."

He sat next to me on the bench and watched me play. "Losing the screamers is marvelous. I wish . . . wouldn't it be wonderful if being together made each of us less crazy?"

"It already is wonderful." I shot him a look. "What color is the world today?"

"Every color." He rubbed his palms against his thighs, as if he was nervous. "It still won't work, Euri. You were in my bed last night, but I still dreamed. Are you ever there?"

"No, I'm only ever in your mind when you're awake. And when you aren't fighting so hard to keep me out."

His shoulders slumped and his head bowed. "If you had any inkling what I dream, you'd run away."

"I have an inkling." I nudged him with my shoulder. "You dream about me."

"I've dreamed about you every night for a thousand years."

"Yes, I know. You think about it a lot." Now was the time. I had to say it. "In last night's dream, you strangled me."

He jerked his head up and looked at me with wide, black eyes. "How do you know?"

I never stopped playing. "It's not just a dream, Zee. You really did strangle me. Last week, you stabbed me. A month ago, the night we were together in Florida, you came into my room and smothered me with your hands. That was the first time." I remembered waking up and feeling glad he was there, then panicking when he wouldn't move his hands from my face. Just about the time I finally understood that he was not fully aware, not really awake, and that he was trying to kill me, I lost consciousness. And when I woke, he was rocking me and crying and berating himself for being a monster. Then he disappeared, until he woke me up again four nights later, strangling me.

Tears instantly popped into his eyes and he stared down at my hands as they flew across the keys. "Why didn't you tell me? How did I not know? I'm in your head as much as you're in mine. Do you never think about it?"

"You've locked me out since Florida."

"I had to, Euri." He swallowed and whispered, "But you didn't keep me out of your thoughts. I was there, so much of the time, and you knew I was. I know you did. Why didn't you think about it? How do you go through something like that and not ever think about it?"

I pretended not to notice when his tears landed in big plops onto the keys. "You said it yourself when we were in Florida. I don't dwell on bad things, Zee. I wake up after those nights and decide not to think about it."

"Just like that."

I shrugged and continued playing. "I've done it my whole life. Thinking about bad things makes more bad things happen."

He stared down at my hands as they moved across the keys, and dripped more tears, which landed on my fingers. "How did I find you? I was asleep. I know where you are in general, like the city, but not exactly. How do I come to you?"

"I don't know, Zee. You wake me up hurting me, and no matter what I say or do, you don't stop until I lose consciousness. When I come round, you're always holding me, crying, terribly upset at what you've done. You move away from me, as if you're afraid of me, and then you disappear."

He was completely blown away. I felt terrible for him, but he needed to know.

Rubbing his eyes with the heels of his hands, he mumbled, "Sometimes I wake up with blood on my hands, and I never know where it comes from. Now I know . . . aw, God, it's *yours*. Christ, *why?* I hate this *so* much."

I was still playing, hoping he'd see that this wasn't the

deal breaker he thought. We would figure out a way around this. We had to. I wasn't going away.

He dropped his hands and blinked at me. "If I stabbed you, how did you live? Why didn't you go to hospital?"

I'd been instructed not to tell anyone, but I was never very good with instructions, and Zee wouldn't believe me unless I told him the truth. I was tired of the lie, of the subterfuge. I'd suffer whatever consequences and not be sorry. I segued into Evanescence's 'My Immortal.' "I heal unnaturally quickly."

"Like we do." He frowned in concentration, swiftly putting two and two together. "You're immortal. Aren't you?"

I nodded and continued playing. "Death pulled me out of the lake and said it wasn't my time. But he was wrong because I was already dead. A woman came then, an angel named Mary Michael, and I remembered her from my dreams, all of my life. She told me I had a purpose, that if I chose to die, I could, but there was a specific reason for me not to."

"Did she tell you about us? About me and my brothers?"

I shook my head. "All she said was that I would make a difference if I lived on. I didn't know your father was Mephistopheles. I only knew he was Death, and it seemed so strange to me that Death would offer me life eternal."

"So you accepted immortality based on nothing but faith."

"My faith is very strong. Not just in God, but in humanity, in life. I see joy. It has a color and a smell and a feel all its own. I decided I wanted to stay and help other people see joy."

His smile was wry, maybe even a little sad. "I'd think you have all the sense of a child if I hadn't lived in your head for so long. There is no one like you anywhere, Euri."

"And no one like you, Xenos."

"I can't believe M did this. How could he be sure we'd find you?"

"He knew what our brains are capable of. Maybe he did something to connect us. Maybe Lucifer did. Or God. Does it matter? I'm here now, and we're going to figure out a way to make it work."

"What if you hated me? What if what we do bothered you far too much to join us? Where did he think you'd go?"

"He said if I changed my mind, if I truly felt I'd made a mistake, I could ask God to take me and he would."

"That's not what we were told. Once an Anabo becomes immortal, they are forever. Otherwise, what's to stop Sasha, for instance, from checking out when she and Jax get in a fight? Or when she's sick to death of what we do. It's a crap life, for sure."

"I don't think Sasha would leave just because Jax is sometimes clueless, or because she had a bad day. I don't intend to leave."

He sat up straighter. "We're going to have to talk about you staying, Euri. I really don't think you—"

"I meant leave life." I played on. "And it's not that simple to do. There's a process. I'd have to sincerely want to leave. I'd have to go to holy ground and pray. I'd have to . . . well, I'd have to off myself."

"That makes no sense. The definition of immortal is that you can't die."

"I can if I'm on holy ground and ask God and am sincere about wanting to."

"Suicide is a mortal sin. It doesn't necessarily mean a one-way ticket to Hell, courtesy of my father, but it's a reservation."

"You just said it's a mortal sin. I'm now immortal. It's a way back."

"For an Anabo, I suppose it would be."

I stopped playing and he began a Schubert piece I'd long loved. "Have you always played?"

"Since I was a boy. They didn't have pianos back then, but my father brought me a guitar, and a flute and a whole host of other instruments that have long since become obsolete. Someday I'll take you downstairs to the music room and show you my collection."

"You still have those instruments?"

"Yes." He glanced sideways at me. "Don't you have your first piano?"

"It's the one at Longbourne, a very old Steinway. I think my great great great grandfather bought it for his daughter."

"Who was Jane."

"It's strange, isn't it?"

"You look exactly like her. Do you know?"

"I know. There's a portrait of her and her twin, Georgiana, in the gallery hall at Longbourne. And there are photographs."

I closed my eyes and listened to him play. He had a way about him that was unique, something indefinable, the gift that separates a born musician from one who reads music. He loved it so much, it was part of him, and his technique was masterful and achingly beautiful.

Floating on the notes of the piece, I smiled. "It was only a week after I died and came back when I first heard you, late at night. You played guitar and sang really old James Taylor, from the beginning. 'Fire and Rain.' Which is a perfect song for you, now that I think on it. You sat on the roof of this house and looked out across the mountains. It was summertime and the moon was full. I had never seen anything lovelier, or heard music played with such emotion. It was so beautiful. You came to me in little waves after that, a snippet here and there. Always when you were playing. One afternoon, I was having tea with my cousin in Kensington when you came to me playing Aerosmith guitar at volume ten."

"Aerosmith must always be played at volume ten."

"Months passed and you began to come to me for longer periods of time, and not just when you were playing. Then it was like it had always been with Sophie, and I wasn't merely aware of you, but it was as if I saw the world as you saw it. I experienced your life as you lived it."

He kept playing, all his concentration on the keys, but I suspected he could play this piece blindfolded. "You must have been frightened."

"I suppose it's the curse or the reward of insanity. Nothing scares me. At least, nothing in my head. Anything can happen when you're crazy."

"I'm not sure what we have is crazy. I realize we're both mad to some degree, but this connection . . . it's not a lie. It's not an illusion. In almost a year, we've been physically together a week, maybe two, total, yet we know each other as if we'd been together for years."

"We have. Two years, anyway. It's been almost that long since Sophie died."

"I wasn't aware of you until after the Panama takedown." He smiled, still playing his piano. "You said something to me while I was in the shower."

I rested my hand on his thigh. His muscles tightened and relaxed as he worked the pedals. "I was a trifle shocked. I've not seen many willies, being that I only ever slept with Miles, and even though the blokes in Arcadia tend to wee on the edges of roadways, I don't look. It's ghastly rude, really. So, you see, I'm a bit of a novice. I don't look at dirty pictures or anything like that. Not that I'm opposed, just that I spend all my time playing music. At any rate, I was rather intrigued. It must be strange to have something like that between your legs all the time."

He chuckled. "When I'm dressed, it's not really . . . I thought I was imagining you, that the voice was something from the depths of my mind, a new kind of insanity, and it made me sad."

"Panama was the tipping point and the reason I agreed to the tour, so I could come to America and find out if you were real."

"You're a naughty girl who wanted to see me naked again."

I laughed and he played and we sat like that for a lovely while, until he said seriously, "So you chose immortality over going with your sister."

"She would have wanted me to stay."

"How do you know?"

I looked up at him. "She was the other half of me. I knew her as well as I know myself. If we'd been switched, I'd have felt the same for her."

He looked across the bedroom at the wall of mahogany shelves that held myriad books, stacks of journals, several photographs, and his elaborate sound system. "I met with M while you were asleep. He followed you from Austin to Telluride, to keep an eye on you, he said. He appeared to you in New Mexico, which I thought was strange because none of us are allowed to interfere in humanity. He kept you from harm by telling you to hitch a ride with a different man than the one you were with. Now I know why he could do that with impunity. You're not human. He can interfere all he likes." He stopped playing and turned to look at me. "So can I."

"What do you mean?" I was alarmed, he looked that intense.

"What do you want, Euri?"

"To stay with you."

"Forever? It's a long time."

"Forever."

"Suppose I can't fix this horrible thing that's wrong with me? What if I attack you in your sleep, in my sleep, every night for all time?"

"I still want to stay."

"Doesn't it concern you?"

"I'm immortal. You can't kill me, after all."

"But I must want to if I dream it over and over. It should bother you that I try. I can't understand why this doesn't scare the shit out of you. Why would you want to be with me?" He teared up again. *"Why?"* he whispered.

"Because it's meant to be, and I know, somewhere in my soul, that I'm the answer. I'm what you need. You're why I was compelled to stay alive. In return, you'll look after me and keep me from losing my shit and hitching rides with strangers."

"And kill you in my sleep." He slid from the bench and walked to the draperies and opened them, then stood and stared out at the mountains, covered in January snow. "These dreams have plagued me all of my life and my hatred of them is indescribable. I've spent every single night being scared to death of myself. Now, knowing I'm actually acting out those dreams, that I've physically harmed you . . ." He huffed out a breath and I knew he was fighting tears. He was badass and strong and take-no-prisoners, but underneath it all, he was a gentle soul. It was why I wanted to stay, why I loved him. But I didn't tell him that. He'd say I saw everyone through rose-colored glasses. He could never see himself as I saw him.

"My worst fears are coming true. Now I'm freaked that the other things in my head will happen. How could I have such horrible thoughts? You've been in here with me, Euri. You know I sometimes go off to a place I can't even speak of, it's so disturbing."

"It's not your imagination bringing you all those images, Zee. They're a reflection of what's happening in real life, as if your mind is a satellite dish, collecting all this information, and the worst of it, the things your soul can't comprehend, or maybe the things God most wants you to fix, play in your head. The past few months, whenever you go off, when you slip over the line into your madness in all its glory, you're always in Azbekastan."

"If what you say is true, why am *I* committing the violence? Why is it *me* killing little kids?" He cried in earnest now. "It's *horrible*. I'm a *monster*."

"You have such intense empathy, you not only see what's happening, you channel the feelings of the men committing those unspeakable massacres. When you think about it, when it comes to you and you can't make it stop, you feel worse than a monster. That tells me that the soldiers in Azbekastan don't want to do what they're doing."

He looked as if I was speaking some alien language he'd never heard. What I said was nothing he'd ever considered before.

And while I watched, I saw hope flicker in his eyes.

"It's the same thing that happens with me, Zee. When you're in my head, you not only know what I'm doing, you know how I feel about it. If I'm happy, you feel it, too. And when I'm with you, I feel as you do. The difference between you and I is that you're the only one I channel. You pick up random strangers."

"If I could stop, I would."

"Maybe it's not such a bad thing."

"Easy for you to say." Tears filled his eyes again. "Jesus, when I think of all the poor souls . . . and I'm there when they die, in such horrible conditions, with so much misery."

He quickly turned back to the window, took a great deep breath and let it out, his shoulders sagging. He seemed so defeated. "All I ever wanted was just to feel normal. To watch a movie without hearing the screams. To sleep all night and not dream at all. To sit by the ocean and hear nothing but waves." He glanced at me, still sitting on the piano bench. "To be with you and just . . . be."

I went to stand beside him, slid my arms around his

middle and rested my head on his shoulder while I looked out at the spectacular view. It had snowed the night before, blanketing the world in white. I felt his strong arm slide across my shoulders to pull me closer. We stood there for a long time and I had never felt so at peace. This is where I belonged. It remained to be seen how I could convince him of it. "You want the wrong things, Zee. You have a gift, and because it's so strong, it manifests itself in any way it likes because you allow it. You should embrace the gift, but put a leash on it and use it for positive purposes."

"You make it sound so easy. You're far too simplified."

"I don't believe it will be easy." I looked up at him. "But it's not complicated. Not if you're serious about it."

"Of course I'm serious."

"Are you? Or are you feeling a tad sorry for yourself that you can't be like the others, that God made you this way?"

He dropped his arm and moved away from me, headed back to the bathroom.

"I've made you angry."

"No," he said as he went into the bath and through to his clothes cupboard that was essentially another room, it was so spacious. "I'm hungry."

I followed and watched him sit on a long bench in the center of the room and tie the laces on his athletic shoes. It smelled of hot cross buns and some delightful cologne and maybe a smidge of sweat. How lovely it was, his clothes all defined by style and color. There were suits and tuxedos and jeans and ski pants and hiking boots and Italian leather loafers and shitkickers. There was flannel and polos and dress shirts, and in the drawers were T-shirts and boxers and briefs and handkerchiefs and cufflinks. It was a feast for the senses, and there he was in the midst of it all, in his gym pants with a hole in the knee and dilapidated Nikes and a T-shirt from a Rolling Stones concert in 1976 that may have been red at one time, but was now some muted shade of pick-a-color. He was absolutely magnificent. I wished all over again that he would make love to me. Kiss me. Hold me. My body hummed with sexual awareness. But I said nothing, because he'd leave as quickly as possible. For a guy who was dying for sex, he was more skittish than a nun in a brothel. "You're not particularly fond of bridges, are you?"

He unbent from tying his shoes. "I assume you mean pointless conversations that connect those with meaning, not roads across rivers."

I nodded and stepped aside when he went to the basin to brush his teeth.

He turned toward me and said with toothpaste in his mouth, "You're hungry, too, yesh?"

"Yes."

After he spit and rinsed, he dried his mouth with a hand towel and leaned against the cabinet. "We've got to figure out a way to get you back to Arcadia."

"I don't want to go back. I want to stay here, with you."

"I think you have to, Euri, at least for the time being. For one thing, you can't leave John high and dry. Don't you want to see the tour through to the end?"

I looked down at his shoes and thought about it for a moment. "Yes, I do. I'm still a little off center, Zee. Not thinking straight."

He nodded. "And if you go back, it'll give me more time to work things out."

Walking to him, I didn't stop until my breasts were pressed against his chest. I looked up into his midnight black eyes. "What you mean is you need time to devise a strategy to keep me as far away from you as possible. How're you going to do it, Zee? Set me up as a psychic on a corner in New Orleans? Take me back to England so my papa can lock me up and throw away the key? Anything in the real world is bound to get dodgy. People will start to notice I'm eternally eighteen. Or will you let me be here, on Mephisto Mountain? Will you pawn me off on one of your brothers? It doesn't appear you can bend the rules like that, but you could try. Or you could make me be a Lumina and work down in a basement office, despite my lack of any skills other than piano and mental telepathy."

"Mental telepathy is a skill, a gift. We could definitely use you."

"Silly man, the only one I can read is you. The Luminas wouldn't like me because they're all bright, scientific, mathematics types. I'm a daydreamer who barely passed algebra."

"You write code. You can hack with the best of them. How'd you get to be a computer geek, anyway?"

"Lots of downtime on tour. I was always with adults who ramble on about dreary things like opera theory or Parliament. I had a laptop with me, always, and I gamed and tried to get into forums talking about gaming, but was trolled mercilessly because I'm a girl. So I learned how to hack into the forums under an alias IP address, and then I hacked into all sorts of databases, just to see if I could. Miles taught me some things, as well."

He said quietly, "You *could* be a Lumina, you know."

"I *could* do many things, but what I *will* do is be here, with you."

He stared down at me for the longest time. "Don't do this to me," he whispered. "I can't bear it, Euri."

And I knew what he meant. "I will come to be with you and I will never leave you."

He swallowed and rubbed his eyes with a thumb and forefinger. He cleared his throat. "Phoenix will need to plan how to take you out. You can't just disappear. We'll have to ask M for a doppelganger so your dad will have a body to bury." He frowned. "What about your dad? Don't you want to go home and see him one last time?"

"Actually, I think that might make this more difficult. As for him, he's remarrying and all his concentration is in that direction. Poor man was married to my horrid mother all those years, he deserves a bit of happiness. She's a lady who's bound to be nice to him and give him an heir to become the next earl."

His frown became a scowl. "Jane's parents scarcely noticed she was gone, they were so caught up in their son."

"Who became my great great grandfather."

"Do the inheritance laws in England bother you?"

"Not really. It's tradition. And I've no desire to be an earl, or a countess, or even Lady Euri." I smiled up at him and rested my hands on his biceps. "I'm going to be a Mephisto, which is much more badass and important than some stodgy aristocrat."

Ah, that made him smile. He really needed to do that more often. "When it's time, I'm sure you'll make an excellent Mephisto. For now, you need to go back."

"I will, but in a month, when the band finishes its tour in New York, after the last concert, I'm coming to stay. I'll sleep in another room if you insist, but I'll never leave you alone, Zee. I'll either be in your head or in your life. You can't get rid of me."

"The last thing I want is to get rid of you, Euri, but surely you understand my hesitation." He took a deep breath and let it out slowly. "I fucking choked you last night."

"And today, I'm right as rain."

He hesitantly slid his arms around me, and when I put mine around him, he gave in and held me tight. "Stubborn Brit," he mumbled against my hair, "you're going to regret it."

"I will never regret this, Zee. We may not always see eye to eye, we may both check out at times, but I'll never wish I hadn't stayed with you."

He held me closer. "I'm going to get you underwear and a cheeseburger. Don't answer my door or leave the room. I'm not ready for them to know."

"You're avoiding interference from the others. You do everything by yourself. Maybe you should let them be more involved."

He dropped his arms and stepped away from me and disappeared. No goodbye, no response to what I'd just said. What a strange guy he was, no doubt because he'd been so alone for so long. When he was done with a conversation, he was done.

Then again, it was oddly refreshing.

Smiling to myself, I went to his sound system and began learning how to turn it on. I'm certain flying a Royal Navy jet would have been simpler.

I'd just figured out how to access his iTunes and chose 'Demons' from Imagine Dragons because the song simply screamed Zee, when I heard the door open.

Before I could even turn, Sasha said, "Oh, my God, *no* way."

When I turned round, she went pale and stepped back, her smoky blue eyes wide with shock. "*Jane*," she said on a breath. "Sweet Mary, you're *Jane*."

Bollocks. I hadn't thought to be discovered. Would she

out me to the others? All I could do was step up, be honest and hope she'd honor a plea for confidentiality. "Actually, no, I'm Euri. Jane was my great great aunt, or maybe great great great. Anyway, a long ago ancestor. It's very odd and strange, I realize. Do close the door, won't you? Zee is keen to keep me secret for now."

"I'm so sorry. I knocked and got no answer, and I wondered if he was gone, so I came in to check. He disappears, you see, and they always make me come to check because he won't get mad at me if it turns out he's here and just off in . . . wherever it is that his mind goes." She smiled nervously, closed the door, then advanced, inspecting every inch of me.

It was dreadfully rude of me, but I couldn't stop staring at her. She was surrounded by an ethereal light, almost a glow, as if something inside of her was lit. It was extraordinary and mesmerizing. I'd long thought her to be lovely, but seeing her through Zee's eyes, I'd never fully appreciated this amazing light. I was also Anabo. I wondered if I glowed like this? The idea made me smile, almost laugh.

"You're for Zee?" This evidently confused her, possibly because she thought Jane had been intended for Phoenix, so why would her double not be also intended for Phoenix? She didn't know Jane had been intended for Zee all along. No one did, except Zee.

"Yes, I'm here for Zee. Or maybe he's here for me. It's a very long story and there's no time, really. He's popped off to steal knickers and bring us lunch and he's bound to be back soon."

She came closer and reached out a hand to pet my hair. "Amazing. You look just like her. You're so beautiful." Tears formed in her eyes and slipped out and rolled down her pretty cheeks. "I'm so glad for Zee. He's always been . . . " She dropped her hand. "Where did he find—"

"It's a terribly complicated story. I will tell you all of it when I am back, I promise."

"Back? Where are you going?"

"I'm in a band and Zee wants me to go with them for the next month, and then I'll be here."

"So you know—"

"Everything. You're Sasha and you're married to Jax. Or not married. Whatever it is that Mephisto do, you are that. I know all of it."

"And you're on board with joining us?"

"Of course. Zee is a splendid bloke and I shall love to be here with him. He may take a bit of romancing, because he is a hard case, but I'm not worried."

Now she was grinning at me. "Awesome."

I touched her arm and began leading her back to the door. "I'm sorry to be so rude. I'm not, usually. But it's a delicate situation with Zee. You understand."

"Yes," she said, turning when we reached the door. "I'm happy to know you, Euri. And I'm dying to hear how you and Zee found each other."

I smiled at her. "I'm mad as a hatter, just as he is."

Her smile faded. "You mean—"

"Yes, that's what I mean. Strangely, when we're together, it's not so bad. It's as if we were made for each other."

"I've begun to wonder if all of us were made especially for the Mephisto. It's a little too convenient, you know?"

"Indeed." I reached for the doorknob. "We will discuss it at length when I return, and get to the bottom of it, eh? It was grand meeting you, Sasha. This will be our secret, won't it? Even Jax mustn't know."

"I tell him everything, but he won't breathe a word, I promise."

"Well, then, I shall look forward to getting to know you better very soon."

She embraced me and, in return, I patted her rather awkwardly.

I am British, after all.

CHAPTER 7

"I screwed up. I see that now. I should have asked Phoenix for help. I suck at plans. And now I know you suck at lying. I can't believe you told John you weren't aware of anything for two days. He's liable to call your dad, and then he'll be over here trying to take you back to England and have you committed or something horrible like that, and then what will we do, Euri? You'll go walkabout and how will you find me, across the ocean? Do you think he'll call your dad? No, he wouldn't. He needs you to play. That song you cut with them is like number five on Billboard, and *Rolling Stone* says Arcadia is the best indie band going right now, mostly because of you. No way John's sending you back to England."

He paced back and forth in front of the bench where I sat, outside the bus terminal in Las Vegas. I was enjoying people watching. "If you sat here all day, you'd see the whole world walk by."

"Will you focus? He's going to be here any minute. Shouldn't you at least *try* to look worried or concerned? And really, why *aren't* you worried or concerned? It's freaking me the fuck out that you'll be on your own again. What if you check out? I about lost my mind for two days and *then* I found out you'd hitched rides, which is how people get murdered by serial killers, or raped or robbed or left for dead in a ditch. Jesus, Euri, maybe I'd better just take you back home."

"It's all going to be okay, Zee. I have this little GPS thing in my phone and you have the program to follow it, so even if I go walkabout again, you can find me. If all else fails, go to sleep. You seem perfectly able to find me when you're asleep."

"That's not funny."

"I wasn't being funny."

"Surely now that he knows you check out sometimes, he'll keep a closer watch on you. Jamison is a stand-up guy. He's also pretty righteous on guitar."

"He's going to want to kiss me. Will that upset you?"

"Like a *kiss?* Or a friendly, glad you're okay kiss?"

"He'll want it to be a kiss, with tongues and hands and such."

He stopped pacing. "Shit, I wish I had a cigarette, and I don't even smoke. What kind of kiss do you want, Euri?"

I looked up at him from behind a pair of Sasha's shades. "From him, only a friendly one. From you, I'd like to take all of your clothes off and lay you down and kiss every inch of you. And then I'd want tongues and hands and such."

He smiled. I'd known he would. He really fretted more than an old woman, like Mrs. Beardsley who lived at Longbourne and was always fearful of another air raid, even though the last one had been in 1943.

"You're a naughty girl, aren't you?"

"Yes, very."

He sobered slightly. "Were you this way with Miles?"

"Not at all. He was terribly shy and reserved and always seemed a trifle awkward and embarrassed about things."

"Then why did you sleep with him?"

"Because it was . . . comforting. Familiar. It was nice to feel close to him like that."

Now he was frowning, his delightful smile all gone. "Sex should be wild and hot and furiously passionate and it should last as long as it needs to last for everybody to get off. Are you telling me you never had a climax with Miles?"

"Of course not. It takes me a quarter hour at least, and he generally lasted about three minutes."

He began to pace again. "Not a hard act to follow. So there's that." He stopped. "You do realize that sex with me isn't going to be . . . what did you say? Comforting? Familiar? I don't really think those will be the adjectives that come to mind."

"It's certain to be quite jolly," I assured him.

He started again, walking back and forth, back and

forth. "Didn't you tell him? It's important for a woman to say what she wants. We're not mind readers, you know." I cocked a brow and he stopped and said, "Okay, so I can read your mind, but evidently only long distance. When you're with me, I'm as clueless as the next guy." He resumed pacing. "Maybe Miles would have tried harder, or not been so shy about it if you'd talked to him."

Now I knew, all I had to do to get him talking was mention sex. I guessed maybe it was natural, under the circumstances. He hadn't had sex in months, which was very out of character for him. Zee thoroughly enjoyed the carnal side of life.

"I should like not to talk about Miles. I know what he did was wrong, that he was weak and lost his faith, but he was my closest friend. After Sophie died, he was all I had, my only solace. He was a lovely man and we will not remember him otherwise."

"You can remember him however you like. I didn't know him at all. I'm just sorry that you had lousy sex. You'll climb into bed with me with low expectations."

"Then you can prove me wrong. What's the problem, oh great sex god?"

He stopped pacing, looked at me, and then he laughed. Laughed and laughed, and I almost cried with joy, it sounded so wonderful.

Abandoning his pacing, he sat next to me and held my hand. "We'll talk on the phone every night."

"Right-o."

"You'll tell me if anything's wrong, if there's a problem?"

"I'll tell you."

He was coming closer, practically squishing me, he pressed against me so hard. "I don't want to leave you here. I have a bad feeling."

For the first time, I paid serious attention. I was concerned. "Your sixth sense? Is it telling you something's wrong?"

He squeezed my hand. "Nah, I think it's just me being revoltingly needy and obsessed."

"If I weren't so very aristocratic and stuffy because I was raised to keep a stiff upper lip, I'd be equally needy and obsessive. It's something of a burden, if you must know. I frequently wish I might let loose a bit."

"Wonder how you'll react when we're in bed together?" He spoke in a British falsetto that was astonishingly spot-on. "I say, sir, what a jolly good orgasm that was. Might we have tea and a biscuit now?"

I laughed, and so did he, and we sat there and held hands and smiled at each other like new lovers. It was marvelous.

After a while, he looked down at our hands. "I've never had anything like . . . well, *anybody*, and it's just all kind of so new to think about, and you're just barely with me, and now you have to leave." Taking me by surprise, he put his arms around me and practically dragged me onto his lap.

"I'll come back, Zee. I promise. Don't fret. We'll talk . . . *umph* . . . every day."

He was far stronger than he realized, I think, because he didn't seem aware that he was squeezing the air from my lungs. Before I could protest, however, almost as soon as he'd pulled me to his lap, he set me off of it and said softly, "Jamison's driving up in that limo. I'm fading out so only you can see me. Don't talk to me or he'll think for sure you're totally wack." He kissed my nose. "Bye."

"Goodbye, love. Do ring me up after tonight's show, won't you?"

"Yes," he whispered, moving to stand at the opposite end of the bench.

As I predicted, John was very enthusiastic about seeing me, and I just barely deflected his kiss, managing to turn it into a friendly buss. Over his shoulder, I saw Zee scowling. He was not keen on John manhandling me.

"Are you all right?" John asked, taking my hand, leading me to the limo. "I've called a friend, who recommended several doctors here in Vegas and a few in L.A. since we're headed there tomorrow."

I took a seat in the limo and waited for him to follow before I shook my head and smiled at him. "I'm fine, John, really."

"Euri, you checked out for two days. That's not fine. How do you know someone didn't put something in your drink? You said you woke up in a motel in Albuquerque, but how did you get there?"

"I am apparently not being clear about what happened. I knew where I was. I just needed some time. I needed sleep. I am sincerely sorry for leaving like that and I promise not to do it again. I just . . . had to get away."

He accepted it because he wanted to. Even added his own spin to make it all okay. "You've not had a break since you came to the States for your piano tour. I should have seen how stressed you were." He paused and looked out the limo window as we passed a billboard announcing Arcadia would play tonight at The Palms. "Although, honestly? You didn't seem stressed. You're always a little vague, Euri, and you smile a lot, like you have tremendous internal peace and happiness. You just don't strike me as the sort who ever needs to twist off." He turned to look at me again. "Is it drugs? Alcohol? Have you gone off on a bender or a trip or something? Did you do anything that might show up in a magazine, or online?"

I smiled at the ridiculousness of it and shook my head. "It's all good, John. I'm back and I'm fine. No need for a physician. Let's just go to rehearsal and forget about it, eh?"

He nodded, but he never let go of my hand.

We'd made a good plan. If we'd stuck to it, I suppose one could say we were mature adults who knew how to restrain ourselves from impulsive behavior.

But let's be honest. We were masses of hormones and loneliness and fear. We were afraid of what lived in our heads, of what unforeseen path it might take. Would our time together be shortened by insanity?

We never said it aloud, but I know he was as afraid of it as I.

We talked after the Vegas concert. We talked the next morning while I walked around the grounds at The Palms, dodging a couple of overeager fans.

We talked while I rode the band bus to L.A.

Then we didn't talk because I had to rehearse. We were playing at Fawkes, a famous old club on Sunset where legendary musicians had played. I was extremely excited about it and said so to John, who laughed and said, "This old dive? Smells like the bottom of an ashtray, with some stale beer thrown in for good measure."

"Yes, it's wonderful!"

Joe, my favorite roadie, nodded. "It's a real cool place, Euri. Don't listen to Jamison. He'd carp and bitch about his granny's house, and she lives in a mansion in Boston."

We were in a nicer than usual hotel in L.A. and when I asked why, John said, "Don't you know? 'Send Me Down' reached number one this morning. We've had a call from every major record label and some indies. I expect all of them to be at tonight's gig. Sam and I decided we should look a little less desperate while we're in Los Angeles."

I was happy for him and the rest of the band, and Sam, our manager, because this could only mean more money and fame and maybe a European tour, which John had talked about a lot. I felt only slightly guilty about leaving. I'd agreed to be with the band until New York, and he knew I would probably want to go back to England after that.

Or maybe he didn't. Maybe he thought I wanted all of this as much as he did. He maybe didn't know that, for me, it was always and forever about the music. I wanted to make it, and if people wanted to hear it, that made me happy. I didn't care one way or the other if they paid for it. Logically, I knew we had to take money to pay expenses, but I certainly wasn't looking to make a fortune. I already had one. But even had I been a poor urchin with nothing, I'd still not care about anything but the music.

Probably because I am mad.

As Zee is mad.

I dressed with extra care that night, because we would be in a famous venue instilled with the spirits of all the greats who'd been there before. I also dressed carefully because I knew Zee and I were destined to wind up in his bed, and I wanted to look pretty for him. I wore the knickers he'd brought to me, a wisp of black silk that tied with satin ribbons on each side. They were clearly made for sex and not real life. That's why he'd also brought me a pair of ordinary knickers, which I'd worn to meet John at the bus terminal.

Before I dressed, Zee had pulled the black silk ones from his pocket and grinned at me and dared me to put them on.

Of course I did, and he took one look and went in the bathroom and closed the door and said, "Take them off. Get dressed. Shit. What was I thinking? Jesus. I'm gonna have blue balls again. I haven't had blue balls since I was twelve years old, too sheltered and ignorant to know I could take care of the problem myself."

"Didn't your older brothers tell you?"

"It never came up, no pun intended. Are you dressed yet?"

I'd said yes, and he came out and we'd left just after.

Wearing them now, I felt very sexy, as if I had a secret. I'd worn my very most proper dress and shoes. I looked as all well-heeled young Brit aristocrats should look, and underneath it all, I wore a pair of black silk knickers that slid against my skin in a sensuous whisper.

In the green room before the front band took the stage, while everyone else ate burgers and drank craft beer and smoked weed, I sat at the upright and played Mozart. Tonight, everything would change. Tonight, he would come to Fawkes. He would take me with him to Colorado and make love to me for hours and hours.

He just didn't know it yet.

I played and lost touch with anything around me. All the others in the green room faded away and it was only Zee. For the first time in weeks, I was in his head full stop, with no barrier. He was walking down Santa Monica, toward a restaurant. Lily's. He'd had a good day, not as bedeviled by his madness as usual. He was lighthearted and as close to happy as he was able. He was thinking of me. He was looking forward to the concert tonight because, like me, he was all about the music. He'd long been an Arcadia fan, and with me playing in the band, he was exceptionally anticipatory.

He walked inside Lily's, following a blue-eyed blonde, checking out her bum. He liked what he saw. She turned and smiled at him and he imagined having sex with her, but in his imagination, she became me. He laughed to himself, or maybe *at* himself as he walked further into the restaurant and saw his brother, who'd just finished eating. Alone.

Phoenix stood, and as he met Zee's gaze, a terrible

knowledge landed in Zee's consciousness, causing the screams to escalate to a fever pitch, so loud, they nearly drowned out my piano. He was breathless and unbearably devastated. His brother had betrayed him.

I played on.

And lived in his mind while my heart broke for him.

~~ ZEE ~~

With the usual screamers in my head, blessedly overshadowed by Euri's Mozart, I walked into Lily's, a favorite of mine and my brothers' where I'd decided to eat while I waited until time to go to Fawkes. I walked in behind a long-legged blonde, and couldn't help noticing she was built very nicely. My mind generally takes me to nudity and sex when presented with a hot girl, and tonight was no exception.

But my imagination turned her into Euri, and that made me laugh.

I watched her walk away, appreciating the sway of her hips in that way short dress.

Then I looked up, about to greet the hostess and give her an outrageous tip to get me ahead of all the people waiting for a table, and that's when I saw Phoenix. He was just getting up from a table where he'd eaten all alone.

Our eyes met across a sea of people, and I *knew*.

Fuck, for real, I *knew*, and every cell in my body went ape-shit. My head exploded, and the screaming went from a low hum to volume ten, drowning out Euri's piano.

Turning, I walked out and down the street, swallowing hard, clenching my hands into fists, fighting to get control. My coat flew out behind me in the strong Santa Ana winds. I heard him running after me, and when he caught up, I said, "Go with me to Fawkes."

"Zee, I—"

"Just go with me, Phoenix, and don't say anything."

Fawkes on Sunset was way too far to walk, but I wasn't ready to be there yet. I had to let this settle in my mind, had to make some sense of it. My brother had betrayed me. He'd done something that could never be undone, never be made right.

Ten minutes into our silent walk down Santa Monica, I came to a dead stop in front of Fred's Dry Cleaners, grabbed his arm and pulled him around to face me. "How did you know? I was so fucking careful, made damn sure I never let it show. How did you know she wasn't . . . that I was . . ."

"A message from Lucifer the day we were to be married."

He fucked her. My Anabo. All these years, over a century, I thought he didn't know she was intended for me, but he *did* know. He knew and he took her anyway. He took what wasn't his. "So you knew when you . . . when—"

"Yes, brother, I knew. And I did it anyway. I never had a clue that you knew she was for you. All this time, I—"

"You've lived with the guilt. You gave up everything as some sort of twisted atonement. Did you plan to ever tell me?"

Above the noise in my head, the endless screaming, and the swelling crescendo of Euri's piano, I could hear his convulsive swallowing. The most stoic of all my brothers, the one who'd gone without sex for over a century because of guilt over Jane's murder at Eryx's hand, looked on the verge of tears. Maybe if I hadn't been so blown away and gut-hurt, I'd have found that kind of touching. As it was, I couldn't get past the realization that he'd betrayed me in the worst possible way.

Each of us had one shot at Heaven, at peace, and that was to earn the love of a woman. Since ordinary women were way too scared to stick around long enough to fall in love, our only hope were the Anabo. None of us had ever found one, ever seen one, until I found Jane. But I didn't claim her. How could I? I hid that she was mine, that I'd been the one to catch her scent. And just as I'd planned, Phoenix found her and assumed she was his. None of my brothers knew Phoenix had been duped. Or so I thought. I knew now, Phoenix had known all along.

He swallowed again, his dark eyes filled with regret. "That night, after . . . I was eaten up with guilt. I realized what a horrible mistake I'd made, how badly I'd betrayed you, and her, and I left. I told her to pack, that I'd be back to get her, but I wasn't going back. I walked around London, wishing I had it to do over again, that I could change it. I tried to gather the courage to find you and tell you, but I couldn't do it. I figured one of you would go to her, eventually, and take her home and look after her. I thought you'd realize I'd gotten it wrong, that she was intended for you all along, and you'd be with her and she'd finally be happy. She was never happy with me, Zee. She tried, and I know she loved me, but it was never right and I didn't know why until that day. I was headed into a church to off myself, was actually on the steps of St. Paul's, when a group of guys jumped me, hauled me into an alley, and beat the shit out of me. They were Lucifer's. I was told I wouldn't be allowed to die until I made it right with you. And with her."

"And while you were getting your ass handed to you, she was with Eryx." Being murdered with no chance of resurrection, no hope of becoming Mephisto; Phoenix's or anyone else's.

He scrubbed his hands across his face and shoved his hair back, out of his eyes, which were suspiciously wet. "How did *you* know she was yours?"

"I'm reconnaissance, remember? I went to all the houses, checked out all the lost souls before the takedown at the Rothschild ball. I saw her and thought she was Georgiana, and was confused, because she had no shadow. She glowed. I got closer and she smelled like the ocean. There's no ocean in Yorkshire. And I knew."

"Why didn't you tell us? Why didn't you claim her?"

I turned and began walking again. "Because I was afraid I'd kill her."

He caught up to me. "What? *Kill* her? Why, Zee?"

"I knew what she would look like. I dream about her every damn night of my life and have for centuries. And I always kill her. When I saw the dancing instructor who was Skia, I followed him and he led me to Georgiana. Finally, my dream made sense. She was so beautiful, but she was lost, and I thought, this is my mind's fucked up way of telling me I can't have what I want. I found perfection, and I'd have to kill her. When I went back for reconnaissance, when I found Jane and realized they were twins, realized she *did* exist, just as she was in my head, I knew if I claimed her, if I talked to her, I'd be obsessed. I'd take her home and bind her to me, and then I'd kill her."

"In your dream, after you kill her, don't you bring her back?"

"She's already resurrected. She's mine. She's Mephisto. I carry her into a church and lay her on the altar and smother her with my hands. I'm on fire and in so much pain, but I can't die until she's gone."

"You couldn't kill her if she was resurrected. Why would you dream something that can't happen? Why are you afraid of committing a murder that would be impossible?"

I stopped walking again, this time in front of a sushi bar. "For a guy who reads a lot, you're way behind on metaphors. I don't think I'd kill her in a literal way. I'd kill her because of *what I am*. She'd have only me – you've said it yourself. Once they're immortal and Mephisto, they're stuck with us."

Leaning back against the building, next to a metal fish, I laid bare my soul. "I'm not right in the head, Phoenix. I've known since I was a kid, long before I made the jump. If you knew . . . there are things in my head no one could fathom, no one would believe. Some days, it's all I can do to get out of bed. Some days, the noise is so loud, so disturbing and horrible, even the music can't drown it out. I've tried every drug known to man and they do nothing. Heroin, weed, coke. I've popped a thousand pills. Nothing. Booze makes it worse. I can never get away from it. The only thing that makes life tolerable is music." Especially Euri's music, and most especially, Euri, but I didn't say that. I was nowhere close to ready to tell my brothers about Euri.

He was looking at me with pity, which I despised, but I owed him an explanation because as much as he'd betrayed me and made the worst possible decision, which ultimately led to Jane's death, I had begun it all by tricking him.

And so I continued. "It all got worse after Mana died, but it really cranked up when we left Kyanos. I realized other people don't hear someone screaming all day and all night. They don't hear snatches of conversations that aren't real, that are going on in someone else's head. They don't ever see the whole world in monochrome. Sometimes, everything is red, or purple, or black and white. And sometimes, especially late at night when I wake up and know I've been sleepwalking, I find blood on my hands. I don't know where it comes from." I'd die a thousand deaths before I ever admitted that I *did* know. It was a shameful, horrible thing. I was still reeling from all that Euri had told me. I couldn't stand to see the look on my brothers' faces if they knew what I'd done to my Anabo.

And that I'd agreed to be with her for all time.

I wondered all over again what the hell I was thinking. She'd made it seem possible, but now, in the cold light of rational thought, it seemed like the worst idea ever.

It didn't matter that I didn't confess whose blood was on my hands. Phoenix looked horrified enough.

"I'm fucking crazy. What woman could live with this and not die a little more every day? Think about Jane. She was fine and kind and capable of deep, profound love. Now imagine she loved me. She wakes up in the middle of the night and what am I doing? I walk through some days without complete awareness. So she talks to me, kisses me, makes love to me, and I'm not even there. Her soul would shrivel and die."

I convinced myself while I spoke that I really had lost all mental capability when I agreed to bring Euri to Colorado, to be with me. She was already crazy. What could living with me do to her?

I pushed away from the wall and continued down the street. "I will never have a mate." I faced that depressing truth once again, and my bubble of hope dissolved like the fizz in the last glass of cheap champagne. "I've known it my whole life. When I found Jane, I thought about ways I could make sure she wasn't at the ball, to keep her from any of you, but as much as it would have been best for her, and for my brothers, I couldn't let her go. If I couldn't have her for my own, I could at least have her in my life. I could see her every day. I could love her as my family. It seemed like such a good idea. And in the end, I'm as responsible for her death as you are. The irony isn't lost on me."

Walking along Santa Monica with Phoenix, the grim reality of what I was came crashing down and I fought the depths of despair that threatened to suck me under.

We walked in silence for a long time, and after an ambulance screamed past, Phoenix said, "She smelled like heather. How did she have a scent if she wasn't for me?"

"The night of the ball, before we all left for London, I took a bunch of heather and mixed it in with the fresh flowers that were scattered around the matrons' room. I knew she'd be in there, because she couldn't walk, because her family tried to hide her away and shuffle her off where they wouldn't have to see her. I felt so bad for her. And I knew you would be the one to take all the old ladies outside before we set the fire. I knew you'd find her, and smell the heather. She loved it as much as you do, and she pinned sprigs of it to her hat. You never questioned that she was yours. Until tonight, when I walked into Lily's, I didn't know you were ever aware that she wasn't."

"And you knew tonight because—"

"You planned to tell me. I don't know how or why I know some things and not others. It just pops into my head and I know. I walked into Lily's and saw you and I knew."

"I don't know how I can ever express how sorry I am, Zee."

"You've spent over one hundred twenty five years being sorry. For fuck's sake, don't spend any more time wallowing around in this, Phoenix. What good does it do? She'll always be dead and I'll always be crazy. What happened is as much my fault as yours. If I'd stepped up and said, here she is and I can't claim her, if I'd been honest, maybe things would have been different."

"But I knew and I still—"

"You're a selfish bastard, I won't argue that, but it's not like any of us were born to be choirboys. If any of the others had been sucked in as you were, if I'd tricked any of them like I did you, I have no doubt they'd have done the same thing. I know for sure Denys would have. He was crazy for her, did you know?"

His eyes widened. "I had no idea."

"I think because I never claimed her, she was sort of a free agent. That's the only way I can explain how he was attracted to her in the first place. He became obsessed. He went to see her behind your back. Did you know?"

"No."

As we walked, I knew he was turning all of this over in his head, realizing the significance of things he'd passed over as unimportant. He was waking up after being asleep for over a century, discovering he'd been the absent brother all these years. Oh, he was there physically. He planned all of our takedowns. He stayed behind when we went out looking for girls, wrapped up in guilt and grief and his endless martyrdom. I could feel the realizations as they hit him, one after the other. He wasn't simply sorry for what he'd done. For the first time since Jane died, he wasn't looking at how it affected him. It was as if he unfolded from a fetal position, stood up, looked around and saw the rest of the world once again.

Phoenix would no longer be an island. "You're having an epiphany, aren't you?"

"Yeah, you could say that. And I always thought I was so smart. Turns out, I'm the village idiot."

I smiled at him. "Welcome back." I grasped his shoulder and squeezed.

My brother stopped me and hugged me and he cried. Just a little, but enough that he was embarrassed.

I stepped back and said, "I love you, Phoenix, just like I love all my brothers. It's not in the cards for me to be with someone, but you can. You have Mariah. Don't screw this up. She has problems, but so do you. And you're both fixers who want to pick up what's broken and make it work again, make something ugly into something beautiful. You're perfect together because you have all the years ahead to fix each other."

He looked like he'd lost his last friend. "I'm releasing my claim to Mariah."

The fuck? "For a brilliant mind, you can be so fucking stupid. What, you think she's like a dog or a cat you can hand over to someone else? Mariah's a fully functioning intelligent human being with her own ideas about who she'll be with."

"I understand it looks impossible, but time changes things, Zee. If she could be claimed by you or Ty or Denys, who's to say it wouldn't work out?"

"Do you think giving her up absolves you of what you did with Jane? Because it doesn't."

"What will?"

"You're gonna have to figure that out for yourself. Don't you think there'll come a time when you regret disclaiming her?" Would there be a time when I regretted not accepting Euri? *Shit, yes*. I'd only made the decision ten minutes ago and I was already regretting it. How could I let her go? *Where* would she go?

It occurred to me that M had made her immortal because he knew I'd be faced with this dilemma. Well, he'd have to accept that it wasn't going to work out. As would she. At some point, she would tire of the world and ask God to take her to Heaven. She would be with Sophie. And that was where she belonged, where her myopic vision of the world and its inhabitants would not be a product of her mind, but reality. Souls in Heaven would be just as she saw them. She'd no longer be mad – her reality would be real. I had to let her go. She'd be away from me and my polluted life. She'd be glad.

I heard her falter on the piano.

Euri never faltered.

She knew my thoughts. I had hurt her.

The screams were intolerable. Like people dying. Tortured. In horrendous pain.

I did my best to ignore it and pay attention to my brother. For all that he'd fucked me over in the worst way a guy could fuck over another guy, especially his own brother, I couldn't stay angry with him, or even hurt. He'd suffered for more than a hundred years over Jane, and it was time to lay her to rest, once and for all.

"It's not like I want to." He looked away from me and watched the cars zip past. "I'm convinced she'll be happier with somebody else."

"You're convinced you don't have what it takes to step up. You judge Denys because he can't let go of the booze, but you're no different. Instead of alcohol, you're addicted to strangling yourself, living like a damned monk. You think if you let go of that, you'll hate yourself even more than you do now."

"You don't know me, Zee. Nobody does."

"You may be more screwed up in the head than I am." I took off walking again and when I was a block ahead, Phoenix transported to catch up and walked beside me in silence. "No arguing?"

"No."

"How do you propose for this to work? None of us are attracted to her. We can't be. You claimed her the night you shouted at her and called her a whore."

"Yeah, that was romantic. I'm a real catch, aren't I?"

"The thought of her with anybody else made you lose your shit. Why do you imagine for even a second that you can step aside and let her be with one of us instead of you?" Why did I think I could say goodbye to Euri? I really was completely batshit.

"It's not about me. It's her, and what she needs. I'm not it. I know I can never make her happy. As soon as I tell her everything, about you and Jane – all of it – Lucifer will release my claim and make it so she could be with any one of us."

Shaking my head, I said, "That's maybe the worst idea I've ever heard. It's also completely pointless. Do you *seriously* think she'd fall for me, or Ty, or Denys when she's already falling for you?"

"She's not falling for me. I'm just the one closest to her right now, somebody she feels comfortable talking to."

I cut the air with my hand. "All right, then. You tell her all about Jane, and me, and what you did. Tell her you've asked Lucifer to take away your claim so we can all have a shot. When it blows up in your face, I'll be a total asswipe and say I told you so."

"It'll be hard. It'll be damn near impossible, but for her sake—"

"*What* is *wrong* with you?" I stopped dead and he had to back up. "If you're so convinced you can't be the guy she needs, then fucking *change. Be* that guy, Phoenix. If you throw away the miracle that is Mariah without even trying, than yeah, you're right – you *are* a worthless piece of shit." I'd have given anything for even the *dream* of the ability to change, to make myself into a guy who deserved Euri. To lose the crazy. But God in his infinite wisdom made me this way. There was no changing for me. Phoenix could give it his best shot, and he might make it, but he apparently didn't have the stones even to try.

He said nothing. Just stared at me.

"You have no idea who you are, do you?"

"No, Dr. Phil, but I'm sure you'll tell me soon enough."

That pissed me off. "Fuck you, man. I'm going to Fawkes. Like now. If you want to go with me and be stupid some more, I'll be at the back entrance." I disappeared.

I didn't expect him to follow, but he did.

Seconds later, he stood next to me at the alley entrance of Fawkes. A guy was banging some chick against the back of the building, and I could see it bothered my brother. I ignored them and knocked, the door opened, and a blond guy almost as big as us smiled at me. "Zeenose, my man, glad you could make it. We got a surprise for you."

"Hey, Kel." I met his fist bump. "I hate surprises."

While Kel laughed, we stepped inside and the door closed behind us.

"This is my brother, Phoenix."

They shook hands, then Kel turned and led us through the trunks, cases and miles of cord crowding the narrow space backstage. "John got himself a new bird. She's British, and so hot, but man, wait 'til you hear her voice, and she's righteous on keyboard. Funny story. She's a concert pianist and has been since she was like ten. Kind of a prodigy. Anyway, she bugged out from a performance in New York and went to see Arcadia at Blackbriar. John asked her to play for him, and the audience went nuts, so he talked her into joining the band."

Shit, shit, *shit.* I'd been so caught up in what just went down with Phoenix, I hadn't been thinking, hadn't realized he was about to see Euri. He would know. He would see she was Anabo.

Fuck.

I'd have to act like I'd never seen her before. I'd have to give no clue that I'd caught her scent. Dammit, why hadn't I remembered? I'd been upset. And all through it, I'd heard her piano. Oh, for fuck's sake.

Hoping to appear as clueless about her as possible, I asked Kel, "She abandoned her career to play in a band?"

Kel shot me a look. "She's kind of different, if you know what I mean."

She was way more than different. She was meant to be mine. She had a mind like mine. She could hear me from two thousand miles away. We were now stopped at the door that led to the green room. "No, I don't know what you mean. Different like mentally challenged?"

Kel glanced at Phoenix, then dropped his voice and said to me, "Like skating close to batshit."

"Most musicians are batshit."

"True, but she's just . . . different. You'll see. Come on and see John and meet her." He opened the door and walked into a narrow hallway.

We followed and Phoenix whispered, "Should I go out front?"

Ordinarily, I'd have said it didn't matter, he could go wherever he liked, but the instant we walked into that hallway, I felt the whisper of something I'd never known before. It came at me so fast, I blinked as if against the wind. My heart beat faster, harder, and my muscles bunched into tight knots. "No, stay with me."

Kel stopped at a door, knocked twice, then opened it and waved us inside. This was the practice studio, which also served as a green room, a place to hang out before the club's evening line-up began. Arcadia was headlining, but a front band would play a few sets first, and that meant a lot of people in the room.

I was aware of only one.

She sat at an upright piano and continued the Mozart piece, her back to us, her unbound hair long and golden blond with a slight curl.

I spoke to John, but I have no idea what we talked about. Whatever I said, it was rote. John had been a doctoral candidate at MIT whose garage band went viral, and now here he was, touring the country instead of becoming a professor. It was just as well. Eventually, he was bound to get nailed for hacking, and some guy in a suit would send him to prison.

She was reaching the crescendo. Goddamn she was fucking glorious on the piano. My heart stuttered a little, and to my incredulous horror, tears popped into my eyes. Good Christ, I was turning into a crybaby nancy boy. I fake yawned and rubbed my eyes, hoping with every drop of testosterone in me that no one noticed I was overcome by an emotion that laid me low.

"I want you to meet Euri," John said, nodding toward her. "She's amazing, and dude, she writes code like a poet."

I knew that. I'd seen her website, a fantastical explosion of color and beautiful poetry, stunning photographs and subtle announcements of upcoming tour dates. She'd built it herself. I'd been in her head when she hacked into the 66X boards, searching for Eryx. She had a natural affinity for coding, and hacking, and writing music. In keeping with my attempt to throw Phoenix off, to make sure he didn't know I already knew about Euri, I asked, "Her name is Yuri? That's like a Russian guy name."

"Her parents had the bad judgment to name her Euripides, and she goes by Euri."

The piece she played ended on a somber note, and she stayed where she was until it faded. A few of the guys clapped, and one of them said, "Holy shit, that was gorgeous."

Turning on the piano bench, she stood and walked toward us.

I could barely breathe.

Dressed in a very short pink dress with no sleeves and a pair of towering black heels, she was graceful, refined and elegant. Her legs went right up to her neck. Her eyes were cornflower blue in a perfect, beautiful face. She looked like she'd stepped out of Buckingham Palace. Like she was classic royalty.

Except she had a tattoo of a question mark on her right forearm, a tiny diamond stud that winked at me from the right side of her nose, and streaks of pink in the long, blond hair framing her face.

She reached us and John made introductions, but she never spared even a glance for Phoenix, or John. She was completely focused on me, and as usual, a quick study. She played along. "Have we met?" she asked in her soft, cultured voice.

Aware of my brother's shock and dismay, because she really was a mirror image of Jane, I lied. "No."

"You're very familiar. Why are you wearing a diamond in one ear? Did you lose the other one? Or is this from your girlfriend, like in *The Breakfast Club*, and she's wearing the other one right now and thinking of you?"

Clever minx. It killed me not to smile, or laugh. "I don't have a girlfriend." I didn't want a girlfriend. I wanted her. I wanted her with me, always, asleep and awake. She would not be a girlfriend. She'd be my whole life. My world.

"That's unfortunate for every other girl in the world, but extremely marvelous for me." She stepped closer and despite her height, even in the shoes, she still had to look up at me. "You smell like hot cross buns, delicious and yeasty. How peculiar."

Of course I did. And now that she'd pointed out my scent, there could be no doubt in Phoenix's mind that she was for me.

Fuck. I was doomed. They'd never let me walk away from her. They'd insist that I try. And I'd fail, and hurt her in the process.

But to be fair, I hadn't known how very much I would want her. I didn't remember wanting Jane like this. If I had, I could never have kept myself from claiming her. I could never have stood by and watched Phoenix court her. When he took her to bed, I would have killed him. Dragged him inside a church and burned myself alive to make sure he died.

But I had let Jane go. I'd wanted her, but nothing like this.

Euri smelled like the ocean, fresh and clean and bracing. I would take her, right now, and we'd leave and go to Kyanos. I'd let her listen to the sea, to the waves crashing against the cliffs, and maybe she'd hear the voice. We'd stay there forever, just me and this girl I'd dreamed of all of my life, over a thousand years, this girl who'd been in my head for months and months. I'd make love to her every day and night. I would love her more than anyone or anything. I would fight the insanity and I'd win. Sweet Jesus, I wanted it to be so. I wanted it so much, wanted *her* so much. It became increasingly difficult not to snatch her against me and disappear from this room, from L.A., from humanity.

Something in her expression told me that she was well aware of my thoughts. That tiny smile played around the edge of her perfect lips, as if we shared a private joke. "Why is your name a letter?"

"It's short for Xenos."

"Which is Greek for crazy and mixed up. Are you crazy?"

Her eyes were laughing now. We were definitely sharing

a private joke. I said seriously, "Chances are excellent. Most crazies don't realize their shortcomings."

"I've been told I'm one note short of a symphony. I have dreams, sometimes when I'm not sleeping. Music fixes it."

Not once in my life had I ever considered that when I finally found my Anabo, she would be crazy like me. Either God was a grand jokester, or he really did work in mysterious ways. I didn't know if the two of us would be happy together, or more miserable. What I did know was that I couldn't fight this any longer. I'd take her and make her mine.

"Do you play?" she asked with a twinkle.

"Yes."

"What do you play?"

"Everything."

"No one can play everything. I think you'll need to demonstrate." She knew my thoughts. She knew of my music room in the Mephisto mansion, and that I would want to take her there and prove I could play every instrument ever invented. It'd take a while. I'd make love to her on the piano. I'd take her while we listened to Hendrix loud enough to blow her clothes off. We'd hole up in there and not come out for a week.

But not yet. And dammit, I couldn't think about that right now. I'd get a hard-on for sure and that would be humiliating. And so obvious.

I cursed my dick and wished I didn't have to leave immediately, but it was too late. I'd let my imagination run away with me, remembered how she looked in those black silk panties, fantasized about her dressed in only the wannabe underwear on top of the baby grand in the music room. Her long honey-gold hair would tease her naked breasts, sweep across the gleaming black lacquer, twine around my hand when I kissed her.

Clearing my throat, I stepped back and said, "I think I need to leave." I turned and walked out, forcing myself to think about anything that wasn't remotely related to sex.

So, of course, the fucking couple in the alley were now making out, about to go at it again. The guy was one horny bastard. And that chick's ass had to be killing her the way he was rubbing her against the bricks. What a wanker.

"Unfuckingbelievable," I said as soon as Phoenix came outside to stand next to me.

"I assume you're talking about Euri and not that girl's ass, which has gotta be rubbed raw from those bricks."

In my desperation, I invented a problem, something for Phoenix to focus on besides Euri. Besides that she was meant for me.

For me. It was a travesty, and I wanted to dance a jig and laugh my head off and shout to the whole wide world that she was mine, *all mine.*

I didn't dance or laugh. I went for my most serious expression and introspective voice. "We need to call a war room meeting with our father. We need to find out what he's up to. In nine hundred years, we found only one Anabo. Now, in less than two years, we've found four. And how coincidental is it that tonight, of all nights, we meet Euri? He's jacking with us, Phoenix. And I have to wonder if Lucifer is aware, because if he isn't, if M is interfering, this could end badly."

"How could M have anything to do with it? Anabo come from God. Last time I checked, M and God aren't golf buddies."

"I don't know. That's the point. I think we should ask him and make him tell us what's going on."

He wasn't buying any of it. He lifted a brow and said, "Or, we could not look a gift horse in the mouth."

"What are the odds she'd walk into my life tonight? What are the chances she'd be crazy like me?" I looked at him. "What the fuck?"

"I don't know, brother. Let's go inside, I'll have a whiskey, we'll see her with the band, and we'll talk about it."

"What's to talk about? I'm just as wack as I was when I found Jane. Nothing's changed."

"It appears she may be as wack as you are. Maybe she's what you need, Zee. If anyone could understand you, maybe it's her. You'll never know if you don't try. Come on, have some faith. Let's go see her sing, and you can think about your next move."

Shaking myself out of my self-centered thoughts, I stepped up and did what I had to do to make sure Phoenix sealed the deal with Mariah. I'd had my doubts in the beginning, but he'd proven beyond any doubt that he was gone for her. He'd love her and make it work. He just needed a push. Looking him right in the eye, I said evenly, "The last thing I need is a head case like me. Not interested. The more I think about it, the more I think maybe Mariah and I would be good together. Coming from her background, she may be the only Anabo I'll ever find who could survive me. So you do what you have to do to release your claim, and count me in. I'll win. She already likes me." That should do it. Just the thought of me touching his Anabo was bound to make him nuts, would ensure he'd take her to bed tonight and mark her as his forever and ever, amen.

I glanced at the couple, who were about to go at it again, and said in a loud voice, "For fuck's sake, man, get a damned hotel room."

Then I disappeared, and left Phoenix staring at the guy, who would of course think he was the one who told him to get a room. Good. My brother needed a fight to get his blood up. Then he'd go home and make love to Mariah and all would be right in his world. And hers. I was very fond of Mariah, felt as if she were my sister already. She'd had a shit-show of a life and deserved peace of mind and joy. Incredibly, I thought Phoenix would be all that to her. They were destined to be stupidly happy for all eternity.

As for me, I went home, to the kitchen, and asked Hans for something to eat. I had missed dinner. I was starving.

I went to the TV room and watched *Die Hard* while I ate the giant sandwich he made for me and drank a ginormous glass of milk. Always liked Bruce Willis.

The screamers had quieted down significantly. I watched the movie and waited until I heard Euri begin to play the first Arcadia set. While I slowly ate the orange sections Hans had added to my plate, I closed my eyes and was with her onstage, could see her slender fingers fly across the keys, heard her compelling voice when she sang backup to John, saw John look at her with such longing, it made me break out in a sweat.

The demon that was my insatiable need for her wouldn't stop tormenting me. I swallowed the last of the orange and popped upstairs to brush my teeth. I would kiss her tonight. I had to kiss her tonight. I stared in the mirror after I was done drying my face and silently told myself to be easy, go slowly, be gentle, not get carried away. A kiss. Just one kiss and nothing more.

The road to Hell was laid with more pavestones of my good intentions.

I popped back to Fawkes, to the front of the club, where Kel and another bouncer were hanging out, watching for underage kids and suspicious types and über drunk people who needed to be cut off. I looked toward the stage and heard the crowd chanting her name. *Eur-ee! Eur-ee!* She played and sang and took her cues from John, and sometimes she smiled at the teeming sea of people in the club, which sent them into louder screams. She was a sensation, mostly because of her enormous talent and ability, but also because she was beautiful and mysterious. I recalled the *Rolling Stone* article about John and Arcadia. The writer had devoted two paragraphs just to Euri, touching on her career as a concert pianist, her aristocratic status in England, that she was a personal friend of the royals, that her father was a noted Greek scholar at Oxford, as well as a prominent member of Parliament. He gave no really personal information about her, and that inevitably led to conjecture and increased interest.

I doubted she had any idea she was becoming a celebrity, already all over the Internet and destined to be on a few magazine covers. I decided she would hate that and made a note to myself to talk to her about it. Give her some ways to avoid it.

I also wondered if she was aware of John's feelings. He was obviously in love with her, but Euri tended to see what she wanted to see and discount the rest. Miles had got it right – she saw everyone through some magical portal that made them into who she wanted them to be. Including me.

I drifted closer to the stage, jostled by the crowd, not caring, my focus entirely on her. The music was exceptionally awesome tonight, and some part of me that was still rational tucked that away to think about later.

They played without a break for over two hours, then the lights went out and they left the stage. They'd come back for an encore, but no way I could wait that long. I popped to the back hallway and stood in an alcove where the club stored extra chairs. She knew. She came there directly and when she stood in front of me and laid her soft hand in mine, the screaming stopped.

I could hear her breath, short and fast. Her perfect breasts with just a shadow of cleavage rose and fell rapidly. Her eyes were clear and lucid and stared into mine with grave intensity.

"Go tell John you're sick and I'm taking you home with me to take care of you."

She turned and walked away, back to the green room. Moments later, she reappeared in the hallway, a leather backpack slung over one shoulder. When she was near, I took her hand again.

"Euri?"

She looked over her shoulder at John, whose heart was in his eyes. "I have to go now."

"Don't. Let me take care of you. He's not what you need, Euri."

Her warm fingers tightened around mine. "I have to go."

I walked her toward the rear exit, and as soon as we were where no one could see us, I transported to Colorado, to the sanctuary of my room. I didn't think about it, didn't ask, didn't say a word. As soon as we arrived, I shoved the backpack off of her shoulder, pulled her into my arms and kissed her.

CHAPTER 8

~~ EURI ~~

I knew kissing him would be different than Miles, but I never expected it to be this different. It wasn't gentle and easy. He wasn't uncertain or shy. I was hot from the inside out, surrounded by the scent of aftershave and hot cross buns, drowning in sensation, in the feel of his large, hard body enveloping mine with solid heat, in the taste of him, in his touch, his strong, quick fingers caressing my back, bared because he'd lowered the zipper. I was destined to be naked very soon.

I'd never wanted anything as much as I wanted Zee. I'd never felt desire as I did now. All conscious thought was shoved aside and I ran on pure instinct.

When I moved my arms, the dress slid from me in a soft whoosh of silk. He lifted his mouth from mine. "All I intended was a kiss."

That was my cue to step away, put my dress back on and tell him to take me to the hotel in L.A. But I didn't do that. Why would I? I'd wanted this to happen for months and months.

I reached between us and felt him through his jeans. I knew just what he looked like, but I was anxious to see him in the flesh, long and hard and hot. I wanted to feel of him, taste him, take all of him inside of me. "This is for me," I murmured against his throat, "and I want it."

Surprising me, he released me, stepped back and the candles on the mantel lit, allowing me to see his handsome face, his serious expression. "Don't jack with me, Euri. Don't ever fucking jack with me."

I lifted a brow and threw it back at him. “Don’t accuse me of being a bloody tease.”

I heard him swallow. He was more nervous than he was letting on.

He didn’t want to. He was trying to start a row so he’d have an excuse not to. That hurt. That bloody *killed* me. Here I was, practically naked with a hot son of Hell who’d shagged thousands of girls, and it appeared I would have to be the instigator. *This* after practically begging for months and months.

It’s rare that I am angry, but the entire situation infuriated me. “Miles was shy and tentative and apologetic, as if he was *sorry* about it all, and I was endlessly frustrated, always wanting more.” I looked at the very significant bulge in his jeans before I said, “We will be together for the rest of time. We’ll have sex thousands, maybe millions of times, and it is *not* going to be me always begging for it.”

He was so still. His face gave no clue to his feelings. I waited and suppressed the impulse to jump on him. I wanted him so much. My body hummed and needed and he was just standing there staring at me. I’d give him five more seconds, and then I would put my dress back on and demand he return me to L.A. I’d tell him to sod off.

One, heartbeat, *two,* heartbeat, *three,* heartbeat, *four,* heartbeat, *five.*

Bugger.

I bent to pick up my dress. I stepped into it and pulled it up and slid my arms through and reached around to zip it.

“What are you doing?”

“I’m going to get laid.” I have no idea where that came from, but once it was out there, I had to back it up. “John won’t be bloody afraid of me. He doesn’t know what I am. He only knows *who* I am. He’ll take my clothes off and fuck me until I can’t breathe, I know he will.” I moved close to him and glared. “He won’t treat me like I’m some sodding holy vagina of Anabo purity.”

His eyes narrowed. He looked dangerous. “Is that what you think this is about?”

“The only other alternative is that you don’t want to because you don’t find me attractive, and if that’s how it is, we're all done forever and I want to leave. Now."

"Do you *seriously* believe I don't want to?" He was clearly incredulous.

"Yes, Xenos, this is *seriously* what I believe. Because I am standing here waiting and you're standing there doing nothing. This is my best clue that you don't want to."

"Shit." He turned away from me. Actually turned his back on me.

My fury ramped up to rage. I will never know what possessed me, and I'm certain every single one of my aristocratic ancestors fairly spun in their graves when I unzipped the dress, let it fall, then jumped on his back. I threw my legs around him, stabbed him in the gut with my heels, and wrapped my arms around his neck and choked him. I was only slightly surprised at my strength, mostly because I was so hurt and angry. "How *dare* you turn your back on me? You arrogant *son of a bitch.*"

He grasped my arms and forced me to loosen my chokehold, and then he said, "You're going to feel really foolish in about one minute."

I dug one of my heels into his belly. "You're going to be eviscerated in thirty seconds."

"Are you crying, Euri?"

"What if I am?"

"Are you so mad, you're crying?" He slid his hands beneath my knees and held me against him.

"Yes." I sniffed, trying to stop. "No. I'm crying because I'm a silly git. I want you so much, have imagined what it would be like at least a million times, dreamed about it, over and over. And now you turn your back on me? You're cruel and heartless and I think I hate you."

He turned his head so we were nose to nose. "If I lay you down and take you, there's no going back because you'll be marked. Once that happens, you can't return to the real world. You can never be entirely safe anywhere on the planet except here, and Kyanos. These are the only places Eryx can't find, can't get to. You're always in danger of him capturing you, taking you where he lives, where he has everything on lockdown so you can't transport, can't escape. If you're marked, you're here forever. You'll be all done with John and Arcadia and the real world."

I deflated, and I suppose I did feel a bit foolish. Overreaction much? "Oh." I dropped my chin to his shoulder. "How does sex mark me?"

"My semen will burn a mark on your womb. The mark is how we can find you anywhere in the world. Once you're marked, you can find any of us."

Bollocks. I cried again, harder this time. I moved my hands to his shoulders and pushed until he let go of my legs and I slid down his back.

Turning, he drew me close and held me and shushed my crying. "It'll happen, Euri. You can't possibly know how much I want you, but I can wait until it's the right time, until you're rea—"

"I don't have a womb." I buried my face in his shoulder and sobbed. It's not my nature to feel sorry for myself, but at that moment, I was swamped with self-pity.

He continued holding me, stroking my hair. "I don't understand. How can you not have a womb?"

I never ever allowed myself to think about it, but the mention sent memories skittering across my mind in swift flashes, like a misbehaving child hurrying to do something forbidden as fast as possible before she's stopped. Needles and screams and Mum and the doctor with his cold instruments and a nurse with the face of an angel and evil in her hands. Restraints and fading in and out of consciousness. My father's fury. Mother's banishment. Sophie knowing, because she was with me in spirit. Sophie crying.

I sucked in a breath and forced the memories to stop by mentally playing a Chopin polonaise. "My mother took me to Sweden when I was fourteen and had a back-alley doctor remove my uterus. She thought it best that I never have children, because I'm mentally unstable."

He pulled me close against him, so tight I could scarcely breathe, and didn't say anything at all. Just held me while I cried, and eventually we wound up in one of the chairs in front of the fireplace, me on his lap and his arms around me.

We stayed like that for a very long time. At some point, he mentally switched on the sound system and we were surrounded by Beethoven, courtesy of the London

Philharmonic. And me.

He nuzzled my neck beneath my hair. "I'll talk to M. There's a solution. We'll figure it out."

I shifted in his lap. "I'm sorry."

"Christ, Euri, this isn't something to apolo—"

"I'm apologizing for jumping you."

He kissed my neck. "Don't. You had every right and reason. I should be the one apologizing."

"But you won't?"

"No, because I'm not sorry. You're all I've ever wanted. Ever. If you don't know that by now, you're just being a girl."

"Then you're just being a guy."

"It works out nice, yeah?" He kissed me, soft and easy, his lips warm and lovely against my mouth. His big hands moved across my bared skin and I decided he was entirely too dressed, especially considering I wore only the pretend-to-be knickers and my bra.

He smelled so wonderful and was hot to the touch of my palms and fingertips. I pulled away from his kiss and moved in his lap, until I was straddling him in the chair. After I kicked off my shoes, I began to unbutton his blue pinstriped oxford, revealing his wide, solid chest as I went. He seemed bemused by my fascination with his body.

"You've seen this all before," he murmured.

"I've never touched you, or seen you naked in person." Awash in desire, I swallowed and my smile faded. I was in awe. He was magnificent. When I had him unbuttoned, I climbed from his lap, tugged his boots off, then pulled him to a stand and pushed the shirt from his shoulders. As I reached for his jeans and unbuttoned and unzipped him, I glanced up and noticed he looked extremely anxious. "Are you shy, Xenos?"

"No, I'm just not used to being the passive one. I'm always the one driving things forward."

"So girls don't typically take your pants off?"

"They don't usually have an opportunity. I'm way too fast for any interference."

"But you're letting me?"

"I'm ill-prepared for you, Euri. If I'd known we were going to have sex for the very first time, I'd have done a lot more. I'd have champagne and roses and chocolates and an entire playlist of songs that would have deep and special meaning as the years go by. I'd have clean sheets and nice smelly stuff in the shower. I'd be way more romantic. I'd—"

"Probably get so worked up, you'd come way too soon. Isn't it marvelous how things work out so well if you just let them?" I moved closer and slipped my hand inside of his boxers. *"Oh, my."* I began to smile again. He was so very hard and ready, and I would never see his excitement for me as anything other than the most righteous and beautiful compliment. Sure he'd shagged lots of other girls, but this was for me. This was mine and I would be ever vigilant in adoring him for it.

He sucked in a fast breath. "You know your way around, don't you?"

I stroked him softly, peeling away his jeans with my free hand, letting them fall to his ankles so that all he wore was a pair of white boxers. "I've seen you do it enough times, I know just where to go, just the way you like it."

He gave me a look. "And all this time, I thought you weren't watching."

"As if." I grasped his boxers and eased them from his hips, until they fell with the puddle of jeans. He stepped out and I led him to the bed, where he sat at the edge and I stood between his knees and admired his well-formed chest and arms. He was so beautiful. I looked my fill and he sat still and let me. I focused on the unusual, artistic *M* on his right bicep.

"It's a birthmark," he whispered. "We all have one."

"Like my *A*."

He nodded. "My turn." He set his warm hands at my waist and looked at my knickers. "You wore the black silk ones."

"Because I knew we'd be together tonight."

"How did you know? We agreed to wait until you're here for good."

"I have a sixth sense, remember?"

"Can you tell the future?"

"I know what's in your mind, Zee, even what you might not be conscious of. You intended this to happen since we were standing at the bus terminal when John tried to kiss me. You want to make it permanent, make sure I don't look away, feel confident in my total devotion to you."

"Yet you were so sure I didn't want you after all?"

"I was confused. And hurt. People do stupid bad things when they're hurt."

Looking up at me, he said soberly, "There is nothing on the face of the Earth as beautiful as you. And because of who you are, what you mean to me, I am completely out of my depth and don't know what to do."

"In almost ten centuries, you've been with thousands of women, Zee. This is a major part of you, what you love as much as music. I'm no different." I stroked his head, running my fingers through his short, dark hair.

"That's it, you see. You *are* different."

"Why? Because you remember my name?"

I was trying to be funny, but he looked up at me with those great dark eyes and said with a rough voice, "Because I want to love you. I don't know how to do that. I don't know anything about girls except sex, and I want this to be so much more than that."

"For now, let's just let it be about sex. The rest will come later."

"Will it?"

He was so terribly insecure, so fretful and afraid. I felt like a heinous bitch for yelling at him, for jumping him. All along, he was trying to protect me, thinking I'd be marked, and left with no choice but to stay here. Granted, he could have said so, instead of saying absolutely nothing and letting me draw my own conclusions. We'd have to work on communicating when we were together. Clearly the mind reading thing didn't work one-on-one. I moved closer and cradled his head against my breasts. "Let's just go slow and take our time and not overthink it."

He chuckled low in his throat and it came out almost as a growl. He was capable of very bad things, but I wasn't afraid. On the contrary, I was intrigued by what he might do to me. Goosebumps spread across my body when he said, "I'm way beyond taking it slow, Euripides." He slid his hands down my waist to my hips and untied both sides of the knickers at the same time, then whisked the silk from my body, tossed it aside, and drew me down. I bent my legs and placed a knee on either side of his thighs, and the long length of him slid inside of me with minimal effort, my body welcoming his as if it had been waiting. I breathed out a glad sigh and wrapped my arms around him and we kissed.

It was glorious. I reveled in the scent of hot cross buns and his cologne and the musky smell of him and me joined together.

I'm not sure how he accomplished it without me realizing, but suddenly, my bra was sliding down my arms and off and sailing across the room to land on his desk. I looked at him with wide eyes and he lifted his brows in a comical expression of innocence. Then he lowered his gaze to my breasts and any pretense of innocence fled. "Perfect."

"You're slightly prejudiced."

"No, I'm completely objective. I'm a breast man, you know."

I smoothed his hair and whispered, "Liar. It's a lady's bum that does things to you."

With a devilish smile, he moved his hands from massaging my breasts around to my backside, which he pretended to seriously inspect. I thought maybe he'd tease me a bit, but he swiftly lost his smile, his expression became deadly serious and in a blink, he had me on my back in the center of the bed while he loomed large above me, sliding his body into mine. "You want this, don't you?"

Was he funning me? "More than I want anything else."

"Are you sure?"

I didn't understand. How could he doubt it? He was pounding into me so hard, my body moved across the bed and he had to pull me back. My heart beat wildly and my breaths came faster, making it difficult to speak. "I'm . . . sure."

He covered me and kissed me, his hand in my hair while his tongue tangled with mine and his cock moved against my sex with astonishing precision, building my desire in a relentless rhythm of I'll-make-you-orgasm-so-hard. I was tremendously hot, from the inside, out. "Zee, I'm so . . ." I became frantic and frenzied, reaching for a climax that eluded me.

"Not yet," he said against my ear. "Last with me. Stay with me."

His kisses were lusciously passionate and all-consuming. Breathtaking. "So . . . hot. Zee, I'm so hot." I could scarcely catch my breath.

"It's Mephisto," he murmured. "You're already turning." He kissed me again and again. He whispered extremely nasty things into my ear, things I'd blush to hear if I were fully dressed. Naked, sweaty and a hair's breadth from a shattering orgasm, his guttural words were my undoing. The last of my control left me and I felt like I was flying.

I'd never had an orgasm with anyone. I thought it'd be pretty much the same as it was when I was alone. I was a million kinds of wrong. I felt like I was flying apart and at the same time, I couldn't cling to him tightly enough. I panted and cried out and my whole body shook and writhed beneath him. It was indescribable.

When I began to calm, I looked up and saw his expression was one of ultimate male satisfaction, which I attributed to his own climax, but then he closed his eyes and went completely still and I felt him move inside of me. When he opened his eyes, the expression on his handsome face was pure lusty gratification. He whispered, "I've never had sex like this."

I slipped my arms around his neck and he embraced me and we stayed like that for a long time, him still inside of me, our bodies perfectly aligned, skin to skin. I remembered feeling close to Miles after sex, but this was so much more, such a feeling of absolute affinity.

"No burn?" he whispered into my hair. He'd been as hopeful as I that it might still work.

"No burn. You said I can't be Mephisto, but you said this heat from the inside is because I'm becoming Mephisto. So which is it?"

"You can't be marked, but you can definitely be Mephisto. You will be." He raised up and propped his head in his hand to look down into my face. "Because you're immortal, Mephisto is permanent, and you'll develop all the characteristics, like the ability to transport, and superhuman hearing and the ability to see in the dark. Probably the most significant change will be in your attitude toward the lost souls. You won't feel sorry for them like you did before."

"I was pretty close to going there already, because of what I saw through you."

"It'll be more pronounced. And you'll be able to see the shadow across their eyes. It's how we know they've lost their soul." He reached over and gently smoothed my hair away from my face, tracing the edge of my jaw, then down to my throat. "You'll be enormously hungry. Being Mephisto requires colossal energy, and the only way to get it is through calories. You need to eat a lot of protein."

"But if I'm not marked, how—"

"I don't know, Euri. I'll ask M. There's bound to be a way around the problem." He was quiet for a while, running his fingers across my body, intently staring at my breasts as he made soft circles around them. "Eryx can sense the mark. That's how he found Jane. We didn't know it, and Phoenix had no clue, which is why he left her in that hotel room by herself."

"So because I have no mark, Eryx won't find me when I go back to L.A. and continue the tour. Well, now, that seems like a happy ending to a problem." I smiled. "I'm not really afraid of him, you know."

"You should be. He has no conscience, Euri. He will do anything without compunction, without flinching."

"He can't kill me. If I'm alive, if I can come back to you, I'll always be okay. Do you believe me?"

He laid his head down next to mine and wrapped his arms around me and drew me close until my head rested in the nook between his neck and shoulder. I loved the nook. I wanted to never leave.

"If by some horrible twist of fate or a tear in the universe or just a gross mistake, you were taken by Eryx, never, ever let him know what you're capable of. He would try to use it for his own gain. Or he'd use it against you to make you lose your grip completely. And never tell him of the Mephisto Covenant. If he knew we could be redeemed through an Anabo, he'd do everything in his power to find the others and kill them, to keep us from finding them."

"What others?"

He didn't answer.

I moved my head so I could see his face. "Zee, what others? Do you know there are others?"

"I can't say. Don't make me."

Maybe Sasha was on to something. Had we been born by grand design, our purpose to find these brothers and love them and join the fight against Eryx's quest for world domination? I supposed I didn't really care. I was happy to have found Zee, and no matter how difficult our relationship might be, I wanted to be with him.

He drew me back to his shoulder and we laid together for a while, slowly learning one another's bodies with our fingertips.

"Zee?"

"Hmm?"

"Is it a dream of yours to have children?"

He slid his leg between mine and pulled me toward him so we were completely entwined. "I've never thought about children. Ever in a thousand years. For us, it's not possible to have children without a willing Anabo, and I have always been certain there would be no one for me. My hopes and dreams were centered around you, being here with me, staying longer than one night. Babies never entered my mind." He stroked my hair and sighed, as if he was very satisfied. And complete. "I am absolutely mentally ill, Euri. I'm so afraid this will end badly."

"There is no end, so good and bad are just words. I'm willing to go the distance with you."

"Even though I'm insane?"

I moved so I could look into his eyes. "Even though you're insane. Even though you want to believe there's a way to save me from you, or lessen how much you want me."

"You heard all of what Phoenix and I talked about, didn't you?"

I nodded. "You're an unusual bloke, Zee. Most wouldn't have forgiven him so readily."

He slipped his fingers into my hair and slowly combed through, all the way to the ends. He did it again and said, "What's the point staying angry and resentful? He's suffered enough. And in the end, he's my brother and I love him. Besides, he has Mariah and I want them to be happy together. I'll think of it as a gift, so he can make a clean start and not have to worry about me, or Jane, or any of the past."

“Someday, will you tell me about Jane?”

“You know the basics. She’s been dead over a hundred years. Let’s leave it alone.”

There were still elements within the history of Jane that bothered him, but I would pick at it another day.

Embarrassing me, my stomach growled.

“Are you hungry, Lady Euri?”

“I’d enjoy a bite to eat, but I’m certain that came from you, sir. I’d never be so vulgar.”

He smiled as he released me and rolled off the bed. I watched him pull on his jeans, without his knickers. “Aren’t you worried your . . . that you’ll get caught in the zipper?”

“I’m an old pro at this. No worries.” He disappeared without a shirt or shoes.

I sat up and looked around the room and smiled. What an extraordinary night this was. I supposed I should put my clothes back on, but I didn’t want to. Not yet. I looked toward the fireplace, the grate laid with fresh wood, and wished it was lit.

Imagine my astonishment when the logs immediately caught fire. I laughed out loud. Then I looked at each unlit candle in the room and lit all of them, laughing again. How marvelous! I willed the lamp on his desk to switch on, then off. I turned my focus to his music system and paused the London Philharmonic.

Twenty minutes later, when he reappeared holding a tray laden with delicious smelling food that included a pizza, I was busily making the draperies open and close, laughing all the while.

He set the tray down on the table between the chairs in front of the fireplace and watched. “It’s fun, is it?”

“Jolly fun! This probably became old to you centuries ago, but it’s all new to me.” I sat on my heels and said, “Watch the piano.” I played Beethoven’s Fifth from the middle of the bed. I looked at him and loved that he smiled, that he looked so happy and carefree. It couldn’t last, but that was okay. We’d be happy when we could, and let the rest take care of itself.

I had one more thing I wanted to try. In the middle of my telepathic recital, I stopped playing and switched my concentration to the zipper of his jeans. It slowly lowered, the button popped free of the buttonhole and, while he stood there in total shock and awe, his pants fell off.

He started laughing and as he stepped free of the bunched denim at his feet, he kept laughing. I, of course, was laughing. Then he was launching himself toward the bed, landing on me, and we rolled around, laughing and kissing and, in the end, we had cold pizza.

~~ ZEE ~~

Until that night, I never really knew what it meant to be happy. I'd traveled around in Euri's head for periods of time and experienced her happiness, but I'd never felt my own. I was nervous about the future, of what I would do when I went to sleep, of what might happen to her over the next month during the end of the tour while she was in the real world, of how my brothers would react when they discovered her existence, and that I'd known her for such a long time without telling them. But for once, all the worries didn't get in the way of the here and now.

It wasn't just the sex, although that was amazing, and we racked up three times in as many hours, which was not something I ever expected to repeat but was something I'd remember forever until I died because holy shit, it was hot. But what really got to me was this feeling of connectedness with her, as if we'd been together always, and yet everything was new. I wasn't one to laugh much, but over and over that night, I'd laugh because she'd do something funny, or make some off the shoulder comment that was as much irreverent as it was stuffy British. She was the eternal optimist, mad in her oblivion, but in the depths of her soul lived happiness and joy. I was smitten, captivated, completely gone for her. And I knew she had me dead to rights – I was doomed to fall hard for her.

I was okay with that. I'd own up to being an idiot with all my talk of not believing in romantic love.

I had, incredibly, an Anabo who made me laugh. I don't suppose I'd ever considered what I'd like in a woman who might actually stay with me, because the idea was so foreign. I was so certain I'd always be alone, what was the point making some lame list of perfect personality traits?

Now I knew that if I ever did, top on the list would he happy, and right after it would be funny. And a close third would be the amazing ability to make a horrible situation not look quite so horrible. Euri was that girl. And she was mine. I was humbled and astonished.

Somewhere around four in the morning, when we finally settled down to sleep, I held her close and said into the dark room, "Are you sorry?"

"No, and I will never be, so don't ask me again."

"If I wake you up—"

"Let's not worry about it, Zee. If you do, you do, and we'll deal with it. I'm thinking tonight, you won't."

"Why?"

"Because you're not miserable right now. You tend to do it when you've had a particularly bad day, when the screamers are more intolerable than usual."

I sighed into her hair. "I can't imagine how I ever thought I could let you go."

"Because you let Jane go. You thought it would be the same with me, but you didn't count on me being as crazy as you are. You're arrogant and alpha and determined to be über masculine at all costs. You're also lonely and sad and convinced you don't deserve an Anabo, mostly because you're mental, but also because you didn't claim Jane, and she died and you feel guilty about it. Phoenix got to openly grieve and express his guilt, but you've had to suffer in silence all these years. Did it never occur to you that what you did was more than difficult? That none of your brothers could have done it? Not one of them are that strong willed. You gave her up because you were certain she'd be unhappy, and then she died, which is way more harsh than being unhappy, and you blame yourself."

"I should blame myself. I'm as much at fault as Phoenix."

"It's neither here nor there, Zee. I'm simply pointing out why you imagined you could not be with me. In reality, you never really had a prayer of ditching me unless I hadn't liked you, and I don't think either of us believes I don't like you."

"I'm afraid as time goes by that you'll be unhappy."

She snuggled closer, wiggling her butt into the bend of my legs, hard against my dick. I was mostly clueless about women, true, but I knew enough to know her movements were not sexual. She wanted to feel closer, which wasn't technically possible. We were tighter than two coats of paint as it was. Nevertheless, I wrapped my arm around her a little more snugly, and slid my leg between hers.

She sighed with satisfaction. "If I'm unhappy, Zee, I will fix it. I won't leave. I won't give up on you, ever."

For someone so off center, she was scary intuitive. She knew my worst fear, and didn't beat me up about it – just acknowledged it, addressed it, and moved on.

"Don't fret," she murmured, stroking my arm. "We will be together and sometimes we'll be happy and sometimes we won't. We're no different than any other couple."

"Except that we're immortal, we hunt people and kill them, and we frequently communicate with the dark angel of death. Also, we're insane."

"Details."

I smiled in the dark and kissed her neck. I was clingy and knew it, but powerless to stop.

Just as I was slipping into sleep, a certain awareness came to me and I knew we had another marked Mephisto. As I'd predicted, Phoenix had taken Mariah to bed.

It made me glad. For both of them. For all of us.

My dreams were the same as usual, but with one marked difference. Euri fought back. She was strong and capable and I was taken by surprise. In the end, I was still stronger, and overpowered her and killed her. Then I was heartbroken and bereft, utterly despondent.

I awoke suddenly, not my usual swim through sludge into consciousness, and was immediately aware that she was crying. I willed a couple of nearby candles to light, raised up and pulled her to her back. Had I attacked her? "Euri? What's wrong?"

She blinked up at me and said, "Sophie."

"Did you dream about Sophie?"

Her nod was slow. "She was with Eryx, in her wheelchair, all slumped over because he took away her pillow."

I smoothed her hair away from her brow. "It's only a dream, Euri, just a way for your subconscious to work through grief and guilt."

Tears formed and fell from the edges of her eyes. "He was so . . ."

"Cruel?"

She rubbed her eyes and shook her head. "Kind. She was upset and trying to tell him she was uncomfortable, and he thought she was hungry, which is why he moved her pillow so he could feed her little biscuits. But he didn't understand she can't eat things that require chewing. He was frustrated, but patient, and she was sad because she's so helpless, because she can't ever be . . . normal."

If it wasn't so heartbreaking, it'd be something like funny. Eryx being kind? Not in this universe. Offering a handicapped girl little cookies? Ludicrous. But Euri was in that netherworld between sleep and awake, still held in the grip of a dream that felt real. "What were you doing in your dream?"

"I was trying to tell Eryx about Sophie, but he couldn't hear me. Sophie couldn't hear me. I was saying words and no sound came out. She looked up at him, and it was as if . . . almost as though she knew him. She trusted him." She turned to look at me and blinked. "She liked him, Zee. Why would I dream such a thing? Do you suppose it's because there's a side to Eryx no one knows? Is it possible?"

"No, baby, it's impossible. It's your nature to want him to be something he's not, to hope for a better outcome to the inevitable, and so you had this dream."

She sniffed. "I wish it could be different, Zee."

"I know, but we'll be all right. Everything will work out. You believe me, don't you?"

I hit the right note, I suppose. Turning toward me, she whispered, "I believe you. I always believe you." She snuggled in and I held her close until her breathing was even. I snuffed the candles, drifted off again, and blessedly didn't dream anymore.

When I next awoke, it was to a red morning, always the worst of my color days. I sat up and saw her standing naked at the window, looking out at the snow. It was red. Like blood. The fucking mountains were covered in blood.

I stared at her and tried so hard to stop it, but as always, I was powerless against the madness. My eyes remained open, but I didn't see her, or my room, or the mountains. All I could see and hear was what violated my brain, intruded into my psyche, fucked with my soul. Curling into myself, I gradually ceased to be me and became a monster.

I hit the woman. Over and over. She screams and tries to escape from me, but I am so much stronger, so angry, so determined to kill her. Her children, five of them with big, dark eyes, stand by and watch me kill her. A man, her husband, I suppose, bursts through a door and I stab him. I shove the kids outside and whistle for my death squad compatriots. While they take aim and shoot the little ones, I walk away, headed for another house, another family that must die because they are not pure, because they worship the wrong God, because a tyrant says they must die. He says I must kill them or my entire family will die. It's mine or theirs, and I will do anything to protect my family. I don't want to cry. It's emasculating and I'm ashamed, but I do. I hate what I have become. Everything I believed and thought was real has turned out to be a lie.

I glance over my shoulder and see the death squad throw the bodies on the cart, an old coal wagon drawn by a mule. Modern times and we still use a goddamned mule to pull a cart to load up dead bodies. The future is right here in front of me. Starvation, disease, misery, and death. A backward slide into ignorance and superstition. All humanity is doomed.

I've had enough. Watching them throw the last little body on the cart, I decide Hell could not be worse than the world as it is. I pull my pistol from its holster and point it toward the others, men who were my friends, who joined this fight with me to make our lives better, who are not yet as disillusioned as me. I shout obscenities at them and when they realize I am about to begin firing at them, they take aim at me and—

"Xenos! *Stop it!* Look at me!" Euri was on top of me, straddling my chest, holding my head, shouting. She was red. Covered in blood. Unclean. Soiled by the murders of all those little ones with those big, dark eyes, looking so lost and haunted and desperate.

I moved her off of me, got off the bed, then picked her up and took her to the bathroom, to the shower. I ignored everything she said. I had to get her clean. She'd be fresh and uncontaminated again, washed free of all this blood, this horror. She was perfect, my Anabo, pure of spirit and kind and good and everything I would never be.

She stopped fighting me when I got in the shower and set her on her feet and washed her with my hands, rubbing her body all over, again and again, until the blood began to leave, flowing down the drain in swirling circles of despair.

Slowly, her color returned, and she stood before me with the warm water running in tiny rivers down her sleek, beautiful body. "Kiss me," she said.

And I did. I made my way back to the here and now, and knew I was out of the grip of my madness, at least for a while. Red days were more rare than the other color days, but always horrific, knocking me out of reality completely. I usually went to Kyanos to weather through them, never quite sure what I might do in reality, always sure I would scare the shit out of anyone who saw me, including my brothers. Today, I hadn't left. I'd had an episode right in front of Euri. She'd been inside my head during red days, but I was certain seeing me in person had to be freaky scary. But she stayed. She was here, with me, even knowing I was this completely fucked up.

I kissed her for a long, long time, drawing strength and solace from her arms, her touch, her lips. What would ordinarily control my mind all day and sometimes into the night had come and gone in less than an hour. Because of Euri. When I finally lifted my head and looked down into her cornflower blue eyes, I knew that I loved her. I had loved her all along and would love her until the end of time. The sudden awareness was nothing like I'd imagined. It wasn't huge and grand, but soft and quiet, and I felt at peace. I wasn't anxious, wasn't afraid.

"It's never going to go away," she said gently, "but we can make it not so bad."

We. Amazing how one tiny word could mean everything. Holding her close, with her heart beating next to mine, I knew what joy felt like. "I love you."

Her arms tightened around me. "I love you, Zee."

Backing her up against the glass, I lifted her and she wrapped those long legs around my middle and I kissed her and made love to her and when she came, while her body caressed mine with wave after wave of her climax, she made that funny little noise again, a sharp intake of breath that ended in a quarter beat musical note. Like a little bird. I would never ever get tired of hearing it. I lost myself in her, and was awed all over again at how much more incredible sex was with Euri. Thousands of girls in my lifetime and I couldn't remember even one.

There was only Euri.

CHAPTER 9

He took me for pancakes at the Dream Café in Hollywood. He wore his Wayfarers and a Lakers cap and a long sleeved T-shirt from a Jimi Hendrix concert. I was still in my pink dress, but wearing new knickers, which Zee had lifted for me earlier.

At a table in the center of the small, bright café, he watched me eat, looking very serious. "There are a couple of guys outside who're going to take our picture when we leave."

"How very strange. Are they paparazzi?"

"Yes. You're about to be famous, Euri."

"Oh, go on."

He pulled his cell phone from his pocket and handed it to me. I had over three hundred thousand followers on Twitter. At the end of last week, I had maybe four thousand. There was a hashtag #LadyEuriRocks , and photos of me from last night's concert were all over Instagram. The Arcadia Facebook page now had over a million likes. I handed the phone back to him. "I don't get it."

"I didn't think you would, which is why I brought you to this place where people go to be noticed so we can go over the protocol."

I laughed. "You're funning me." He was not smiling. I stopped laughing. "You're not joking. Okay. Protocol, as soon as I eat the rest of your pancakes."

He watched me switch our plates and make short work of his short stack. And the extra rasher of streaky bacon. After that, I ate his scrambled eggs and toast. I was eyeing the parsley garnish when he pulled his plate away and waved at the waitress. "We'll need another order of pancakes," he said, patting his belly. "I ate my girlfriend's. My bad."

The waitress seemed almost afraid of him, and when she returned with another plate, she set it down in the middle of the table and booked it back to the kitchen.

"What's wrong with her?" I asked.

"It's me and my brothers. We generally make people anxious, but some people are way more attuned to what we are, and they give us a wide berth. It's why I wear shades even inside if I'm in public."

I looked at him carefully. "Take off the shades for a moment."

He lowered them from his eyes and blinked at me. "You can see that they're black, but you probably can't see that they're scary because you're Anabo. Regular people are generally afraid of our eyes. It's why we always hunt for girls at night, in dark places like swanky restaurants and clubs."

Laughing, I almost spit out my juice. "*Swanky?* Did you just say *swanky?*"

He grinned. "Don't tell me you don't know what swanky means."

"Of course I know. It's just so old school. And perhaps the funniest word in the English language." I watched him replace the shades. "Your eyes aren't black, Zee. They're dark grey. And I don't think they're scary. They're beautiful."

"They're grey? Are you sure?"

"Yes, I'm sure. Does this mean you're redeemed? Because you love me? Shouldn't there be angels singing and trumpets and archangels pronouncing you're now a candidate for Heaven?" I looked up, as if there really might be angels flying around the ceiling at the Dream Café.

"It stands to reason my redemption would be anticlimactic. Everything else in my life is manically dramatic. I have to say, I've never felt this way before."

"Happy?"

"Yeah. It's weird." He handed me the pancakes, which I got busy buttering and drowning in copious amounts of syrup. While I ate them with tremendous enjoyment, he drank his coffee and watched me with a little smile.

"You're not disgusted, are you?" I asked around a bite.

"Kind of turned on, actually. Your mouth does interesting things when you eat. I'm imagining all the marvelous things you could do with that mouth."

"Behave."

"Good call. Cripes, I'm getting another hard-on. I haven't been this randy since we moved to Greece and I saw my first woman."

"Sent you off, did she?"

"I came in my tunic. Made a spot and I was terribly humiliated."

"Poor Zee." I dropped a shoe and lifted my foot to his crotch and wiggled my toes. He really did have an erection. I instantly dropped my foot.

"Are you disgusted?"

"I'd abandon the rest of these pancakes if you'd take me back to your room right now."

"You have to meet John in an hour."

"All I need is fifteen minutes."

"Behave." He smiled, then shifted in his chair and turned his attention to the wide windows at the front of the restaurant. "Okay, so those guys will take our picture. Probably taking it now, really. They're going to want to know who I am. I'm going to be with you a lot over the next month, so we need a story. Jamison thinks I live here, because I always see Arcadia at Fawkes, and that's where I met him, and continue to see him every time he's here. Our story is that I met you last night, we went out after the concert and now we're friends."

I swallowed a bite and took a drink of my orange juice. "Just friends?"

"That's the story. John will want it to be up for conjecture, so it looks like you're available, and he'll look like a definite possibility. This stuff sells music, Euri. The more mystery and seductive information, even if it's all bullshit, the better it is for the band. Jamison's a good guy and even without you, Arcadia is awesome. I don't want to fuck it up for him."

I smiled as I finished the pancakes and sat back, finally feeling satisfied. "For a son of Hell, you're a very nice bloke."

"It's entirely selfish. I like the band and I'm a music snob, so I have a vested interest in their success."

"All right, so you're a fan boy computer geek who hacks, which is why you're friends with John, right?"

"Right."

"Do you work?"

"I'm a trust fund bum kinda guy who's taking an extended break from college. That's why I can take off and travel with you to Arcadia gigs."

"Will you ride the bus with us?"

He looked at me and shook his head. "John wouldn't like it, and because I can't, you can't ride the bus anymore. Until you've been Mephisto a long time, until you know what you're capable of and how to control it, you're at too much risk to be among ordinary people for long periods on your own."

"For instance?"

"You're not going to be tolerant of lost souls. When you see one, and it's inevitable that you will, your instinct will be to give chase and capture. You'll want to take them to Hell on Earth right then, immediately, and it takes some self-control to not do that. We can't give in to instinct because every human we take out has to have a doppelganger, a body left for the living to see and bury. Until you know how to keep yourself from capturing lost souls, you need me to be with you in the real world. I think you're okay during rehearsals and performances, but otherwise, I'll be with you."

"This is all so very strange. I can't imagine feeling compelled to capture someone."

"You probably couldn't imagine making my pants fall off, but . . ." He smiled. "The other problem is that you're more unpredictable than the other Anabo because you're wack. Suppose you go walkabout again, while you're on the bus? You can transport now, so you might pop off and wind up God knows where. If you don't have your phone with you, there's no GPS and I can't find you. Have you tried to transport yet?"

"No. I've been with you since you first kissed me and turned me into Mephisto, and I wouldn't want to transport away from you. I don't want to be away from you at all."

He grinned. Like a little boy. Like he was shy and almost embarrassed. "Aw, go on."

I returned his smile, despite the lump in my throat. He wanted to be loved so badly. He was so alone, and thinking of him fighting his mental issues for centuries, all by himself, made my heart hurt for him. "Are you fishing for sentimentals, Xenos?"

He leaned in and whispered, "Tell me you love me again."

"I love you again."

We laughed together and I had never been happier than I was at that exact moment. I decided I'd have lots more moments. Life was grand.

~~ ZEE ~~

There is a duality to all things. It's the nature of the universe. Or maybe God just has a thing for push-pull. The old adage, what goes up, must come down, applies across the board, always, so I knew as the day progressed that this bubble of euphoria couldn't last. I didn't know what would stick a pin in my big happy balloon, but I was prepared for it.

Or so I thought.

I hadn't foreseen a gigantic motherfuckin' pin. Turns out, even for a glass-half-empty doomsday pessimist negative naysayer like me, something could be light-years worse than I ever imagined.

I'd taken her to meet with John and, while he wasn't happy about her revised travel arrangements, he was glad she would be continuing until the last scheduled concert, which would be in three weeks at Blackbriar in New York. The band was in L.A. another night, so while she was at rehearsal and sound check, I went home and had a visit with Key. I knew Phoenix would tell him about Euri, and I wanted to take the offensive, instead of getting blindsided. Key was a hard guy, never said a lot, and he rarely hung out with any of us. Of course, neither did I, but Kyros was the oldest, our de facto leader. I wished sometimes he would lighten up, be a little warmer, more approachable. He was effing hard to talk to.

I found him in his room, getting dressed for the winter ball at Jordan's school, which he would attend because he went everywhere with her. Like Euri, she was immortal and Mephisto, so being in the real world was dicey. I thought it was pretty funny, a guy like Key going to high school. I was certain all those kids were scared shitless of him. He was a tiny bit scarier than the rest of us, maybe because of his long hair, but most likely because he rarely smiled and had a way of staring hard at a person that was a little freaky.

Today, however, he seemed almost lighthearted. I knocked and he opened the door in only a towel. His hair was loose, like he'd just blow-dried it. "Hey, I'm getting dressed. Come on in."

I followed him to his closet, looking around his room as we went. None of us spent much time in any of the other suites. We hung out in the TV room, or the game room where there was a pool table, or in the gym, working out. I noticed Key had at least fifteen snapshots of Jordan all over his room, and that made me want to laugh. Mister Solemn was completely gone for her.

I leaned against the doorjamb of his closet and, while he pulled on a pair of boxers, then tux pants, I told him about Euri. He stopped in mid-zip and looked at me with that classic hard Key stare. "Why am I just now finding out about her? You met her last night, it's late afternoon the *next day*, and you're just now telling me?"

I shrugged. "It's not that important."

"Are you fucking with me, Xenos? *Not that important?* There's *nothing* more important than Anabo. You find one, you know she's meant for you, and it's not that *important?* Jesus, brother, you make me afraid for you. I mean, really, I do not understand you at all."

This would probably have been a good time to confess everything, but I didn't want to. I wanted to keep Euri a secret from my brothers a little while longer. They had to know she existed, because Phoenix had met her, and as soon as he emerged from Mariah's room, he was bound to announce it to any and all, but they didn't have to know how long I had known her, or that I was crazy in love with her. I wanted to hold that close and examine it, revel in it, before anyone else knew. I was wildly happy, and I worried one of them would say or do something to lessen my elation. Especially Denys. He was always the jokester, always laughing, but beneath his gregarious nature, he was bitter and angry. He'd be glad for me, but at the same time, he'd be more angry. I didn't want that weighing on me. Not yet. I just wanted to be with Euri without interference or interruption. I was going to the concert tonight, and then she'd come home with me. And no one would know. Just me and her.

Key was staring hard at me, obviously aggravated. I had to say something. "I know it's important in the long run, but for now, I'm going to let it ride, let things settle with Jordan and Mariah before I do anything. Euri is touring with Arcadia, and I'm not going to screw that up for her."

He went back to dressing and, as he slid his dress shirt on, he asked, "When's the tour over?"

"In three weeks, in New York. I was thinking maybe we'd all go to the last one, and afterward, I'll ask her to go with me."

"Where?"

"Shit, I don't know, Key. I'll think about it. I'll figure something out."

"Get Phoenix to help. He's always good with plans." Finishing with his shirt buttons, he looked at me. "He marked Mariah. I thought it'd take months, and it took, what, like five days?" He actually grinned as he put in his diamond stud cufflinks. I'd given them to him for his birthday over fifty years ago. It pleased me that he still wore them. "We need to make sure she's okay. I'm a little preoccupied. Would you mind checking on her?"

"I don't mind."

He was ready. He pulled his hair into a ponytail, then looked in the mirror. "Oh, hell, these pants are wrinkled."

"Pop down to Mathilda and get her to press them again."

He did and I followed, mostly because I was highly entertained by my hard-ass brother wigging out about his pants.

It got even better when he asked Sasha to tie his bowtie. He looked in the mirror in the front hall and shook his head. "It's crooked." He untied it and went to stand in front of her again. By the third retry, she was scowling at him. "Call M. He's a dapper dresser and bound to know how to do this."

Jax was sitting on the stairs, laughing.

Deacon stood beneath the portrait of Jane and slowly shook his turbaned head. "Vanity is destructive to the spirit. You dishonor all men by your obsession with appearance."

While Sasha tried the bowtie again, Key ignored Deacon and glanced in the mirror. "Maybe I should wear my hair down. Sasha, which looks better? And, dammit, these pants are still wrinkled. I'm gonna look like a hobo and Jordan will be embarrassed."

Sasha glanced at me and rolled her eyes. "Jordan would be nuts for you if you showed up dressed in an Elvis suit. You look fine."

"Fine? Just, *fine?*"

Now she was laughing. "Okay, you look very handsome and hot." She waggled her brows. "I'd do you."

"Not while I'm alive," Jax said.

That got Key to stop fretting. He looked down at her and began to laugh.

Deacon shook his head again and went toward the dining room. Moments later, I heard the distinctive clink of silver as he set the table for dinner.

In my head, Euri was practicing. She was letting her mind wander and it was incredibly sexy. I had to make myself stop thinking about her. Damned dick was always popping up at the worst times.

I put my hands in my pockets and said, "I'm going up to check on Mariah. Anybody care to join me?"

Jax instantly shook his head.

Sasha said, "I'd rather ask Deacon his thoughts on alcohol and hear his lecture."

Denys had just popped in and he held up his hands in mock defense. "Go in her room and face Phoenix? They're probably naked and he's bound to beat the shit out of anybody who questions her wellbeing. No thanks."

I sighed dramatically. "I guess it's up to me, then."

"He won't beat you up, Zee," Kyros assured me as he

rebound his hair for the umpteenth time.

"Damn straight," I said. "I can kick his ass any day of the week." Before anyone could point out that I was full of it, I popped up to the third floor, outside of Mariah's room. I knocked and heard Phoenix tell me to come in. When I opened the door, it was clear he hadn't expected me. Probably thought it would be Mathilda, who'd taken a special interest in looking after Mariah.

I walked to the bed and stared down at the two of them, Mariah's face half buried in Phoenix's neck, her long, dark hair spilling across the pillows. She wasn't as beautiful as her sister, but she was built better. Jordan was a little thing, not so curvy, but with a face like the Madonna. Of course neither of them, nor Sasha, were as perfect as Euri, but I admitted to extreme prejudice.

I met my brother's solemn gaze, remembering what he'd said last night, about giving up his claim to Mariah. He hadn't waited even six hours before he marked her. She wasn't immortal yet, so she could be claimed and marked by another Mephisto, but the likelihood of that happening was less than zero. Phoenix would kill anybody who touched her. With as straight a face as I could muster, I said, "I assume this means your plan is null and void."

Looking humble and maybe a tad sheepish, he nodded.

"You do realize I'd never have gone through with it, right? I only said as much because I knew it'd make you crazy, make you do exactly what you did. You're the most hardheaded, stubborn asshole on God's earth. It takes something extreme and harsh to get you to pay attention." My attention turned to Mariah. "It's our duty to ensure the comfort and happiness of all Anabo, Mariah, and I was chosen to do the honors. Are you well? Is everything okay? You have only to say the word, and he'll be dealt with accordingly."

She turned her head to look up at me and said, "I'm horribly embarrassed, but that's not his fault."

"Why are you embarrassed?"

"Because I'm in bed, naked, with your naked brother, and you're here looking at us, and everyone in the house knows what happened last night."

"Of course we know," I said reasonably. "He marked you.

This is how it works." At least, this is how it usually worked. It appeared God hadn't planned for alternatives, like an Anabo having a lunatic mother who had her uterus removed before she was even through adolescence. "Perhaps it'll make you feel better that no one will know about any subsequent sex. Unless you yell a lot." I thought of Euri's sweet little chirp at the end of her climax and my cock jumped at the memory. Jesus, I was turning into a pubescent again, getting hard at just the thought of sex. "Some girls like to yell, which seems a little overdramatic to me, but whatever. Are you happy?"

She'd turned her face into Phoenix's neck again, but I could see she was ten shades of red. "Very," she said, her voice muffled.

"Good." I remembered I was teaching her to play the piano. She had a natural affinity to music, and a killer voice. I imagined she would join our band of musicians that included several Luminas, and now would include Euri. That made me enormously glad. Hoping to make Mariah less uncomfortable, I said, "Don't forget to practice your scales. Every day. Lesson on Wednesday at nine. Be sharp." I paused. "B sharp. Get it?"

"I get it. I'll be sharp. Thank you for the TV."

I glanced at the flat screen I'd installed above her mantel yesterday afternoon. "Welcome. I also bought you a laptop, which you need to let me teach you how to use. Phoenix will do it wrong."

Clearly offended, he said, "I beg your pardon. I'm not some Luddite who doesn't know—"

"You're an amateur. She needs me to teach her."

"Fine."

"Fine." I turned away and headed for the door. "Try and make it downstairs for dinner. Key is leaving just after to go with Jordan to her school's winter ball. He's asked Sasha fifty times to adjust his bowtie, and Mathilda is about to bean him with a skillet because he keeps freaking out that his tux trousers are wrinkled. He's put his hair in a ponytail ten times, taken it down ten times, and now he's wondering if he should pull it back again. It'd be pathetic if it wasn't so funny."

As I closed the door, I heard them laughing. I hadn't

heard my brother laugh in a long, long time.

I smiled all the way down the stairs.

At dinner, I was relieved that Phoenix was so caught up in Mariah, he seemed to have forgotten about meeting Euri, and Key became more wound up and obsessed about the dance, so he also appeared to have forgotten about her. No one looked too closely at me, so no one noticed anything different about my eyes.

I ate Hans's delicious schnitzel and listened to my brothers give Key a hard time. I listened to them tease Mariah and Phoenix, then laugh when she blushed, and laugh harder when she asked if she could eat Phoenix's schnitzel. Mariah thought we were laughing because she had a major love affair with food and we liked to tease her about it. I think maybe she grew up hungry, and she was painfully poor, so she was always extremely enthusiastic when it came to meals. She took our laughter in stride, probably because she never caught on that we were snickering over sexual innuendos. Sasha knew, and shot all of us a quelling look. Not that we paid her any mind. Poor Sasha – had to put up with our immaturity on a daily basis. I suspected once all the new Anabo were here for good, we'd have to grow up. Some.

While I ate dessert, peach pie with ice cream, I was aware of the people in the green room at Fawkes as they chattered and laughed around Euri, who played Weird Al songs while some guys from the warm up band sang.

Everyone there was laughing.

Everyone here was laughing.

We were all happy.

And then, in keeping with the duality of life, we weren't.

CHAPTER 10

~~ EURI ~~

The way Zee and I were connected was a mystery to me, but I was certain it was not something that happened randomly. I was convinced that God, or Mephistopheles, or maybe even Lucifer had made this happen. We each had the mind for it, an ability that most did not, so with a little tweaking, it was logical. Weird. Very, very odd and curious, but strangely reasonable. It had brought us together, which was undoubtedly part of the reason, but this ability of ours was too precise and strong not to have a specific purpose. I didn't spend a lot of time analyzing it because it's not my nature to question. I'm curious, but not overly. I take things as they come, usually at face value. I'd become accustomed to Zee in my thoughts when we were apart. He'd become a part of me as I was a part of him.

Which is why, when he stopped being there, I was lost.

We were halfway through our playlist when Zee looked up at me from the sea of faces in Fawkes and pointed to his phone. He had to leave. He disappeared, and I continued playing.

Another hour passed. I kept waiting to hear him, to feel his presence in my psyche, but nothing happened. I grew concerned, then worried, then afraid. By the time we went back out for an encore performance, I was shaky. He wasn't blocking me. He wasn't doing this on purpose. He simply wasn't there.

John took my hand and pulled me behind the front speakers. Over the din of the screaming crowd, he asked, "Are you feeling okay? You're very pale."

"I'm good for two songs," I said, trying to smile and failing miserably. "If you blokes want to play 'Home by Never', I'll just duck out." It was a long drawn out song, filled with a guitar solo and an entire segment for Garrison, the drummer. Fans loved it. The band loved playing it. I would lose my mind if I had to stick around that long.

"I think we'll play the usual encore, then get out of here." He nodded toward the bass player. "Pogo wants to head up the street and see Ben Folds."

So I stayed and played the encore, and as soon as we were done, I gathered up my backpack, got in the limo to the hotel, and went to my room, vaguely aware of a huge crowd of people in the lobby, yelling at us as we passed through to the elevators. I changed into jeans, a loose blouse and some flats, then packed my backpack with clean knickers and a bra, a Coldplay T-shirt, a clean blouse for tomorrow, and some toiletries and cosmetics.

When I was done, I sat at my practice keyboard and played, hoping if I was quiet and alone, I'd know his thoughts.

I still heard nothing.

Frustrated, I stopped playing and sat on the chair by the window and called him. Again. No answer. This was déjà vu of the night Miles would never answer his phone or any texts.

Afraid he might be having another episode, I had to know if Zee was okay. When he had them, I knew what horrors were in his head, but maybe tonight was something different. Maybe he had gone walkabout.

For a long time, I stared out at the lights of L.A. and reviewed my options. In the end, only one was logical. If he wouldn't come to me, I'd go to him.

With a deep breath, I looked toward the bathroom, then stood and closed my eyes as I'd seen Zee do when he transported, and imagined I was in the bathroom. After a familiar rush, I opened my eyes and stood in front of the basin.

I practiced a few more times, and even though I knew I would certainly require more training at this, I took my handbag, the backpack, and a chance. Closing my eyes again, I imagined I was in Zee's room, enormously relieved when I opened my eyes and saw his piano. Unfortunately, I landed on his desk, almost immediately lost my balance, and slid to the floor.

It was dark and he wasn't there, so after I picked myself up and lit a few candles, I sat at the bench and began to play. If he didn't show up within half an hour, I'd leave his room and find one of his brothers and our secret would be out, but it would be a small price to pay for finding him. I was extremely worried.

I'd just finished playing a Strauss waltz when he appeared. My relief was short lived, however, because clearly something was horribly wrong.

Zee stared at me with no expression on his face.

I slid from the bench and stood next to him. "What's happened?"He looked through me and I understood why he wasn't in my thoughts. He'd completely shut down. Checked out.

I led him to the chairs in front of the fireplace, and lit the fire and all the candles around the room. I went to the intercom and pressed a button I was almost certain would call the housekeeper. She answered, obviously crying, "Aye, Master Zee, what is it I can do for ye?"

"Can you come to his room and bring tea?"

Her reply was long in coming. "Who would you be, missy?"

"Bring up the tea and I'll introduce myself."

"Aye, I'll be there."

I went to sit by Zee and held his hand, and he began to speak, so softly, so disjointed and halting, I could barely make out what he was saying. Something about Key and Jordan and Eryx and dying.

When Mathilda arrived at the door, I let her in and waited for her reaction.

Eyes wide, plump hands clutching the tea tray, she whispered, "*Jane.* God's blood, ye've returned from the grave."

I closed the door behind her and led her to the little table between the fireplace chairs. She set the tray down and I gently guided her into the unoccupied chair. "I'm Lady Euri Rutledge. Jane was my ancestor. And you see, I am Anabo, and Zee found me and we have an agreement that I will be here forever starting in three weeks. Until then, he doesn't want anyone to know, but Sasha knows because she caught me here. I met Phoenix last night, and he's bound to tell the others about me, but he doesn't know that Zee and I have an understanding, you understand? So you mustn't say anything." I began to pour the tea.

She blinked up at me. I was certain she was rarely dumbfounded, and it was upsetting to her. I handed Zee the teacup and he drank it mindlessly, staring at the fire, mumbling about Key and Jordan.

I sat on the small footstool I pulled away from his chair and looked at Mathilda, noticing she smelled like gingerbread. Her long dress was brown bombazine, a fabric popular in the 1800s. I knew her story from Zee. She'd killed her employer, an earl, while he was raping her daughter, who died later that night. Mathilda was tried, convicted and executed. Not a candidate for Hell, but unable to breach Heaven because of her anger toward God, her spirit was sent to the Mephisto in hopes she could make her peace through work and interaction with the Luminas, who were live angels. She'd been with the brothers since 1852 and still showed no sign of forgiving God for taking her daughter, which made me wonder if any of the Purgatories had ever turned a page and ascended to Heaven. Deacon was a Moor who'd been with them over eight hundred years.

Glancing at Zee, I then turned my attention to Mathilda. "He's not here. He's gone off somewhere in his mind. And you were crying. What's happened?"

The older woman began to cry again, dabbing at her kindly brown eyes with the hem of her crisp white apron. "Do ye know of Kyros? And Jordan?"

"I know everything," I assured her.

"Miss Jordan attacked Eryx at her dance tonight, and Key took her back to the White House. She was to see her papa, then come here, and Master Kyros planned to tell her it was all over, that she couldn't go back. The Mephisto had a meeting and everyone agreed. The real world was too much for her." She sniffed and frowned at the same time. "And Eryx wouldn't stop pesterin' the puir lamb." She blinked at me. "He thought she'd finally give in and go with him. Imagine that, Lady Euri."

"Is he in love with her?"

She guffawed. "He's unable to love anything or anyone. Not even himself. I believe he's never met a girl who stands up to him the way Jordan does. She's a sight to see. Strong, because God made her that way so she could be with Master Kyros. He's a hard one, strong and quiet and he does what's best for the family, even when it hurts him." She cried harder and buried her face in her apron, muffling her voice. "He loved Eryx so. They were closest in age and always together. When Eryx . . . after he became the lost soul that he is, Key had to hate him, had to vow to fight him." She looked at me and swallowed. "All these years, he's done what he had to do, even while it broke him over and over to know his beloved brother is a monster. It all came crashing down tonight. Eryx went to Miss Jordan and convinced her there was some hope for him if only she'd share her light, if she'd care for him and kiss him."

I recoiled and sat up straighter and couldn't help a slight squeak in my voice. "No, Mathilda, she didn't."

The older woman nodded slowly, tears streaking down her pink cheeks. "Aye, milady, she did. For Key, because he loved Eryx, because he missed him, she believed Eryx. She took a chance, and lost what she is. She's not Anabo and she's not Mephisto. But she's immortal."

"So she's like him?"

Mathilda nodded and dabbed at her eyes again. "The only way to save her is to take her back to God, ask him to accept her into Heaven."

I already knew the answer, but asked anyway "Who will take her?"

"They have a plan to rescue her from Eryx's castle in Romania tomorrow, then Key will take her to a church and ask God's mercy on her."

"He loves her. Doesn't he? He can go in the church. Can't he?"

She slowly shook her head. "I believe he does, but he has yet to acknowledge it. He's been alone so long, had to be strong and always set himself apart from the others, not too close because he had to make all the hard decisions." She glanced at Zee. "He's been alone as well, Lady Euri. I'm sorry I'm so upset right now, because I'd want you to know how happy I am for Xenos. He's so very tortured and bedeviled by the break in his brain." She looked at me again. "Do ye ken what's in his mind?"

I nodded. "My brain is broken in the same way."

She stared at me for a long time. "God is good, Lady Euri."

I stood and poured Zee some more tea. He looked at the cup, then up at me. He saw me. He knew me. He was coming back.

His eyes were filled with pain. I set the cup aside, fell to my knees between his thighs, and wrapped my arms around him. When I lifted my head again, Mathilda and the tea tray were gone.

He told me what had happened, with me still on my knees, my arms around his middle and my head on his chest. His voice rumbled against my cheek and I listened and said nothing, even though I knew already that this was the worst thing that had ever happened to him, to his brothers. Even losing Jane wasn't this devastating. Kyros was the glue that held them together, the father figure they needed in the absence of Mephistopheles in their daily lives.

And tomorrow, he would die to save Jordan.

When he was done and all was silent, I rose up and looked into his beautiful eyes. "He must love her, Zee. Why else would he sacrifice himself for her?"

"It's not just for her. If she stays with Eryx, she will help him. She may give him children, and God only knows what they would be. Key is doing this for us and all of humanity."

"But he's mostly doing it for her."

"How do you know?"

I reached up and smoothed his hair. "Because he loves her. He just doesn't know it yet. It will happen for him like it happened for Ajax. He'll die and come back redeemed."

"I wish you would be right. He's been there my whole life, and if he's not any more," he took a deep breath and let it out slowly, "it'll feel like the world has stopped turning. Like my center of gravity will be altered."

I got to my feet and held out a hand. "Let's go to bed."

He took my hand and stood, but he looked anxious. "I lost you for a while tonight. How did you get here? Did you transport all on your own?"

"Yes. I was worried about you."

He drew me close and embraced me. "I'm glad you're here, but I'm afraid of what will happen when I go to sleep."

"It's been a particularly brutal day for you, hasn't it?"

"This was the best and the worst day of my entire life." He led me toward the bathroom. "Maybe I should go sleep somewhere else tonight."

"Why? You'll just pop in here in your sleep if it turns out to be one of those nights."

Standing at the basin, reaching for his toothbrush, he said, "I don't actually think I'll get any sleep tonight, so it's a moot point."

Turning, I walked back to his bed to get my backpack, then went to the other basin to wash my face and brush my teeth. When he went in his cupboard, I followed. We undressed, I slipped into my T-shirt and he pulled on a pair of gym pants, then we went to bed and just as we had the night before, he pulled me close so that we were spooned together. I drifted off, and when I woke a few hours later, Zee had moved to the other side of the bed and was crying into his pillow. Deep, soulful, heartrending sobs.

I stayed where I was and let him cry, gave him space and time.

When he was quieter, I slowly made my way toward him, until he turned and pulled me next to him. He was so tense, I think every muscle in his long, hard body was stretched taut. I plastered myself against him and didn't say anything except, "I love you."

I felt him relax, little by little, and he eventually fell asleep. I remained wide awake, listening to his even breaths and the wind outside the windows. I wondered how his other brothers and Sasha were doing? How was Key doing? I had never met him, but I knew him as Zee knew him, and because Zee loved him, I loved him. It wasn't terribly complicated. I loved Zee, so anyone important to him was important to me.

Lying next to him, I watched him sleep. He was

splendidly beautiful, truly, his face square and masculine, covered right now with the beginnings of a beard. His lips were full and could curve into a gorgeous smile. The diamond in his ear was a contrast to his skin in the dark. He'd told me Phoenix had an elaborate brooch made for Jane before she died, a gift for her arrival at the Mephisto house in Yorkshire, which is where they lived until they moved to Colorado to get away from the bad memories. He didn't want the brooch, and asked Zee to get rid of it for him. Instead, Zee took one of the diamonds and had it made into a stud for his ear. He said it made him remember, and because he believed remembering someone was a form of respect and honor, he would never forget her.

In a warm swell of affection, I reached out to pet him.

He mumbled something, then pulled me closer, and I finally went back to sleep.

When Deacon announced breakfast at seven, I woke and Zee turned his head on his pillow and blinked at me. "How did you sleep?"

"Very well," I assured him.

His eyes reflected bewilderment, as if he couldn't quite grasp reality. I held my breath, wondering if he was slipping into a color day. Then he swallowed and blinked again and said softly, "The dream was different, Euri. For the first time in a thousand years, I didn't take you in the church and kill the both of us."

"You love me. I love you. You're on the other side of hope now, and that makes all the difference." I could see he was bemused, but not happy. "If you didn't dream the usual, what *did* you dream?"

"You ran from me, into the church, and I chased, but by the time I got inside, you were gone. You asked God to take you out." He swallowed again. "You left me."

"You're just feeling anxious because this is all so new."

He turned and stared up at the ceiling. "It was so terrible, Euri. I've never felt like that before. Absolutely gutted."

"It will never happen, Xenos. Never in a million years. I told you, I'll never leave you, and I won't. No matter what happens, I'm here with you forever. You believe me, don't you?"

He nodded, then rolled out of bed and went into the bathroom. When he came out, he was dressed in jeans and a long-sleeved Arcadia T-shirt. Standing beside the bed, he bent and stroked my hair. "I'm going down for breakfast, because he's going to be gone. I want to spend as much time with him as I can."

"No need to worry after me, Zee. I'll pop back to my hotel room and get some breakfast with the band."

"Don't ride the bus to San Francisco, Euri. Promise me you won't. I want to take you."

"You're going to be pretty busy today."

"I want you to go with me."

"What? How? I'm not trained for—"

"After we get Jordan away from Eryx, after Key takes her to . . ." He paused and took a deep breath. "I have to take Jordan's doppelganger to her room at the White House. I want you to go with me. Will you?"

He would be tremendously upset. He was asking for my help to keep him sane enough to do his job. I got off the bed and slipped my arms around his middle. "Of course I'll go with you."

"Good. When it's done, I'll take you to San Francisco for rehearsal."

He kissed me, then turned away. I watched him leave the room before I went to get dressed.

Ten minutes later, I closed my eyes and popped back to the hotel in L.A. It was an hour earlier than Colorado, so just a little past six. The red message light was blinking on the phone, and when I called to collect the message, John said, "Euri, I guess you must be with Zee tonight. I was hoping we could make more progress on that song we started. Also, your father called me. Said he can't reach your cell. I can't either. Did you forget to charge it again? Anyway, your dad saw a photo of you in one of those gossipy London newspapers, and he's extremely worried about what your sudden fame might do to your family name. He's kind of uptight, isn't he? You should call him, preferably soon. Call me when you're back. Maybe we can have breakfast."

I was about to ring off when the recording indicated a second message, after which a soft, feminine voice without a trace of an accent said, "Euri, I apologize for intruding. I know you're terribly busy and likely deluged with fangirls, but this isn't about Arcadia. It's a personal matter. I came across a photograph of you, taken last year, I think in St. Tropez. You were in a bikini with some others on a boat, and I noticed your tattoo, which is very unique."

I glanced at my forearm. A question mark was not remotely unique. Mine and Zee's were alike, but the concept of a question mark was hardly distinctive. The lead singer of the Goo Goo Dolls had a question mark tat. What did this girl want? Maybe backstage passes. She probably had a crush on Pogo, the bass player. He'd morphed out of his MIT geekdom and turned into more of a hot nerd. Girls went for his rust colored beard and green eyes.

She continued, "I'm wondering if your tattoo is actually a birthmark, because I have one just like it, in the exact same place, beneath my right breast. A very beautiful, cursive letter *A*, surrounded by lines that resemble the rays of the sun."

My heart sped up and I became slightly breathless. *Anabo.* My birthmark was the sign of the Anabo. This girl who called me out of the blue was not a fan, but an Anabo.

Scrambling to retrieve the hotel pen and paper on the desk, I waited for her to leave a number, ready to write it down.

"I just think it's odd, the little A, and wonder if we're somehow related. We look nothing alike, but still, it's a strange coincidence. I attend school in New York and will be at the Arcadia concert at Blackbriar. I would love to meet you, if possible. I'll contact you then, and hopefully you'll agree to visit with me. My name is August. Actually Augustine, but everyone calls me August."

I was still waiting, holding the pen at the ready, when I realized she had rung off. She didn't leave a number or give me any indication of how to reach her, and I was determined to do so. If she was Anabo, she deserved the opportunity to meet the Mephisto and see for herself if she wanted to join in the war against Eryx.

I set the phone back in its cradle and wondered which Mephisto would catch her scent. It had to be either Ty or Denys. Despite the sadness of the day, I allowed myself a small smile. *August.* What an unusual and lovely name. A bit antiquated, but oddly compelling.

After a shower, I dressed in a pale pink cashmere sweater and a pair of jeans I'd bought in Austin before I went walkabout. I called John and we went downstairs for breakfast.

Nothing could have prepared me for what awaited us as the elevator doors opened. A thousand flashes went off, blinding us, and a roar of deafening voices rolled toward us.

John grabbed my shoulder and pulled me back. "What should we do?"

I pressed a button and the doors closed. "We'll go back upstairs and call room service."

He drew a shaky breath. "Maybe it's time to hire some security."

I expected Zee to break down after he came back from Romania, after seeing Kyros for the last time, but he didn't. When he returned to his bedroom, his solemn face belied his inner turmoil.

He came to stand behind me at the piano. "You were with me, weren't you? I heard you playing. It made it not quite as horrible." His hands rested on my shoulders and I could feel the tension in him. "You saw what we did?"

Still playing, I nodded. "You blew up his castle. Was he inside?"

"Yes, and a lot of his Skia. They'll be back, but not for a few weeks. It takes a while to reanimate."

"So no one needs to worry about Eryx for a while."

"Right. It makes me less anxious about you still being out there."

It was very strange to think of the world as 'out there', or 'real', but at some point, I'd crossed over to this realm and now everything else was different. I no longer fit in that world.

He squeezed my shoulders. "Are you ready to do this?"

I lifted my fingers from the keys, turned on the bench and stood. "I'm ready."

He took my hand and we popped away from his suite and into a dark, cold room in the basement of the mansion with stone walls and many wooden shelves, all large enough for a human body. At the moment, there was only one. He dropped my hand and slipped his arms beneath her, then said, "Hold on to me."

Wrapping my fingers around his bicep, I asked, "What if there's someone in her room?"

"I have us under a cloak, so we're invisible to humans. If someone is there, we'll wait until they leave and I'll have to put her somewhere else in the house, where no one would have looked since last night. Be careful moving around because even though you're invisible, you still have mass and can make noise if you bump into something."

After I nodded my understanding, he closed his eyes and all was dark. When I could see again, we were in Jordan's bedroom in the White House. Zee laid her doppelganger on the bed, then arranged the covers and her hair and her body to look natural, as if she'd simply slipped into death while she was asleep.

He came back to me. "Does she look okay?"

"Yes." She was so beautiful. Jordan had that kind of face one could stare at for hours in complete wonder and awe. I realized I might never meet her, never know her. I looked up into Zee's eyes and knew he was thinking the same thing. He said tightly, "Some days, I really hate everything."

"I know, love." I looked again at Jordan's body double just as the bedroom door opened and an older, mannish woman stepped inside the room. She smiled as she came to the bed. "Upsy daisy, young lady! I let you sleep in, but it's time to rise and shine and . . ." She came to a halt next to the bed, bent and touched the doppelganger's cold face, and instantly began to cry. "*Dear, sweet Jesus.*" Turning, she hurried out.

"Let's go," Zee said, reaching for my hand.

"Wait."

"Why? He's going to be terribly upset. I don't want to see it."

I dropped his hand. "I understand. Go home and I'll be there in just a minute."

"Why would you want to see the man's heart break? He's got so many troubles, and he lost his wife, and now Jordan.

The man will likely fall to pieces. He deserves his privacy, Euri."

"I want to know for Jordan. It's my way of honoring her." I didn't say that I was extremely optimistic that she might return, with Kyros redeemed. There was a better than good chance that she wouldn't, and I didn't want to get his hopes up, but I remained encouraged, and I knew she would want to know every detail about her father. I looked up into Zee's worried eyes. "It's okay. I know how to get back."

He let out a deep breath and took my hand again. "If you're staying, I'm staying."

A few moments later, I almost wished I hadn't felt compelled to stay. President Ellis came into Jordan's room, lifted her body from the bed and sobbed. The mannish woman stood in the doorway and cried. Within a few minutes, the room was filled with other White House staff, all of them crying. I wondered if Jordan, wherever she was, knew how very much she was loved. All of these people, particularly her father, were devastated by her passing.

I couldn't help thinking of my own father. How would he react when I 'died' in a few weeks? I didn't doubt he'd be sad and upset. For all that he was a serious, undemonstrative man, he loved me. I loved him. But he would move on, and hopefully find happiness with Mrs. Carlisle, the widow he would marry in the spring. A new beginning for my dad.

There was an attractive woman who hovered near the fireplace whose eyes I couldn't see very well. I squinted and realized her eyes were shaded, as if a small cloud floated just in front of them. A lost soul.

I started toward her, but Zee grasped my arm and jerked me back. "No, Euri. Leave it."

"But she's—"

"Remember, we can't take them out until we have an exit strategy for them and a doppelganger. She's only one of several who're on the White House staff and in the president's cabinet. Phoenix had an elaborate takedown planned for next week, at Jordan's birthday party, but that's obviously off now. Instead, we'll have to plan a takedown at her funeral."

It took a hefty dose of willpower not to take off after the

woman. I was a bit confused and very disturbed by my anger at her, my dislike and aversion to her very existence. I had never felt this way before and I didn't like it. But it appeared I was unable to alter the feeling. I didn't even know the woman's name and I despised her. I felt a violence in me I'd never known before.

Determined to get past it, I refocused on Jordan's father. "Losing so many at the same moment he's burying his daughter will make it that much harder for President Ellis."

"It can't be helped. There are enough of them that it's best to do a group takedown, so Phoenix will come up with something." His hand tightened around mine. "There's also a Skia on staff, and if he comes in, he'll see us. They're immortal and can see past our cloak. We should go now."

I agreed and we popped back to his room.

After he went to tell Jax it was done, Zee sat at his piano and played while I lay on the bed and listened.

In the middle of a Beatles song, I said, "Let's go to Cologne and visit the cathedral. You can go inside now. Maybe being there would make you feel a little better."

He never missed a note. "I want to, but not right now. Something's coming."

"Good or bad?"

"Too soon to tell. Let's just sit tight for a while."

An hour passed. Then half of another.

I was about to suggest we get something to eat when I heard Sasha shouting, "They're here! Oh my God, Key and Jordan! *They're back!* They're in her room!"

I heard the thunder of many footsteps in the hall, on the stairway. Zee turned to me and the smile on his face was beautiful. He hauled me to my feet and crushed me in an embrace. With my face scrunched against his shoulder, I said, "Go see them."

"I'll be right back." He released me and rushed for the door. When he opened it, I heard the excited voices and happy crying of the Purgatories and Luminas and the Mephisto.

It was a joyful, exuberant moment, and I wished that I were a part of it. I suppose I was, in a weird way. It was a bit perverse that I knew all of them and they did not know me.

I lay down again and, possibly because I hadn't slept well the night before, I drifted off. When I awoke, it was dark and Zee was sitting on one of the fireplace chairs, staring at the ashes in the grate. I sat up and rubbed my eyes. A glance at the clock told me I'd been asleep almost three hours. "I've missed rehearsal."

"I called John and told him you're unwell, that you won't be at tonight's performance."

Despite my laissez faire personality, there are certain things I find intolerable. One of them is being dictated to, or managed. "You could have asked."

"Yeah, I could have, but you were asleep."

"I was asleep, not dead." I swung my legs over and got to my feet. "I'm going to San Francisco."

"No, you're not. You don't know where it is. You'll get lost."

I headed for the door. "I'll ask Sasha to take me."

"She'll take you to San Jose, or San Antonio."

"I'll ask Jax." I was almost to the door.

"No one will take you."

Hearing something in his voice, I slowed. "Why?"

"They're all too upset."

I turned. "What's happened?"

He was still staring at the ashes. "Turns out, Mariah is immortal and she transported to Erinýes so she could see Jordan one last time before we rescued her and Key took her away."

I walked back toward him. "Was she blown up with the castle?"

"No." He rubbed his forehead. "Jordan tricked her and she went to Hell on Earth. She can't leave. She's there until Lucifer goes to get her." He looked up at me and, even in the dark, I could see the horror in his eyes. "Phoenix followed, to be with her until they're rescued. M went immediately to Lucifer, but he's so angry, he said he wasn't sure how long he'd leave them there. No one is to go there, but it hasn't ever been an issue because no one in their right mind would ever want to. When Mariah died, Mary Michael took her there to show her what Eryx does to people, hoping to convince her to be resurrected and stay with us. Because Mary Michael is an angel, she doesn't have the same rules we do. "

"How did Mariah die?"

"Denys took her to a pub in London where he got drunk and passed out on a sofa in the manager's office with one of the barmaids. With no one to protect her, Eryx abducted Mariah and killed her."

Quiet, gentle Mariah. She'd had a horrible life, terribly abused, and it was a travesty of cruelty that this had happened to her. "Eryx brought her back? I don't understand. I thought he wanted all the Anabo to be dead, except Jordan."

"He was so obsessed with Jordan, so certain she would be with him, he thought it would make her feel more settled to stay with him if she had her sister with her. He didn't realize when he kissed her and made her believe he could change that Jordan would become just like him, her soul obliterated of any light at all. Jordan didn't care about Mariah, so they plotted to get rid of her, to ensure she never came back to the Mephisto, and that's how she ended up in the worst place on this planet. I can't even begin to imagine how terrified she must be. Of any of us, she's the most . . . it would be the most . . . shit, Euri, it's the worst thing. The worst fucking thing."

"But Jordan is back. Is she . . ."

"God gave her a second chance and returned her to Anabo. She's how she was before, and Key's eyes are grey. Swear to God, he almost glows. It's like you can see divinity in his smile." He looked down at his hands, gripping his thighs as if he were trying to contain himself. "Then Phoenix started looking for Mariah and that's when Jordan remembered where she is. She's in hysterics. Made herself sick from crying so hard."

"She shouldn't blame herself. She was another person for a while."

"Guilt isn't always justified."

I honestly didn't know what to say. I busied myself with the fireplace, moved the screen and scooped the ashes into the ashbin, then laid fresh logs from the small stand close by, and stood back and imagined they were lit. When the logs were aflame, I took the other chair and sat down.

"Thank you," he murmured.

"You're welcome."

"I don't want to be alone, Euri."

"I understand."

"You're not still cross, are you?"

"No." I looked at him. "Maybe you and your brothers should visit Lucifer and ask him to go for them now. If he knew what Mariah's life has been, surely he wouldn't leave her there any longer."

"Oh, he knows. Lucifer knows everything about everyone. But he's always been rigid about rules. We planned to ask anyway, but M said no, that it'd just make him more angry, and he might leave them there even longer. All we can do is wait."

CHAPTER 11

The wait dragged on for another entire day, and when Phoenix and Mariah were finally delivered back to Mephisto Mountain over thirty-six hours after the nightmare began, she had gone walkabout in her mind. Her eyes were open but she saw nothing, knew no one. I couldn't begin to imagine the horrors of Hell on Earth. The Skia could never die, and with nothing to eat, they must be living skeletons. And they'd be enraged at their captivity in a pit many miles beneath the surface of the earth. I had no doubt they attacked and tortured Mariah and Phoenix.

As soon as they returned, after Zee and the others had barely had a look at Mariah, Phoenix took her into her bedroom on the third floor, closed the door and wouldn't allow anyone inside. Not even Mathilda, who stood in the hallway and cried and wrung her apron. Phoenix went to the kitchen and carried meals back to her room.

After four days of this, Key demanded Phoenix allow him to see her. When Key openly cried because Phoenix still refused to let Jordan see Mariah, Phoenix finally relented. After that, everyone went to visit, and when Phoenix decided they'd been there long enough, he made them leave. If they didn't go right away, he picked them up and carried them to the hallway and slammed the door in their face. He insisted that no one cry or say anything negative while in her room. Zee said he was quiet and soft and gentle when he was with her, but outside of Mariah's room, he became a tyrant, shouting and demanding and cursing everyone on Mephisto Mountain. He got in daily brawls with his brothers, particularly Zee, who invariably pointed out what a tool he was being, and that if Mariah was actually present, she'd hate what he had become. It was a horrible time.

I spent non-travel days with the band in rehearsals, and as we made our way back across the United States, despite all the trauma in the Mephisto house, I grew more anxious to be done with Arcadia and start my new life with Zee. I slowly decamped from the band, until everything I had brought to America was in Zee's spacious cupboard. Mathilda was kind enough to do my laundry, and never mentioned it to anyone. I still took a room in every city where the band stopped, because it wasn't possible to explain where I stayed. I think John assumed Zee stayed with me, but he never mentioned it.

With all the screaming female fans' attention, with groupies vying for a chance to shag him every night, John quickly fell out of love with me, just as I'd known he would. He'd never truly felt anything close to love for me. It was all about how we looked together. He liked who I was and what I brought to the band, something no other band could claim. That I was a concert pianist who could play any piece of music ever written was at the bottom of the list of my desirable qualities.

I was always okay with John's somewhat paternalistic, even overbearing ways. All I cared about was the music, and I generally went along with whatever he wanted. Except sleeping with him. Or kissing him. Or allowing him to hint to fans or the media that there was something between us besides friendship. I told him after a gig one night, "The next time you insinuate we're hooked up, I will call the editor of the *London Sun*, who's a family friend, and tell him you have no pecker." His eyes widened. "I'll say you lost it in an accident. You'll never get laid again as long as you live. Leave off, John. Let's be the friends we've always been, shall we?"

He laughed, but he agreed.

Zee came to every concert and delivered me to every rehearsal, then returned to collect me when we were done. Pretending we were normal began to grate on me, and I was ready to be done with the real world and the constant façade I lived behind.

Two weeks after Phoenix and Mariah returned, I was

eating a late supper with Zee in his room, unwinding after a particularly difficult concert in Chicago. We'd been rushed by the crowd and Pogo lost his shit and punched a bloke and the coppers came and it was bloody hell to keep them from arresting him. John was certain there would be a lawsuit. Pogo said John should sue the security firm he'd hired. That the audience was able to rush the stage at all was unacceptable. I thought it extremely strange that people who professed to love the band would harm us. As if this would make them somehow closer to us. I didn't understand fans, or what drove them to the lengths they took. We were strangers to them, yet they believed we were friends, that they knew us very well, when in reality, all they knew was what we chose to show them, and most of it was a lie.

I would not be the least tiny bit sad to walk away from Arcadia. It had become something besides the music. Some of the others in the band were becoming aggravated with John, resentful that he spent less and less time talking about Arcadia and more time talking about himself, how his career was skyrocketing, as if everyone else was there for his benefit, to prop him up and make him look good.

Yes, I was definitely ready to walk away.

I made myself stop thinking about it while I finished my sandwich, drank half of Zee's milk and ate all of his cookies. Then I sat back in the chair and sighed. "I am certain Phoenix has forgotten I exist, so he wouldn't have told anyone about me."

"Truth."

"I think the time has come that you should tell them."

"They already know."

"What?" I sat up and leaned over the armrest to look at him. He wasn't wearing a shirt. Just his ratty gym pants. I made myself concentrate on his face, but my attention kept straying to his chest. His arms. His thighs beneath the faded blue fabric. The lovely bulge in his gym pants, which could make me . . . "When did you tell them? Why didn't you tell me?"

He knew I was looking. He kindly pretended not to notice. "I told Key before Jordan's dance. He told everyone else."

"Do they know I come here to be with you and sleep with you every night?"

Avoiding my eyes, he concentrated entirely too carefully on the strawberries Hans had sent up. I grew tense, waiting to hear what he would say.

"They think you're traveling with Arcadia, that I'm not planning to approach you until after the last concert. They think we've only ever met the one time, when Phoenix and I came to Fawkes."

"I see." I looked at the fire. Sasha had kept her promise. "No, actually, I don't see. Why are you still keeping me a secret?"

He stood and went to the piano and began to play. I remained on my chair and waited.

He was done with my favorite Brahms piece and halfway into 'Clocks' before he finally said, "I don't want to share you. I know it's absurd and childish, but I've been all alone for so long, Euri. I wanted these few weeks to be just you and me, and I wanted you to live what bits of life on the outside are left to you. I want you to talk to your dad, and do anything else you're inclined to do before you're dead to the world and can't. Call your cousin. Go see Miles's dad. Send a letter to the queen. Whatever. Once my brothers and Sasha and Jordan know you're immortal, that you already know so much, they may demand that you leave the real world immediately. At a minimum, they'll want you to begin training. They'll expect things of you, and I don't want that. Not yet."

They would lay claim to me in a way he wouldn't like. He was possessive of me, which didn't bother me, but it was bound to be a problem going forward. "What happens after the last concert? Have you asked M for a doppelganger?"

"Not yet." Now he was playing something I didn't recognize. Something he'd written. It was, unsurprisingly, dark and sad. "I thought you and I would discuss it, later, and decide how best to do it. As for after the concert, you'll go back to your hotel and I'll come for you."

"And I'll die in my room?"

"Maybe. Or perhaps you'll drown while swimming in the hotel pool. Let's think about it later. For now, I want to just be with you."

Mentally, emotionally, and physically exhausted, I leaned my head back and dozed a bit, then jerked awake from an erotic dream. It made me a trifle needy, made me think of things that couldn't happen. Zee and I had been practically platonic since all the trouble began, because it seemed crass and unfeeling to enjoy something as intimate and indulgent as sex when others in the family were suffering. He'd told me that Key had yet to mark Jordan. When I saw them through Zee's eyes while I played during rehearsals, I could almost feel the sexual tension. They wanted it badly, but as long as Jordan's sister was lost in her own mind, I knew Jordan and Kyros wouldn't be hitting the sheets.

And for the foreseeable future, it appeared Zee and I would remain likewise celibate.

Or so I thought.

When we went to bed, he stayed on his side and I on mine, just as we did every night. We always woke up wrapped up in each other, but we began the night without touching. He never said it aloud, but I knew we were still far too new and raw in our relationship to withstand touching and nothing else. Zee was a carnal male and I was quickly beginning to believe I was an utter failure at my birthright of reserved British. What I was unable to do in reality I had great fun imagining in my mind.

I lay there and listened to the wind at the windows, harkening a blizzard that had been forecast for over a week. The Mephisto house was high in the Rockies, in deep wilderness, hidden by Lucifer's magic from humanity and Eryx and anyone who was not Mephisto, Lumina or Purgatory. This didn't alter its presence in the atmosphere of the planet, and weather affected the buildings and residents of Mephisto Mountain as surely as it did anywhere on Earth. I was unused to so much snow, and was fascinated by it. Zee had promised we would go out in it when I was here permanently, when Mariah was better.

I hoped she would be better. I secretly worried she would check out, that what had happened to her was too grievous to overcome. Zee told me that because Mariah had been sexually abused, she was afraid of all men, except Phoenix. Two days ago, Phoenix had broken down and told Key she was raped repeatedly in Hell on Earth, that by the time he arrived, she was already gone away to another place in her head. Phoenix was eaten up with grief, and it was not at all surprising to anyone that he was unable to control his temper, that he flew into furious rages and broke things and shouted at people. I think everyone on Mephisto Mountain believed that unless God or Lucifer erased her memory of her time in Hell on Earth, she would likely never regain consciousness. Some things are simply too horrific to be borne.

Listening as the wind grew stronger, I said a prayer for Mariah, and Phoenix, and finally, I drifted off to sleep.

When I awoke, I don't know how much later, Zee was kissing my neck. I'd been having a colorful dream, so waking to his lovely mouth on me didn't seem odd in the least. "Are you asleep?" I whispered.

He didn't answer. His big hands moved across my body with firm certainty, sliding my camisole off, massaging my breasts, running his fingers beneath the edges of my knickers, then tearing the seams when they took too long to remove. His warm fingers stroked and tweaked my sex, and he murmured unintelligible words of encouragement, as if he wanted me to climax immediately.

I tugged his arm so he would come closer. He never said a word. He stretched above me and kissed me slowly, sliding his tongue against mine with languid sensuality, his stiff erection filling me with the familiarity of many times, despite our newness to one another.

He was asleep. I knew it. Instead of killing me in his sleep, now he made love to me. I would much prefer him to be awake, but in light of our self-imposed celibacy, I understood why this was happening, and the bloody truth was, I wanted this far more than I could have dreamed even a week ago. There was an element of intimate knowledge about how we came together that transcended thought or emotion. It felt as though we became one being, our minds melding into a single line of exquisite lust.

Then things got a bit dodgy, and I kept reminding myself that he was asleep, that he didn't know what he was doing, that this was him unconsciously acting out his fantasies. I suppose I could have woken him. I could have left the bed and gone in the bathroom and waited for him to settle back down into a hard sleep. But I didn't do any of that. I confess to a wicked curiosity to see where his fantasies would take him. Where they'd take *me.*

He slipped from the bed and went in the dark into the bathroom, into his cupboard. I heard him opening and closing drawers and when he returned to bed, he had a long string of my pearls and two of his black silk bowties.

I was torn between alarm and hypnotic fascination. What I knew of sex beyond the basic fundamentals could scarce fill a teaspoon. I couldn't imagine what he intended to do. If he were awake, I would ask. That he was doing all of this within his dream world, within his subconscious, added an element of surrealism to it all. I willed the candles on the mantel to light and his looming figure was cast into relief against the soft glow. My belly shivered and my entire body was covered in goosebumps.

Back on the bed, he tugged me to a sit, then moved to settle behind me until my bum was nestled in the V of his long legs. I could feel his erection pressing against my spine, hard and hot. I rested my hands on his muscled thighs and waited to see what he would do. I hadn't noticed a hairbrush, but he must have brought one because now he was slowly brushing my hair, from the crown all the way to the ends. I heard his breathing escalate. I realized my hair, long as it was, covered his very hard penis and with every stroke of the brush, it swept across the sensitive skin, bringing him further along the road to pleasure.

I'd long loved having my hair brushed, so I sat still and enjoyed. After a while, he gathered up my hair and tied it back with his bowtie. I hadn't seen it going that way. I'd imagined he would tie me up, or some such. Then he slipped the other bowtie across my eyes and tied it behind my head. I let it happen. He drew me backward, into him, and while one hand gently moved across my breasts, squeezing and smoothing and cupping, his other hand dropped between my legs and his quick, clever fingers brought me ever closer to orgasm. He'd stop just as I balanced at the edge and whisper in my ear, "Not yet, angel." My breath became labored and he chuckled against my neck. "You want it bad, don't you?"

I didn't answer. I was afraid I'd wake him up and he'd stop.

I thought I was close, but I was wrong. I discovered this only a few minutes later, after he gently but firmly laid me on my stomach and hitched up my hips. I was certain I looked ridiculous, my arse waving about in the air like that, but Zee didn't concur. He murmured a great lot of wicked things, including how badly he wanted to fuck me. "I'll never tire of this," he said softly while he dragged the pearls across my buttocks, then around my waist, and finally, through the cleft of my sex.

I cried out, shaking with the effort it took not to climax. Not yet. I wanted him inside of me when I went off.

"For all eternity, Euri, the millionth time with you will be as amazing as the first. God, I love you." He moved on top of me and while he continued pulling the pearls, he pushed into me with a deep, guttural exclamation of satisfaction.

In my darkness, with one of my senses handicapped, the others became sharper, making everything more intensely sensual. His smell, his heat, his touch, his erotically charged words of love, his large body covering mine while the length of him moved in and out of me with languid purpose in every thrust. I couldn't quite figure out how he managed to move the pearls without interfering with our coupling, but it wasn't more than a flash of curiosity. I didn't really care *how* he was making this happen, only that he didn't stop. He took me to the edge over and over, and just as I was about to come, he would stop and kiss my neck with an open mouth, most likely leaving a mark, after which he would murmur, "Not yet, love. You've been a very naughty girl, trying to come before I say you will."

I risked speaking, because I was certain if he woke up, he wouldn't stop. Not now. "Please, Xenos, you've got to let me. I'm so close, and this hurts."

"What hurts?" He nuzzled my neck, kissed my cheek, made me turn my head so he could kiss me full on the mouth. "I will never hurt you. Never. Tell me what hurts."

"I can't stand it."

"Ah, but you can last as long as me, can't you?"

"No," I whispered into the sheets.

The pearls were suddenly tossed aside – I knew because I heard them skitter across the rug to the wood floor – and he plunged into me harder and rougher, over and over, until I lost all control and began to shake and quiver and moan as wave upon wave of bliss swept over me. I couldn't get enough of him, and I pushed back against his groin, greedily taking all of him inside. I clawed at the bowtie to uncover my eyes and turned my head just in time to see him climax. He was staring right at me, and his big body went stiff and still and I felt him jerk and move within me. When it was over, we were both breathing as hard as if we'd just run several times around the mountain. As one, we splayed across the bed on our backs and stared at each other in the warm candle glow.

I whispered, "You're awake, aren't you? You've been awake the whole time."

He swallowed and grasped my hand. "Guilty. I thought I'd go mad, wanting you."

"I hate to break it to you, but you are already quite mad."

"It's worse when I am so needy and you're right here and I can smell you and see your big eyes watching every move I make."

"Am I so obvious, then?"

"You're incapable of anything else, Euri." He sighed. "I feel rotten about this, though. It was marvelous. The best sex I've ever had. *Ever*. But it shouldn't have happened. Phoenix is in a living hell, and it's not right for us to be this sublimely happy."

"I can pretend to be miserable if it will make you feel better."

He smiled at me. "Nah, you're a terrible liar. I'd never believe you're miserable."

I rolled toward him and he gathered me close. I was in the nook. I loved the nook. I never wanted to leave. "Since when are you so adventuresome?"

"Since I saw what you imagined in your own sweet head."

"I never . . . oh, well, yes, I suppose I did imagine what it would be like to have something, um, some object other than . . . I don't remember pearls."

"Ah, right. That must have been my own overactive

imagination from when you unpacked those beauties and held them up to show me. You said they belonged to the queen and she gifted them to you on your sixteenth birthday. I suppose my dark side ran away with the notion of sexualizing pristine monarchy pearls. It was wrong of me. I will not apologize."

"They were Queen Victoria's, and are quite valuable."

"Now they are yours and have been intimate with your very lovely lady parts, which means they are priceless. I may start carrying them in my pocket."

I laughed and he held me tighter and after a little while, we went back to sleep.

~~ ZEE ~~

A knock on my door woke me. I heard the wind howling at the window, heard Euri's soft exclamation of displeasure when I drew away from her and left our snug little cocoon in the middle of the bed, heard my heart beat faster when I realized it wasn't Mathilda at my door, but Key. I had a rare moment of gratitude for my ability to know things.

I went to the door, opened it a crack so he could see I was naked and hopefully not ask to come in, and sleepily asked what he wanted.

He held up his phone. "It's all over the Internet."

"You woke me up before the fucking chickens to tell me about something on the Internet? Seriously, Kyros? You gotta get a life, man." He needed to get laid, but I didn't say that. I was blunt, not cruel.

"Your Anabo was involved in an altercation during an Arcadia concert last night."

"I'm aware. I was there."

"She could have been killed."

"But she wasn't."

He bent his head and swiped the screen, then held it up to show me. "This is a fifteen year old girl in Minsk."

I leaned on the door and squinted at the screen. "Yeah, so?"

"Look at her torso. She has the sign of the Anabo."

I stood straight and looked more closely at his phone. "I can find her."

"No need. She has the sign, but she's not Anabo." He swiped the screen and held up the phone again. "This one is seventeen. She lives in Bulgaria." He swiped again. "Here's one in Manila. And here's the entire cheer squad at Gopher Pass High School in Kentucky."

I was still half asleep. "I don't get it. Cut to the chase, bro."

"They're tattoos, Zee. These girls and hundreds, maybe thousands, have gotten tattoos beneath their right breasts. They got the idea after seeing your Euri's photograph. She was on a boat in a bikini with some upper crust Brits in St. Tropez, and the picture has gone viral. Everyone assumes it's a tat, and now it's a big deal to get a Lady Euri tat."

I was waking up rather quickly now, alert enough to get why this was a catastrophe in the making. "Eryx will be back soon."

"Yes, and he will know exactly where to find Euri, won't he? Do you have the smallest notion of how pissed off he's going to be when he comes back? He'll be infinity enraged not only because we blew him up, but we wiped out Erinýes, took all of his work. And worst of all, we reclaimed Jordan. He will be all about revenge, Zee. Your Anabo is at great, terrible risk. I'm calling a war room meeting and we'll vote on whether to allow you to wait. I don't actually know why you would want to."

I had to admit defeat. With the world's population of teenage girls getting Anabo tats, I didn't have much of a choice. It was only six days until the Blackbriar concert, but it was a week I'd wanted us to have, just the two of us. I hated to share her with them. Nevertheless, I stepped back, opened the door a slight bit more, and let him see Euri, who looked exceptionally lovely beneath the covers, her golden hair across my pillow. She was smiling in her sleep. As she did. I noticed she had marks on her neck. Mine. And that made *me* smile.

"I'll be damned," Key whispered. He continued staring at her while he asked, "When did this happen?"

"It's a long story."

"I've got time."

"I'll get dressed and meet you in the library."

Jax appeared out of the gloom of the hallway, wearing

boxers, his hair sticking up at odd angles. "What's happening?" He peered into my room and grinned. "So now Kyros knows."

"Wait, *what?*" I was shocked. "Are you saying *you* knew?"

He nodded as he yawned. "Sasha busted in on Euri a few weeks ago, and she swore her to secrecy, but Sasha and I have no secrets."

"You knew and didn't tell me?" Key looked like he'd blow a gasket.

"I didn't see why you needed to know before Zee was ready for you to know. And Sasha made me promise not to tell. No offense, Key, but I don't sleep with you, so she wins."

Key was obviously stunned. Then he was mad. "I will see both of you in the library and we'll get to the bottom of this." He glanced at Euri again and his face softened. "She's exactly like Jane."

"Not exactly," I said. "She's crazy."

"For you?"

"That, too, but I meant it literally. She's completely wack."

"How are you sleeping with her without marking her?"

"Same way you're sleeping with Jordan."

An expression of pain crossed his features and he ran a hand through his long hair. "She cries all the time. I don't know how much longer I can take it. If Mariah would show any sign of change . . ." He looked at me, then at Euri. "*She's* not crying. She's got love bites on her neck. She looks blissfully happy, and I know what an animal you are, so what gives? Are you having sex with her, or not?"

I would have loved to tell my brother it was none of his fucking business, but in truth, it *was* his business. And every other Mephisto's business. The Mephisto mark was crucial, and since Euri was unable to have one, we'd have to figure out a workaround. "Yes, but she can't be marked."

"Why?"

Jax leaned close and whispered, "She has no womb."

I glared at him. "How the fuck do you know?"

He shrugged. "Logical deduction, which you've just verified. So what happened? Cancer? Did she have to have it removed because she had cancer?"

"No, her mother thought she shouldn't be able to procreate because she's mentally unbalanced."

"Good *God.*" Key looked thunderstruck. "Isn't her mother dead?"

"Look, I'll tell you the whole long story if you'll get out of my doorway. I don't want to wake her up. She needs rest. It's hard for her, being in the real world."

They both left, and ten minutes later, when I popped down to the library, Key was already there, wearing a long dark velvet robe, pacing back and forth in front of the fireplace, which Deacon had just finished lighting. The candles around the room were lit, lending a warm glow to the spines of all the books. I liked the library, but didn't spend much time there. I spent most of my downtime in the music room.

Deacon returned with a tray that held a silver coffee pot and china cups, which he set on one of the library tables. I poured myself a cup, dropped in some sugar, stirred, and took a seat on one of the leather wingbacks in front of the fireplace. I was still trying to wake up.

As soon as Jax arrived, Key looked hard at me. "Talk now."

I did. I talked through another cup of coffee and right up until the grandfather clock struck the half hour after six. They both listened and nobody said anything until I was done.

Actually, nobody said anything for several minutes after. The first twilight of dawn lit the sky through the wide library windows and Jax smiled at me. "I've only just realized that your eyes are gray. You love her, don't you?"

"So what if I do?"

"It means you're invincible because now there's no way Eryx can take you out."

Key was pacing again, his robe swirling around his ankles as he walked. "I can't get past M making her immortal. He did it almost two years ago, even before we found Sasha."

I hadn't told them about the other Anabo. M told me it was my secret to keep and I'd never mention it. He had a good reason. If the others knew, they'd spend all their time searching, instead of working to inhibit Eryx. That was our function, our purpose for being, and finding Anabo was secondary.

Except that it wasn't. For me, finding Euri meant everything.

"Can you really read her mind?" Jax asked.

"Not really. Not when we're together. When we're apart, especially when either of us are making music, I can see what she sees, be in her enough to know what's happening to her. If she speaks, I hear her, and same with her. We talk on the phone a lot. It's easier."

"Does she channel anyone else?"

"She shared this with her sister before she died."

"So M or Lucifer or maybe even God made her mind connect to yours after the sister died," Key said. "I wonder why?"

Jax leaned back in his chair and gazed up at the portrait above the fireplace. "If she was never found, she had no reason to be immortal. M had to make a snap decision when her fucked up mother drove her into a lake and drowned her and once he decided to bring her back, he probably thought they needed to be connected to make sure her immortality wasn't for nothing."

"What if she hated Zee? What if what we do was such a turn off for her, she absolutely didn't want to be here?"

"M told her she could be taken out anytime she wants," I said. "She has to go to holy ground and ask God, then off herself. Evidently, they all have this exit strategy."

They both stared at me as if I'd just told them we had one minute to live.

I shrugged. "She seemed pretty sure about it, but ask M if you want."

They looked at each other, then Key poured himself another cup of coffee, which he carried back and forth between the long, leather sofa and the picture of Tolstoy that hung toward the far west end of the library. "Every Anabo we've found has been accidental, but with Euri, you were bound to know she's Anabo. You go to so many concerts, there was always a good chance you'd see her in person and know. So why would M connect the two of you after he brought her back?"

I wished I didn't have to go into it, but maybe it was best

to say it now, get it over with, so I'd never have to talk about it again. Maybe it'd be better for Phoenix if they knew the truth. Maybe they'd understand his motivations a little better.

I drained the last of my coffee, which wasn't helping me stay awake. Stress and sex made me tired and all I wanted to do was go back to bed, to hold Euri and slip into deep sleep. "Jane was meant for me." I held up my hand before they could ask their questions and quickly, succinctly explained what happened. "M was afraid I'd do the same with Euri, that I'd not claim her if I found her all on my own. I am certain he did something to connect us so I'd be drawn in and completely unable to resist her." I shrugged. "It doesn't matter how or why, does it? She's mine now, and I intend to ask M for an end run around the inability to mark her. It's especially crucial for Euri. She's gone walkabout before and I had no idea where she was. More than any of us, she needs a mark so we can find her if she pops off into la-la land again."

"Does she know she's crazy?"

I looked at Jax and smiled. "She does, but she doesn't know just how off she really is."

"What do you mean?"

"She loves me. That makes her certifiable." I set down the cup and popped back to my room, where I intended to climb into bed with Euri, who would be snuggled in, warm and soft and inviting.

Except that she wasn't.

Instead, I found her out of the covers, clutching my pillow, her head rolling from side to side and her expression one of tense fear. She was in the midst of a nightmare.

I moved to her side of the bed and bent low, gently shaking her shoulder. "Euri, wake up. *Now*, Euri. Wake up *now*."

Her eyes opened wide and she was instantly aware of me standing over her. She drew a deep breath, her face crumpled and she launched herself into my arms, crying and shaky, trying to tell me something, but she was crying too hard. I lay her down and stretched out beside her, covering us up, gathering her close, petting her hair, hoping to calm her. "It's all okay. I'm right here and nothing will hurt you. It was just a dream. Relax. Shh, there now."

I continued to murmur words of comfort, and when she finally stopped crying, she whispered, "He's so dark, Zee. So unbearably dark."

"Who, Euri? Who did you dream of?" Instead of answering, she began to shake, and I knew she was about to go off again. "Stay right here." I got out of bed and popped to the billiard room and poured a crystal highball almost to the brim with Key's favorite whiskey. I popped back and sat next to her on the bed. "Sit up and drink this."

She pushed herself up, scraped her hair away from her face and blinked at me. "What is it?"

"Single malt scotch. Finest kind. Drink up."

She took the glass and sipped. "This is delicious. It's warm and I'm so bloody cold. It was freezing in my dream. I've never been that cold, like from the inside, out, like death."

"Well, you kicked off the covers and you're naked as the day you were born and there's currently a blizzard blowing outside and this house was built at the turn of the last century. We had central heat put in, but it's still fucking cold." I went to build a fire and when I was done, I turned to see her sitting cross-legged in the center of the bed, dutifully sipping the whiskey. As I moved to sit next to her, she offered the glass to me and after a small drink, I handed it back. "Drink more."

"Bloody hell. You're trying to make me drunk."

"Yes."

The glass slowly emptied and I could see the tension and anxiety gradually leave her body. She handed me the empty glass, then politely burped behind her hand. "My apologies," she murmured, her eyes a bit glassy.

"Let's get back in bed and maybe after you sleep some more, you'll feel better." And I would find out what she had dreamed. It was strange in the extreme for her to have a nightmare. Her mind didn't imagine bad things. I was far more concerned about her than I let on, hopeful that she would regain her equilibrium after she'd slept a while without the nightmare.

But she didn't want to go back to sleep. Even after downing enough whiskey to make a grown man shit-housed, she was still in the grip of whatever had taken over her mind. She twisted the edge of the sheet in her hands and rambled on about it, almost like a stream of consciousness. "I was in Azbekastan, walking down a street, watching men march past in uniform, goose-stepping like the Nazis did. I walked toward an enormous, ornate palace. Inside, it was beautiful, baroque, and very old. I thought of all the kings who'd lived there and it made me all the more angry because they'd been lauded simply because of their birth, because they were firstborn sons. My life was ruined because I was the firstborn son."

Aw, *Christ.* She dreamed of Eryx. It seemed that, in her dream, she *was* Eryx. No wonder she was so upset. I sat there and listened to her with ever increasing dread and horror.

"I found Kovalev in a bathtub, a big golden one with bubbles. He stood and extended his hand and I despised him. I didn't shake his hand. The idiot was standing there, naked, covered in bubbles, and he expected me to shake his hand. I regretted making him immortal. I told him he had a month to finish his job, or he would be sent to convert the assholes in fucking Iran. What the hell was he doing taking a goddamn bubble bath? He said he thought I was dead, which infuriated me. I get so fed up with these imbeciles. He looked afraid, which was his first smart move since I'd returned. The twisted psycho is a sociopath, a serial killer with absolute power. I am certain he gets off on death. The disgusting excuse for a man has had his soldiers killing small children, even babies for fuck's sake. I told him there will be no more killings of anyone whose soul doesn't belong to me. I left and went to my rooms, where I found a girl in my bed. She'd been sent there by my secretary, Mr. Beedle. He knew what I liked, petite and brunette, and he sent this girl for me. But I did not want sex. I didn't want anything but an end to this burning in my belly, this overpowering rage."

Mr. Beedle was a thin, proper Englishman Eryx had conscripted and made Skia in the early part of the nineteenth century. He'd been an under butler for the prince regent and took on much the same role for Eryx. At no time would I ever have mentioned Mr. Beedle, or given him a thought. Yet Euri knew his name, and his duties to Eryx. My skin fairly crawled because I was horribly afraid that this wasn't her imagination. Somehow, incredibly, she'd managed to channel Eryx's thoughts while she was asleep.

Twisting the sheets ever more, she began to shake again and her eyes grew wild. "I had a plan and as soon as I rested, I'd begin. I decided I'd follow the bastards everywhere. They'll wonder what I'm up to, but they'll never know, never guess. I hate them, most especially Kyros. The rat bastard couldn't let me win, not even once. She was mine. She was supposed to be here, with me right now, but instead she's in bed with my fucking brother. He'll pay for stealing her. They'll all pay for what they've done to me. I was so angry, I began to break things. I smashed priceless artifacts and art objects, an ormolu clock, a goddamn swan, a figure of a girl in a long dress holding a fucking parasol. Who bought all these things, these useless bits of expensive crap? A woman. Some wife of some long dead king. He had a woman. He didn't have her stolen away by his son of a bitch brother. I hate him. I hate the whole goddamn fucking world and every fucker on the planet. They will all be sorry they were ever born."

She was slipping off, remembering, experiencing the same feelings she'd had in her dream. "Euri, stop now." She stared at me without seeing me, her mind reliving every moment, compelled to tell me, to purge it from her conscience.

"I talked myself down, reminded myself of the bigger picture. I had to get a grip and remain calm. To further the plan, I can't be out of control like a petulant child. Once Azbekastan is gone, with all those souls to my credit, I may finally be powerful enough to begin the war I've wanted since the start, a war I'm certain to win. But if not, there will be Ravinia. It will be more difficult than Azbekastan, but in the end, they always succumb. Idiot humans never fail to give in. Their greed and selfishness always works for me. I am certain—"

"No more, baby. That's enough." I reached for her and wrapped her up in my arms and rocked her slowly.

She was quiet and pliant against me for a long time

before she said softly, "What happened to me, Zee? How could I dream anything so horrible? Do you think it's real?"

"I don't know," I said, wanting to be honest, but not wanting to alarm her.

"If it's real, it means he's back, and he's in Azbekastan. But what if none of this is real?" She began to cry again. "What if," she whispered, "I've lost it all? What if I'm gone walkabout in my head? Like when I heard that baby. There was no baby, Zee."

She was so worked up, so afraid, I couldn't think what to do except hold her as tightly as possible without breaking her. "It was a dream, Euri. People with no mental issues have wack dreams. It's the brain's way of cleaning the cobwebs, a reboot so you can meet a new day without jumbled thoughts."

"What if it's not that, Zee? What if I can see into his thoughts? What if my dreams every night are what he sees and thinks? I don't think I can stand that."

"Let's wait and see."

"Do you think he's back, reanimated, and in Azbekastan?"

"I'll go tomorrow and find out."

"I want to go with you."

"We'll see." She was still shaking, still completely freaked. I continued holding her and murmured mushy things I'd never say out loud, and after a long time, hoping to head her thoughts into another direction so she wouldn't be afraid to go back to sleep, I said, "Let's talk about your next concerts. Tomorrow night, you're in Cleveland, and the next night, you're in Philadelphia. We'll go early to rehearsals that day and I'll show you lots of interesting things there, like the Liberty Bell. Philadelphia is where the United States began, you know. We'll get a famous Philly cheesesteak, one at each of the competing sandwich stands, and we'll decide which we like best. You'd like that, wouldn't you?"

She nodded and wiped her nose on the back of her hand, like a little child.

"There's a flower farm in Michigan, where thousands of tulips and irises bloom every spring. I'll take you there next month, and we'll stand in the middle and the colors will be so beautiful, won't they?"

"That sounds lovely," she mumbled into my throat, her arms snaking around my neck. "I love you, Zee."

"And I love you. Why don't we lie down and get some more sleep?"

"Okay." She allowed me to lay her down, and as soon as I was beneath the covers with her, she curled into me with a sad sigh and was almost immediately asleep.

Now wide awake, I lay there and held her and stared at my ceiling and wondered what the future would bring.

My phone chirped with a text and I didn't need to look to know it was from Key. He and Jax had decided not to tell the others any of what I had told them about Euri. She had until the Blackbriar concert to be in the real world, but I was to be with her anytime she wasn't here, on Mephisto Mountain, and she had to stop posting on the 66X boards. She was Mephisto now, and forbidden to interfere in humanity. Since Phoenix was lost in his own world, unable and unwilling to do anything but stay with Mariah, Kyros would ask M for a doppelganger. He'd let me know how Euri would die.

I was okay with that. I'd prefer someone else make that call. It made me feel horrible, even knowing it wasn't real, that the flesh and blood Euri would be here with me always, and the death was only a cloned body.

A second chirp was a text from Sasha, who said Euri could call on her anytime and she'd be happy to be of any help.

It had already started. They would invade my life, and all the things I'd spent a thousand years keeping from them would be wide open for them to observe and discuss and offer their advice. They loved me. It would be an honest, sincere wish to help. I simply did not know how to make them believe there was nothing anyone could do to make it different. How did I tell them all to back off and leave me be? All they could do was disrupt the ebb and flow of my insanity, what I'd spent centuries learning to deal with. Euri knew. Euri understood. Euri was all I needed, and they would take her away from me, little bits at a time so that she would never again be mine alone.

I held her closer and petted her silky hair. Tomorrow I'd

go to Azbekastan for reconnaissance, get more details, then tell Key if Kovalev turned out to be Skia. If so, it followed that most of his advisors and assistants would be lost souls. I wondered how much of the population had converted? Was there some sort of edict? Swear fealty to Eryx or die?

I'd thought all those people murdered in my red day visions were executed because they weren't native to Azbekastan and weren't Russian Orthodox. Now I wondered if they were murdered because they refused to pledge their souls to Eryx. Thinking of my red days, of all those small children, innocent women, and hard-working fathers slaughtered, I would be almost glad to discover that Kovalev was Skia. It would give us a reason to interfere, to take him and his minions out and hopefully restore sanity to the people of Azbekastan. To stop the genocide.

Whatever happened, my primary concern was Euri, that I could give her what she needed to see the world through that marvelous filter of joy, her own unique brand of crazy.

My hope for our future and Euri's peace of mind returned moderately when she smiled in her sleep. She was so beautiful; strong and fragile at the same time.

"I love you," I whispered.

She nuzzled my neck and mumbled, "I love you," before slipping back into sleep.

I finally began to relax and it wasn't much longer before I drifted off.

My dream that night was another incarnation, weirder than any before. I followed Euri to the church and when she ran inside, calling God to take her, I saw Eryx at the window. He was crying. I called out to him, but he couldn't hear me. When Euri disappeared, taken away by the angels, he began to scream.

CHAPTER 12

~~ EURI ~~

I decided not to play Cleveland. While Zee grumbled about my nonexistent training and the dreadful, awful danger of accompanying him to Azbekastan, I called John and told him it was a bad day.

"What's going on with you, Euri? Are you in, or out? You missed all of San Francisco two weeks ago, you bugged out from Chicago before the cops were done taking our statements, and now you're blowing off Cleveland. The fans come to see you as much as anyone else in the band, even me. They feel cheated when you're not there."

I waffled a bit. Talking about the fans' expectations was genius because I could easily be made to feel guilty.

Glancing toward the bathroom, I watched Zee while he brushed his teeth. Naked. This is where I belonged. I would play music for him and the rest didn't matter.

I lied, because it was easier than saying I had to pop over to Azbekastan and find out if people there were selling their souls to stay alive. "I can play, John, but I may be sick in the middle of a set, and I suspect fans won't particularly like that part of the playlist." It wasn't altogether a lie. I was feeling lousy because of the whiskey. Were it not for immortality, I'm certain I'd have been throwing up my toenails. As it was, I was merely fighting a lingering headache and a twinge of queasiness.

"You need to see a doctor, Euri. There's something wrong with you." He paused. "Or you need to stay the hell away from Zee. He's a cool guy, but maybe not for you. Ever since you two hooked up, it's been one thing after another."

"Not seeing him is not an option. If you'd prefer I step out of the band now, instead of after we play Blackbriar, say so."

He didn't reply for a while, and then he said softly, "You're leaving the band?"

"I've never made it a secret, John. I agreed to play through the United States tour, and that ends next Saturday night at Blackbriar."

"What will you do? Go back to performing lame piano concerts?"

I would die. And live in Mephisto world forever. "I'm staying with Zee."

"What, like marrying him?"

Zee unbent and looked toward me and smiled through toothpaste foam. And winked. "Yes, like that."

"What does he say about you giving up the band? He's as big a fan as we have, even from the old days when no one had ever heard of us."

I smiled at that. The 'old days' was two years ago. "He's supportive of whatever I want to do, and this is what I want. For me, it was never about the fame or the money. You've known that since the start."

He sighed. "Yeah, I guess I did. Man, I will miss you. Are you sure you won't change your mind?"

"I'm sure."

"You're all over the Internet, you know."

"No, I didn't."

"Every girl in the world is getting a Lady Euri tat."

"It's not as if I invented the question mark."

"No, not that one. The one on your torso, the A."

Bugger. How long, I wondered, before Eryx caught up to me? He was plugged in as much as Zee and I, so he was bound to see all those tats online and know they originated with me. He would investigate, come to see me and determine his options. Would he abduct me and keep me hostage? Perhaps he'd attempt to bamboozle me as he had done to Jordan. Maybe he'd try to kill me, as he had murdered Jane.

I didn't care much, whichever he chose. I was immortal. Mephisto. Zee's love. His lover. I had no womb to mark. Whatever Eryx did to me, I wouldn't allow it to affect me. I would always find my way back to Zee, where everything made sense. I knew Zee was scared to death of what I'd dreamed last night, but there didn't seem to be anything I could say to settle his mind, so I let it go. I didn't like that I'd dreamed of Eryx, whether it was real or not, but I knew who he was, why he was so angry and hateful and violent.

In truth, I felt a bit bad for him, even while I despised him, and despite all the wrong he had done. Even knowing it was because of him that Miles was tempted enough to lose his way. Eryx hadn't ordered the killing of children in Azbekastan. He was not about evil for evil's sake. Only for his own, for his agenda of ruling all mankind. Killing little ones wasn't part of the plan. That was all on Kovalev.

I intended to be there when Kovalev was sent through the gates to Hell on Earth.

John was talking about a new song we'd written in L.A., but had yet to perform. He'd wanted to play it tonight, in Cleveland. "I thought it'd be a good test run, since it's a smaller venue than usual."

"Go ahead."

"Euri, it's a duet."

"Get Pogo to sing my part. He can hit high notes."

John sighed again. "I'll just wait until tomorrow's performance."

"I have to go now. I hope Cleveland is marvelous."

"I'll see you in Philly tomorrow at three o'clock, right?"

"I will be there."

I rung off and went into the bathroom to brush my teeth, gliding my fingertips across Zee's tight bum as I went. "Remember I told you about the girl who left me a message?"

"Right. August. Have you heard from her again?"

"No, but John says girls all over are getting tattoos of my Anabo A. That photo August mentioned must have been seen by more people."

He turned with his comb in his hand. "It's gone viral." While I brushed my teeth, he told me about Key's late night visit and his concerns. He told me about their meeting in the library. Then he went back to combing his hair so it was messy and unkempt looking. He added a bit of bar soap to dull the shine.

After I rinsed, I patted my mouth dry. "So no more posts on 66X?"

"Right. It's not a terrible loss, Euri. I know you meant well, but not one of them heeded your warnings."

I ignored that. "You post as 4Jane on 4chan."

"It's just stuff about music. I'm not trying to interfere in people's spiritual choices." He walked into his closet and I braided my hair while he stepped into a pair of knickers. Wrong of me, or perhaps far too elemental, but I liked watching him adjust all his manly bits. It was such an exercise in habit, something he'd done a thousand years.

Smiling, I turned toward the section of his cupboard that was now mine and sorted through the hanging clothes until I found my oldest sweater, a well-worn blue merino wool. I chose a ragged pair of jeans and my Chucks. I finished by tying a scarf around my head and sliding on a pair of drug store shades. "How do I look?"

"Like a celebrity trying to go incognito."

"Really, Xenos, do be serious."

"I am." He came toward me, removed the shades and slipped a pair of oversized glasses on my face. "They're just glass, but they're old and ugly." He bent and ripped the small hole in my jeans until it was a big hole. Then he closed it up with a length of silver tape. He stepped back and looked at me again. "Change that silk scarf for one of my old knit caps and you're good to go."

I went to one of the drawers and dug around until I found a beret made of green wool. I put it on and turned for inspection. He nodded before he slipped a scruffy grey turtleneck sweater over his head, the collar hiding the tat on his neck. His pants were rugged khaki, like a workman might wear, complete with a few grease stains. While he pulled them on and zipped, he said, "Tell me, in the Azbekastan dialect, that you're looking for work."

I ran over the sentence in my head several times in several different languages before I hit on the correct one. I said it aloud and he grinned. "Sweetheart, you gotta lose the British accent."

It was something of a surprise when I'd realized I could speak any language on Earth. I could see in the dark, hear Hans chopping vegetables in the kitchen, and say *I'll have the prawns* in Swahili. I rather liked becoming Mephisto.

I said something to Zee and he frowned. "You're speaking Swahili, and you said my oxen are at the gate."

I grinned. "It was a metaphor."

He looked down and checked his zipper before he shot me a look. "Behave."

I concentrated carefully, lost my accent and he approved of my second try.

After he'd removed his diamond ear stud, he slid into his oldest pair of boots and tucked a dagger inside.

"Doesn't that hurt?"

"There's a little pocket that keeps the blade from touching me. As soon as you're here for good, we'll get you some boots like this."

"And a knife?"

"Good God." His smile was a trifle wry. "And a knife. You're going to have to train a lot."

"With you?"

"With Jax. He trains everyone."

"I wonder if I'll be any good at it? I was always at the piano, so never was involved in sporting all that much. I like to ride, and I did learn tennis, and I could outrun Miles."

"You'll do fine." He cocked his head. "Interesting that you like to ride. When spring comes and the snow melts, we'll go for a ride. Ty keeps beautiful horses."

"He's always the quiet one, isn't he?"

Zee shrugged. "I think he talks to his animals, and doesn't have much use for people."

"That's odd."

"True. But he's odd. I wonder sometimes if the animals talk back."

"You're funning me, aren't you?"

He nodded. "Mostly. But you and I have strange abilities. Who's to say? I don't think they actually speak to him, but I wonder if he knows what they're thinking." He looked me up and down. "Are you sure you want to do this? I'd really feel better about it if you'd stay behind and not go with me until you've learned more about—"

"I am going with you, so do stop trying to talk me out of it."

"All right. Just do what I do and follow my lead. Remember all we talked about. Don't say anything unless you absolutely have to. Oh, and act like you're hungry."

"I don't have to act. You wouldn't let me eat a second bun at breakfast."

"Now you know why."

"Method acting?"

He grasped my hand, we disappeared from Colorado and materialized in a cesspool of mankind, undoubtedly the most frightening, horrible, desperate stretch of land in all the world. There was no war in Azbekastan, so no rubble from bombs, no sign of distress among the squalid row houses of the village where Zee took us. But lying in the narrow road was an endless row of dead bodies. I was instantly struck by how many children there were, each with a round hole in their forehead. The doors of most of the houses were standing open and there was no sign of life, no movement within or on the street. The weather was cold, but above freezing, and the stench of decaying bodies was unimaginable. I pulled my sweater up to shield my nose and mouth. Flies covered the dead and the trickle of melting snow that made its way through the ridges and cracks of the stone street was tinged red with blood.

"Holy Christ," I whispered, "it's infinitely worse than I'd imagined."

In the edge of dusk, holding hands, we walked along in shock and horror. We passed an elderly woman who crossed herself before she stopped and asked if we had any food. I wanted to take her with us, to protect her, but Zee told her no, then walked on, tugging my hand.

A man in uniform whose eyes were completely shaded, meaning he must be Skia, came toward us from what appeared to be the village square, where many bodies were stacked. "It looks as though my dream wasn't all my imagination."

"Just follow my lead," Zee said under his breath.

"You, there! What are you doing?"

Zee replied in Russian, with the Azbekastan dialect, "We are in need of work."

"Where have you come from?"

"The south. My family are farmers, but all our stores

were taken, so we began walking north, hoping to find food. My wife is pregnant." He drew me close to his side.

"You can help with the dead, and we have food in the commons house, but you'll have to take the oath first."

"We already agreed to it before we left the farm."

"Impossible." The man became instantly angry and shoved Zee. "Liars will be shot."

"We will take the oath again."

He pulled a small book from his pocket and held it out in his palm. I was stunned to see it was a Bible. "Place your hand and forswear your allegiance to God."

Zee did so.

"Now say, *I pledge my life and the hereafter to Eryx DeKyanos, the one true Defender.*"

Defender? Of what? Absurd, yet here we were. Here were hundreds of dead, in the name of the *Defender*, who did not defend anything at all but his own twisted notion of the world.

Zee repeated it, and I followed suit, ignoring my distaste at the sacrilege of swearing the horrible oath on the Bible.

As soon as I said *Defender*, the soldier lifted a handgun, pointed it at my head, and pulled the trigger. It happened in the space of a nanosecond. I had no chance.

And all was darkness.

~~ ZEE ~~

Masking my rage that this asshole fucking shot my love, I said with relative calm, tinged with slight disbelief, "Why did you do that? She was a hard worker."

"She's pregnant, and would eat too much. More than her share."

So much for thinking she'd be spared if it were believed she was pregnant.

"Take her over there, then meet me at the doorway to the commons and you can have some food. Then we will work. We have to burn or bury all the bodies and you have been spared death because you're strong and able."

I nodded as I bent to pick Euri up off of the road. I had no intention of leaving her anywhere. I waited until the soldier turned away, then transported back to Colorado.

Except I didn't transport. I was stuck.

And that's when I began to realize just how much stronger Eryx had become. He must have all of Azbekastan on lockdown. Just like Erinýes, his stronghold in Romania, the Mephisto could pop in, but we couldn't pop out. I'd have to get to the border and into neighboring Ravinia before I could get back home. *Fuck, fuck, fuck.*

While I walked toward the center of the square, I looked at all the bodies and had another grim realization. Eryx had changed his methods, his way of recruiting souls, what he'd done for centuries. Instead of the Skia taking the pledge from a new recruit, then teaching the lost soul how to go out and conscript others, Eryx must now be instructing them to kill the lost souls the instant they swore fealty. His power grew with every soul who passed from this realm to the next because he absorbed them. He had the might of all the souls who'd died before we could take them to Hell on Earth. And now he was speeding up the process by killing them immediately, before we even knew they existed.

This was as depressing as it was daunting. We'd have to figure out some way of defeating his new system.

But first, I had to get Euri and myself out of this village and further along the road toward the border. As long as we were here, there was a chance of Eryx knowing, and I wasn't ready for him to be aware that I knew what he was doing in Azbekastan.

I glanced over my shoulder and saw the soldier talking to the old woman who'd asked us for food. She argued with him as she crossed herself, and he shot her. Was Eryx aware that the soldiers were still indiscriminately murdering people? If what Euri dreamed last night was real, Eryx had instructed Kovalev to back off from killing those who hadn't pledged, but it appeared this soldier hadn't gotten the order.

Eryx's best maneuver was attraction. People had to be sincere when they turned their back on God and swore allegiance to him, and I didn't think relinquishing their souls under duress would work. To win the soul of a human, Eryx had to charm and woo them, had to tell lies they wanted to hear, offer what they wanted most in the world.

The complete devastating carnage of Azbekastan didn't fit with what I knew of Eryx's methods, or how people were persuaded to follow him. It was also extremely bad PR for any future maneuvers he might be planning in other countries. If what Euri saw in her dream was true, Eryx planned to begin working Ravinia sometime soon. He'd have a much more difficult task because once the people of Ravinia knew what happened in Azbekastan, they'd be far less enthusiastic about revolution and following a new leader, someone cherry picked by Eryx.

There would come a time, very soon, when the world would invade and demand Kovalev's head on a pike, and the murders would have to stop. Even countries with the worst human rights atrocities would condemn the murder of every citizen in Azbekastan, even the children. What kind of psycho maniac killed children for fuck's sake?

I thought of the Anonymous ops that attempted to shine a spotlight on what was going on within the closed borders. I hoped there was another one. Soon. Except it appeared there would be no people left to post pictures and reports.

Where did that soldier get his ammunition? There must be a storehouse or armory somewhere that dispensed munitions and weapons. If I could find it, I could blow it up.

I continued walking, allowing the now dark countryside to swallow me, willing Euri to wake up. She'd lost her fake glasses and my cap when she was shot, and her beautiful hair was matted with blood in the back, where the bullet had exited. I tried again to transport and failed again. Azbekastan was tiny, about the size of Long Island, but it was still freaking me out that Eryx could put a lockdown on an entire country. And he was only becoming stronger. How many souls had he absorbed since he made Kovalev Skia and took over Azbekastan?

Almost two hours into my walk, not far from the lights of the next village, Euri stirred in my arms and opened her eyes. "Ow," she whispered.

"Headache?"

"It's bloody awful to be shot." She turned her head slightly. "Where are we?"

"On the road to Perböl."

"The capital? Isn't that what I dreamed? There are

soldiers everywhere."

"We have to see what we're up against." I explained what I'd figured out while she was unconscious.

"Is Perböl on the way to the Ravinian border?"

"Yes. We'll look around for a bit, then head for the border."

"He intends to take over Ravinia next."

"We'll be ready for him. I don't know how, but we'll figure it out. Phoenix will come up with a plan."

"I can walk now, I think."

"It's okay. I kind of like carrying you."

"You're squeezing my boob."

"Oh, sorry. My bad." I increased the pressure of my hand against her very soft breast.

"Perv."

I grinned at her and continued along the road until I heard the sound of a vehicle engine coming from behind us. I put us beneath a cloak and veered into the woods, set her on her feet and we waited behind a large tree. Moments later, a Mercedes sedan rounded the bend in the road. Before it passed us, while it slowed to take the curve, I rushed into the road and waved my arms.

The driver stopped and within seconds, a soldier in a far grander uniform than the one in the village stood in front of me, his rifle trained on my heart. He was lost, but not Skia.

I kept my voice low enough that only he could hear me. "Don't shoot me. I'm your salvation. I can return you to how you were before the pledge, so you can leave here and have a chance at a normal life. You won't lose your soul to Eryx when you die."

He wanted to believe me. More than anything, he wanted to believe he could undo what he had done. They always did. The lost souls always regretted it. The Skia didn't, but that was because they'd already lost their soul when they became immortal. They were like clones of Eryx, bound to do his bidding with no questions asked. But the lost souls still lived a mortal life, their spirits within. They still had the illusion of free will, and they never lost hope that they could regain their freedom.

This one was no different. And due to the nature of how he became lost, he'd not yet been schooled in the ways of the lost souls. He had no idea there were Mephisto who would hunt him down. He still thought his worst enemy was Eryx. I pressed my advantage. "There are others over there in the woods. Go and wait and I'll take care of the immortal."

The rifle barrel dropped a couple of inches. "He'll kill me."

"Not if you run. And you're the one with the gun. Who is in the car?"

"A driver and the mayor of Perböl. He's been touring the countryside, convincing people to take the oath." He looked bitter. "Either they pledge, or they're shot. And now, just in the past two days, it doesn't matter whether they pledge, or not. Kovalev ordered the death squads to kill everyone."

Had Kovalev ignored Eryx's demand that the soldiers stop the murders? This was a clusterfuck of ginormous consequences. Whatever strides Eryx had made by taking over all of Azbekastan were far outweighed by indiscriminate genocide.

The soldier looked scared and desperate. I asked, "Where is your family?"

"All dead."

"You have nothing left here. Run and have a chance of freedom. Stay with him and you're bound to be killed eventually."

That was all it took. He tore off at a dead run, right into the dark forest lining the road, straight to Euri. I heard a scuffle, a grunt, and then her soft whistle of a tune only she and I knew. I wondered what she'd done to him? She had no knife.

I looked toward the car and watched a fat man in a suit climb out of the back and lumber toward me. The fucker had to weigh four hundred pounds, at least. He must eat constantly. All the food he wanted. I thought of all those emaciated kids I'd seen lying dead along the road, and fury nearly choked me.

Before he could demand to know who I was, shots rang out of the woods and Euri stepped into the shadowy light on the road, holding the rifle, pumping bullets into the fat mayor's very large head.

He dropped like a sack of potatoes and I lunged for the car before the driver could take off. He was putting it into drive when I stabbed his arm. He growled at me and reached for a pistol on the dash, but I stabbed him again and shoved him out of the car, moving behind the wheel at the same time. Euri got in and I drove away from the mayor, his driver, and the desperate soldier. I wished we might have taken them all to Hell on Earth, fuck doppelgangers, but with us on lockdown, there was no way to ferry them to the border undetected. They'd regain consciousness far too soon. But I vowed to take out the fat man. He'd spend the rest of eternity in Hell on Earth, with nothing to eat but the carcasses of the lost souls.

I glanced at Euri, who sat with the rifle across her knees. "How'd you learn to shoot like that?"

"Grouse hunting with my father and the queen."

"Some of the things you say would sound ridiculous from anyone else."

"Her Majesty is actually quite a decent shot. Well, she was. She's a bit old now."

"Are you a particular favorite of hers? It sounds as though your family spent more than the usual amount of time with her."

"She's my father's godmother and quite fond of him."

"Will she be terribly upset when you die?"

"I expect so. She came to Sophie's funeral and was sad. She did not attend my mother's funeral, but then, neither did my dad."

"I want to know more about your mother."

"Someday I'll tell you, and you can tell me more about Jane. For now, I believe we've all the unpleasantness we can stand without adding to it." She inspected the gun. "This is a German make. How do you suppose a country that's long been enemies with Germany ended up with German guns for its soldiers?"

"A black market arms dealer probably sold them to Kovalev before he staged his coup to overthrow the Azbekastan government." I smiled at her. "Very astute of you, Euripides."

"There, you see? I will be very good at reconnaissance."

"I never doubted it." I took a turn in the road, then asked, "How did you knock out the soldier?"

"I punched him, which he wasn't expecting, especially

because I was under a cloak and invisible. While he was reeling from that, I beaned him with a rock."

"Did you kill him?"

She shot me an irritable look. "After all this time following you while you chased the lost souls, don't you think I know how it works?"

"I just wanted to know if maybe you accidentally killed him. Most people don't survive being banged on the head with a rock."

"I was like Muhammad Ali. *Float like a butterfly and sting like a bee.*"

Bemused, I asked, "Now how would a girl like you know a quote like that?"

"My uncle, married to my dad's sister, is simply mad about boxing. He has that quote and several others, in frames he keeps in his study."

The more I learned, the more I liked her. And the less certain I was about what was within her mind. There were apparently sides to her I'd not seen before, even though I'd traveled around with her in her head. I never could have imagined she'd be a crack shot, or that she'd unflinchingly shoot a man in the head, even a Skia. "How did you know the fat man was immortal, that he was Skia? You began firing at him while you were still in the dark, in the woods. Our night vision isn't so perfect to tell a man is Skia from over a hundred feet away, in the dark."

She rested the rifle on her knees again and said softly, "I knew because you knew."

"You can't read me when we're together. You just knew, didn't you?"

She shrugged, as if it wasn't a big deal. "All right, yes, I suppose I simply knew. Like I know you're going to get us out of this Godforsaken country."

"Concentrate carefully and see if you can simply know where there might be an armory or munitions warehouse."

I drove another five kilometers before she said, "There's a large building south of here, but I don't know what it is. I get the sense it has cattle, so maybe a milking barn?"

I turned south on the next road and after another three kilometers, we came upon a dairy farm. With a milking barn. "My mind is blown. How did you know?"

She looked at me in the dim glow of the dash lights. "I don't know, Zee. The same way you know what someone is about to say before they say it. The way you know how many lost souls are in a building without ever going inside. It's as if my mind becomes a movie, and I'm traveling along and I see things. I saw this barn, and the shadows of cattle. There may or may not be arms inside, but you did ask about a large building, and here you are."

I was more freaked, and impressed, than I let on. I knew she had certain gifts not afforded ordinary humans, but I had no idea she could do this. The possibilities of what she could do as a Mephisto were endless. Key would be over the moon about her. He loved anything that furthered the cause. He was much more tuned in and passionate about the fight than any of us, I suppose because he was our leader. The success or failure of our efforts could be attributed to his leadership.

I parked the car close to the barn and we were instantly surrounded by bawling cows.

"Poor things need to be milked, Zee. They're in pain."

I saw exactly where this was going and made my best attempt to head it off. "Euri, we've got to go to the capital, do our reconnaissance, and get to Ravinia so we can go home. Key and the others need to know what's happening here as soon as possible. And I absolutely do not want to get caught here by Eryx. Especially right now."

She was already walking toward the barn, holding her smart phone flashlight like a beacon for the cows, which were following. When she had the doors open, the light switched on and the cows clustered at the gate into the milking stall. She opened it and allowed one in, and the gate closed automatically. She climbed up on the fence and watched as each cow was allowed in, via the automatic milking mechanism, and as each of a dozen cows was milked, I swear they sighed with relief.

"How on earth did you know how to activate the machine? Is your uncle also a dairy farmer?"

"Of course not. He's a businessman. But there are dairy cows at Longbourne, and my dad had one of these milking machines installed a few years ago, because the Hedleys were getting too old to milk them the old fashioned way. My father likes producing things at Longbourne, like milk and cheese and butter. We have chickens and geese and goats and sheep. It's a working estate. He was able to restore and renovate all of it after he married my mum, who came from vulgar amounts of money. Her father is arguably the richest man in the U.K., richer even than the queen."

I stood next to where she was perched on the fence and watched as the cows filed into the stall, one by one. "Ty has cows and we have a whole staff of Purgatories who milk them, and the goats, and there are other Purgs who make cheese and butter and such. There's a stone building on the mountain that used to be the dairy, but we converted it to a gym back in the sixties, and added on to the stables, so that's where the cows and goats stay during winter."

"And chickens?"

"And chickens. We buy a lot of groceries, but there are some things we like so much better done the old way."

"Like candles?"

I nodded. "You'll discover how much easier the light is on your eyes. Gaining night vision is a perk, but it also makes you more sensitive to incandescent light. And it's how we lived for so many centuries, it's familiar. Comforting in some weird way."

"It's very odd to think you've been alive so long. You've seen all of modern history, haven't you?"

I looked up at her. "I was around, but not really alive, Euri. I've merely existed, and done my job, and survived as best I could. I only know this because there's such a wide gap between before I knew you, and after." I felt all kinds of awkward, but said anyway, "I'm alive now, thanks to you."

She stroked my hair. As she did. "I love you, Xenos."

"I love you, Euri." We looked at each other for a long while, and despite where we were, and what was to come, I was deeply content. Happy. "Only five cows to go. I'll have a look around." Turning, I walked toward the south side of the barn.

"Do you suppose they shot the family who owned this farm?" she asked over the rhythmic glug and whoosh of the milking machine.

"Maybe they ran away."

While she tended the cows, I poked around the barn and

found a door with a busted lock toward the back. Behind the door, I found the answer to her question. They'd tried to hide, locked themselves inside this closet, hoping the soldiers would go away.

"They're in here," I called over my shoulder.

"Are they . . ?"

I shut the door. "Yes." There was a toddler. A sweet little boy with a hole in his head. A tiny soul who belonged to God because he wasn't old enough to be hurt or jaded or bitter or angry or envious. A baby was incapable of selling its soul. But some asshole soldier shot him anyway. Fucking maniac.

"It's insanity, Zee. This can't continue much longer. The world won't allow it."

"I dread seeing what's happened in the capital."

~~ EURI ~~

Zee's concern about the capital was justified, but not in the way he thought. In Perböl, a city of almost a quarter million, there were no dead bodies on the streets. It was early evening, around eight o'clock local time, and citizens walked through the downtown area, their breath turning to steam in the cold air. I saw only a handful of soldiers, most of them standing in front of the entrances to flats and businesses, watching as people went inside. I assumed they were looking for those who'd yet to take the oath.

It must have been a very boring job because it appeared they were all, every single one who was above the age of sixteen or so, lost souls. "There are so many," I whispered, breathless with dismay, completely dumbfounded that Eryx had managed to convert an entire city.

"He must be killing only the rural lost souls," Zee said. "This way, he stays beneath the radar. The lost souls in the city are bound to his edicts so no one will sound the alarm that their friends and relatives are being slaughtered."

We passed the palace, which rose from the very center of the city, surrounded by a small park with tall trees and a pond with swans. "I've never been here before, but it looks exactly as it did in my dream. I wonder if Eryx is inside?"

He slowed the car and I knew he was concentrating

fiercely before he slowly nodded. "Yes, he is."

"Do you think my dream was real, Zee?"

"I'm afraid it just might be, Euri. If it continues, if you can't lose them, we'll do something to fix it."

"Like what?"

"We'll ask M. He'll know what to do."

"Maybe it's not such a bad thing. If I dream about what he's doing, what he plans, wouldn't that be a help to the Mephisto?"

"Doesn't matter. Nothing is worth your unhappiness."

I stared up at the massive iron gates, affixed with the Azbekastan royal family's coat of arms. There hadn't been a king on the throne since just after World War II, when Azbekastan was included in the countries granted to the Soviets, but the coat of arms remained, a testament to a bygone era. It added to the majesty of the palace, something tourists had paid to see before Kovalev closed the borders.

Zee continued driving and we wound through street after street, eventually leaving behind the old city and traveling into the suburbs, where row houses and flats stretched across the rolling hills of Perböl.

We passed a café with no lights on. "The restaurants are dark and closed. And the markets are all closed. It's just after eight. Why would the markets be closed?"

He pulled into the car park at a market and drove slowly past the window. "There's no food in there. Look, the shelves are empty. I can see the light in the dairy case and there's nothing there."

"Is Kovalev starving them to death?"

"So it seems, but is it on purpose, or because he failed to consider that murdering all the farmers would have an effect on the food supply?"

"Most of Russia's food is imported, and I'm certain it's the same in Azbekastan."

"Kovalev closed the borders almost a year ago, I think before Eryx came into the picture."

"I remember. Miles and I participated in the first Anonymous op, when they opened Internet access and crashed the Azbekastan government's homepage. And despite all the pictures and posts about how horrific it was, nobody did a bloody thing to help."

"The U.N. placed sanctions on Kovalev's regime."

"So they couldn't export anything and make any money? What a joke, and completely worthless punishment. It's a tiny country with almost no natural resources, but it's beautiful, and they have some of the oldest examples of architecture from the Ottoman Empire. They made most of their money from tourism, and the idiot closed the borders."

"I read an article that said Kovalev believed the country could sustain itself without any imports or exports. That's why so many are starving." He scanned the street as we traveled along. "It's as if everyone here is merely waiting to die. It'd be a mercy to them if the soldiers were to shoot them." He glanced at me. "But that would be bad for us. We need to take them to Hell on Earth, sooner than later, but it will be next to impossible since we can't transport."

My creeped out factor rose exponentially every minute we remained in Azbekastan. "Let's get out of here."

He pulled out of the car park, then drove further into the suburbs, toward the edge of the city.

That's when he said quietly, "There's no one here, Euri." He slowed the car and I looked left and right, all along the street. I rolled down the window. There was no noise, no lights on in any of the buildings. Nothing. No dogs barking, no cars, no sign of life. Anywhere.

"Do you think they're inside their homes, hiding?"

He looked at me, his expression grim. "No. I know there's no one here, and I've just realized there hasn't been a living soul since we left the old city."

"Are they dead?"

"No, they're simply not here." He continued driving, searching as we went, concentrating completely. He was searching in his mind, looking for anyone. We were close to the edge of the city, out of residences and into scattered businesses like an auto repair shop and a petrol station. Zee looked at me. "Nobody, Euri. It's a ghost town."

"Where are they? Where did they go?"

"This is fucking eerie. I've never seen anything like it outside of a war zone. People flee from wars and become refugees, and their homes typically get blown up after their gone. But this . . . it's as if all is well, no sign of disturbance, but no people."

"Maybe they fled because they didn't want to take the oath."

"All of them? What are the odds? Some of them would have stayed and taken the oath." He slowed to a stop and put the car in park. "Think with me, Euri."

I closed my eyes and concentrated fiercely. I moved down the road at light speed, passing small houses and fallow fields, until I came to a church, silhouetted against the moonlit sky. It was made of light stone, but had dark streaks, and most of the stained glass windows had been broken. "There's a church," I said, my eyes still closed, "close to the border, fifteen or so kilometers from here. It seems darkened, as if someone tried to burn it, but it's mostly stone with a slate roof. The windows are broken. And there are faces looking out. Lots of faces."

"Are they lost souls?"

"I can't tell. This thing that I do, it's obscure and not always accurate. It's only a shadowy vision that comes at me superfast." My mind continued traveling past the church toward a cluster of lights down the road. I tensed and felt sick. "Zee, there's a field of bodies. Hundreds of dead people." I opened my eyes and swallowed back bile. "That's what happened to all the people from Perböl. They're dead in a barren wheat field."

CHAPTER 13

~~ ZEE ~~

As we reached the outskirts of another village, I slowed and swept my gaze around, shutting my mind off and allowing it to roam freely, to find what was behind the closed doors of the row houses that lined the streets. There were no lights on, not even the streetlights. As I'd known in Perböl, I knew the houses were all empty. There was no sign of life.

And just as Euri had said, in the center of the town, on one side of the village square, was an old stone church with a slate roof, scorch marks where someone had tried to burn it, and broken windows. Of the faces I saw peering out, none belonged to lost souls. I drove closer, and pulled into the small, unpaved lot on the opposite side.

Out of the car, I made sure to take the keys, then I folded her hand in mine and we walked toward three stone steps and double wooden doors. "First time I've ever been inside a church," I whispered. "Kind of fits for me that it'd be this one."

She squeezed my hand as we went up the steps.

Inside, it was gloomy, the back half of the church lit only by a camping lantern someone had hooked onto a candle sconce in the stone wall. A sea of solemn, thin faces turned toward us and a middle-aged man stepped forward, smiling at Euri. "Ah, the beautiful one."

"Have you seen me before?"

"No, but you've a shine to you, like one of the chosen." He turned to me. "You look similar to DeKyanos, but you cannot be him. You're inside the house of God, where he can't be."

"My name is Zee and this is Euri. How long have you been here, and where did you come from?"

"Some are villagers, and the rest of us are from the city, from Perböl. I am Yefim. Three days ago, we were told to evacuate, and we could bring one small bag. We were made to walk twenty kilometers to the border, then given the choice of pledging our lives to DeKyanos and returning to our homes, or leaving the country to take refuge in Ravinia."

"How did you and these others end up here, in this church?"

A fleeting expression of pain crossed his face, then he was back to all business. "They broke us into two groups – those who pledged and those who refused. There were thousands of us, all crowded into what were once barley fields. The group that refused the pledge was much smaller than those who agreed to it, and we thought we'd be allowed to leave, to cross the border." He stopped and swallowed, obviously trying to get himself together. "Instead, as we walked toward the border, the soldiers began shooting, and a crop duster flew over and spread a chemical of some kind that caused people to seizure and die. We ran, and those of us who were lucky made it back here, to this village and the shelter of this church. The soldiers tried to come in, but the doors wouldn't open. They tried to burn us out, but the fire wouldn't stay lit." He looked heavenward. "God protects us here."

Euri turned her head toward me and murmured in French, "Skia can't go in churches?"

"Yes, they can," I replied in French. "Only Eryx and the Mephisto can't, because we're born of Hell."

"You are French?" the man asked.

"Yes," Euri said. "We're with the U.N."

"Can you get us out of the country, to safety?"

"Not just yet," I said. "We'll have to report back and wait for help and supplies."

"We are in severe need of food," Yefim said. "There have been shortages since all the past months, but now, there is nothing anywhere to eat. When they couldn't get inside this church, the soldiers left, but took all the livestock that remained after the last purge, and burned the grain."

Why couldn't the Skia come inside? Euri and I had opened the doors with no problem.

"We need to look around and see what is available now, to determine what's needed."

Yefim, who appeared to be the de facto leader, nodded, and walked with us through the church, through the gaunt faces of the refugees, to the front where there was an altar, a lectern, and at least a dozen candles. Every wall in the church, from floor to ceiling, was covered in icons, flat one dimensional paintings of long dead saints and scary looking men in robes wearing giant crosses. I wished I could look longer and ask Euri questions, but Yefim was waiting to take us through a doorway to the right of the altar. We followed him into an anteroom that was empty except for a multitude of cracker boxes stacked along one wall. "Why aren't you handing out these crackers?"

Yefim gave me a look of censure and shock. "These are communion wafers. They are holy."

I picked up a box and read the print. "They're made at a factory in Italy."

"They represent the body of Christ."

"Under the circumstances, I think God would prefer they represent food for hungry people." I could see he was intent on disagreeing with me. I opted to play along with his dogma. "God protected you from the soldiers. Will you now starve to death when there is food right here? Do you really believe this is what God wants?"

He was torn. He kept moving his gaze from my face to the box of wafers.

Euri took the box, broke the seal, and pulled one out and ate it. She handed one to Yefim. "You see? I am not offending God by eating what was so conveniently left behind."

He crossed himself, then snatched the wafer and ate it in one greedy bite. Then he took the box from her and ate several more. Then he smiled. "Yes, this is right." He gathered up more boxes and left us there while he went back into the main church and called the others to come and have some food. I heard their excited chatter. They evidently didn't share Yefim's paranoia.

"Why couldn't the Skia get inside?" Euri asked while she jiggled the knob of another door.

"I don't know." I was about to move Euri aside and force the door when Key suddenly appeared. I took one look at him and said, "Whoa, shit, bro, you're going to be sorry you did this. Eryx has the whole fucking country on lockdown."

"It's an emergency." He glanced around. "Are we in a church?"

"We are. We wish it was a restaurant or a grocery store because all those people out there haven't had a square meal in months, but it's not. It's a church and all they have are crackers."

"This church isn't locked down," Key said. "He can't lockdown where he can't be. This is holy ground."

"They said the soldiers couldn't get inside and we thought that was weird."

"Must have something to do with the outside on lockdown, but not within the walls of the church." He gave me a wry smile. "God does throw us a bone every so often."

I felt a little better about what we had to do. "So we can use churches to transport lost souls when we do a takedown here." I glanced at Euri, who stood silently by the as yet unopened door, then I said to Key. "We think the people here may be the only ones left who aren't lost. We drove through Perböl and didn't see anyone other than children who weren't lost. They've murdered everyone else, including a lot of the lost souls." I told him of Eryx's new methods.

He ran a hand through his hair and sighed. "We get a step ahead, and he takes three. I knew when he came back he'd be out of control, and he's taken it to another whole level."

"So he's back?"

Key nodded. "Since yesterday. When any of us leave the mountain, he shows up and stays right there and stares. Denys went to buy some new boots at Hogrebe's in Denver, and there was Eryx. Ty went to buy vet supplies in Sacramento, and there was Eryx. I took Jordan for lunch at that little dive we always liked in Seattle, and there was Eryx, eating at the table right behind us."

Euri had dreamed this. Eryx's plan going forward included shadowing the Mephisto, turning up wherever we were, hoping to unnerve us. "Wonder why he thinks we'd be freaked by him showing up and staring at us? I don't give a damn what he does."

"I suppose he's deluded himself into believing he can make us feel guilty." Key took a deep, tired breath. "I'm so sick of all this, Zee. Just so ready to be done."

"When Mariah is better, when Jordan's more herself, take her somewhere for a few days and take a break."

"Wherever we go, Eryx will be there."

"He won't be in your hotel room. When you're in public, ignore him."

He turned to the door Euri had been trying to open and kicked it. It turned out to be a storage room, filled with all the accoutrements needed for a mass, I supposed. Brass crosses and old Bibles and those weird swinging, smoky things I'd seen priests carry in movies. There were candles and candlesticks and lots of banners and runners and shiny purple cloth.

While Euri went inside to poke around, I asked Key, "You said you came because of an emergency. What's happened?"

He held up his phone to show me a photo of Euri in a white dress, singing in front of a choir. Her hair was shorter and she was thinner, but beautiful and smiling like she did, with all the joy in her soul. "How is an old photo of Euri singing with a choir an emergency?"

Key looked at me and said softly, "It's not old. It was taken last Sunday at a church in Stockholm." He lowered his voice to a whisper. "And it's not Euri."

CHAPTER 14

~~ EURI ~~

Back in Zee's room, while he popped downstairs to get us something to eat, I sat at the piano and played Strauss and waited to hear about the emergency.

Kyros sat next to me on the bench. "You have blood in your hair."

"I was shot in the head by a Skia."

"I hate getting shot."

Minutes passed and he watched me play and didn't talk. I remembered he was always quiet unless he had something he considered important enough to say. And to Key, important meant Mephisto. All the rest he left to the others.

"I look forward to meeting Jordan," I said, hoping to draw him out a bit.

No response.

"She's very beautiful."

A nod. He really was remarkably good looking, all that long dark hair and his square jaw and serious dark eyes. I liked watching him with Jordan, who was so petite, especially next to Key.

Strauss segued into Adele.

"I'm so terribly sorry about Mariah. I hope she comes around soon."

He looked up from the keys and met my eyes and said soberly, "She has the gentlest soul of any I've ever known."

"Do you feel guilty about Mariah?"

His gaze instantly fell to the keys again. "Of course not."

"That's lovely for you."

I played on and he was silent until his curiosity got the best of him. "Why do you think I feel guilty?"

"Because you brought her here knowing Phoenix wouldn't be able to leave her alone, and also knowing he's a selfish, hard bloke who forgot a long, long time ago what it means to think of anyone but himself. He abandoned her when she needed him most, just like he did with Jane, and because of that, she's gone walkabout in her head. She may never come back, and so I wondered if you feel the tiniest bit responsible and if you've apologized to Phoenix for setting him up like that."

He was clearly furious, but he didn't leave, didn't shout. He said in a low, modulated voice, "I brought her to be with Jordan. They deserved to be together again."

I drifted into the new music I'd written for Zee, when he was blocking me and I was so alone and sad. "You brought her so Jordan would see what Mariah did for her, the sacrifice she made to ensure Jordan was safe, so she could escape the monstrous guardian they were sent to live with when they were orphaned. Jordan despises Eryx, and when she realized you still love him, in spite of everything, it was a deal breaker. So you found Mariah and brought her here as a way to illustrate to Jordan that nothing is entirely black and white. Eryx is what he is because of the sacrifice he made, losing his soul so his younger brothers might have a chance of redemption and peace. Your plan worked and now you have your Anabo, you're redeemed, and someday, when Mariah is either gone, or back amongst the living, you'll have Jordan the way you want her, happy and free and loving. But your peace came at a high price to Mariah, didn't it?"

"Stop talking."

I played and he fumed. He ran his hand through his hair, and said . . . nothing.

At least ten minutes passed before he deflated from righteous indignation and said glumly, "Okay, all right, you're dead on. I'm drowning in guilt. I take great pains to hide it, but it's eating my lunch. How do you know?"

"Because I know."

"Like Zee knows?"

"No, I just know who you are. I realize it's strange, but

I've come to know all of you through Zee." I nudged him with my shoulder. "You didn't do it for totally selfish reasons, Key. You really did think it was best for Mariah, considering where she lived and what her life was like. And you believed Jordan would feel better about leaving her adoptive father and the real world if she knew she had a biological sister. But more than all of that, you wanted her to love you and not hold your feelings for Eryx against you."

"And then she tried to bring him back to me, and was lost, and then Mariah went after her and ended up in Hell on Earth and lost her mind." He sighed and sounded at wits end. "It's all fucked up and it's all my fault."

"True, but sometimes being the leader means taking calculated risks. You're susceptible to missteps the same as anyone else would be, because you're imperfect. You should apologize to Phoenix, then stop beating yourself up about it."

"Jordan cries all the time. All. The. Time."

"Give her something to concentrate on that isn't her sister."

"Like what?"

"You'll have to figure that out for yourself."

He listened to me play for a few more minutes. "You're enormously talented."

"Thank you."

Zee popped back into his room, carrying a tray filled with sandwiches and crisps and fruit and biscuits and milk.

As he set the tray on his desk, Key said, "Your Anabo is perfect for you. She's not shy about saying what's on her mind."

"She has to because she's fey. All people with the sight have to say what they mean so that nothing is left to conjecture." He glanced at me before he asked Key, "Have you told her?"

"No, I waited for you, so we can discuss what needs to be done."

I stopped playing and swung round on the bench to face the other way. Key did the same and handed me his phone, which had a picture of Sophie in a white sweater dress singing in front of a choir in a church. I stared at it, confused and afraid. "I don't understand. Where is this?

How can she be standing up, singing?" I looked at Key. "How can she be *alive?*"

"It's in Stockholm," Key said. "That picture was taken by one of Arcadia's fans, and posted with a tagline about Lady Euri's doppelganger. It's all over the Internet, along with a rumor that your twin didn't actually die, which then led to people pointing out that she was handicapped, and this girl obviously is not. I sent Jax to Stockholm to find out more. Her name is Sophia Ekstrom, and she lives on a secluded estate outside the city with an older woman who seems to be some kind of nurse, or companion, and several servants. She has a tutor who comes every day, and she takes riding lessons. The only time she leaves the estate is to attend church."

"Is she Anabo?" Zee asked.

"Jax doesn't know because he never actually saw her. He posed as a reporter following up on the photo that went viral and got his information from the caretaker at the estate and a woman at the church. He tried to find Sophia, but couldn't."

I continued staring at the picture, my heart breaking all over again, remembering her beloved face disappearing into the murky gloom of that awful lake, down to the depths. "I wish it was Sophie, more than anything in the world, but I know it's not. She drowned the day my mother drove all of us into a lake. We all drowned. And your father pulled me out and told me it wasn't my time and offered immortality. When he brought me up out of the water, it forced me to let go of Sophie, and she . . ." I took a bracing breath. "She disappeared in the gloom. Her body was found by divers two days later. She's buried at Longbourne."

Zee was tapping the screen on his phone. Then he was talking into it. "We need your help. Can you come to my room, right now?" He ended the call and looked at me. "We could guess the truth and still not know, so I've called M. He'll tell us what happened that day."

A nanosecond later, there was Death, dressed in a dark grey suit, crisp white dress shirt and a striking red silk tie. A jaunty red kerchief peeked from his breast pocket. He was a disarmingly handsome man. Small wonder all the Mephisto were such beautiful creatures. Their mother must have been exquisite.

He smiled at me with what I decided was genuine affection. "Hello, Euri. How is life on this side?"

"Interesting."

"Is Xenos treating you well? I raised my sons to be gentlemen, and I'll be very displeased if he's not given you all due respect."

I thought of the night before, of pearls and black silk bowties and Zee's rough, lusty voice telling me all manner of sexy things. "He's quite lovely, thank you."

M nodded, still smiling. "Now, then, what may I do to help?"

I pointed at Key's phone. "We've discovered a girl in Stockholm who bears a remarkable resemblance to my sister, and since she was Anabo, like me, we're wondering if you brought her back as well."

He lost his smile and became serious. "How do you know she was Anabo?" His rapid glance toward Zee was filled with accusation, which he instantly masked, but I caught it. He had told Zee of other Anabo and sworn him to secrecy.

Key was also aware and said to his father, "Give up the cloak and dagger, Pops. Did you think we wouldn't notice that after a thousand years, there's a sudden abundance of Anabo, all of an age to become Mephisto? I was born at night, but it wasn't last night. So tell me, how many more Anabo are there?"

"Don't get fresh with me, Kyros." He gave his second oldest son a stern look and walked toward the fireplace, where he stared at the small metal statuette of a girl playing a violin that Zee kept on his mantel.

When he didn't speak, I said into the silence, "Sophie had the Anabo birthmark, just like me. That's how I know she was Anabo."

He cleared his throat and remained at the mantel, staring at the girl with the violin. "Your mother was a truly terrible person."

"Yes, she was."

"All of the Anabo have had difficulties because of their parents."

I glanced at Zee before I said, "M, everyone in the world has problems because of their parents. Even great parents cause problems for their children. It's part of the human condition."

"If your naiveté wasn't so endearing, it'd be so very sad. Most parental difficulties are centered around arguments about career choices, money, boyfriends and girlfriends, which university to choose, unmet expectations, disappointment. They quarrel over sibling rivalries and petty jealousies and wounded feelings. But there's generally always love and affection. It's the glue that binds a family."

He turned to face me. "Your mother was a selfish sociopathic murderer who should have been prosecuted and sent to prison. Your father knew what she did, but because of the family name, he didn't call the police or pursue having her charged with attempted murder. He could have divorced her and ensured she had no rights to visit you or Sophie, but again, because of the family name, he didn't do that. Which is how she was able to abduct your sister and coerce you into taking that fateful drive. Mary Michael was hysterical, and begged me to step in, to do something, but because we are forbidden to interfere in humanity, I couldn't do anything until you were dead."

I turned around and began to play. It was my solace, always, and this was so painful to hear, to remember.

He came closer, almost to my back. "You have a gift, one that God gave you. I don't know why or what purpose it might serve, but I couldn't let you die without offering you the opportunity to find out."

"I lost my connection to Sophie, I thought because she was dead, but that wasn't the reason, was it?" I lost my fight for reserve and began to cry. "Did you connect me to Zee?"

"No. That was Lucifer. Centuries ago, he told Xenos he'd do something to help him with his mental instability, and that turned out to be you."

I played happy music, wanting to find my equilibrium, but it sounded false and wrong. Like the joke was on me. I switched to a pensive piece and took several deep breaths, trying to control myself and stop crying. "Where is my sister?"

When he failed to answer, I stopped playing and swiveled around to look up into his face. "She's with Eryx, isn't she?"

His nod was slow. "He took her from Stockholm to the palace in Perböl late this afternoon. It's what she wanted, Euri. She's the one who posted that photo online. She knew he'd notice all the hubbub about you and your Anabo tat, that he'd be thinking of some way to sabotage you before you could become Mephisto. She knew he'd come to her, to discover her real identity, and once he knew she was Anabo, he'd take her with him."

"Are you telling me she *wanted* to go with Eryx?"

"It's been her plan since she became immortal and learned about him."

"How does she know about Eryx?"

"I told her. She's worked tirelessly to catch up, relearning to walk and talk and take care of herself. And from the start, when she learned of this other side of reality, of Eryx and the lost souls and the Mephisto, she became convinced she could alter the course of the war, from the inside. She asks me questions and I'm as truthful as I can be."

I was stunned. And furious. "My sister going to be with Eryx, hoping to change him, is like sending a lamb to live with a lion to teach him to be a vegetarian." I narrowed my eyes. "And how did she learn about Eryx? Did you tell her? Was that the plan from the start? Bring her back to life so she could be a sacrificial lamb?"

Zee moved to face his father. "Is that how it was? You told me that you and Lucifer had all but given up on us winning the war. Was Sophie your secret weapon? Was she a throw-away because of her disability? Collateral damage? How did you convince her to accept immortality?"

"Those are a lot of accusations, Xenos." He looked at Key. "Call him off."

"No." Key stood and said, "I think you've got some explaining to do, and it needs to happen now."

M looked from Key, to Zee, and finally, to me. He sighed, as if he was very tired. Extremely depressed. His black eyes reflected a certain pain, the kind suffered by the lonely and misunderstood. "She has your gift, Euri."

I deflated and was a bit breathless. "She channels Eryx?"

"No, but she dreams of him when she sleeps. She has

since she came back. She asked me if it's real, what she sees in her dreams, and I told her the truth."

"Lucifer did this?"

"I can't say because I don't know. Does it matter?"

"Because she has the gift, because she's fey, and because she's no longer mortal, he's using her."

M's smile was wry. "He uses all of us."

I had dreamed of Eryx. Was she closer to me now? Was I dreaming her dreams, as I'd once seen her life as it happened?

"She says she visits you sometimes, that you meet while she dreams."

So my mirror episodes were real, just as I'd thought. "Why was she in Stockholm? Why didn't you bring her here from the start? How do you know she isn't meant for Ty, or Denys?"

He rubbed his whiskers and said, "Because I know. She died, and I had scarce moments to decide what to do. Lucifer came to me and said to bring her back, that she would be part of the solution, that because of her unique qualities, she would be a savior of sorts. She would offer something no other Anabo could."

I whispered, "The purest heart."

Zee said, "All Anabo are pure of heart, without jealousy or resentment."

"Maybe so, but we're still human, and survival is instinctive in all of us. Except Sophie." I looked at Zee and knew he would understand. "The car was sinking and I turned for her and she shook her head. She looked toward our mother." I was overwhelmed with the memory. "She wanted me to save Mum, instead of her. She was willing to sacrifice herself for the woman who stole her life from her."

"But you didn't allow her to do that."

I slowly shook my head. "Sophie deserved a chance. She was so bright and beautiful, so happy and at peace, despite everything that happened to her." It was why I gave a part of myself to her during every visit we had. I looked again at M. "Now she's with the worst evil the world has ever known. I can't begin to imagine what you were thinking, letting her do this."

"All I did was bring her back without physical or mental

limitations and provide her a place to become the person she was meant to be, before your mother changed her life. I spared no expense and she lived as close as possible to the manner in which she was accustomed. She had privacy, constant care, and all sorts of exercises for her body and mind. Her happiness in the simplest of things was humbling, even for a reprobate like me. She had the choice to come here, Euri. All along, I told her I would bring her to my sons, that she would be welcome here. I told her she would be with you. She could make a difference by living here and working with the Luminas."

"And she chose Eryx?" Key said, dropping back to sit beside me again. "I'm missing something. I really don't get it. Was she fully aware of who we are and what we do? Was she maybe confused and thought he was the good guy?"

"No, she wasn't confused. When he came back, just yesterday, she knew. She called me and said he was back, that he was in Romania debating whether to rebuild, or move on. For the moment, he decided to go to Azbekastan. He turned Kovalev to Skia about a month before he discovered Jordan. Once he met her and became obsessed, he let things slide in Azbekastan, and without the benefit of any human decency after he sold his soul, Kovalev's dark nature took over. That's when the genocide began in earnest. Anyone who refused the pledge was killed. The fool was unaware that none of them really pledged. Strong-arming a person into relinquishing their very essence will never work. Azbekastan is a complete disaster for Eryx. Sophie said now, when he's as low as possible, was the perfect time for her to meet him, to gain his trust. So she posted the photo and took steps to ensure it went viral. Barely five hours afterward, he showed up in Stockholm and took her back to Azbekastan."

"Does she intend to make him believe she's there to help him?"

"On the contrary. She says she'll be truthful and honest."

"He'll make her leave," Key said. "No way he'll want a happy child of God hanging around while he plots the downfall of mankind."

"Time will tell."

I got to my feet and looked from Key to M. "Surely you're

not suggesting that we *leave her there?*"

"It's what she wants," M said.

"She has no life experience! How could she possibly know what she wants?" He gave me a patient look, which I, of course, took as patronizing. "You, sir, can sod off if you believe I'll sit still while my twin sacrifices her soul to a monster." I looked at Zee. "I'm going back to Azbekastan."

He had that patient Zee look, the one that ordinarily made me feel better, but at the moment only served to fan the flames of my rage and frustration. I had to see Sophie. Had to rescue her. Had to fix what was broken. "You're either with me, or against me. Decide now."

He looked at M. "Does Sophie have a legit way out if she wants one?"

"Mary Michael and her band of angels are keeping tabs, and the instant Sophie wants out, I'll be alerted. I'll go and get her immediately."

Zee looked at me and said gently, "Her whole life has been decided for her, from the moment she was born, really. For the first time, she has the ability to make the decision for herself. You think it's the wrong decision and maybe I do, too, but is it our call to make? There are undoubtedly a lot of people who'd tell you to stay away from me, maybe even some in my own family, but here you are. It's your decision, not theirs." He held up a hand when I started to argue. "I'm not comparing myself to Eryx. It's worse, I know. She's in grave danger. There are a million things that could go wrong. She may be damaged beyond repair, but that's what you thought before, when you thought she was dead. Doesn't she deserve the right to make this call on her own?"

I looked at Key, then at M. They both were looking at me with what I'd have to call trepidation. They expected me to go off and argue with Zee.

Instead, I sat on the bench again and stared at the intricate pattern of Zee's rug and remembered all of my life with Sophie. My awake dreams of her. She loved when George took her through the secluded, beautiful park that surrounded Hawthorn House. He would tell her stories and she was in love with his kindness and his deep, beautiful voice and his strong, sure hands. She would daydream that she was well, that she could walk and talk, and in her dreams, she held hands with George and told him how very much he meant to her.

I remembered her hurt when Miles and I had sex the first time. I hadn't known she was that far developed. It wasn't until then that I realized my sister had the same hormone driven needs and thoughts that I had.

I wondered what went through her mind now? Did she sincerely believe she could save Eryx from himself? Did she imagine herself saving the world? I was tremendously heartbroken to realize that I did not know. Resurrected Sophie was a stranger to me. Our visits through the mirror were always somewhat ethereal and unreal, and we talked about all the things we wished we might have done when she was alive, because I assumed she was dead and she never said any different. I remembered that she said she regretted never having the chance to kiss anyone, that she would like to know what that felt like.

I looked up at M, who was still staring at me. "If he kisses her, won't the result be the same as it was with Jordan?"

"I don't think so. Jordan was Mephisto when she kissed Eryx. And she gave him her trust. Sophie is not Mephisto, and she knows not to trust him. She's dreamed of him for two years, so she knows him as no other. As well as you know Xenos."

"I have to go there and see for myself that she's not being hurt or misused. I have to know if he's being cruel to her. She doesn't know, you see. She only knew our mother was cruel. She made excuses for everyone else. They hurt her in the first two sanatoriums my father took her to, but she believed it was accidental. She couldn't see the smug, evil satisfaction in their faces, or read the intent in their hearts. She believes everyone has joy, that all they need to do is recognize it. She might not see just how awful Eryx is, until it's too late."

"She sees much more than you know." M came a bit closer. "And what if she's right, Euri? Suppose she *does* make a difference?"

"You're endlessly hopeful because he's your son. Your first concern isn't Sophie." I looked at Zee. "I'm going to spy on her and Eryx. By myself. He will never know I'm there because I have no mark. There's a chapel in the palace where I can most likely transport back here, but if not, there's a cathedral just down the avenue."

He looked toward Key. "I need to talk to Euri. Go away." He nodded at M. "You, too."

Key stood and had that hard look on his face. The one that meant business. "She's Mephisto now, so where she goes is important for us to know. She can't just take off on a mission like this without permission"

"I go on missions like this all the time and you never know. If you've got complaints about how I do my job, fuck off. Nothing's changing." He took a menacing step toward Key. "Leave. Now."

M disappeared, but Kyros didn't. He stood a bit straighter and leveled a look at me. "If you go off without permission, if something happens to you, like he captures and holds you, don't be surprised when no one comes for you. Whatever you do, it's on your own and the Mephisto will have no part of it."

Zee took another step toward him. "You can be a real son of a bitch sometimes, brother. You think I'd let her stay a captive of Eryx? Seriously?"

Key had no response. He also didn't leave.

"Take your control freak ass and get the hell out. Do it now, Kyros."

I suppose Key realized Zee was close to losing it. He gave him a patient look and said, "Go with her. She has no idea what he's capable of." Then he disappeared.

Zee immediately said, "You're not going anywhere until you've eaten and taken a shower. And while you're doing that, I'll figure out how I can go without getting caught. He's evidently tracking all of us right now."

"Then why didn't he show up when we were in Azbekastan? We were there for hours and hours."

"Probably because he was too busy following my brothers." He shrugged. "And he's always ignored me. I think he worries I can read his mind, which freaks him out."

Taking a sandwich, I began to eat and ditched my manners and talked around a very large bite. "I don' fink you sh'd go."

"What you fink doesn't matter. I'm going."

I took another bite. "How'm I s'pposed to shpy if he knows we're there?" I swallowed, then gulped down some milk.

"I doubt he'll know because, like I said, he pays no attention to me." He wasn't eating. I held out the other half of my sandwich, but he ignored it and said, "It doesn't really matter because whether or not he figures out I'm there, there is absolutely no way I'm letting you go alone."

"I don't need your permission."

"And I don't need yours. If you go, I'm going with you. End of story."

"Then it's pointless for me to go."

"Then don't go."

"I *have* to go. I have to see her. Why are you being so stubborn?"

He sat next to me on the bench. "There is nothing in the universe more important to me than you. There's nothing I do that will ever be as essential as keeping you from harm and doing everything in my power to ensure your well-being and happiness. I would die for you. I'd do anything for you. But I will never, for all the rest of time, knowingly let you walk into danger. Do you understand what I'm saying to you?"

"Yes." I ate the rest of the sandwich. And the crisps.

It was completely quiet except for my chewing until he finally said, "Aren't you going to argue?"

"Do you want me to argue?" I ate a biscuit, then shot him an accusatory look. "Oh, bollocks, now I begin to understand. This is a ploy to get in a row so we can have make-up sex, isn't it?"

My attempt at humor failed miserably. He still had that serious death stare.

I swallowed the last bite of my cookie. "No argument, Xenos. And no make-up sex." I polished off the milk, then stood and went toward the bath. "I'll be in the shower. Eat your sandwich. And drink your milk. You need your strength to go back to Azbekastan."

He made no reply and my curiosity made me turn to look at him. His wonderful face was solemn, his dark eyes earnest, but I sensed his underlying anxiety.

Then, I understood. It wasn't only Eryx he was afraid of. It was Sophie. He feared I'd leave him, that I'd align my loyalty and love with her and shove him aside. He feared I'd not love him anymore. Of course it was irrational, but fears like this are rarely rational. They're visceral and real, and never to be mocked. If he needed me to verify my feelings for him every day for the rest of time, I'd do it. Because I loved him, and never wanted him to be unhappy or feel less than grounded.

Walking back to him, I stood between his thighs, cradled his head against my breasts and stroked his soft, silky hair. "I love you more than I will ever love anyone or anything. Do you believe me?"

It took him a moment to answer. He wrapped his arms around me and burrowed his face against my breasts, making his voice muffled. "Don't leave."

"I told you, I will never leave you, no matter what. But I have to go see about my sister. If it were your brother, wouldn't you go?"

His nod was slight.

"Of course you would. Now I'm going to shower and you're going with me."

"To Azbekastan?"

"That too."

He lifted his head and looked up at me. "You want me to shower with you?"

"Yes, and we may inadvertently have a shag, like we did last night." I sat next to him and handed him his sandwich. "Eat your dinner, Zee. I'll wait."

At no other time in the history of mankind has a sandwich been eaten that swiftly.

Almost three hours later, we transported back to the place I'd thought not to return until it was time to take all the lost souls to Hell on Earth. By now, it was the edge of dawn and Perböl was still mostly asleep. The palace guards were clustered around a small gatehouse on the eastern side of the grounds, drinking coffee and smoking. The majority of the population were lost souls, subdued and not a threat. The only possibility of attack was from outside of Azbekastan, a U.N. task force perhaps, or troops from neighboring Ravinia, sent to unseat Kovalev and restore order. Until that happened, the guards had little to do. The risk was evidently so low, the gates behind them were open.

From our observation spot within the shadows of the buildings across the boulevard fronting the palace, we watched the perimeter and the roof to see if other guards were more vigilant. In ten minutes, we saw exactly none. Zee whispered, "Do any of them look Skia to you?"

I shook my head. "The shade is light and I can see their eyes."

"That's what I think, so let's do this. Ready?"

"Ready."

"Hold my hand and don't say a word." I felt a chill when we went beneath a cloak, then we moved inhumanly fast toward the open gates. We carefully wound our way through the guards, careful not to touch, then hurried toward a side door of the palace that led through a narrow passageway into the grand reception hall at the front. He tugged me behind an enormous screen, painted with wood nymphs and faeries.

"How did you know where to go?"

"I've been here before. In 1743 we took down half of the palace staff and servants. Eryx turned the head butler to Skia and he converted as many as he could." He glanced at the ceiling that soared above us, filled with paintings of long dead kings and queens of Azbekastan, lined with gilded molding. The paint was faded and doomed to disintegrate from disrepair and neglect if Kovalev remained in power.

Zee drew me closer and whispered into my ear, "Close your eyes and do what you do. If you can't pinpoint where she is, we'll need to go to plan b."

"What's plan b?"

"We don't have one, so do your best."

I stayed close to him while I shut my eyes and concentrated carefully, urging my mind to travel across the grand hall, through a narrow hallway that led past a library, a study, a morning room, the chapel, and then a set of stairs, one of many. At the landing, my mind didn't wait or observe. I hadn't that kind of control. I turned to the right and raced down the hallway, turned and darted down another, around and around and up another flight of stairs and down more hallways. I knew the doors I passed were bedrooms, that there were people inside, but none were my sister. I would know. I continued through long corridors and narrow passageways and wide galleries until I came to a renovated, more modern section of the palace. It was familiar to me because I'd seen this in my dream last night. This is where Eryx came, where he found Kovalev in the bathtub.

My mind slowed slightly and moved along the hallway. I passed through a closed door and on the other side, my sister stood at the window, looking toward the eastern sky. To the sunrise.

"You've found her, haven't you?" Zee asked.

I nodded and held his hand more tightly. "Go with me." With my eyes still closed, I transported to the hall outside her room. When I opened my eyes, we were still behind the screen. *"Bugger."*

"Lockdown, remember?" His eyes were laughing at me. "Come on. We'll have to walk."

"It's a long way."

"You want me to carry you?"

I shot him a look and he grinned. "So, that's a no?"

"Zee, be serious."

Instantly, he sobered, but I caught the unmistakable twinkle in his eyes. Crazy hot shower sex meant he'd be in a devilishly good mood for hours and hours. I suspect I might have felt the same, except when I thought about Sophie living in this cold, run down palace with a douchecanoe like Eryx, it was impossible to feel anything but complete anxiety.

"We're still under a cloak, so be careful not to bump into anything. Most everyone in the palace is probably Skia, but just in case, we'll at least be invisible to some."

"Where is Eryx?"

"He's here, upstairs somewhere, walking around. Pacing, actually."

"Do you think he knows you're here?"

"If he knew, he'd be right here, right now. But his mind is on other things besides the Mephisto right now."

"Oh?"

"He has an Anabo under his roof. He's no doubt wondering how he can best use that to his advantage. He's curious if we know about her, if we'll try to rescue her. And he wants to know if she can give him the son he wants so desperately."

A *child?* Sophie having a *child?* With *Eryx?* "Hyperbole."

Zee shook his head. "He wants a miniature Eryx, a little man he can mold into his own image, who can go out and sucker the humans. He thinks if he has a son with an Anabo, the child will have all the best characteristics of her, and his own dark intentions."

"He'd be disarmingly sincere and charming and diabolical at the same time?"

"That's what Eryx thinks." He took my hand and we stepped out from behind the screen, moving as quickly and quietly as possible across the grand hall and through the palace, following the path I'd taken in my head. We were still in the old section when he whispered, "Cripes, you weren't kidding. We've walked a mile already."

I tugged his hand and he didn't say anything else. We finally arrived in the renovated section of the palace and within a few minutes, we stood in front of Sophie's door. Zee pulled me aside and whispered, "Someone's in there with her."

I listened and heard nothing but soft shuffling, like someone walking in house slippers. An attempt to make my mind pass through the door again failed, which didn't surprise me. My ability to see certain things was dodgy at the best of times, and it only ever seemed to work when I wanted to see something very far away. "Is it Eryx?"

He shook his head. "It's a maid, or a servant of some kind. An underling sort."

Then I heard a female voice. An American. "He'll be tired of you in a week. It's not as though you can continue touring, and as soon as you stop, you won't be such a big deal, will you? You'll be a has-been and he'll ditch you."

"You're terribly worried about me, which I'd ordinarily find generous and thoughtful, but your concern isn't about me at all. I have no words of comfort for you. No matter what you do to me, what you say, how violently you dislike my presence, I'm staying with him for the foreseeable future."

"Bitch. Whore. You're a cunt."

"Yes, you've said so already. Perhaps you might consult the online urban dictionary and discover some new and different vulgar insults. Go ahead. I'll wait here."

"God, you're a self-righteous bitch with a stick up your ass."

"If I did indeed have a stick, I would consider beating you about the head with it as a means to get you out of my room. I intend to take a shower and dress. Leave. Now."

"If you don't—"

"Oh, do sod off, Alissa. Give up and accept that I'm here."

I was astonished. My sister just told someone to sod off. I jerked a look at Zee, who lifted his brows.

"You're going to wish I was your friend when he gives you the boot, and it's inevitable. All he sees in you now is that you're famous. Everybody wants you and he thinks he does, too, but it's only a momentary interest."

"You are so very tiresome. As I've said, again and again, I am *not* Lady Euri. She is my twin. I'm not famous or talented or anything except determined to keep Eryx from sucking the souls from people."

"It's not so bad. Maybe you should try it."

"You've all the warmth and kindness of a wounded rhinoceros, Alissa. Your every waking thought is bitter, angry, and miserable. Not so bad? You've quite forgotten what it is to be human."

"Seriously, you're getting naked right now?"

"I told you I want to take a shower and since you won't leave, I'll have to work-around."

Again, I shot a look at Zee and he shrugged.

"He won't like that you have blond hair. He's very particular. And you're tall. And your boobs are . . . well, he'll probably like those."

Zee's brows shot up again, this time in a *Hmm, isn't that interesting?* expression. I pinched his arm.

"But if you think you can hold his attention longer than a week, maybe a month, tops, you're so way wrong."

"Is it all you think about?"

"What?"

"Eryx. And sex. And hoping he'll notice your existence? I realize you're but a clone of him, but you do still have some measure of autonomy. Do something. Take up sculpting. Paint. Write poetry. Garden. Cook. Learn bookkeeping. It's no wonder you're desperately miserable. What did you like to do before you met Eryx?"

There was a long pause, then Alissa said, "I was in the graduate program at Harvard. I would have been a biomedical engineer. Instead, I'm a lackey to a guy who doesn't remember I'm alive. I spend my days surfing the web, buying endless cosmetics and clothes and anything that might make him notice me."

"Why doesn't he send you out to recruit? He sends all his immortals out. Why not you?"

"He wants me near because he likes sex, and when he's tired and not up for going out trolling, he comes to me. I'm a convenience. A concubine."

"You just said you go to great lengths to get him to notice you."

"Wow, what you don't know about guys and sex is epic. He comes into my bed and wakes me up and ten minutes later, he's done and gone. I could be anybody. I had a boyfriend in Boston. He loved me. He made love to me. I stalk him on the Internet. He's married now, with three kids, lives in a two story house in Georgetown, and works in Washington. His wife looks so much like me, it's scary. Except now she's middle-aged."

"How long ago did you become immortal?"

"Twenty years."

I heard the water turn on in the shower, then the shower door as it closed.

"Maybe I *will* find something to do."

"Yes, that'd be lovely. Then I can take a shower without an audience."

"Why are you doing that to your hair?"

"It's called shampoo."

"You're a real smartass. I meant, why are you shampooing it that way?"

"It's how it was done for me when I couldn't do it myself.

Honestly, Alissa, this is beyond rude and exceedingly awkward. Do go away."

"I'm lonely. I'll stay and go with you to breakfast."

A deep, masculine voice with just a hint of an accent said, "Alissa, go to your room and leave Sophie alone."

I leaned in and whispered, "Eryx?"

Zee nodded. And gripped my hand a bit tighter before pulling me toward the room next door. He must have known it was empty before he opened the door. We slipped inside just as Sophie's door opened and we heard Alissa's footsteps as she walked away down the hall. We moved closer to the wall separating the rooms and stood immobilized while we listened.

"What are you doing to your hair?"

"I realize I'm your captive, but I still have the expectation of privacy. Step back, Eryx. I'll be out in a moment."

"No, really, why are you all bent over like that? The soap's getting in your eyes."

"They're closed."

"Look, if you'd stand up straight and lean your head back, you'd get it clean and not get soap all in your face. Here, let me show you."

"No touching, Eryx."

"It's not a sexual thing, Sophie. I was just trying to be helpful."

"Everything about you is sexual. You popped into my room uninvited without notice, wearing only a . . . whatever that is. Back off." There was a pause. "Is that a kilt?"

"It is. Do you like it?"

"I'm British. And female. Of course I like it."

"There, you see? We will be friends, after all."

"You're missing significant elements, like a shirt and a coat and a tie and a sporran and socks and shoes and empathy and the ability to see reality."

"I was in a hurry. I'll wear the whole get-up for you later, if you like. And I can't really help it, you know. I lost all hope of humanity when I jumped to my death a thousand years ago."

"Oh, bugger, here you are playing the martyr, as if this might elicit sympathy. Or perhaps you hope it'll induce me to give you a shag. Leave off, because no matter what else happens between us, I will never feel sorry for you, Eryx."

"Then why are you here?"

"You abducted me and brought me here. Less than twenty-four hours ago. Have you already forgotten?"

"Of course not. But why were you so compliant? Like you were waiting for me. Like you *wanted* me to come for you."

"I did want you to come for me."

"Why?"

"It's my purpose. And I don't have anything else to do."

"Didn't my father offer to take you to live with my brothers?"

"Yes, and with Euri, but I will never be Mephisto, so I thought I'd see what it's like to live with you."

"Do you truly believe you can stop me, just by being here?"

"I think I can stop you by loving you."

Then there was only silence. I looked up at Zee and saw pain and despair in his eyes. He slowly shook his head. Sophie was setting herself up.

"Do you mean romantically? Or platonically?"

"I don't know. I suppose if we have sex, it will be a romantic sort of love. If not, then you'll be my friend that I love."

"It's not this simple."

"Isn't it? What's complicated about it? You, of course, will never love me, or anyone. You're incapable. But as it stands, I'm pretty sure the only people who love you are your parents and Kyros. You need someone who cares about you. It's not as though the lost souls care. They despise you, actually. And while the immortals fawn over you, it's only for opportunity, always jockeying for position as the leader of the pack. None of them care a whit about you. It's rather ironic, all those souls to your credit, and they revile you."

"But you don't?"

"No, I don't, but I'm also impervious to your charms, to any carrot you might dangle in hopes of me handing you my soul. I know you as well as anyone has ever known you, and you desperately need someone to love you."

Eryx laughed. "And you've decided it has to be you?"

"Yes."

"How do you know me so well, Sophie?"

There was silence before she said, "I dream about you. Every night since I became immortal, I dream about you."

"That's odd."

"Why?"

"I've had a dream or two about you. I thought the girl in my dreams was . . . someone who looks like you. Her name was Jane."

"She was my ancestor. You murdered her."

"She lost herself, lost Anabo, and when she realized she could never go back, that Phoenix was lost to her forever, she lost her mind. It was a mercy to kill her."

Zee looked down into my eyes and I could see his torment. He would always feel responsible for what happened to Jane.

"Suppose I don't allow you to stay?" Eryx asked. His tone was different. He was connected in a way he had not been before.

"Then I will go away."

"Just like that?"

"No, you'll have to transport me somewhere. I have no means, no money, and the whole world thinks I'm dead, so since you brought me here, you'll have to take me out."

"Where would you go?"

"To see my sister. Then I'd go to God."

"You wouldn't stay immortal and fight me? Wouldn't you join the Mephisto?"

"No. M said I can never be Mephisto, only a Lumina, one of the immortal angels who live there and help them with all the nonviolent parts of fighting you. I have no skill sets, and no desire to be a Lumina, but mostly, I can't endure these dreams without some purpose behind the agony of living inside your head every night. So I'd see Euri one last time, then I'd go to God."

"Agony? Really?"

"You live it, Eryx. And I am infinitely perplexed that you have no idea how very twisted you are, or how lost you are from all that matters."

"Are you going to start spouting religious canon at me?"

"I don't know any religious doctrine well enough to lecture you on it, and please, don't insult my intelligence this way. I'm well aware your interest in religion is somewhere around your interest in feminine hygiene products."

"Actually, I'd find those far more interesting than some religious balderdash."

"I really wish you'd get out of here. I'm a modest person and it's unsettling to shower with you as my audience."

He ignored her request. "How do you know what you dream is real?"

"Because every dream unfolds in real life just as it does in my mind. I dream as if I am you, so when I wake up, I know your thoughts, your motivations, your innermost desires and needs. I'm with you when you plan, when you eat and get pissed on too much wine, when you wee, when you shag a girl. I was with you when you took Jordan, and when you came back and became aware that your home was gone. And that you'd lost Jordan. I know exactly what you thought about that. I have been with you for two years."

"Why? *How?*" He sounded a little panicked now. "Did Mephistopheles do something when he brought you back?"

"He didn't bring me back."

"God, then."

"No."

There was a pause. "Lucifer."

"I didn't want to come back, wasn't at all interested in immortality. M and Mary Michael tried to talk me into it, but I was ready to go to Heaven. I didn't have an easy life, Eryx. And so I said no, let me die, let me go, and then everything was dark and I was terribly cold and Lucifer was there. He wanted me to stay, very badly. He's quite sincere in his belief that I have a gift that will save humanity."

"And connected us so you could spy on me in your dreams."

"I have the sight, which is why he was so determined to convince me to come back. He connected me to you, but it can only work one way because you aren't fey. As for spying, he has no idea what I dream and we do not communicate, so what I learn of you remains in my head. It's just me, Eryx. Tuck your paranoia away. I will stay with you as long as you'll allow me. I will try to love you, give you all of what I have, and be your friend."

I looked up at Zee and he sighed. He slowly shook his head. He didn't think she had a prayer of changing Eryx. I whispered, "Not even a little bit?"

"Not even." He gripped my hand tighter. "Have you heard enough? Can we go now?"

"One more minute."

He nodded and we continued listening.

"This was Lucifer's grand plan for you? To come here and be my friend?" He laughed, but it had a hollow ring to it, as if he was scared to death and trying to make it sound as though he wasn't at all afraid.

"He told M he would attempt to win the war without violence. He seemed quite taken with the notion of introducing me into your life. I will become your Achilles heel."

"Do you believe it? Do you think you can alter my life and change my goal?"

"It's doubtful and a bit dodgy."

"Then why did you do it? Why did you agree to come back?"

"For Euri. She needs me to be alive. Lucifer reminded me of our connection and said she would suffer if I was gone. I don't always dream of you. Sometimes, I dream I see Euri. She always gives me a piece of her, just as she did when we were both alive. Without her, without the energy she gives me, I'd be unable to stay, and vice versa. I give her sanity. I ground her. We're dependent on each other for survival."

I sharply inhaled and shot a confused look at Zee. Was this true? How had I never known? I gave pieces of me to her, but I never realized she did the same for me. Was Sophie the reason I wasn't completely mad? I was humbled. Laid low. Stunned.

Zee slid his arm around me and drew me close and kissed my forehead.

It was quiet for a long time and I shot a questioning look at Zee. He whispered, "He's processing it. His mind is blown, and that's not easy to do. Also, she's probably shaving her legs and he's watching her. I watch you when you shave your legs. There's something extremely appealing about it."

Coincidentally, Eryx said just then, "Have you cut yourself?"

"So it seems. There are many things I've yet to master."

"Let me fix it for you."

"I've fixed it myself. See? It's already healing. Do you intend to make me leave?"

The water stopped, the shower door opened, and I swear I heard Eryx swallow. "I don't . . . you aren't . . . what did you say?"

"I asked if your intention is to make me leave. And why are you turning your back on me now? The horse has left the barn already."

"You're too distracting. Hurry up and put that robe on."

"What's this? Alissa was so sure you'd not find me attractive. Something about being blond and tall?"

"I do tend to like petite brunettes, but you're naked. And very beautiful. And saying you love me."

"I don't love you. Not yet."

"This is absurd. I'm taking you back to Stockholm. Or to your sister. Where is she?"

"Next door, eavesdropping on us. With Zee."

I gasped and froze in fear when a door opened into the bedroom where we stood. It led to the bathroom, which was shared with Sophie's bedroom. Eryx's kilt rode low on his hips and I was petrified that it would slide right off and he'd be naked. I'd never noticed when I saw him through Zee's eyes, but in person, he was deadly beautiful.

Except his eyes. They were flat and lifeless, black as sin at midnight.

"Hello, brother," he said to Zee, leaning against the doorjamb while Sophie came toward me with open arms, wearing a terrycloth robe and a wide, happy smile.

Holding her close, practically squeezing her to death, I was so overcome that I couldn't speak.

Zee asked Sophie, "How did you know we were here?"

"I saw you sneak across the lawn and decided you must be here to rescue me, but I don't want to be rescued. You understand, don't you?"

"No," he said. "We understand your thinking, but you're misguided because Eryx is hopeless, and it's a sad waste of your life to try. Come with us and be happy."

She pulled back from my arms to stare into my eyes. "You understand, don't you?"

I nodded, but said, "What happens if you fail?"

Sophie shrugged. "Nothing ventured, nothing gained."

"You would be so happy with the Mephisto. I know you would. There's a Lumina there who's so much like George. You'd be his friend, Sophie."

"I'll be Eryx's friend."

I shot a glance at him, aware he looked a trifle smug. "Do you understand what he is, love? Do you know what he's done in the world, the misery he's caused?"

Sophie hugged me again and said into my hair, "I know more than anyone who and what he is, and I still want to stay. I'll be just fine, Euri. I've always been fine."

"There's a difference between fine and happy. You've never been truly happy, and you deserve that, more than anyone I've ever known."

She pulled back again and blinked at me, as if she was confused. "Why do I deserve it more?"

"Because you're all that's good, the best of mankind."

Her arms fell away and she smiled at me as she stepped back. Toward Eryx. I couldn't quite believe this was happening. My sister was choosing Eryx – *Eryx!* – over me. I wasn't hurt. I was gobsmacked. Perhaps even angry. I had fully expected to take her home with Zee and me, to Mephisto Mountain. We'd meet the family together. She'd move into one of those empty bedrooms upstairs. She'd be one of us. She'd be my sister, my friend.

Instead, she wanted to stay here and tilt at windmills.

"I don't think a person's soul makes them more or less entitled to happiness," she said. "Does Eryx deserve misery because his soul is dark?"

"He's doomed to it, whether he deserves it or not."

"You're missing my point. Nobody *deserves* unhappiness."

"Even those who mete it out? Those who ensure the misery of others? Like our mum?"

"What she did to others is why she was unhappy. Instant karma."

Eryx pushed away from the door and moved to stand just behind Sophie. "What did your mother do?"

I narrowed my eyes at him. "She drowned Sophie when she was six years old."

"How did she live to eighteen if she was drowned?"

"She was resuscitated and lived the rest of her mortal life in a wheelchair, unable to speak. When we were eighteen, Mum finished the task by driving the three of us into a lake. I believe she thought she could escape a sinking car, but she was wrong. We all drowned."

He smiled at Sophie, and if I hadn't known better, I'd think it was genuine. He appeared to be sincerely pleased for her. "How magnificent of my father to offer life immortal after your mother succeeded in murdering you. Has it been marvelous to walk and talk?"

She nodded and didn't flinch when he took her hand. "I've especially enjoyed riding a horse. I'd like to try other things, and see all the places I only ever saw on the telly, like the Grand Canyon, and St. Mark's Square."

"So you weren't teasing when you said you've never been kissed?"

"No, I was completely serious."

Eryx was looking at her like she was the most fascinating creature he'd ever seen. Her openness of heart and soul intrigued him. She kept nothing guarded, nothing hidden. He really didn't know what to do with that.

I suspected Eryx was in for a lot of surprises, not all of them pleasant.

I glanced at Zee and saw him become focused on a spot toward the top of the wall. A red spot. When I looked up at it, I knew it was growing in his mind.

Holy hell and damn, he was sliding into a red day.

I couldn't let Eryx see him do this. I had no idea if he could use it against the Mephisto. I didn't even care at that moment. All I could think was, I have to get him out of here, away from anyone who might see him or interfere in his madness. He had to come out of it because he wanted to, had to find his way through the fog on his own. I could help him back to reality, but not here, not in this cold palace where he was surrounded by enemies.

Standing straighter, I grasped his hand more firmly and said, "Will you call me, Sophie? I'll spend every moment of every day wondering about you, hoping and praying you're safe."

Eryx said, very seriously, "She'll come to no harm from me. We'll come to one of your concerts and you can see for yourself that I'm not the monster you believe me to be."

As if. He didn't know I'd traveled across Azbekastan and seen the horrors he had brought to the people. He didn't know I'd dreamed of him, saw into his thoughts, knew his motivations. But I didn't say that. It was best if he didn't know we'd been here already, that we were putting together a blueprint of how to take down all of his minions in this barren wasteland of humanity.

I didn't want to look at his eyes, so I kept mine on Sophie and said, "You'll have to do it soon. I've only two performances left. The last is at Blackbriar in New York on Saturday night."

Sophie smiled. "We will be there."

It was a bit of an out of body experience because it was so foreign to my inclination, which was to snatch my sister close and run with her as far away from here as possible, but I turned and walked out, holding Zee's hand, and left my twin, whom I'd spent my life protecting, with the worst threat to all mankind.

By the time we'd walked back through the castle, down the stairs, into the little chapel, Zee was completely gone. His breathing was crazy fast, his eyes were unfocused and glassy, and he clung to my hand like a drowning man. As soon as we cleared the doorway of the chapel and stood on holy ground, I transported both of us back to Colorado, to the sanctuary of walls and privacy and music. Zee collapsed to the floor, dragging me down with him, and began to cry, sobbing the name of God with his face smashed against the rug, begging for help, for peace, for an end to what his mind brought to him. I could only wonder what horrors he witnessed. And he was a part of it, not a spectator, but a participant.

I rolled him to his back, straddled his chest, and smoothed his hair. While he cried, while his soul was awash in anguish, I called his name, softly at first, then louder, and finally, I practically shouted. "Xenos! Wake up! Stop this! *Come back to me.*"

He was deeper into the red than I'd ever seen him. An

hour stretched into two and his big body jerked and folded in half, shoving me aside. I scrambled to climb back on top of him, and he grabbed my arms and looked up at me and didn't see me. He was somewhere else in the world, living inside the head of someone doing something truly horrific. I started to cry at the unfairness of it. Why would a gentle, loving man such as Zee have this terrible curse? I decided I would go all over the world in search of a way to help him learn to corral his insanity, to use this sight for a purpose, for good. The problem was that when he went into a red day, his mind was completely overtaken by the thoughts and life of another. He became that other person, and he lost all touch with reality.

The physicality of me stroking him, touching him, the pressure and weight of my body on his always eventually got through, and he would finally come back to himself. This time, he took a lot longer, but I never gave up. He threw me off of him several times, and I climbed right back on. I willed his sound system to turn on and enveloped the room in Brahms, his favorite piece.

I was exhausted and hoarse from crying and calling his name before he blinked and his eyes began to focus.

As he'd done every time before, he set me aside, got to his feet, then picked me up and took me to the shower. He thought I was covered in blood. I passively went along while he stood me beneath the water, still fully clothed, and began to wash me clean. He took each article of clothing from my body and tossed it aside and rubbed my skin until it tingled. Only when he was confident the blood was gone, that I was safe from the contamination of fury and death, did he begin to regain lucidity.

When he was back, when he was aware of his surroundings, he crushed me against him and cried again, but not because of what he saw in his mind. His emotions were a runaway train, unstoppable. He murmured, "I love you," over and over, then whispered against my neck, "You didn't leave me. You didn't . . ."

"I'll never leave you, Zee. Never, ever."

"Even for her?" he mumbled.

"Even for her."

"You said you give pieces of yourself to her, that you

want to fix her. But you're here, with me, and no part of you is missing. No part of you isn't mine. I can't survive without you, Euri. Do you know?"

"Yes, love, I know," I whispered. "You're the other half of my soul, Zee, and I can't survive without you. Do you believe me?"

He cried harder and held me tighter.

And I knew that he finally, at long last, understood who I was and what I was about.

CHAPTER 15

~~ ZEE ~~

We went to bed and I finally got a grip and stopped crying. I couldn't remember ever losing it like that before. And I know I'd never been that vulnerable. There was no corner of my soul that Euri had not seen, and yet she was here, with me. She loved me. She chose me over her twin. She left Sophie with Eryx because she had to make a choice – and she chose me.

It was ridiculous to think of her love for me and her twin in black and white terms. I knew this. She didn't love Sophie any less than she always had, and there was no doubt we'd have mountains of issues and problems going forward. Her sister, an Anabo of the purest heart, was living with Eryx, whose one goal in life was to kill Lucifer and take over Hell. Of course Euri would be afraid and anxious and would undoubtedly insist we go to extraordinary lengths to ensure she was well and unharmed. And when things weren't going well, which was inevitable because of Eryx, we'd have more issues and trauma. But none of that really mattered. All that mattered was that Euri walked away from Sophie because I needed her. I knew now, without a shadow of doubt, that she would never leave me. I'd banished the worst of my demons, and I was practically dizzy with euphoria.

I made love to Euri slowly, so slowly, and in the soft light of the candles on the mantel, she smiled up at me and said, in Swahili, "I love you and your oxen."

And I replied, "My oxen will be at the gate when you wake up. With all my love."

And she came for me, with that hitch of breath and sweet quarter note. Like a little bird.

In my dreams that night, for the first time in a thousand years, it wasn't me running into the church. I stood behind the altar and waited for Euri. The doors opened and she rushed down the aisle, crying, arms wide. I opened mine, expecting her, anticipating holding her, but she stopped at the altar and fell to her knees and begged God to take her home, that she couldn't go on, didn't have the strength.

And I realized this wasn't Euri. This was Sophie. A light came from above and I stepped back, awed by a host of angels, led by my mother, who lifted Sophie and took her away.

The doors opened again and, just as Sophie's last cry reverberated through the cathedral, Eryx stood at the threshold and screamed her name, begged her to come back. He ran inside and was instantly consumed by fire. He fell to the floor, crying her name, tearing his clothes, pleading for her not to leave him.

I woke on a gasp and all was quiet. I heard the tick-tock of the grandfather clock in the library downstairs, and Euri's soft breath, and a whinny from one of Ty's horses in the stables. I willed the drapes to open and saw that it was snowing. All was peaceful. At the window, I looked out at the snowy night and knew I would never have the dream again. I couldn't be sure, of course, because dreams don't work that way, but I thought perhaps it had never been me, all these years. Maybe I'd been living in Eryx's dream, just as I lived in a stranger's head during my red days.

It didn't matter, really. I would never have that dream again. The curse of my madness would take a new turn, a different direction.

I felt Euri at my back, her soft fingers tracing circles against my skin. I told her my dream, and my thoughts. "Do you think it's possible? Could it be that it was never me at all?"

She moved around me and slipped into my arms and rested her head against my shoulder. "Anything's possible," she whispered, "but how do you know for sure you'll never have the dream again?"

I smoothed her silky hair and smiled. "Because I know."

As I'd promised, I took Euri to see the Liberty Bell in Philadelphia, and we spent some time at the Benjamin Franklin Museum. Then I took her for Philly cheesesteaks, which she didn't love as much as I did, but that didn't stop her from eating one.

The Arcadia concert that night was as wild as any I'd seen, but the new security John had hired did manage to keep the fans off of the stage and away from the band.

The next day, the band traveled to New York, and had the night off before the final concert the next night. Afterward, Euri would go to her hotel room at the Waldorf and die in her sleep, as Jordan had died, the victim of an aneurysm. Key said he and Jordan would take care of her doppelganger.

As soon as she'd checked in at the hotel, I suggested she should call her dad, and they spent an hour on the phone. She told him she loved him, and seemed okay when they ended the call.

On Saturday, I helped her pack all of her things that were in my closet and we carried them to her hotel room. Except the Victoria pearls. Keeping personal items was against Key's rules for people who became immortal and moved to Mephisto Mountain, because taking things out of the real world caused confusion amongst the humans and made the new immortal more aware of their inability to go back, which was counterintuitive to our purpose.

Nevertheless, we stowed the pearls in my underwear drawer. Then we went shopping and she found new clothes to take to her new home. With me.

When we were done and she had all the basic essentials, including girly stuff like make-up and lady razors and the like, I took her for sushi at a midtown restaurant. We were inundated with paparazzi, which was okay because this would be the last of it.

After I'd dropped her at Blackbriar for rehearsal and sound check, I went to Tiffany's and bought her a diamond ring. It was understated but rich, and classically beautiful. Like Euri.

I bought pink roses and peonies in a crystal vase and took them to my room and set them on the piano. Mathilda was there, cleaning and puttering and carrying on about the disgrace of my worn upholstery. "Lady Euri is an aristocrat, Master Xenos. Ye can't have a fine lady like her sitting her bum on a worn chair. Ye go and buy new, as soon as ye can."

"I was waiting for Euri to help me. I think she'll like decorating our room so it's as much hers as it is mine."

Mathilda harrumphed, but nodded agreement. She fluffed the flowers, smoothed the bed, then looked at me and smiled. "'Tis a happy day for ye, Zee."

"Yes, but it'd be happier if Mariah would wake up."

She came around to stand before me and whispered, "Go and see your brother. Ye've no idea what's happened to him."

Curious, I went upstairs to the third floor, outside of Mariah's room, and rapped on the door. At Phoenix's invitation to come in, I went inside and was instantly aware of a strange light. I blinked and moved toward my brother, who sat next to Mariah's bedside, reading a romance novel to her. She sat up against the pillows, her eyes open, but she saw nothing, was unaware of anything.

I went to the opposite side of the bed so I could see Phoenix's face. He looked at me over the top of the book and I knew what Mathilda meant. Phoenix's eyes were gray, and he had that strange light of divinity in his face, just as Kyros had when he came home with Jordan, just as Jax had when he came out of that church in St. Petersburg, holding Sasha's hand. I wondered if my face looked like that the morning I knew I loved Euri?

That's when it hit me that for Jax, Key, and I, our realization of love for another was coupled with the reality of their love for us. In fact, that was the crucial side of the covenant, that we manage to elicit real love from an Anabo, from someone not predisposed through genetics to love us.

"Did she tell you she loved you before she went away?"

"No."

Looking from his face to hers, my confusion must have shown. Phoenix said softly, "In the wee hours this morning, I had a visitor."

"God? Did God visit you?"

"Lucifer."

"Whoa, that's heavy."

"He offered to wake her up if I agreed to go with him."

"And you said yes?"

He nodded. "I was telling her goodbye, even though she can't hear me, and an angel appeared."

"Our mother?"

"Jane."

I hadn't seen that coming. It took me a moment to absorb it. "What did she say?"

"That I'm redeemed. That I'm forgiven."

I leaned against the wall and looked at Mariah. Where was she? What was her reality right now?

"She said you should accept Euri, that she's a kindred spirit."

Key had told me not to say anything to Phoenix about Euri. It wasn't so much that Phoenix would resent my happiness, but that he would be more depressed. He'd reached the end of his rope, Key said. I imagined he must have lost it last night, and Lucifer came to offer him a way out, an end to the endless spiral of misery Mariah was stranded in. And in the midst of it all, while he said goodbye and ripped his heart out, Jane came and brought redemption with her.

And now he could leave and go to Heaven, and there he'd be with Mariah.

He smiled at me. "You've got it all figured out, don't you?"

I nodded. "Except I don't know why you're still here. Why didn't you go last night? Why didn't Jane take you and Mariah with her?"

"I don't know. She disappeared and Lucifer never came back, and so I've been sitting here ever since, feeding Mariah like I always do, reading this book and praying so hard that she'll wake up and know me and not remember what happened to her."

"Whatever happens, I want you to know I'm happy for you."

"No hard feelings, Zee?"

"Like I said before, you spent over a century wearing a

horsehair shirt of guilt. And now, Jane appeared and forgave you. It's all done and tied off."

He nodded and looked at Mariah. "If she'd just wake up."

I never told people things I didn't think they should hear. I didn't say what I saw because it would alter how they reacted and it seemed wrong on a fundamental level. Life happened and people lived it as best they could. Not knowing what was around the corner was the hard part, but it was also sometimes the best part.

Standing there watching Mariah, I knew she was on her way back. She'd gone a very long way away, but she was coming back to life, to Mephisto Mountain. To Phoenix.

I pushed away from the wall and said to my brother, "Don't leave her side, not even to go pee."

He jerked a look at me. "You know?"

I walked toward the door. "See you at dinner, Phoenix."

An hour later, Mathilda bustled through the house, grinning, exclaiming over the miracle. She'd popped up to check on Mariah, and she was awake. In the shower with Phoenix. Laughing.

I went to my room and played the piano and smiled and connected to Euri, who was drinking a craft beer with the band. She knew right away what had happened. She laughed out loud and raised her glass and said, "Here's to every bloke in Christendom who ever loved a girl!"

Mariah wore a black dress and a pair of black heels to dinner. Her convalescence hadn't significantly altered her appearance, but I noticed something I hadn't seen before. An air of peace and calm surrounded her, a serenity that made her incredibly beautiful. And she was very obviously mad about Phoenix.

Holding her hand, sporting a wide smile, he walked her into the dining room and everyone stood and clapped. Jordan rushed toward her and they hugged and cried and Phoenix muttered, "Key should buy stock in Kleenex. We're turning into crybabies."

"Shut up, Phoenix," Jordan said.

"As you wish, sister. Now, stop getting snot all over

Mariah's dress and let her sit down so she can eat. She's been eating gruel for three weeks."

She pulled away and said, "I love you, Mariah. I'm so sor—"

"No, none of that. It was a bad time. You weren't yourself. Let's look ahead and put it behind us, okay?"

"Okay." She swiped at the tears on her cheeks and gave Mariah a watery smile. "We're going to see Euri play in New York later. Do you want to go?"

She shot a look at me, clearly confused, and on instruction from Key not to let on about Euri until later, I said, "Don't read anything into it. She won't know . . . we're just going to see Arcadia. Nothing else. You should go. They're most excellent."

I glanced at Phoenix, who was as clueless about Euri as Mariah. He didn't want to go. He wanted to keep Mariah home, with him, safe and secure. She was only just back from a three-week walkabout in her head. Nevertheless, he knew it was best for her to get out a bit, to feel alive again. He finally said, "Just for a couple of hours, and no alcohol."

Mariah smiled wryly. "Thanks, Dad."

"You're still my patient until I decide you're well. Now sit down and eat. Hans made your favorite. Short ribs."

"How do you know it's my favorite?"

He led her to a chair and pulled it out. "Because I'm the master of observation. Also, Hans told me."

While we took our seats, she looked around at our faces. "Did I really eat gruel for three weeks?"

Deacon said from behind her chair, "No, Anabo, you ate quite well. Phoenix was making a joke." There was a pause, then, "Heh."

It was the Deacon equivalent of laughter, and whatever anxiety remained dissipated.

When dinner was done, we all transported to New York, to Blackbriar. After I had all of my family situated at a table close to the front, and a round of drinks had been procured for everyone except Mariah, who got a Coke, but including Denys, even though he was already halfway trashed, I made my way backstage and found Euri in the green room with the rest of the band. I could tell she was sentimental about leaving. The guys were especially attentive, toasting her with champagne, making wild boasts about how far they'd go to see her play the piano. She was a bit misty, but when she looked across the room at me, she nodded and smiled. She was ready to go. I returned her smile and left through the side door, into the back hall of the club. I nearly ran right into Eryx.

"Hello, brother," he said.

I looked around. "Where's Sophie?"

"I left her up on the catwalk. It's not as if she can be in the crowd. They'd trample her, thinking she's Euri."

"Is she all right?"

He looked bemused. "She appears to be extraordinarily happy and well adjusted."

He was dressed in a black sweater, faded Levis and a pair of well-worn boots. It had been eons since I'd seen him wear anything but a suit, if I didn't count seeing him half dressed in that kilt. Sophie was having some kind of effect on him.

"We left Azbekastan yesterday and are staying in her house in Stockholm."

"So you abandoned Azbekastan?"

"Haven't you seen the news?"

"Actually, no." I'd been busy getting Euri ready to live with me on a permanent basis, absorbed in thoughts of her, buying her a ring because I intended to ask her to marry me. We weren't human and didn't live in the world of manmade laws, so marriage had no legal meaning, but it had spiritual significance. We would commit to one another and ask God's blessing. And Lucifer's, which was messed up, but our entire existence was all kinds of bizarre. Sasha and Jax had done it, and I was certain Key and Jordan would, and Phoenix and Mariah. So I would propose to Euri, and give her the ring. And flowers.

But of course I didn't say any of that to Eryx. He really wouldn't get it. Or care.

"Russia sent troops into Azbekastan and took over in Perböl."

I didn't bother acting surprised. "And Kovalev?"

Eryx gave me a cagey look. "Suicide."

"You took him out?"

"I had to. The man was a sick bastard who murdered

children and got off on it."

The irony almost made me laugh. Eryx wanted people's souls, but he abhorred murdering children. I didn't mention what I knew about Azbekastan. If he was aware of what we'd learned, that we knew a large percentage of the people who'd survived Kovalev's genocide were lost souls, he might devise some method of killing them all, to keep us from capturing them.

Taking down all those lost souls in Azbekastan could take a year or more, and it would be tedious, painstaking work, but I'd have Euri with me for reconnaissance and despite the nature of the work, I wouldn't mind so much. I could go anywhere and do anything if I had Euri at my side. "You do realize that Sophie's house and staff are paid for by our father?"

"It's only temporary, until I can rebuild Erinýes, but yes, he told me. He suggested I stay in Stockholm and take a hiatus. I think he believes Sophie will be the change I need to find my way back and be a real boy again."

M never gave up hope that Eryx would not be a lost cause. I guess that came with being a parent. Or maybe he hoped to rid himself of guilt. If Eryx regained even a shred of his humanity, our mother's heart would heal. She saw what Eryx was, what he did to people, and his motivations, and it had to break her. And while she didn't hate M, didn't lay blame at his door, that didn't alter his guilt or his never-ending hope that Eryx would recover some of what he'd lost. I gave Eryx a look. "Is he wrong?"

I nearly choked when he actually looked pensive, as if the thought wasn't completely out there.

Then, he laughed. "Of course he's wrong. I can't stop now, not when I'm this close."

"How close are you?"

He grew serious. "Nervous, Xenos?"

I shrugged. "I'm many things, but never nervous."

"Perhaps you should be at least a little anxious. If I win the war, you lose Euri."

He wanted me to argue, but I didn't care enough. Eryx was a sad, pathetic excuse for a brother and at no time did I ever consider him worthy of argument.

"She's Anabo, without Original Sin. If I win, she goes to

God and you go with all the rest of humanity."

I stepped around him and walked away, but said as I went, "I hope Sophie enjoys the concert. This will be her first. I'll pop up and take her a drink."

Right behind me, he said, "She's probably never had alcohol. Don't take her anything. I'll get her something. I'll take care of her."

"Suit yourself." I pretended not to notice that he sounded like a guy who actually gave a damn. It seemed extremely unlikely, and I naturally wondered what he was up to. Everything he did was suspect, especially when he exhibited characteristics ordinarily considered the better part of humanity, like kindness and concern for someone other than himself.

But I also couldn't forget what had happened with Jordan. He'd been completely obsessed with her, and none of us could quite figure it out. He'd been so certain he could win her, he'd made Mariah immortal so she would stay with him and make Jordan feel more settled. He went to great trouble and showed tremendous restraint in all his efforts to win Jordan, and when she took a chance and believed him, I wasn't sure if he'd known all along it would never work. Had he secretly hoped it might? Did some deeply hidden part of Eryx wish for a chance, for a sliver of light in his soul?

I had always wondered why taking over the reins of Hell was so important to him. Phoenix and Key said it was to fill the void that was his spirit, that he thought he could replace what he'd lost if he ruled all of mankind.

It was a logical assumption, but I wasn't so sure. I had always felt the whisper of something not quite right with what we knew about Eryx, like a solitary wrong note in an entire symphony. There was something to him that we couldn't see or understand. Chances were excellent that Eryx also didn't understand or know. He wasn't one to analyze his motivations.

I took a seat next to Key, who was holding Jordan's hand while they gave each other looks that would be awkward if it wasn't so dark. It didn't take rocket science to figure out what would happen in their bedroom tonight.

The front band was a group from Ireland, with a

drummer and a fiddle player I made a mental note to keep an eye on because they were über talented. When they were done playing, the lights went up for a while and the crowd grew restless, waiting for Arcadia. They began to chant Euri's name. I glanced up and saw Eryx and Sophie perched on the catwalk, their feet dangling below. He was pointing things out and describing them while she paid rapt attention. Thus far, the Mephisto hadn't noticed them. They were cloaked, so no one else could see them, but because of where they sat, close to the ceiling, in the shadows, no one who could see them ever noticed. Except me.

Denys came back from trolling the club, drunker than before. He laughed too loud, called attention to us, and generally was a nuisance. I said to Ty, "If he makes a scene, I'm kicking his ass."

Ty shrugged, all his attention on a tall girl who stood in the crowd of people in the center of Blackbriar, where there were no tables or chairs. "He'll find a girl soon and hit the road."

"He'll miss Arcadia."

Ty shot me a look. "He'll miss it either way. He's too drunk to focus on music."

Denys turned a chair around and straddled it, then said to a brown-haired girl at the table in front of us, "Hey, beautiful, what's your favorite Arcadia song? I bet it's 'Send Me Down', isn't it?"

She ignored him. The girls she shared the table with glanced back at him and smiled, but the one in the middle, the one Denys was hitting on, never moved.

He asked her another question and she ignored him again.

The third time, she got up and left. Denys, not to be dissuaded, got up and followed her.

Arcadia finally started their first set and I lost interest and notice of anything but Euri. She was magnificent, as always, but tonight there was an edge to her music that brought the band's performance to a new level of awesome. The other guys seemed more enthusiastic than they had of late, maybe because they knew this was their last concert on this tour, and the last time with Euri. Whatever the reason, the music was magic and the audience knew it.

When they took a break, because Blackbriar required all performers to break so they could sell more liquor, I stayed in my seat, wanting to give Euri her space. That's when Eryx decided to let the others know he was there, maybe in keeping with his decision to stalk us. He leaned against the wall and watched us, and we mostly ignored him, but his presence clearly upset Mariah. Phoenix pulled her close and whispered something and she relaxed. I think Eryx was pleased to get a reaction. A quarter of an hour later, when Arcadia still hadn't returned to the stage, Phoenix nodded at me. "I'm taking her home. It's been two hours and she's exhausted."

"Thanks for coming."

Phoenix glanced toward the stage. "Good luck, Zee. She's mighty fine."

He didn't know. He would tomorrow. For now, I accepted his well wishes and said goodbye. He took Mariah's hand and led her out of the club, into the darkness where they would pop away from New York and back to Colorado.

Denys returned, even drunker than before, complaining about the girl who ignored him. He said she had a backstage pass and ditched him to go back there during the break, and she was bound to hook up with the bass player. "He's a total nerd, and the ladies are all over that. What gives, man?"

Jax said, with an edge of impatience, "Not every female in the world wants to do you, bro. Move on and find somebody else."

"I guess maybe she's über religious. Has a Star of David on her necklace. Probably she only dates nice Jewish boys her mama picks out."

"You're not nice," Ty said practically, "or Jewish, and no mama anywhere would pick you out for her daughter. Leave it, Denys."

He went for sour grapes. "Yeah, she's kinda on the plump side anyway."

"She has *curves*," Sasha said, scowling at him. "Where do you get off, Judgy McJudgerson? Since she didn't swoon into your arms, now there's something wrong with her?"

"Calm down, Sasha," Jax said, "and ease up."

She rounded on him and frowned. "He hides behind that

laugh and his jokes, but deep down, he's lonely and jealous and a spoiled brat. You all spoiled him when he was little, then spent the next thousand years giving him anything he wanted. Now, he can't deal with not having what he wants most of all, what no one can give him. Maybe if somebody, *anybody*, told him to step off and made him be accountable, he'd sober up, get off the pity party train, and *do* something. Everyone else in this family does works outside of just going on takedowns. All he does is chase girls and get drunk, and you're doing him no favors by enabling him to go on like this. Wake up, Ajax!"

We'd all grown accustomed to Sasha giving us lectures, but I hadn't ever heard her say something like this. Neither had anyone else, so we all sat in awe and shock.

Except Denys. He stood and swayed a little before he said, "Sorry if I offended you. I'll take myself away and stop ruining your party."

"Now you're a martyr," she said with heavy disgust in her voice. "I wonder who you really are, Denys?"

He grinned at her, because that's how Denys dealt with anything unpleasant. "I'm not sure, Sasha. Let me think . . ." He tipped his head back and tapped his chin, as if giving it a great deal of thought.

His eyes widened, he lost his grin, and I realized, entirely too late, that he saw Sophie.

With Eryx.

I hastened to say, "She's not Euri."

Key stood and moved close to Denys. "She's Euri's twin."

He looked at Key, then at me, and the fury in his eyes made me recoil. "She's Anabo and she's with Eryx, and *you're okay with that?* What the fuck is *wrong* with you?"

"It's what she wants," I said.

He was so drunk, he had no filter at all. Looking up at Sophie, he shouted, "Are you stupid or just an idiot? *Fuck you!* Fuck the whole fuckin' world! You want my brother? The one without a fucking *soul?* You'll get what you ask for! You'll pray for death because he will *lay waste* to you and everything you love."

People turned to watch with an array of expressions: fear, anticipation, shock, anger. They of course couldn't see Sophie, or Eryx, so Denys appeared completely nutso, shouting at the empty catwalk.

Jordan stood and said, "Freeze everyone, Kyros. Do it now."

He waved his arms and all noise instantly stopped. No voices, no clink of glasses and ice, no footsteps. There was no movement anywhere.

Except there was. There, at the back of the club, in the dark shadows beneath the mezzanine.

It was the brown-haired girl, hurrying toward the door. The only way she could not be frozen was if she was Skia, or Anabo. I jerked a look up at Eryx, who slowly shook his head.

She wasn't Skia, which meant she was Anabo.

Denys had missed it entirely because he was so caught up in his rage against us for allowing an Anabo to be with Eryx. And because he was drunk. An Anabo, perhaps meant for him, and even after following her around, he missed it, didn't see her glow because he was so fucking drunk. We hadn't seen it because she'd never turned, and we never saw her face.

I was about to tell Key that I would go after her, when Euri appeared, looking panicked. "What's happening? In the green room, all the guys are fro—" She looked around at the people in the club. "Everyone's frozen. Why?"

Wide-eyed, Ty looked from Euri to me and said, "I'm going to go out on a limb and guess that you didn't meet Euri just the one time."

"It's a long story. One for later."

Euri said to me, "Did you see August? She was already spooked, then everybody froze and she ran away. Did you see her? Did she come this way?"

So the Jewish girl was August, who'd called Euri so many weeks ago and said she'd be at this concert. Who had an Anabo birthmark. And now she was gone. "She ran out the front door."

"Wait," Denys said, blinking, trying desperately to make his alcohol-infused brain stop stuttering. "Are you saying that girl is Anabo?"

Key said to Euri, "You know that girl? Her name is August? Why didn't you tell us? It's absolutely imperative that we're all made aware when an Anabo is found."

Euri ignored him. "She ran before I learned her last name. She was so afraid."

"Well, duh," Sasha said. "Everyone freezing in place is über freaky." She nudged Jax. "Let's go find her. She can't have gone far."

"I don't even know what she looks like. I wasn't paying attention and she never turned around."

From above, Eryx said, "I saw her. I'll find her."

In unison, we all said, *"No!"*

He raised his hands as if in surrender. "No worries. I'll bring her right back here so you can tell her she's destined to become immortal and tied to either the alky or the giant. It'll just make her day, I'm sure."

"Maybe it will, Señor Sarcastic," Sophie said. "You know, it wouldn't kill you to feel something for your brothers besides disdain."

He smiled. "I don't have feelings, remember?"

She looked down at us and said, "It's a moot point anyway. Denys has gone off to find her."

I looked all around and realized she was right. Denys was gone.

Euri said, "Zee, please, go with me to look for her. Denys is . . . he might have some trouble."

"What she means," Eryx said, "is that the Anabo is gone forever and for good if drunk Denys is in charge of finding her. He couldn't find his ass with both hands. Why'd you let him become an alcoholic, Kyros? He looks up to you. It's just too bad you never took the time away from fighting me to be a real brother to him."

"Fuck you," Key said, and flipped him off. "Go back under your rock and leave us be."

Naturally Eryx took that as a taunt, an invitation for a fight, so he popped down to where we stood, and took a swing at Kyros. And made it. He knocked him backward and he stumbled into some of the frozen concertgoers.

Jordan moved between them. "I punched you out once, remember?"

Eryx grinned. "Sure do."

"I'll do it again if you don't back off."

"Go ahead. Give it your best shot."

Jordan was winding up to do just that when Euri moved

next to Eryx and said, "It's no good, you know."

"What's no good?"

"You and my sister." She lowered her voice, but I heard her say, "I won't let her stay with you. She's too pure of heart, and you'll destroy her. Give her back. Do it now. Tell her she has to go with me."

He forgot Jordan, and Key, and everything on earth except Euri and her demand. I watched the play of emotions as they crossed his face, reaction he felt on a primitive level, what he felt too acutely to inhibit or hide. He definitely had feelings, and he wasn't giving Sophie up. "No. You need to back off."

"Your entire being is selfish. You have no idea what she is, or what she can do. She needs kindness and compassion. What will you give her? You're incapable of anything but selfish greed, a slave to your never-ending need to *be* somebody. You'll tire of her and then what? You'll turn her into a needy, helpless doormat, just like Alissa."

"That's an insult to your sister. She will never lose her soul. Alissa handed hers over within an hour of meeting me. She and Sophie are from different planets."

"This isn't negotiable, Eryx. I will get her away from you, whether you like it, or not."

He stepped closer, his mouth set in a firm line of anger, his eyes snapping with fury.

She stood straighter and her hands clenched into fists.

Shit was about to get real, and the freeze wouldn't last all that much longer. And I knew Euri was fighting a losing battle. As long as Sophie was determined to stay with him, there wasn't much Euri could do. And picking a fight with Eryx was never a sound idea.

She was saying, "Does Sophie know the truth about Jane?" when I moved toward her and reached for her arm so I could pull her back and diffuse the arc of rage forming between them.

But before I could even touch her, Eryx did something with his hand, something to Euri's neck, and she collapsed at his feet. He seemed shocked and shot me a surprised look. "I wanted her to stop talking. All I did was pop her larynx, to make her stop talking. She had to stop. I don't know what . . ." He bent to feel her pulse and I shoved him out of the way.

I felt her neck, then bent and listened to her heart.

Silence.

I picked her up and held her next to me and knew, because I always fucking know every goddamn thing, that she was gone. The world dropped out from beneath my feet. I felt like I was falling. Drowning. Dying. I was in shock, unable to speak.

"How?" Eryx asked. "She's immortal. How can she be gone?"

M appeared, pale as a ghost, looking horrified. "Who's dead?" He saw Euri in my arms and closed his eyes and took a deep, long breath. "What happened?"

"I popped her in the throat," Eryx said, "so she'd stop talking, and she fell down and she's . . . but I don't know how. She's *immortal.*"

M came close to me and met my eyes and I saw so much sorrow there. It barely registered. I was in a fuzzy fog of disbelief. This could not really be happening.

He said softly, "Euri wasn't brought back by God. The Anabo are all brought back by the grace of God through the Mephisto."

"I'm not Mephisto, but I brought back Mariah," Eryx said.

"You shared your energy with her, but trust me, God is who gave her new life. He is who gave all the Anabo immortality. Except Euri and Sophie. They were killed by their mother, and were only eighteen. They weren't supposed to die, and it was so unexpected, we had to hurry to make a decision. Did we bring them back, or let them go? Lucifer was insistent that we bring them back, and we didn't know then that it was something to ask of God. Lucifer gave them immortality. It's how he was able to connect Euri and Zee, and you and Sophie. And because they were made immortal by darkness, they could be taken out by darkness." He leveled a look at Eryx. "You're darker than Lucifer."

Eryx said to me, "I didn't know, Xenos." His voice dropped to a whisper. "I didn't know." It was as close to an apology as he had ever made.

I didn't care. My love, my darling, my Euri, was gone

from me. Her lovely fingers would never play beautiful music. Her cornflower eyes would never again smile at me, never watch the snow fall while her warm arms enveloped me. I was gutted. Bereft. Lost in dazed confusion.

M said, "Say goodbye to Sophie, Eryx."

Everyone looked up at the catwalk. Sophie was slumped over, extremely still.

Eryx popped up there and gathered her into his arms.

"She will die because she gets her energy from Euri."

"I thought it was bullshit," he said, stroking Sophie's face. "She can't die just because Euri's gone. It's not logical. It makes no sense."

"It's how they were made."

I rocked Euri and prayed to God to give her back. He did not need her like I needed her. I couldn't survive without her. I got to my feet and began walking, thinking to go outside and allow my mind to wander, to find a church. I would take her there and ask God to bring her back, and if he would not, I would ask to be taken with her. I inhaled the warm scent of her, of the ocean and her shampoo. And Prada. I was crying. My heart hurt.

Eryx was right behind me. I don't know why, or what he intended. Did he think I would lead him somewhere that would offer help? Did he think I was capable of saving Sophie?

Then I heard Sophie whisper, "Give Euri to me."

I stopped and turned and we stood there, my brother and I, holding identical women, staring at one another while Sophie grasped Euri's hand and murmured, "I can return to her all that she's given to me, and it will save her. It will bring her back."

Eryx looked down into her face. "And what about you?"

She smiled weakly. "I'll go to God, where I wanted to be from the start."

He clutched her more tightly. He was beginning to feel the sting of loss, something he was wholly ill equipped to handle, even to recognize. He'd lost Jordan, but he'd never really had her. She'd never given him what Sophie gave him – unconditional friendship. She would be his companion and friend despite who and what he was. And now she was dying and he began to realize just what was slipping away. He was desperate to make this stop happening. "But she can't live without you. M said so."

"She can live, but she'll be lost in her head."

"No, she won't." I clasped Euri ever tighter against me. "I will be with her always, and I won't let her be lost."

"He loves her, Eryx. He needs her."

"But *I* need *you.*"

"No, you want me, which is entirely not the same at all." She touched his face. "You'll find who you need, someday. I think she'll be as strong as you, and have a beautiful name, and you will never see it coming."

"What are you talking about? Her name is Sophie. I'm not letting you sacrifice yourself for her. You can't leave me."

She continued stroking his cheek, until she didn't. Her arm fell and her head lolled to one side and at the same time, Euri stirred in my arms.

Many moments passed while he stared down at her face before he said, in a tight, raw voice, "I have to go now."

"You can't take her with you."

He hugged her to him and said, "I can and I will. Leave me be, Xenos. Just . . . let me be." And with that, he disappeared, taking Sophie with him.

I looked down at Euri and my heart sang with joy.

She slipped her arms around my neck. "Don't cry, love. It's all going to be okay. Do you believe me?"

She didn't finish her concert. We went back to Colorado, to the privacy of our rooms, and she cried for her twin, and maybe a little, I think, for Eryx. And when she was spent, I put her to bed, climbed in next to her, and held her in my arms. She nuzzled my neck and ran her fingers across my belly, down to encircle my cock while she whispered, "Make love to me, Zee. I want to feel alive."

I did, and she gazed up at me in the darkness of our room and whispered, "I will always love you." And when I came, I heard her say, "Sophie gave me more than her life." I knew in the next moment what she meant. She was marked as Mephisto. She had a womb. I would never lose her, would always know where to find her if she ever went walkabout again. My joy was complete.

Wrapped up in one another, we drifted off.

I'd been asleep many hours when I awoke to an empty bed. Instantly alert, I sat up and saw her sliding one of my T-shirts over her head. "Did I hurt you?"

"You never do. Not any more. Not since you stopped having the dream."

She went toward the door. "Where are you going?"

"The baby, Zee. I have to find the baby."

Oh, no. Was this what Sophie had meant? Would Euri go walkabout more often? I climbed from bed, hurried to put on my sweat pants, then followed her down the hallway.

She was very determined. "It's coming from down there. Don't you hear it?"

"No, love, but let's go and see."

She slowed and frowned at me. "You don't believe me, do you? You think this is like before, when I imagined a baby."

"If you think there's a baby, let's find out, because you'll never be settled until you're sure."

Denys's door opened and he stood there, buck naked, his eyes bloodshot and his hands shaky. "What the hell's going on?"

I assumed by the looks of him that he'd not found August. Or maybe he found her and she told him to stay away from her. Denys had a long, hard road ahead of him. Whether August was meant for him or not, he had to find a way to get off the booze. Because Sasha was right – he was a pathetic excuse for a man, and we'd all contributed to that.

Euri said as she walked past, "Do get some trousers, won't you? Your willie's out."

She kept going and I said, "Seriously, Denys, grow up."

He slammed his door.

She was almost to the end of our corridor when she stopped and pointed at Ty's door. "In there. Ty has a baby."

I didn't hear anything, but I knocked on his door anyway and hoped he'd understand. We'd all have to make concessions for Euri's madness.

Ty opened the door and I was surprised to see he was wide awake, although he was only wearing a pair of plaid flannel pajama pants. Candles were lit, he had a roaring fire going, Gretchen was lying on the hearth, and a little pug snoozed on the rug.

And right there, next to the pug dog, was a cradle. The one we'd all been swaddled in after we were born. He'd gotten the cradle from the stone house on Kyanos. For the baby. Which he held in his gigantic arms.

I stared in complete and total shock. The boy was so wee, his skin the color of milk in coffee, his eyes as blue as a summer sky, his silky hair dark and curly. He had fat rosy cheeks and he waved his tiny fists around and made sweet little baby sounds of pleasure. He was entirely surrounded by the light of divinity. The glow of Anabo.

I met my brother's eyes.

He grinned at me. "Say hello to Jamie."

I looked further into his room, expecting a baby-mama, but there was no one there. Just my oversize brother and this tiny infant. "Where'd you get a baby?"

The child gripped Ty's thumb with both of his miniature hands. "After I left the concert, I went to rescue some bait dogs in a village outside of Mexico City, and Jamie was in one of the kennels." Suddenly emotional, he sniffed. "The little pug was with him, curled around him, keeping him warm."

"You have to take him back and find his family," Euri said. "His mother is probably frantic."

"His mother is dead. His whole family was murdered by the Garza cartel and Jamie is all that's left."

"How do you know?" I asked.

Ty looked up from the bundle in his arms. "I asked M. He said because Jamie is Anabo, and has no family, he should stay with us."

"Does Key know?"

"Not yet. He and Jordan . . . I don't think he would care about anything in the universe tonight."

He'd marked her. Finally. I'd been asleep and missed it. Concentrating, I looked at Euri and was aware of another Mephisto, who was Jordan. Four girls, four new Mephisto, four brothers redeemed.

I had absolutely no idea what Jamie might mean to us and to humanity in the future, but I was certain he would be beloved. Just standing there in Ty's doorway, I felt the pull of his spirit so strongly, it made me smile, made me happy.

Euri slipped her arm around me while she gently stroked the baby's downy head. "Doesn't he have any nappies? He's bound to wee." She smiled up at my brother. "Or something worse."

"Mathilda will be here shortly with diapers."

Jamie began to cry and the pug jumped to attention and began running around Ty's feet, barking. Ty looked down at the dog and said, "Good boy. Sit."

And the dog sat.

But the baby didn't stop crying, and within moments, we were surrounded by the rest of our family, all in various states of dress, some with eyes swollen from sleep, and some with crazy hot sex hair. We were an odd lot, standing there staring at Jamie. My heart nearly beat itself right out of my chest, I was that overcome.

After Ty repeated his story for them, I asked, "What about when you find an Anabo?" Because I knew one was out there for him, one he was bound to find soon. "What if she's not into raising a baby?"

"God wouldn't send me a girl who could turn her back on Jamie. Or Gretchen or this little pug dog." Ty looked at Sasha and Jax, Mariah and Phoenix, Jordan and Key, and then he focused on Euri, who was cooing at the baby while she petted his soft head. "I think we get what we need." He met my gaze and smiled.

Then, as Euri predicted, Jamie did wee, and we all ducked and laughed.

ABOUT THE AUTHOR

Stephanie Feagan is a RITA® award winning author of romantic fiction who lives in the outback of west Texas with her beloved husband and a mean cat. For information about upcoming releases, and to sign up for her newsletter, please visit her website.

BOOKS IN THE MEPHISTO COVENANT SERIES

Book One - *The Mephisto Covenant: The Redemption of Ajax*
Egmont USA Available in hardcover, trade paperback, and eBook.

Book Two - *The Mephisto Kiss: The Redemption of Kyros*
Egmont USA Available in hardcover and eBook.

Book Three - *Only You*
Pink Publishing, LLC Available in trade paperback and eBook

***Written and published as Young Adult novels under the pseudonym Trinity Faegen. Each Mephisto story is standalone and can be read satisfactorily without having read previous books.

Coming in 2015!

The next book in The Mephisto Covenant series . . .
It Had To Be You
He's only twelve steps from everlasting love.

Made in the USA
Lexington, KY
29 November 2017